HARD
WINTER

T0191148

HARD WINTER

WILLIAM W. JOHNSTONE
and J.A. JOHNSTONE

PINNACLE BOOKS
Kensington Publishing Corp.
www.kensingtonbooks.com

PROLOGUE

From the December issue
of **Big Sky Monthly Magazine**
by Paula Schraeder

Not much happens in Cutthroat County, Montana—
1,197 square miles and a population, countywide, of
under 400—in winter. Some say not much happens
there in spring, summer, or fall, either. At least, they
used to; but that was before; over the past year, things
abruptly turned as dangerously exciting as—take your
pick—the 1870s–1890s, the late 1960s, or driving through
a construction zone between Butte and Bozeman on I-90
over Fourth of July weekend. But Cutthroat County and
the county seat of Basin Creek might be settling down.

The county elections are over, and Sheriff John T.
Drew easily won reelection in November. After a wild
summer, covered in previous issues of this magazine (not
to mention cable news organizations, *Time*, *Newsweek*,
the *New York Times*, the *Washington Post*, *Huffington
Post*, London's *Telegraph*, every newspaper, TV and
radio station in Montana, and most media outlets across
the Rocky Mountain West) and likened, by one local

who asked not to be identified, to "one of 'em spaghetti Westerns I watched as a kid—but with a higher body count!"

Once again my editor sent me to our state's smallest but wildest county during the November elections. Elison Dempsey, head of the quasi-military vigilante group called the Citizens Action Network, was resigned to his fate as the losing candidate for sheriff.

"Drew bought the election," Dempsey told me at the Busted Stirrup bar, "and he didn't have to spend a dime."

The tall man, wearing a mix of khaki and camo topped by a 10X Resistol cowboy hat, was referring to the shooting of Sheriff's Deputy Mary Broadbent by a man later identified by the Federal Bureau of Investigation as Santiago Scholz, a notorious hired assassin suspected of murdering at least thirteen people in five countries. After killing Harry Sweet, a hired hand working for the late Garland Foster, and state trooper Lon Hemby and then stealing the dead thirty-two-year-old's cruiser— Scholz kidnapped William "Billy" Drew, the Cutthroat County sheriff's son; Alyson Maddox, daughter of Circle M ranch owner Ashton Maddox, among Montana's biggest and most famous cattle legacies; and forty-seven-year-old Taisie Neal, Ashton Maddox's attorney. While attempting to flee Cutthroat County with his hostages, Scholz was killed instantly by a single shot fired by Nathaniel Harrigan of Montana's Department of Criminal Investigation, DCI Lieutenant Will Ambrose said.

"That's what did you in," Rudy Pierce, owner of Pierce's Car, Truck & Tractor Repair, called out to Dempsey from the other side of the bar. (The watering hole wasn't crowded, and if Cutthroat County is known for anything other than the state fish that bring tourists by the hundreds during the summer, it is eavesdroppers and wannabe stand-up comedians.) "Harry Sweet and that dead cop woulda voted for you. Maybe Foster, too."

"The cop didn't live here," another bar patron informed us.

Pierce shrugged before adding, "Since when did that stop anyone from voting in this county? Remember back in '72. Nah, you wouldn't. You wasn't even in Montana then. You wasn't even born then."

Which prompted chuckles from everyone in the Busted Stirrup that evening except Dempsey and me.

"What I'm telling the lady," Dempsey said, "is that with all the news networks and newspapers repeating all this Old West in the New West stuff, I didn't have a chance. But me and C.A.N. aren't going anywhere. C.A.N. is needed in this lawless country."

"And you can't afford to go nowhere after spending all that money for a losing cause," another patron quipped.

"I've lived in this state long enough to know Cutthroat County needs better law and order than it has or no tourists will be coming up here to wet flies—and we depend on tourists. Not cattlemen. And not quick-triggered sheriffs who think they're John Wayne." He slipped off the barstool. "Don't misquote me, lady," Dempsey said, paid his tab, and stormed out of the saloon.

In case you've forgotten—which no one in this county has—here's the rest of the summer's body count.

Garland Foster died of a broken neck after falling down the stairs of his ranch house shortly after the shooting of Scholz and the rescue of the hostages. Coroner George J. White, who lives in Havre (about a three-hour drive northeast in Hill County), ruled the death accidental. Maddox's attempt to buy Foster's ranch, now known more for wind turbines than sheep or cattle, has been stalled as the deceased left a TODD (Transfer of Death Deed) to a son, Cain Foster, whose whereabouts have not been determined as of press time. A TODD allows the deceased owner(s) to transfer said property to a designated beneficiary or beneficiaries without probate.

Ashton Maddox, whose name was recognized statewide and across the Rocky Mountains long before a killer wanted by Interpol was killed here, had refused to talk to me in previous visits, but he did sit down with me at Basin Creek's Wild Bunch Casino on this trip north.

"Did the election results suit you?" I asked.

He sipped his bottle of Moose Drool. (I am told he prefers expensive bourbon, but beer is the only alcohol available at the Wild Bunch.) "Since I didn't vote, I can't complain one way or the other," he said.

"You didn't vote?"

He let out a mirthless laugh. "There didn't seem to be much point. And a Maddox will never vote for a Drew."

"Even after Drew helped—" I began, but the rancher cut me off.

"*Helped.* That's the key word, miss. *Helped.* I credit DCI for bringing that [expletive] to justice and saving the state the expense of a trial."

"But you backed Dempsey. Why not vote—"

He interrupted again.

"I did until I realized he was an incompetent moron who hired men even more worthless than he is for his *CANT* squad of imbeciles."

Time to change the subject.

"How's your daughter?"

Alyson Maddox works at Denver International Airport as a flight controller.

"Back in Denver," Maddox told me. "She's a Maddox. She'll be fine." He started to raise the beer bottle to his lips, but paused and stared at me. "You haven't talked to her, have you?"

I was honest. "She hasn't taken my calls, and she hasn't returned my messages."

He drank and smiled. "That's my girl."

"But you're talking to me," I let him know.

"But not about Aly. Just what I've already told you. She's a Maddox. She'll be fine."

"And your attorney?"

He shrugged and finished his beer.

"She hasn't talked to me since I did the wrap-up article for the September issue," I informed him.

"She told you all you needed to know then."

I had to agree, and realizing the fruitlessness of pursuing anything further along those lines, I asked about his ranch.

"Most of my cowhands headed south for warmer country the first of last month," he said. "Cowboys like warmer climes. So we'll have a skeleton crew till spring. My accountant likes that."

"How does your accountant like your trying to buy Garland Foster's ranch?"

He seemed now to regret having polished off his beer, but did not ask for another. In fact, he asked the waitress for the check when she asked if he'd care for another drink.

"What makes you think I'm interested in that Don Quixote's spread?"

"Public record."

He shrugged, started to rise from his chair, but settled back into it. "It's property adjacent to the Circle M," he said. "I'd rather have Black Angus beef grazing on that than see more wind machines go up."

"Will you keep the turbines?"

He laughed, relaxed again (from one Moose Drool?), and leaned forward. "I haven't bought the place yet. Might not get a chance. Foster's kid is the owner—if he can be found."

"Will you really not keep those wind turbines?" I repeated. "If you are able to buy the property?"

"I don't think the government or my attorney, and especially not my accountant, will let me tear them down. If I can afford the place."

I start with another question, but he raises his hand to shush me, and this time he stands up, picking up his cowboy hat he had laid, crown down, atop the table. I'm no expert on cowboy hats, but I'd say it was multiple *X*'s more than the one Elison Dempsey wears.

"That'll have to do, miss." Maddox concludes the interview. "You're lucky you got what I gave you. I'm not one to talk to the press."

George Grimes, on the other hand, is.

Grimes, a retired Texas Ranger whose brand of justice inspired the hit movie *Beretta Law,* was hired as a special investigator for C.A.N. He, too, played a hand in ending the brief run of terror in Cutthroat County, and he was eager to tell his side of the story to me, over about a pack and a half of cigarettes and a fifth of Jack Daniel's.

The celebrity is good for quotes—but this magazine

has a limit in what profanity is acceptable, and we prefer to stick to the facts.

For here are the facts—none from George Grimes.

Broadbent, whom Ambrose and Drew credited to helping break the case despite her critical injuries, was discharged from the Clark Fork Medical Center in Missoula two days before the election and is undergoing rehabilitation and confined to desk duty at the sheriff's office until cleared by Noam Haddad, Clark Fork's chief neurosurgeon, and Drew.

"We're not rushing her into anything," Drew told me while climbing into his Interceptor the afternoon after the election. "She's too good a cop to lose."

"You're not shorthanded?" I asked.

He smiled, then shrugged. "Well, we've just had one dusting of snow so far. But I've got a good deputy in Denton Creel, and we have plenty of volunteers for search and rescue."

"Have you hired George Grimes as a special deputy?" I ask.

"Not a chance."

That contradicted what George Grimes told me, but I didn't believe that or anything else he said.

The sheriff closed the SUV's door, but rolled down the window. "The county budget can't afford him. And our newspaper doesn't have enough advertising to pay for all the pages he would fill up if he had a badge."

Grimes came up from Texas and has not left. He is renting an efficiency apartment at Basin Creek Apartments.

"Wasn't he a key to solving the crime spree this summer?" I asked.

Drew sighed. "Too many people, county, state, and federal employees and plenty of local volunteers, helped.

If I singled any of those out, excepting Deputy Broadbent and DCI's Nat Harrigan, I'd leave someone out. So we'll just leave it at that, Miss Schraeder."

I started to ask another question, but he started up his engine and rolled up the window. As I stepped back, though, the window rolled back down, and he leaned out a bit and smiled.

"You and that magazine of yours like to paint Cutthroat County as some backward, 1890s town, the last vestige of the Wild West. It's usually really quiet here. If you want a different kind of story, come up in January—if you have four-wheel drive and chains and aren't afraid of freezing temperatures.

"I never really understood why kids do these kinds of things, but the Always Winter Downhill Run brings in a handful of crazy kids who like to test their skills and show off their daring on snowboards, snowshoes, skis, and snowmobiles."

"Do you compete?" I asked.

He laughed. "I said kids, ma'am. I know you'll find this hard to believe, since Drews have lived in this part of Montana since the early 1800s, but I really don't like cold weather. And I spend enough time with the county's search and rescue unit, though the highway department has the worst of it. Clearing roads of snow and ice. But every fall and winter, hunters get lost, drivers get stranded, and idiots—and even experienced outdoorsmen and -women—get in over their heads. But kids seem to like the adventure—stupidity, if you ask me—of showing off at eleven thousand feet. ESPN had a segment on that two years ago. Come on up. Put something different in your magazine, something that'll show folks that Cutthroat County isn't a Clint Eastwood Western movie on acid. But dress warmly."

I have heard about this event, and I conceded that it sounded like a fun event to cover. Adventurous young men and women, testing their skills and levels of daring on snowboards, skis, and such, or racing snowmobiles despite the threats of avalanches. Trying not to be over-matched at the top of the Always Winter range.

Providing no one put me on skis, boards, or snowmobile.

"I'll pitch it to my editor," I told him. "Ashton Maddox told me that his job is mostly staying warm in winter, that he runs a skeleton crew that mainly tries to keep cattle from freezing."

"That can be a full-time job," the sheriff conceded—about as much of a compliment that a Drew can give a Maddox, I suppose.

"It's cold enough in Billings for me."

"And it's usually colder here. High-country enthusiasts often find themselves overmatched. But, again, the high-way department has the hard job of clearing the roads. And I have a pretty good search and rescue team."

"You aren't making this assignment so appealing, you know," I said with a smile.

"Then get a fishing license and come up in the summer. The cutthroat trout here are amazing. There's no better place to wet a line than Cutthroat County."

He was smiling when we shook hands.

"That ought to be on the back of that T-shirt they sell at the Wantlands Mercantile," I told him. "Instead of that BUT WATCH YOUR BACK one."

That's the T-shirt, in all sizes, long-sleeve and regu-lar, for both sexes and in multiple colors—black is the best-selling—with Welcome to Cutthroat County We're named after Montana's state fish on the front along with a colorful image of the trout and a bearded, blackhearted cowboy stenciled on the back, teeth gripping a giant knife in his mouth and the But watch your back warning.

"I don't think Maudie would sell as many of those, but you can ask her on your way back to Billings." Drew said. He gave me that charming smile, pushed the button to close the window, then stopped it. Pointing at my car, he said, "Anyway, if you get the assignment and want to come up in January, let me know. We'll show you the fun side—for stupid kids, anyway—of Cutthroat County. But I wouldn't drive up in that Camry if I were you. We might not be able to dig you out till June. Maybe even July."

DAY ONE

THURSDAY

CHAPTER 1

The numbing wind kept blowing stinging snow and ice at the main base for the Always Winter Downhill Run, and John T. Drew and his son had been working most of the day covering the portable grandstands with tarps, securing them firmly so it would not take fourteen hours of shoveling snow and ice to make them ready for what few spectators, mostly parents of the younger kids, who had enough gumption to drive up to this bitterly cold wasteland in the name of fun and entertainment and athletes pushing their limits.

Finishing the knot, Drew felt mighty glad that he had been able to tie it with thickly gloved hands. Last year, he'd dang near came close to getting frostbite when he had to remove the winterproof gloves to get that last tie-down tight enough. At least that's how he felt, anyway.

Billy said something, but Drew could not read his son's lips, since he could not see the boy's face through the three-hole, full-face ski mask and frosty ski goggles.

Billy pointed to the Interceptor. He said something, and Drew figured Billy said it could wait till they were in the SUV—maybe ten minutes after the heater could be felt—because he shrugged and went back to tying his end down.

Nodding, Drew went back to work, too. This storm wasn't supposed to last long, and another storm moving down from Alberta was expected to bypass Basin Creek and most of the county. That would be good for the thirteen men and women, mostly boys and girls, who had signed up to compete in this year's annual event that attracted kids and a few adults with more polar bear and musk ox in their blood to think this was a fun thing to do to start off a new year.

The stands, which came from the high school football field, also were rented for the Fourth of July rodeo each year. Drew liked the rodeo better than this catastrophe of an event. But at least the only media covering this year's annual display of Cutthroat County craziness was some high school kid dumb enough to come up for the ten bucks Carl Lorimer would pay him to write up an article and take photographs for the *Basin River Weekly Item* and maybe the girl from *Big Sky Monthly Magazine*— providing she didn't turn chicken-livered (or wise beyond her years), hang a sharp U-turn, and skedaddle back to the low country of Yellowstone County, where the high today, according to the Weather Channel this morning, was expected to be a balmy twenty-six degrees. The year ESPN and *Sports Illustrated* decided to give the event publicity had been nothing more than complete insanity.

Straightening, Drew beat the snow and ice off his gloves and looked at his son, who had finished his job.

"What do you think?" he shouted over the wind.

"I'd say it's good enough." Billy yelled that loud enough to hear.

"I figured you would." With a grin that Billy couldn't see because of Drew's own winter wraps, Drew hooked a thumb toward the Interceptor. "Let's get lower than two miles elevation."

The SUV started and the heat blasted them as they shed parkas, masks, and wet gloves, which they tossed into the back seat. The defroster began melting the windshield ice, and Drew opened a thermos of hot chocolate, which was only lukewarm by now, and handed it to his son, then buckled himself in.

"What is it that those sheepdogs carry in Switzerland?"

Drew rubbed the feeling back into his hands, then turned toward his son.

"Sheepdogs?"

"You know what I mean!"

"Saint Bernards. And it's brandy."

"Well. Brandy would be better than this."

"You've never had brandy." Drew laughed. "I don't think I've ever had brandy." It did sound warm, though. He hit the wipers, which cleared off enough melting mush so he could see. "What was it you asked me back there?"

He thanked his son when he passed the thermos, then drank some weak hot chocolate made from a mix—and lukewarm was an overstatement.

"Nothing." Billy took the thermos his father held back toward him.

"What was it you asked?"

His son, who had finished the first semester of his junior year at the University of Wyoming, sighed. "I was just wondering if you thought Mr. Maddox would be coming up to the run."

Drew couldn't hide his grin.

"A Maddox making a Drew nervous?" Before Billy could complain, Drew added, "Your grandfathers and great-grandfathers are turning over in their graves."

Billy changed the subject. "How much is the county paying me for helping you out today, by the way?"

"Nothing. The Always Winter Downhill Run is a five-oh-one-C-three. You know what that is, or do they teach those things for youngsters studying outdoor recreation and tourism management?"

"It's a nonprofit. Sorta like being a county sheriff, I guess."

Drew laughed. "Nonprofits make more money, son."

He shifted the SUV into reverse, backing up and hearing the ice crunch under the tires, turning the wheels sharply, then putting the Ford into first gear. Drew never liked driving down from what some people considered a ski resort but he thought of as more of a death trap. He kept the Interceptor in low four-wheel drive and never topped fifteen miles an hour for the first nerve-wracking few miles downhill.

They didn't talk. Not now. Though keeping one hand on the gearshift, Drew practically hugged the steering wheel and stared at the whiteness in front of him.

"I thought this storm was supposed to miss us," Billy said after a while.

"That's what the weatherman at Great Falls said," Drew whispered, before biting his lower lip as he downshifted but kept his foot on the brake pedal on a hairpin turn.

The forecast might still be right. Town was about sixty-five hundred feet lower, and it might be clear as a

July morning when they climbed off this mountain, though it would still be freezing.

Brandy, he thought. Maybe he would try some when they reached Basin Creek. He wondered if they had that on the back bar at the Busted Stirrup.

When they reached an elevation too low for aspens and the snow and sleet lessened and the visibility rose, he breathed a bit easier, but he still kept his eyes focused on the road and the SUV in four-wheel drive.

"I saw Alyson Maddox at the grocery yesterday," he said.

Billy waited a long moment before responding: "Who?"

"Alyson Maddox. Does she ski?"

"Snowboards." Billy quickly added. "Or so I hear tell."

"Guess she came up on vacation or comp time."

"Flights might be all grounded at DIA," Billy suggested.

Drew tried not to snicker at that bit of logic from a junior, third-string catcher for the Wyoming Cowboys. He didn't say that George Grimes had told Drew that he had seen Billy and Alyson at Mack McDonald's beaver pond, oh, roughly two hours after Drew had held the door open for her as she left Outlaw Grocery & Liquor with a shopping bag full of apples, cookies, and napkins—like she was going on a picnic. In winter.

His smile faded. Times like this, he really wished his wife were still alive. Boys, even college-age juniors, could talk to their mothers about girls and such. He wondered what Rebecca, killed in a single-car accident, would have told Billy. *Alyson Maddox is a pretty girl, smart, and . . . how many years older than you? You'd*

be wise to court her. Or: *This isn't a fairy tale, son. And
you'd best remember that Drews and Maddoxes haven't
been on social terms in something like one hundred and
eighty years.*

He tried to think of some wise counsel he could offer
Billy. Then he waited for his son to say something. The
only sounds were from an icy mix pelting the Interceptor and snow crunching beneath the SUV's tires and
chains.

"You don't think they'd cancel the run, do you?"
Billy asked after a lengthy silence.

Drew breathed easier.

"Depends, as always, on weather." He laughed at an
almost forgotten memory. "They canceled it when I was
ten years old. That was when the only events were
skiing and snowshoeing. My daddy, your granddaddy,
was sheriff then. Chuckie Corvallis and Fergie Trent decided they were going up to compete anyway."

Billy perked up. "Mr. Corvallis . . . that old man who
smokes like a chimney—and the game warden?"

"Chuckie only smoked a pack a day back then. And
it was Trent's daddy. He wasn't a game warden, but I
imagine whoever was the game warden then would
have loved to have stopped that old poacher."

His son's face brightened. "You're kidding."

Drew shook his head and focused on the road.

"Someone tipped Daddy off. Even back then,
Chuckie couldn't keep his mouth shut, and Daddy
cussed and cussed and said he ought to let those two
stay up on those mountains till the snow melted, and
then he'd let the buzzards and silvertips have them for
supper. There wasn't a search and rescue outfit, per se,

back then, so Daddy had to round up anyone he could find, and they drove up in the county's dump truck."

He remembered pleading with his father to let him ride up there with them. John had always wanted to ride in a dump truck, but his father was as mad as Drews could get. Then, seeing how worried his mother was, John had started fearing the worst things that could happen. Mostly that those silvertip bears and carrion would be feasting on his father and the three cowpunchers he had pulled out of what was then Jimbo Bell's two-bit bar—Monty, the oldest boy, had turned that into a grocery and liquor store when he learned that he couldn't compete with the Wild Bunch and Busted Stirrup.

John relayed what he remembered, leaving out his own fears, smiling and picturing what must have been going on inside that dump truck as his hard rock of a father and three drunken cowhands went up this very road, only back then it wasn't paved.

"What happened?" Billy asked when John paused to get around the last hairpin turn.

"It was right about here that Daddy found them." He pointed as much as he could toward the left-hand side of the road. "Slid into a snowbank. Trent had stolen his father's Chevy pickup. Kids didn't even put chains on the tires.

"They had tried to walk up the rest of the way, then gave up and were snowshoeing down when they saw the lights of the dump truck.

"Well, Daddy scared the crap out of them, then made them climb into the back of the dump truck. Said there wasn't room for them up front, and there probably wasn't. Not with those cowhands and Daddy, who was about the size of a three-year-old Brahman bull. I'm surprised they weren't frozen solid by the time Daddy pulled into Basin Creek."

John shook his head and chuckled.

"The newspaper printed the next week that Fergie Trent won that year's Downhill championship. Since when Sheriff Drew stopped the truck, hit the lever, and emptied the bed, Fergie was the first one through the dump gate."

They both laughed.

"Is that true?" Billy asked. "Or did you make it up?"

"I don't have the gift of gab that your granddaddy had," John answered. "But it's in the bound volumes of the old newspapers at the library. Look it up yourself."

"That's funny," Billy said.

John nodded. "Folks talked about that for years." He wondered how stories like that got lost over time, but the violent stories of Cutthroat County went on forever. Well, maybe he could understand that after all. He remembered all those Wild West stories. The funny ones didn't come so clear after a few months or so. He was surprised he even managed to dig up that one.

"I don't think either of them could sit for a week after their dads got through with them."

It was good to hear his son laugh with him. After all, with what Billy had been through this past summer, being kidnapped along with Alyson Maddox by that deadly hired assassin, John had worried that, once the adrenaline wore off, Billy would falter, flounder, fall apart. But his grades had been solid, Bs all the way around in five classes this past semester, and he had looked pretty good in fall baseball practice. Probably would hold on to his job as bullpen catcher, maybe get a bit more playing time since last season's backup had transferred to a smaller school in South Dakota, the freshman signee had decided to play pro ball in Mexico, and the starter was battling a hamstring injury.

"Wanna grab something to eat for an early supper?" John asked.

"Sure. Where you thinking?"

John smiled. "Not that chophouse in Bozeman. Our options are limited." He wasn't about to drive to Medicine Pass to eat at Jimmie's Chinese. John had thought about grilling steaks, but after getting those stands weatherproofed for the crazy run scheduled for Saturday, he really didn't want to be outside in a biting Montana wind any more than he had to.

"Guess the Wild Bunch," Billy said. "Maybe I can ask Mr. Corvallis if that story you told me is true."

A retort had not formed in John's mind when the Interceptor's radio crackled. Someone was calling the sheriff's office emergency line.

"Cutthroat County Sheriff's Department." He heard Mary Broadbent answer the call, which automatically went to all units. It had to be a local call. 9-1-1 calls were relayed to Cut Bank in Glacier County.

"Yeah." The sound of glass breaking came through clearer than the voice. "Two cowhands are tearing up the Busted Stirrup." The next noise sounded like wood breaking, and the caller cursed, cried out, then swore some more. After a string of blasphemy, the voice demanded, "If you don't get someone over here, I'm breaking out my sixteen-gauge pump."

"Calm down, Bull," Mary told the bartender, Bull Resnick. At least that joint's owner, Cindy Kristiansen, who also ran the Basin Creek Apartments, wasn't working.

She wouldn't have called the sheriff's department. She would have already had that shotgun in her hands. "I'll call Derrick Taylor now."

Good girl, Drew thought. Taylor was constable for Basin Creek, so a barroom brawl at the Busted Stirrup fell in his jurisdiction, though the county sheriff's department often assisted in things like this.

"That piece of lard drove up to Havre this morning to see his ex-wife!" Resnick followed that with a booming string of profanity. "Why the . . ."—The next bit of profanity was garbled by static, breaking glass, and curses—"called you?"

Call Denton Creel, Drew silently mouthed. *Be smart, Mary. Be smart.*

Before Mary could respond, the bartender said, "You'd better bring in the National Guard. The guy who started the fight is Colter Norris."

John and his son said the same curse word at the same time.

"Otherwise, I would have already sprayed both of those"—static did not quite bleep out the curse—"with six-shot already."

Colter Norris was foreman of Ashton Maddox's ranch. He was old, ornery and tough as nails, and hard to provoke, but when he got riled or drunk, especially during winter when there wasn't much for a cowboy to do but get just drunk enough to keep a job and hang on till spring, he could level a joint like the Busted Stirrup in half an hour.

"Hang tight, Bull," Mary told him. More garble. Then ". . . on the way."

Slowing the Interceptor, Drew grabbed the mic. "Mary," he said urgently. "Get Denton. Send Denton."

She did not respond.

"Mary," he tried again. "I'm twenty minutes away."

That was a lie. Drew felt hopeless. Twenty minutes. That was like twenty thousand miles. And twenty minutes wouldn't get him to Neely Road, the local name for Montana Highway 60. If he could be at the Busted Stirrup in forty-five minutes, it would be a miracle.

When no response came, he radioed for Deputy Denton Creel, knowing that, this being Creel's day off, he wouldn't be near a sheriff's radio. He pointed at the cell phone.

"Billy, call Denton now."

Drew couldn't dial and drive down this mountain road at the same time, and he had never been bright enough to figure out how to get the stupid cell phone to call with a verbal command.

Denton answered on the third ring. Billy had put the call on speakerphone.

"John. What is it?"

"Denton. Colter Norris is tearing up the Busted Stirrup. Derrick's off on vacation. I need you to get there ASAP."

"You're breaking . . . John. Repeat."

Drew swore, then repeated what he had said, only louder.

He held his breath.

"John . . ." More garbled nonsense followed. ". . . dropped off . . . Connie Good . . . hour away."

The sigh sounded like a volcano erupting. Drew had caught just enough to understand Denton Creel's response.

He had dropped off Connie Good Stabbing, a Blackfoot woman and alcoholic who got special treatment among county and tribal officials because, well, she had had a rough life—and she was the daughter of a Blackfoot legend, Drew's good friend Hassun.

And the Blackfoot Indian Reservation bordered Cutthroat County on the north. Creel was about an hour from Basin Creek in the best conditions. He'd get there about the same time Drew could.

"Hang up," Drew told his son. "And hold on."

He pressed down the accelerator.

CHAPTER 2

John Drew would blow his top.

That's one thing Mary Broadbent knew for certain. He might be mad enough to fire her or—even worse—dump her. But her boss, her lover, was way up in the Always Winter peaks, and knowing how long it generally took Sheriff John T. Drew and Billy to get everything protected from the snow already falling, he wouldn't be able to get to Basin Creek in an hour, and that's if Johnny hadn't been lying to her about being twenty minutes away.

Besides, twenty minutes would be too late for the Busted Stirrup—and Mary's landlady owned that bar.

"What choice do I have?"

She was surprised to hear her own voice. It sounded like that time she had gone into that cave on a grade-school field trip to Lewis & Clark Caverns State Park near Whitehall, when Monty Jefferson had dared her to yell "Charley Parker is a big dummy!" in one of the limestone chambers. The echoes scared the dickens out of everyone, especially their elderly teacher.

Mary wasn't cleared by her doctors yet to do much of

anything. She still needed the walking cane, but at least she had graduated from wheelchairs and walkers. Buckling on the belt that carried the Glock Model 17 took longer than she anticipated, but her vision was clear and she didn't feel dizzy or show signs of another tear-inducing headache. The bulletproof vest went on easily, and she stepped out into the hallway.

So far, so good.

Once she made it to the staircase, Mary felt better, but kept one hand on her cane and the other on the guardrail as she made her way down to the ground floor. It wasn't like she was coming down the Empire State Building. County offices in the Cutthroat County Courthouse/Basin Creek Municipal Building were on the second story.

But she did run into the clerk, James Alder, who was entering the old building as Mary was walking toward the front door.

"Hey, Mary," he said, greeting her warmly. Then he noticed the vest and belt. His smile faded. "Any trouble?"

"I'm just building up my strength," she said. "Getting myself back into shape." She tugged on the front of the belt and smiled. "Need to lose some weight."

Building up my strength . . . ? Getting back into shape . . . ? Need to lose weight . . . ? What a bunch of horse hockey to say!

Maybe that bullet to her brain had shattered her ability to tell lies all so smoothly. Lose weight? She had lost twenty-two-point-four-six pounds in that Missoula hospital. And at five foot two, she needed all the weight and muscle she could stand.

Alder was staring after her as she went out the front

door. She whispered a barnyard oath and moved down the wheelchair ramp, clutching the rail with her left hand.

She didn't hear the door to the creaky old building open, though, and she wasn't about to look back—just in case John Alder was staring after her.

Seeing her Ford, she decided not to take it. She wasn't cleared to drive, either, but the Busted Stirrup wasn't more than a couple of blocks away.

Mary made a beeline for the saloon.

It sucked being an invalid.

She had to catch her breath before she got to the street in front of the bar, and inhaling frigid air burned like whiskey going down the wrong way. Glass exploded, and the patrons who had escaped the melee inside and several passersby gasped and pointed at the barstool that crashed onto a dusting of snow.

Mary thought about quitting, but then she whispered "Semper fi" and crossed the icy street.

Bull Resnick had left the war zone and now screamed into his cell phone, calling Colter Norris every four-letter word in the book. He had to be talking to Cindy Kristiansen. That wasn't good. The landlady would give Mary grief till the end of days, and she probably was loading an assault rifle at this very minute to come and protect her property and fill the Circle M foreman full of holes. But Cindy was eighty-two years old, so it might take her a while to make it from her apartment.

"Derrick not's here!" the bartender yelled into his phone. "Denton Creel's not here! And the sheriff is up in the Always Winters . . . !" He held the phone away from his ear to keep from going deaf, then brought the phone closer to his mouth and roared, "What could I do? You want me to shoot someone who rides for the Circle M?

Not meaning any disrespect, but you don't pay me enough to do that, Miss Cindy."

He moved the phone away.

Mary crossed the street and pushed a gawking, gangly ninth-grader named Harry Evarts aside.

It could have been worse. This could have been going on on a Friday or Saturday night. But on a weekday afternoon, on a cold, wintry day, there were no more than ten spectators, and that included the Evarts kid. She didn't spot Basin Creek's newspaper editor among the faces.

"Let me through." She tried to sound like Clint Eastwood or Robert De Niro, but figured she came more across as Shirley Temple or Doris Day.

"Hold on." Bull Resnick lowered the phone. He stared uncomprehendingly . . . unbelievingly . . . then spoke hurriedly into the phone. "Miss Cindy, I gotta go. Deputy Broadbent just showed up." He slipped the phone into a back pocket in his Wranglers and hurried toward Mary.

"Deputy . . . you can't . . . I mean . . ."

Mary stared him down.

"Is anyone else inside other than Colter Norris?" She hoped her voice didn't squeak. She hoped her eyes managed to tell this fellow about her age that she was up to the task at hand.

"He knocked out one of the seasonal Circle M hirelings. A Mexican. I can't remember his name."

Glass shattered inside.

Mary shook her head. "The county ought to fine Ashton Maddox."

Someone in the crowd said, "Aw, Colter ain't done nothin' like this in a dog's age."

"He's probably just ticked off like everyone else since COVID," Henry Richey muttered. Richey was the county tax accessor. The Busted Stirrup's value was going down quickly. Richey smiled at Mary. "I called . . ."

But a cowboy with a blackening eye interrupted him.

"Nah," the cowboy said. "Colt's just ringin' in the new year."

"Well," Bull Resnick said, "if he ain't under arrest before Miss Cindy gets here, he's gonna be ringin' in the new year in hell."

Mary got the hint. "Stand back," she said, though the onlookers had already moved to a mostly safe position on what passed for a sidewalk in Basin Creek. Owners of the pickups and SUVs parked in the lot had backed their vehicles up to protect them from thrown beer or whiskey bottles, or—she took in the barstool in the snow—anything that Colter Norris could get his hands on.

She started toward the door to the bar.

In her first year on the force—like two deputies and a sheriff made a *force*—she had seen John Drew take care of Colter Norris when the foreman was mad-drunk after losing a Super Bowl bet. John and Mary had gone through the door, which was off its hinges, quickly, and John had ordered Mary to keep him covered and not accidentally put a bullet in his back. He'd just walked straight up to the slim but tough-as-nails foreman, drew his pistol, screamed at Norris not to move an inch, then when he got up close to him, he'd swung the barrel of his gun and knocked the drunk out before he knew what had happened.

"Take command," Drew told her later that night in his office after the doctor had ruled that Colter Norris probably wouldn't even have a headache—from either all the booze he'd had at the Busted Stirrup or the walnut-sized knot and cut that required three stitches on his noggin—when he woke up the next afternoon.

"A guy like Colter, he doesn't expect someone to just walk right up to him and put him down" was Johnny's lesson. "Because he's got his pride. And mostly because he's drunk as a skunk."

He had finished typing the report, printed it out, and passed the paper to Mary for proofreading.

"But you have to read the situation. And know who you're going up against. I wouldn't have done that against most drunks in a bar. Cowboys I don't know . . . or a reservation Indian, I'm trying something different."

"What about Hells Angels?" she had asked.

He had given her that charming smile of his, the one that hypnotized her.

"Hells Angels? I'm calling in the Marines."

"Semper fi," she had told him.

Shards of busted bottles and glasses crunched as Mary rounded the bar. A quick glance found the Mexican hired by Ashton Maddox as a winter hand. Conscious now, he leaned against an overturned table, holding his bandanna against a bloody cut across the corner of his left eye. Blood dribbled down his cheek and chin and stained his ripped plaid woolen shirt. His left hand clutched a crucifix that hung over his neck on a rawhide cord.

He shook his head at Mary and then shrugged.

"Where's Grimes?" Colter Norris bellowed. "I thought Grimes would come in after me."

Mary decided against the tactical maneuver she remembered John Drew using against that drunk. For one reason, she was already out of breath from walking in the freezing wind from the courthouse to the bar. For another, she was dizzy and her pulse had to be beating at around one-twenty-plus. Her fingertip reader, issued by one of her doctors, would have revealed her exact heart rate, oxygen level, blood pressure, and whether she was alive or almost dead. She didn't care about all that. She just wasn't certain how long she could keep her balance.

"Grimes isn't," she tried, then lost the train of thought.

"Grimes isn't a man," Colter Norris said. "He's a . . ."

She couldn't quite grasp what the Circle M foreman said, but knew it wasn't a phrase spoken in polite company.

"I wanted to kill Grimes." Norris slurred his words.

There was just enough light for Mary to make out the cowhand's eyes. He weaved now, shaking his head wildly, then lowered it and let out a wretched burp. For a second, Mary thought he might throw up. She prayed that he would just pass out.

"Colter," she spoke softly but loud enough for him to hear. "You've wrecked this place."

That was an understatement.

"Let's call it a day, shall we?" She wondered what had happened to her original plan: to charge in here like John Wayne or John Drew, pound that drunk to the floor with a Glock, and drag his sorry carcass to the jail, which most people claimed could not hold a flea for five seconds. She kept trying to remind herself that she was a Marine.

Yeah. She was a Marine. And a sheriff's deputy. With a portion of her brain removed, plastic surgery covering a hole in her head, and steel plates and pins that felt like rusty metal grinding against her temple most mornings when she first woke up. It wasn't morning, but the grinding was working overtime.

Colter Norris came in and out of focus.

"You should've brought Grimes with you," Colter said, still slurring his words. "That's why I started this fight." He waved vaguely at the cowboy he had knocked senseless. "I ain't got nothin' against Pablo. He's a good ol' boy. Hard worker. Handles horses better than most wranglers I've worked with." He turned and grinned at the bleeding man he had coldcocked. "You're *muy* . . . *muy* . . . *muy* something another, Pablo."

"*Gracias, amigo*," Pablo, if that was really the hired hand's name, whispered, but without much conviction.

"But . . ." Colter pointed a shaking long, gnarly finger at Mary. "But . . . you . . . you ain't George Grimes."

"Why don't we go find George Grimes?" Mary said. "I wouldn't mind seeing you kick that blowhard all the way back to Texas."

She wasn't even joking.

Norris shook his head.

"No dice, girly. You ain't foolin' me." He shot a quick glance toward the unhinged door. "Where the devil is Grimes? Where's that louse of a sheriff, that boss of yours?"

He turned back, stared at Mary, and shook his head.

He swore softly, then moved his right hand behind his back.

"I wanted to shoot George Grimes in the belly," he said. "That's all I wanted."

He sighed. Mary wet her lips.

"But I guess it'll have to be you."

She saw him pull a long-barreled, single-action Colt from the back of his waist. Only then did she drop her cane and try to jerk her Glock from the holster.

CHAPTER 3

In the dining room of the big house that usually felt even bigger, and all so vacant, Ashton Maddox reached across the dining room table and topped off Taisie Neal's glass with more of the expensive and excellent—if he could believe the wineshop gent in Great Falls—Shiraz.

Taisie looked up from her plate and said, "Ash, I have to drive home."

He started to say "You don't have to," but stopped himself. That would have been a mistake. Instead, he turned to his daughter and poured some wine into her glass. She didn't protest. But she wasn't driving off the ranch. Instead, he asked Aly, "How's your . . . chicken?"

"It's fine, Daddy. Thanks for grilling it for me."

Well, Ashton figured he ought to be thankful that his only daughter had sworn off just red meat. At least she wasn't one of those veggie idiots eating tofu, whatever that was, and crap like that.

"This steak is delicious," Taisie said.

Ashton set the wine bottle down and looked at his lawyer.

"It ought to be," he said as he reached for his glass of

Blanton's Single Barrel bourbon, which cost him even more than the bottle of Australian wine. "It's Circle M Black Angus."

They were eating supper early so Taisie wouldn't have to drive back to Basin Creek in the dark, though the county had done a pretty good job of keeping the paved roads in good condition. And according to the weather forecasters, this latest storm coming down from Canada should move through fast and keep predominantly west. Kalispell, Coeur d'Alene, and down the Bitterroots were expected to get the worst of the storm. Oh, Cutthroat County would get its share of snow. February was usually when this country got started to get hammered, and that hammer rarely stopped ringing until April, sometimes not until May.

Taisie set her knife and fork on her plate and found a napkin. She hadn't eaten but half the T-bone, but then Ashton had served steaks that filled the entire plates. Side dishes—mashed potatoes with gravy and green beans—and biscuits were on a separate plate. He should have told Yukon Hearst, the ranch's cook, that he was feeding two lovely young women and not half-starved, gluttonous cowboys.

"How long are you here, Alyson?" Taisie asked.

His young daughter dabbed her mouth with the napkin and set it on the table. Little wonder she was so thin. She hardly put a dent in the boneless chicken breast or the veggies.

"I'll leave Sunday," she said. "My flight out of Great Falls is scheduled to leave at two-twentyish. I just have to turn in my rental, and Great Falls is pretty easy to manage." She smiled. "It's a tad smaller than DIA."

"I know." Taisie laughed. "Two-hour flight?"

"Yes, ma'am."

Taisie had made those flights often, Ashton knew. He sipped his bourbon neat. This late afternoon supper had gone better than he had expected. His lover and his daughter were carrying on polite conversations, and since Aly had arrived on Tuesday, she had not once brought up her mother—wherever the devil she was. His private investigator, Malachi Pry, had yet to get any leads on where Patricia Maddox had gone, but Ashton still kept paying the Great Falls detective, who had worked for police departments in St. Louis and Dallas before getting fed up with crime-ridden cities and moving to Montana to escape crime and heat. Well, he certainly had gotten away from heat.

He pushed those thoughts out of his head, killed the bourbon, and said, "Who wants dessert?"

"I'm stuffed," Aly protested.

"Me, too," Taisie said with a smile.

He had gotten the cake from a bakery in Great Falls. It was too good of a cake—chocolate, even—to give to the boys in the bunkhouse. Too expensive, too. Well, it wasn't like he couldn't afford it, but his special supper seemed to have been all for nothing.

Except that Alyson had not yet tried to claw out Taisie's eyeballs. His daughter remained devoted to her mother, whom Ashton—nor anyone else in the county—had not seen in ages.

His cell phone buzzed, and he swore underneath his breath, then reached inside his vest pocket and saw the name on the screen. "What the . . ." He rose, backing up toward the bar with his empty glass in one hand and punched the phone while bringing it to his ear.

"Excuse me," he told the women. Why on earth would the county tax assessor be calling him?

"Richey," Ashton said, "what's up?"

"Ash, you better get to the Busted Stirrup ASAP—while there's still something left of the bar."

He could make out several voices, not the words, just the commotion, but he was grinding his teeth because Henry Richey didn't know him well enough to call him Ash. He might let Ashton slide, but that crooked politician ought to be calling him *Mister* Maddox.

"What's going on?"

"Colter Norris is tearing the place down."

He let that sink in and walked away from the dining room to the big plateglass window in the living room. Running his tongue over his lips, he studied the pickups parked near the bunkhouse.

"Hold on for a sec, Henry." Covering the mouthpiece of the cell phone, he turned back to the table and found his daughter.

"Sweetheart, can you do me a favor?" He didn't wait for a reply. "Run down to the bunkhouse. Ask Dante Crump where Colter is. And come back lickety-split."

He waited till Alyson had found her parka and was out the door. Taisie sat in her chair, staring hard at Ashton, but not saying a word.

"How bad?" he asked the caller.

"He hasn't shot anyone, but he's knocked out some teeth, ran everyone out of the joint—there's at least one of your riders he put to the floor—and he's begging for George Grimes, that Texas hardcase, to come haul him off to jail."

Ashton was about to ask about law enforcement, but the tax man beat him to that salient point.

"I don't know where Denton Creel is, but our local constable is on vacation, Derrick Taylor, told me he was driving up to see his ex."

"Drew?" Ashton didn't even like saying the county sheriff's name.

"Getting the ski area ready for the big weekend show."

Ashton swore softly and started for the coatrack, swiping the keys to his SUV off the table.

"Bouncer? Anybody there man enough to handle Colter?"

Henry Richey chuckled like this was some joke. "Not this side of Malmstrom Air Force Base."

Wise guy. Maybe Richey ought to apply for a job on . . . Ashton could not think of any modern-day late-night talk show. He had stopped watching those after Johnny Carson hung it up.

He hit the speaker function on the phone, which he set on the bar, and found his sheepskin-lined coat and pulled that on, grabbed his billfold, which he slid into the back pocket of his jeans, and then settled his 20X black Stetson on his head. Taisie was coming toward him now, concern showing in her eyes.

He mouthed, *It's all right.*

But he knew, and so did Taisie, that was a bald-faced lie.

"I'm on my way, Henry," he said, and grabbed the phone. "Don't let anybody go inside that bar till I get there." He ended the call before that gutless wonder could protest that he had no authority when it came to that.

"What's happening?" Taisie asked.

Ashton sighed. "Cowboys are still cowboys."

Alyson came back into the house. "Dante says Colter drove to town with Mateo Balcázar."

He couldn't contain the sigh or the curse.

That Mexican knew his way around horses, and he wasn't afraid of cold weather, either. Ashton couldn't say that about some of the native Montana boys that hired on for the Circle M.

"Is Colter—"

Ashton cut off his daughter. "He's just doing what cowboys do every now and then. You two stay here. Clear the table if you don't mind. I won't be gone long."

Just long enough to beat Colter Norris within an inch of his life, pay a king's ransom to Cindy Kristiansen, and spend who knew how much money paying off doctor's bills for every scratch, bruise, and hangnail for the next month or so.

"Don't wait up for me."

He went through the door, slammed it shut to cut off any protest those two women might start, hurried in the freezing wind to the Ford Expedition, and climbed into it. He cursed for the entire drive to the first gate, looked at the SUV's clock, and wondered how long Cutthroat County Sheriff John T. Drew would be stuck up in the Always Winter range. If the lawman was up in the high country, his deputy off somewhere, and the town constable chasing a skirt up in Hill County, Ashton might be able to sweep all this under the carpet, pay off a few folks—though that old Kristiansen wench would demand a small fortune for that two-bit claptrap of a saloon.

He might be able to get this buried and forgotten.

But by the time he was on the county highway, he remembered someone else he might have to deal with.

Nah. That Broadbent gal was still walking wounded, half dead, confined to desk duty, and moving around like a zombie. Which she probably was after taking a nine-millimeter slug to the brain.

He didn't convince himself of anything, though.

So he punched the gas pedal to the floor.

He had driven like he was leading the Indianapolis 500.

Even if he had a Porsche on a summer day, he would not have been able to break his speed record for covering all those miles between the Circle M and Basin Creek proper. Later, he would think Ford might want to use him in a TV commercial. But that thought would not come till much later, and he would forget it just days afterward.

Not four hundred people—men, women, and kids—in the whole dang county, which covered roughly three-quarters of a million acres, and it looked like two hundred of those souls were lined up in front of the Busted Stirrup, which was far more than busted when the Expedition slid to a stop. That shack was practically kaput.

Ashton exited the Expedition, pushed a teenage boy out of his path, and tried not to look anyone in the eye as he made it to the grounds. He caught a glimpse of Henry Richey, but the county employee was on his cell phone, probably trying to get CNN or ESPN to cover the brawl. At least Richey was too busy talking to get in Ashton's way.

Bull Resnick came up to Ashton, though.

That was just like that booze pourer. He should have

tried to jump Colter Norris. The barkeep stopped and hooked his thumb toward the building.

"That Mex is still in there, Mr. Maddox," Resnick said. "Norris just went ballistic. He knocked your Mexican out, then busted every piece of furniture and glassware and a few heads, screaming that he was gonna kill George Grimes."

Well, that made paying all those bills a little more acceptable to Ashton.

"I take it that that loudmouthed pile of Texas dung is nowhere near here," Ashton said.

"No one's seen him," the beer jerker answered.

Ashton's eyes swept the parking lots and vehicles, mostly trucks, on the streets. He didn't see any of the county sheriff's rigs.

That was a good sign, too.

"Anybody left inside?" Ashton asked. "Other than my hired man Balcázar?"

The bartender seemed to go pale.

"Yes, sir, Mr. Maddox." His voice had dropped to a whisper.

"Deputy Broadbent went inside . . . not two minutes ago."

Swearing, Ashton pushed Resnick out of his way and ran to the busted front door of the saloon.

He caught just a few words—"it'll have to be you"—before he stormed into the dimly lit barn. He saw the deputy first, trying to get her weapon out of the holster.

"No!" he screamed, and then found his foreman, Colter Norris, holding a cocked Colt in his right hand.

"Colter!" he roared. "Drop that gun, buster, or I'll ram that barrel down your throat!"

Colter Norris turned and aimed the hogleg at Ashton,

who walked calmly, though his nerves were tense, until he stood in front of Sheriff's Deputy Mary Broadbent. He had no idea how the young blonde was still standing. At least, her service weapon remained holstered. And now Colter would have to shoot down Ashton before he could harm the brave, but stupid, young woman.

He had taken five steps toward his foreman when he saw Mateo Balcázar, legs spread-eagled on the sawdust-covered floor, eyes fluttering and a wicked cut underneath one of them, looking half dead and trying to comprehend how he wound up in this position in this state—in what was barely a town in a big state of mostly nothing. He was a long way from Harlingen County.

"I'm . . ." Colter faltered. "I'm gonna kill that . . . Ranger."

Ashton sighed. Colter Norris had gotten through the election, Thanksgiving, Christmas, and even New Year's Eve . . . only to fall to the lure of those old demons and tie one on for the ages.

"Kill an ex-Texas Ranger?" Ashton shook his head, then pointed at the Circle M rider and hooked a thumb back toward the deputy. "Those don't look like Texas Rangers to me, buster. They look like a man I pay to work just like I pay you to work. And a brave woman who lacks the sense of a jenny." He stood just a foot in front of the foreman now.

"Drop that pistol, Colter. Drop it now, or so help me, I'm dropping you. To what's left of a floor. And off the Circle M payroll."

Colter Norris's dull eyes blinked. He seemed to realize he was holding a .45.

"Ease the hammer down first, Colter," Maddox

whispered. And when the foreman had complied, Maddox held out his left hand.

"I'll take the Colt, Colter."

He felt the cold metal in his gloved hand, and only then did he feel his pulse starting to slow, but it had a long way to go till it reached what Maddox would consider normal.

"Now walk over to the front door and wait for the deputy. Then you're going to jail. You savvy?"

"Yes, sir, Mr. Maddox."

He watched the leathery old cowpuncher do as he was told, to the letter, and then Ashton moved back to the winter hire, and helped Mateo Balcázar to his feet.

"Can you walk?" he asked.

"Sí. Muchas gracias, patrón."

Ashton only shrugged. He found the deputy again.

"You all right?" he asked.

"I think so," she managed to say.

Ashton tried to smile at her before he waved at his foreman. "He's all yours, Deputy." He started to apologize for Norris's tomfoolery but decided against that. A Maddox, his father had drilled into him, never apologizes. Because a Maddox is never wrong.

He had to smile at the cheers the crowd gave when Deputy Broadbent walked behind Colter Norris out of the Busted Stirrup. Well, Ashton would let that girl reap the glory. She had, after all, the guts to go in after Norris when no man in town had dared try it.

A good bracer of pricy bourbon would hit the spot right about now, but that would have to wait. He needed to get Mateo Balcázar patched up. But he was feeling good right now, and he was wondering how much he would embellish his story when he was back at the Circle M with his daughter and Taisie.

The good feeling disappeared when he heard the wailing of a siren and saw the Cutthroat County Ford SUV slide to a stop next to Ashton's Expedition.

Out stepped Sheriff John T. Drew and his boy.

CHAPTER 4

Homesick?

Lying on the couch, head resting on a pillow from his bed, with some CNN anchor talking about whatever the devil was going on in Yemen, George Grimes smiled at the most satisfying sound in the world.

Popping open a cold beer.

Well, maybe not as good as opening a new bottle of Jack Daniel's, but the sour mash would come later. He used the remote to change the channel to the first bowl game he could find—not the Rose or Sugar but some Podunk game sponsored by a corporation that started with a *S* and ended with a *T*, and Grimes figured that he could fill in two letters that defined the company to a *T*.

He had never heard of the two colleges playing and didn't care about the score. Just killing time on another red-letter day in Cutthroat County. Too cold to go outside, he figured, and as some smart aleck had told him the other day, "Sonny, it ain't even cold here yet."

Well, it sure felt frigid to a Texan.

Which is why he thought he must be homesick. It got cold in Texas. Don't let anyone tell some bragging Montanan any different, and ice storms wreaked havoc across the Lone Star State. But it was different up here in northwestern Montana. The freezing temps and snow wore on George Grimes, but beyond that, well, a man couldn't find good Tex-Mex chow in this part of the country—not even any Mexican food, or what would pass for Mexican food to a Texan. And while he wasn't partial to Chinese food—there weren't too many Chinese restaurants in most of the towns he had been stationed at during his Rangering years—he knew what good Chinese tasted like. Dallas had some real good joints, he recalled, but even the worst chow mein he had there was light years ahead of what he had sampled up in Medicine Pass.

It had been exciting when he first got up here, hired to assist the Citizens Action Network, a bunch of yahoos and punks led by Elison Dempsey, that cowardly weasel. But things had turned out all right. Grimes had made some headlines, got to talk on the cable networks and local affiliates, got his name in newspapers again, and an old friend, one of the few down in the Big Bend area who still talked to Grimes, had mailed him some clippings from the El Paso and Alpine newspapers and a bigger one in that Dallas rag.

He kept expecting some Hollywood producer to call him up and talk about a sequel to *Beretta Justice*, but maybe that would come later. The film had been a minor hit, or so he was told, though the box office results did not change the amount of money he had gotten. He should have found a better agent.

The team in blue and white scored, and Grimes saw the score. Forty-two to thirteen. Three minutes left in the fourth quarter. Not worth watching, so he turned to the Weather Channel and hit the button to get the local

temperatures, or as close to local as he could find in this
speck on the map, which was Great Falls. Thirty-three
degrees there. A warm January day. Folks had told him
that the weather was usually six or seven degrees warmer
in Great Falls than it was in Basin Creek.

He switched to CNN, downed his beer, and burped.
Maybe he would take a nap. Dream of summer. Or
some blond bimbo with giant breasts. The thought, or
maybe the four beers he had already had, made him
sleepy, and he was about to switch off the boob tube
when he saw some reporter standing outside in front
of what looked to be a courthouse and read the dateline
on the bottom:

MILK RIVER CITY, MONTANA

That was just up the road—well, nothing here was
just up or down from anywhere. On the Canadian
border. And there were flashing emergency lights all
around the bundled-up reporter, some young woman
who looked like she hated her job choice. But despite
being bundled up, she sure was a lot better looking than
any college football player or a bunch of sobbing
women from some terrorist strike in the Middle East or
North Africa or wherever the Sam Hill Yemen was.

Grimes hit the button to unmute the TV.

"That's right, Larry, a spokesman for the US Marshals Service has confirmed that two vehicles will be
used to drive the Chadwick gang to the federal correc-
tional facilities, where Rupert Chadwick and his uncles,
Lyle Baxter and Hemingway Jones, were sentenced by
Judge Linda Mae Applebee."

"Two vans?" The anchor sounded skeptical. "For three prisoners?"

"As you know," the woman explained, "Rupert Chadwick topped the FBI's Most Wanted List, and Baxter and Jones were sixth and tenth. These men are ruthless, and the judge, FBI, and federal marshals wanted to keep Chadwick away from his uncles."

"Why drive them? Wouldn't airplanes be faster?"

The woman seemed to wish the anchor would cut this interview short. Grimes enjoyed watching her suffer.

"Planes are grounded here, Larry," she told the dumb jerk sitting at a desk and being warmed by studio lights. "They will be taken to Deer Lodge."

"After being sentenced to life in prison with no chance of parole," Larry the Dufus told viewers. "How far is that drive, Clarissa?"

Clarissa, Grimes thought. Why don't you take off that hood? *Why don't you take off that entire parka so I can bet a better look at you?*

"Officials aren't giving out any details," Clarissa said, "but as one special agent told me, 'The Chadwick gang has many friends in this part of the country. We just want to get these three fiends behind bars as fast as we can.' That's a direct quote."

"So they can live out the rest of their lives behind bars." The anchor looked straight into the camera, giving his stern preacher look.

"Maybe not," Clarissa said, sounding better now that she realized this interview was about to be over. "A Justice Department spokeswoman said that this trial in Milk River City was just the first case, where the Chadwick gang will be brought to trial, and that the US District Court gets the next one. And that prosecutor has already pointed out that he will be seeking the death penalty for Rupert Chadwick, Lyle Baxter and Hemingway Jones."

"Thank you, Clarissa." The anchor smiled. "Go find yourself a warm Montana saloon and some hot chocolate—or something that will warm you even better."

"Thank you, Larry. It'll be on my expense account."

They laughed. The pretty chick disappeared, and Larry the Dumb Oaf said, "Earlier today in Washington, Senate Majority Leader –"

Larry vanished with a blip and a blackout after Grimes shut off the TV, then he climbed off the couch and moved to the end table, opened a drawer, and pulled out a Montana map.

It took him a while, but he found Milk River City, which got a bigger dot than Basin Creek but not as big as Miles City or Choteau or Havre. He had seen signs for Milk River City on State Highway 60, and, sure enough, the map said that would be one route to take, though it was a long one. Pick up US 287, then cut down to I-15 to Helena, cut west on US 12 to I-90, then down to the prison in Deer Lodge. That would likely be the way to go. But it would also be a predictable route. Or take a little road and wander across what looked like no man's land—like most of Montana looked like—toward I-15. Or other routes. If George Grimes were running this operation, he'd take them down to Cut Bank, hold them in the jail there and wait out the winter, then get a helicopter to haul those dirtbags to the pen.

Cut Bank interested him. He had driven up there in the fall, found a cheap but dependable hooker. Yeah, that's where George Grimes would take those rabid dogs, let them rot in jail while he found that big-boned gal.

Thinking about another beer, he glanced at his wristwatch and figured that Jack Daniel's Time came early during the first week of the New Year. He was heading toward the bottle when someone tapped on the door.

George Grimes didn't get many social visits.

He pulled out the Colt, a long-barreled .45-caliber he had placed underneath the pillow cushion, and walked softly to the door.

"Ranger Grimes."

He recognized the voice but didn't lower the hammer on the Colt. That would be Cindy Kristiansen, his landlady, too old for Grimes, too bony, too, but he liked her because the rent was cheap and she called him Ranger.

He still looked through the peephole and turned the deadbolt, then slowly cracked the door.

She was alone, so he opened the door. Her eyes fell to the cocked .45 in his big hand.

"You never know, ma'am," Grimes explained. "Texas Rangers are always prepared."

She smiled. He waited, trying to look patient and pleased, but he was breathing in frigid air and his throat was pleading for the thawing smoothness of Jack D.

"Ranger Grimes, I hate to be a bother, but Mr. Resnick, the bartender working at the Busted Stirrup Saloon—you know I own that place, I must've told you . . ."

"Yes, ma'am, you did." Grimes gave as close to a friendly look as he could manage when he was letting precious heat out of his efficiency apartment.

"Well, he called a moment ago and said that Colter Norris was tearing the bar apart."

Colter Norris. It took a moment to place the name.

"That rawboned old fart who works for Maddox?"

"Yes, the very one."

He couldn't cut off the laugh. "Miss Cindy, I don't see how much damage a puny cuss like that cowhand could do. A fart would knock him over."

She sighed. "Ranger Grimes, you haven't been in Cutthroat County long enough, if you don't mind my saying so."

He did mind, but he'd give her a free pass this time.

"He can be terrible when he is in his cups, Ranger Grimes, and that bar I own brings in more money than rent at these apartments or my Social Security check."

Grimes had no doubt about that. That joint was a gold mine in this Podunk burg.

"Well, it turns out," the puny old gal went on, "that our town constable, who is pretty much worthless, is out of town, and so are Deputy Creel and Sheriff Drew. And you know, your neighbor, poor Mary Broadbent, she can't do much but answer the telephone and file papers for Sheriff Drew these days, God bless her strong heart."

The smile spread across Grimes's beard-stubbled face.

"Would you like me to teach Colter what's-his-name some manners, Miss Cindy?"

She sighed. "God bless you, Ranger Grimes. If you could just go over to the Busted Stirrup and mop up what's left of my floor with that no-account cur's face, I'd surely appreciate it."

"I'd be my pleasure, Miss Grace. Let me pull on my boots, grab a coat, and I'll drive right over there."

The day, he decided, was picking up. He didn't even feel cold when, with boots and winter coat and Stetson on, he walked out of his apartment.

His ancient landlady had gone back to her apartment

by the time he had bundled up for Montana weather. He locked his apartment and hurried to his Dodge Ram, only to find that the lock was frozen. He had to lean close, light his cigarette lighter, and hold it close to the keyhole, freezing his ears off, but at least the snow had stopped falling. That Bic worked its magic, and he climbed into the rig, slammed the door closed, and lit a cigarette for himself.

His pickup was all Texas. Warm-blooded. It took him several minutes before the engine caught and the heater finally began blowing cold air onto him.

Why couldn't some city in New Orleans have wanted him to come fight crime? Or a city in the Arizona desert that had plenty of swimming pools—though he didn't like to swim—and about a zillion Arizona State coeds in skimpy clothes?

Worst thing about it all was that by the time the Ram had heated up, he was already at the Busted Stirrup—or what was left of it. He swore and shook his head, then cursed himself a bit for doubting his old landlady. One guy had done that much damage? That cowpoke who looked thin enough that it wouldn't take more than a fart to knock down?

And Grimes was just looking at the outside of the building.

Worst of all, he was too late. That sad excuse of a deputy was leading the Circle M hired man toward that big SUV the head-man law dog had climbed out of with his college-boy son. Some of the gawking spectators were moving on, but the big man of the ranch—and some said of the entire county—was here, too, and he looked madder than a hornet.

Things might get right interesting, Grimes figured,

but he wasn't going to get out of the truck now that it was warming up inside. He wasn't until he saw the pipsqueak newspaper man, Lorimer, who published the piece of crud that passed in these parts for a newspaper. Well, the *Weekly Item* wasn't exactly *Texas Monthly*, Grimes told himself, but he might get his name in the paper. And as an old Ranger had told Grimes when he was just a state trooper, you never knew who was gonna read something in a newspaper.

Jack Daniel's would have to wait.

Grimes stepped out of the truck, jerked up his collar, and pulled down the brim of his hat, and walked toward what he figured would be center stage in Basin Creek for a while. He could stand the freezing wind for a bit.

CHAPTER 5

She was in for it. Mary Broadbent knew that without John T. Drew saying a word, but the sheriff wasn't one to chew out anyone, other than a perp, in front of a crowd.

Ashton Maddox stopped and let Mary escort Colter Norris toward Cutthroat County's top peace officer.

"Did you read him his rights?" Drew asked, but his eyes bored so hard into Mary that it made the bullet wound in her head seem trivial.

"Yes," she whispered. Her heart raced, her head pounded, and despite the freezing wind, she thought she was sweating.

Drew made no response. He simply reached over, took Colter Norris's shoulder, and pulled him toward the Ford.

"Colter Norris," Drew said, "you are being placed under arrest for assault and battery, reckless endangerment, assault on a peace officer, and destruction of private property. More charges may be filed before we're finished with our investigation."

He did a quick search while he said by rote, "You have the right to remain silent . . ."

She had already read the Circle M foreman his rights, had told John Drew that, but she could figure it out—even with a patched-up hole in her head.

John T. Drew would be the arresting officer on the record books. That wasn't for glory. That was for Mary's own protection. She hadn't been cleared for anything but minor desk duty. John would tell her all about that . . . later. If he were still speaking to her. If he had not severed her employment with Cutthroat County. Or called an end to their relationship.

She felt sick.

Later that night, in the sheriff's SUV in front of her apartment, Drew said everything that Mary figured he would say.

"You're on desk duty. Desk duty. That doesn't mean you can go on calls."

She played it meekly, whispering, "I know."

"You know how insurance companies are. They're just looking for a way not to pay anything. Fall out of your chair in the office, fall down those outdated stairs, and they'll pay you anything to keep from going bankrupt. But get hurt, just a sprained finger, doing something you're not supposed to be doing, and so long, insurance. *Try explaining that to our county manager.*"

"I know. I'm sorry."

He swore and shook his head. "You scared the crap out of me. Do you know that?"

"Yes." That's when she figured she needed to fight back. "But I also knew that Denton and Taylor were out of town. And you were in the Always Winters. I couldn't let Norris tear the place apart—or put some drunk in the Choteau hospital."

"You don't know Colter Norris."

That's when she snapped back. "I've been on this force for two-plus years, John. I've seen Colter Norris on a tear. Once a year. New Year's or his birthday. Always one or the other. Not the Fourth of July. Not during the rodeo. Not on payday like most of the cowboys around here. Just once. I've seen how you handled him, and I've even helped bring him in before. What did you want me to do? Let George Grimes try to take him?"

He stared into her eyes long and hard, and finally let his façade crack.

"What am I gonna do with you?" he whispered.

She smiled. "The same thing I'm gonna do with you—when this headache passes."

He leaned over and kissed her cheek.

"I'd pay money to see Colter Norris and George Grimes go head-to-head."

"I wouldn't." She opened the door. "Pick me up in the morning?"

"You bet."

But that was later that night, after things had settled down. At that moment in the afternoon, Mary thought her heart might blow a gasket. This was no way to ring in a new year.

Drew had just started frisking the drunken cowboy when Ashton Maddox walked up to him.

"I'd like to bail him out," the rancher said.

"You can't bail him out till after he's been arraigned and bail has been set," Drew told him without turning away from Norris, who didn't look nearly as intimidating as he had inside the Busted Stirrup.

"Maybe I'll call Judge Olson."

"Call Jorn," Drew snapped. "Call Murdoch, too. But you can't bail him out till he's been arraigned."

Murdoch Robeson was Cutthroat County's prosecuting attorney, though he lived down the road a ways in Choteau in Teton County. Jorn Olson was the judge, but fat chance of getting him to answer the phone after five in the afternoon.

Drew opened the back door to the Interceptor, ducking Norris's head so he wouldn't get a concussion, and then slammed the door shut. Turning, he put his hands on his hips and stared hard at Ashton Maddox.

"He's going to sleep it off," Drew said forcefully. "In jail." He tilted his head toward the bar. "And that's gonna be paid for. One way or the other."

"It won't be the first time I've paid to have that gin mill remodeled," Maddox said.

"You might be paying more than just carpenters." Drew tilted his head toward the Mexican.

"He rides for the Circle M," Maddox said. "He knows I'll pay wages and his doctor bills."

"Good." Drew walked away from the Interceptor, pulling out a notebook from his back pocket and a digital recording device from his shirt pocket. "But first he's giving a statement." He stopped to turn back to Mary.

"I guess it'll be all right for you to take some statements from witnesses, Deputy. Just make sure you get signatures and do this *by the book*."

Mary Broadbent breathed in and out. *Well*, she thought, *I still have a job.*

She didn't feel steady, but, using her cane, she managed to walk toward Bull Resnick.

Denton Creel arrived ten or twelve minutes later, and Drew let him finish getting statements from patrons who had witnessed RAMPAGE AT THE BUSTED STIRRUP, which would be the headline in the Carl Lorimer's *Weekly Item* the next week. Drew gave his son the digital camera he stored in the glove box and asked him to take photos of the Mexican cowboy Norris had throttled and of the inside and exterior damage wreaked upon the bar, then run over to his office.

"Those photos are evidence, Billy," he said. "Do a good job."

"You bet!"

If he still weren't so mad at Mary Broadbent—or maybe still worried sick over all the ways this incident could have played out—he might have laughed.

Colter Norris didn't say a word, but he never had a gift for gab, as Drew drove the short distance to the Cutthroat County Courthouse/Basin Creek Municipal Building. He had to guide the ranch foreman up the stairs to the sheriff's office for the fingerprinting and head shots with another digital camera, and then tag and file every single thing in Norris's possession. That included the revolver the wiry little man had carried into the bar.

He unloaded the cartridges, putting those in a bag, and then looked into the cowhand's face.

"You're in big trouble for carrying this inside the Busted Stirrup," Drew told him.

The man laughed, turned, and spit on the floor. He cursed and said, "You forget. I ain't got to have no permit to carry in Montana no more. I can carry it anywhere, Drew. Even inside a bar. I don't need no permit. And I don't need no background check."

Drew nodded. "No, sir, you don't. But you do need a permit to carry a weapon, openly or concealed, in a state game preserve.

The drunken cowpuncher squinted. "Huh?" he finally said.

"What I just told you. Montana law prohibits the carrying of a firearm, concealed or in clear view, without a permit from the director of Fish, Wildlife, and Parks, in a state game preserve."

"Game preserve?"

"You forget that part of our fair city falls inside the Basin River State Preserve so we still have cutthroat, and nobody wants to see our West Slope cutthroat go extinct. Yes, sir, you're in big trouble. You're lucky you're not facing a federal rap on this." He paused. "Though maybe I'll call the US Forest Service and see what they think."

He got what he wanted. Colter Norris's face paled.

Once Drew got him out of his ruined cowboy duds and into Cutthroat County's finest orange jumpsuit, he led him to the basement jail and locked him up in the big cell.

"It's cold down here," Norris complained.

Drew laughed. "Colter, the sun's hardly down. You think it's cold *now*?"

He locked the door, tested it, and walked back toward

the stairs. "But if I don't forget, I'll send down a blanket before I leave to my nice, warm house."

Ashton Maddox had helped himself to what the Cutthroat County Sheriff's Department called coffee. The girl deputy, Broadbent, came into the office, saw him, but said nothing and sat at her desk, turning on the computer and pulling out her notebook. He didn't ask if she wanted coffee.

The sheriff came up a few minutes later, glancing at his deputy before his eyes locked on Maddox.

"You still here?"

No, Maddox thought about saying, *I'm a mirage.* He finished the cold coffee and set the mug on John T. Drew's desk. "Can I . . . ?" No, he decided he wasn't going to ask the sheriff anything. Asking a Drew was beneath a Maddox, no matter how much the sheriff had helped with getting Aly and Taisie out of that psycho killer's clutches this past summer. "I'd like to talk to my foreman."

Drew seemed to debate that as he unbuckled his gun belt, storing it in a locked safe, then removed his hat and coat and hung those up.

"I guess that'll be all right."

That surprised Ashton. He thought for sure that Drew would make up some excuse.

"You know the way to the pit, don't you?"

Ashton hadn't answer. He remembered Drew's daddy throwing him in that dank, cavernous cell back when he had been drag racing Rudy Pierce on Highway 76. That old hard rock had not arrested Rudy, of course, though that might have been because not even a sheriff's patrol car could catch up with Rudy's Z/28. That kid should have gone into the moonshine-running business instead of settling down to fix cars, trucks, tractors, and lawn mowers.

"Yeah. I remember."

He had also gone to the basement more times than he could count to chew the hide off other Circle M riders who couldn't hold their liquor or let an insult, said in jest, pass without busting noses or knocking some molars loose.

"Keep it short," Drew told him. "We'll be locking up as soon as Mary finishes her report. Hate for you to have to spend the night here, too."

"I won't be long." He was at the door when Drew called his name.

Turning, he saw the sheriff unplugging a portable space heater, then bring the contraption and the remote control across the cramped office.

"If you don't mind, bring this down to Colter. The remote's easy enough to figure out, and there's an outlet in the wall just across from the cell door."

Maddox slipped the remote control into his coat pocket and grabbed the cord and device in his left hand. He opened the door and stepped into the hall. "I won't be long."

He headed to the staircase and heard the door to the sheriff's office close behind him.

He flipped the light switch before he descended into the basement, his winter boots echoing down the cavernous, chilly stairs. The sheriff had been kind enough to leave the lights on in the basement, and Colter Norris was sitting on a blanket on the floor, testing his jaw. He stopped when he saw Ashton and grabbed the bars behind him to pull himself to his feet.

Maddox found the outlet, plugged in the unit, and brought it as close to the cell as the cord would reach. He figured out the remote, turned on the heater, and, hearing the motor whirl, passed the remote through the bars.

His foreman took the piece of cheap plastic, looked at it, and then stared through the ancient bars at his boss.

"You're the best foreman I've had," Ashton told him, "and, most likely, the best one I'll ever have. But you pull a stunt like this again, and I'm sending you packing."

The wiry man just nodded.

"You need anything?" Maddox swore softly. "You're in here till the judge can get down and get you arraigned. Snowstorm isn't supposed to last long, so that might be tomorrow, but knowing how our judge works, he might keep you in here over the weekend."

"I've been in jail before," Norris told him. "I'll—"

"You're not breaking out." Maddox waved his finger at the foreman. It was known throughout most of Montana that the decrepit jail cells in Cutthroat County couldn't hold a lame cockroach for more than twenty minutes. "What were you thinking?"

The leathery old-timer looked at his scuffed knuckles. "I wanted to give that Texas Ranger a whuppin' he'd remember."

"Mateo Balcázar doesn't look a bit like Grimes."

Norris stared at his boots.

"*Does he?*" The shout bounced across the dark walls.

"I didn't hit that Mexican too hard."

"Hard enough." Maddox shook his head. "Whatever the doctor charges me is coming out of this month's paycheck. Savvy?"

Norris nodded.

"Lord knows how much money I'll be forking over to

Cindy. And I mean it. One more chicken-livered, idiotic stunt like this and you're through with the Circle M. And fat chance of finding any outfit in Montana that'll hire you on after I blackball you."

Ashton turned to spit on the floor, then whirled around and marched to the stairs. He had issued similar threats to Norris before, but this time he really meant it. This was the twenty-first century, not the 1800s, and Ashton had enough problems in his life right then. He didn't need some Wild West cowpuncher acting out some stupid saloon brawl from a 1950s B Western.

He marched up the stairs, turned off the stairs light, found his way into the frigid night, and marched to the snow-covered Ford Expedition. He'd be glad when he got back home, where he could have another good bourbon. He'd be glad when this storm moved out of Cutthroat County.

That big SUV was backing out into the snow-packed road, and George Grimes eased on the brakes until Ashton Maddox was flooring his fancy, hundred-thousand-dollar rig down the street. Chuckling, Grimes wished he could have seen the rancher's face, but he blew that man a kiss for leaving him a good parking place in front of the courthouse.

He hated leaving the Ram, because it had just warmed up enough to suit him, but he grabbed a receipt from the liquor store, stuck it in his pocket, and hurried into the wretched old building. He didn't bother locking the truck. He didn't want to have to burn fuel in his lighter to unfreeze the lock again, and nobody in this dung heap of a town was stupid enough to steal his truck.

He wouldn't call the inside of the building warm, but at least it wasn't snowing indoors. Yet. He came up the stairs and quickly entered the sheriff's office.

John T. Drew looked up from his desk, and his expression caused Grimes to chuckle.

"You don't look happy to see me, Boss Man." He nodded at the pretty deputy and walked over and slapped the receipt on the pile of papers in front of John T. Drew.

The sheriff glanced at the receipt and looked up. "Two liters of Jack Daniel's, a carton of cigarettes, and a case of Coors."

"'Cause that skinflint don't carry Lone Star at what passes for a liquor store in this dung heap of a town."

"When do you plan on returning to Texas?"

Grimes laughed.

"Then you might want to change your residency, put Montana plates on your rig, and get yourself a Montana driver's license—if you can pass the test."

Grimes pointed his trigger finger at the receipt.

"Turn it over, pardner. That's my written statement. Witnessed and signed by your boy deputy." He turned and winked at the cop. "He ain't as pretty as this one."

He chuckled when that tall drink of rotgut turned over the receipt and saw Grimes's chicken scratches and his John Hancock and Denton Creel's tiny little signature.

"It's short," the sheriff said. "I'll say that much."

"Just the facts. Like that *Dragnet* dude said."

Drew slid the paper away. "All right. I'll call you if we need you."

"Not even a thank you, Sheriff?" Grimes chuckled.

"That's all right. I was just doin' my civic duty. This one was on the house. Next time, I'll send you my bill. But I'll give you my New Year's sales rates." He turned, winked at that pretty cop, and headed to the door, but turned back before his hand reached the handle.

"I thought this storm was movin' through. It's still a blizzard out there."

"It's not a blizzard," Sheriff Drew told him without looking up from the other papers on his desk. "At the Busted Stirrup, you could hear some old-timers tell you about the real storms we've had here. But there's no telling when that'll reopen."

Grimes laughed. "Drop by my pad, lawman, and I'll tell you about some kicker bars where I knocked down the walls in some parts of Austin decent folks don't know about and in West Texas where there weren't no decent folks."

He opened the door and was stepping outside when he heard the pretty cop say, "Thank you for your assistance, Ranger Grimes."

That stunned him. He must have looked right then like Carter McDonald in third grade after Grimes had punched the wannabe bully in the nose on the school playground.

Slowly, he turned back and looked at the deputy. She still wasn't a bad-looking woman, even with that ugly patch over her head.

He started to thank her but held back and just nodded at her, then stepped outside and closed the door.

1894

▲

JANUARY

CHAPTER 6

"What do you mean Carlton Boone wants to see me?" Murdo Maddox roared at that stupid Ben Penny, one of the Circle M's hired hands, who was standing on the porch of Murdo's home. "*In town?*"

He could have invited the dollar-a-day waddie inside, gotten him out of that icy wind, but he didn't see any point in that. Before the hand could answer, Murdo fired another question.

"And what the Sam Hill were you doing in town anyway, Penny? This ain't Sunday, is it?"

"No, sir," Penny said, trembling more from the fear of that legendary Maddox wrath than the frigid wind and the threat of more snow. About a foot already covered the ground, and some of the drifts had to be taller than Murdo himself. But at least this winter wasn't shaping up to be another 1886–1887 storm—the one folks called the "Big Die-Up" because it had practically wiped out ranches south of here, from below the Blackfoot River all the way to southern Colorado. The prairie states from the Dakotas to Kansas had also been hit hard. That murderous winter had almost wrecked the entire cattle business across the West—from Kansas to the Canadian border.

"It's . . ." Ben Penny's face reddened.

"Tuesday," Murdo informed him.

"Yes, sir."

Murdo thought about slamming the door in his face, but then he started thinking like a Maddox. Carlton Boone was a rancher down south. Carlton Boone had been struggling to keep that banker in Helena from calling in Boone's note and calling his bluff. Carlton Boone might be ready to give up, admit that Montana had whipped him good—though he had put up a better fight than many—and was ready to run back home to his mommy in Prowers County, Colorado.

He wet his lips. "He tell you why he needs me to ride to Basin Creek in freezing weather with the threat of snow?" Murdo thought he spoke quietly and as polite as a Maddox could muster, but Ben Penny's face revealed that the cowboy didn't seem to feel that had been the case.

"Said he's got some cattle to sell."

Murdo laughed. Nobody bought cattle at this time of year. Especially cattle owned by a man who was . . . desperate, one more bad break from skedaddling or putting a bullet through his brain.

"He in town?" Murdo asked.

Penny nodded. "Said he'd be at the Swede's saloon till three today. And if you didn't come by then, he'd be payin' a visit to Abe Killone."

Murdo took a step back inside the doorway. The waddie quickly added, "I wasn't in the Swede's place. He caught me at the German's trading post. Just told me to pass that on to you."

He didn't like Boone throwing Abe Killone, the second-largest rancher in the area, in his face. And if

Boone wanted to sell his land—the days of open range pretty much fading with that hard winter of 1886–1887—Murdo had no interest. Oh, he'd pay top price for good land, but the Bar B wasn't good land. Passable land at best. But if the cowboy'd heard right, the rancher was selling his cattle, and Murdo began rethinking his quick dismissal of buying cattle in winter. Oh, it could backfire and put egg on Murdo's face easy enough if this winter turned hard and long. On the other hand, if the snow didn't let up, there was a good chance the army would be begging for beef. And no matter what Murdo told himself about the foolishness of buying meat on the hoof in winter, sometimes foolishness paid off. Sell lame Carlton Boone cattle to the butcher shops and some poor outfits in the county. Keep the Circle M Black Angus for prime spring and summer prices.

"I'm sorry it took me so long to get back from Basin Creek, sir," the cowboy explained, "but it was rough goin' on the road."

Murdo barely heard what the kid said, but he nodded, still thinking, debating with himself, and at length making a decision. "Saddle up Captain Lewis for me, kid. Leave him in the barn. Then you'd best get those supplies unloaded before Jacques blows his top." Jacques was the new cook, hired this fall by foreman Deke Weems. Frenchy wasn't French, and he wasn't much of a cook, but the grub he served was hot and filling, and he could cook up a decent pot of coffee when the mood struck him.

Murdo looked at the clouds again.

"Tell Deke I won't be back till tomorrow. I'll have to spend the night in town."

Actually, he was wondering if he'd be able to spend the night at Jeannie Ashton's place. But that was nothing more than fantasy. He probably wouldn't even be able to see her since her place was south of town, and Ben Penny likely wasn't exaggerating about the condition of the roads.

When the cowboy turned away, Murdo got ready for a wintry ride to Basin Creek, finding his sheepskin coat and woolen scarves, filling his flask with brandy, and throwing some clothes in a carpetbag in case he had to spend more time in Basin Creek than he wanted to.

Bundled up as best he could, he turned down the coal-oil lamps, emptied his coffeepot, and left his home for the barn. Ben Penny had done a good job saddling the stallion, and Murdo tied on his carpetbag, stepped into the stirrup, and pulled himself into the saddle. After pulling up a wool bandanna to cover his mouth and nose, he kicked Captain Lewis into a walk and let the horse follow the tracks Ben Penny's gelding had made up the trail to the main road, then rode to Basin Creek.

He left his horse at Finnian O'Boyle's livery stable, surprised to find it crowded. He was lucky, the stable boy told him, that there were any stalls left.

The sounds of snoring men reached his ears as Murdo started unsaddling the zebra dun. He shuffled to the nearest stall, laying his saddle over the top railing and spying some skinny man wrapped in a blanket, sleeping near his horse.

Turning to Luke Jasper, he asked, "Is your boss trying to give Sissy White some competition?" Sissy ran a boarding house—Basin Creek's only boarding house, if you didn't count the poor excuse for a hotel. By thunder, there wasn't another hotel in all of Cutthroat County.

"Charley blowed all his summer wages," Luke said. "Got too drunk to ride to Texas."

That was Charley Bandanna. He had worked for Murdo two years back. This year he had signed on at Abe Killone's spread. That was one thing about some cowboys. They rode for whoever they felt like. But when a man like Charley Bandanna took your pay, he rode for the brand.

Luke nodded. "Couple of boys are sharin' the stall with him." He pulled a blanked over his shoulders. "They'll need to sleep close to fight off this chill."

"Chill ain't the word for it," Murdo said, before tossing Luke a dime and heading into not chill, but a brutal cold.

He dropped his carpetbag off at Sissy's boarding house, chatting with her briefly, then checked his watch against Sissy's regulator. Murdo was more than an hour late, but then Carlton Boone's deadline had not been reasonable. The lousy rancher probably wanted to think he was making a Maddox sweat. But Murdo would give that two-bit wastrel no satisfaction. He told Sissy he would talk later, that he had to meet a fellow at the Swede's place.

He saw the rancher sipping a beer at a corner table. Carlton Boone was the only person there, except for the Swede, who sat next to the stove, sampling his own whiskey. The Swede jumped up when he realized who had just walked into the dimly lit—and not quite warm—bucket of blood. Murdo wished the rancher had picked the Hangman's Saloon and Gambling Emporium as a meeting place, but he doubted if Boone could afford even a beer down the street.

"Just bring me a coffee, Swede," Murdo said, pulling down his scarves and using his teeth to remove his gloves as he walked to the table.

Carlton Boone looked up slowly. His face showed nothing but defeat.

Silently, Boone motioned at the chair opposite him, and Murdo dragged it out, sat down, took off his hat, and set it on the table.

The Swede came by with a tin cup of coffee and left immediately.

"How you been, Murdo?"

"Passable. You?"

The thin man didn't answer. "I reckon your cowhand got my message to you."

"I'm here."

The rancher sipped his whiskey.

"Sold my place," he said, then chuckled as he killed the liquor in his glass. "Some gent—Mackey's his name—from Helena. He says he's gonna put up a new town there. Something better than Basin Creek."

It wouldn't be hard to make something better than this wreck of a place in the middle of nowhere.

"Ambitious," Murdo said. "What did you have? Two sections? Three?"

"Three." He laughed, but Murdo found no humor in the man's chuckle, his eyes, anywhere. "Yeah. What's that? Eighteen hundred acres and then some? Not enough for a man to make a livin' on in this country."

"Reckon not." Murdo drank some coffee.

He waited, but the rancher just stared at his drink, then refilled the tumbler.

"I got cattle, though."

So it was the cattle he wanted to sell. Good. Murdo

might gamble with some beef, but not for nineteen hundred and twenty acres—"eighteen hundred acres and then some"!—that weren't worth the grass that kept most of the dirt from blowing away.

"How many?" Murdo asked.

"Three hundred."

Murdo would want to count those himself. Boone's math skills had not impressed him so far. Three hundred head? On three sections? No wonder he was busted.

"Herefords."

Better than the Texas longhorns that drovers brought to this country a decade and more ago. But not the Black Angus that Murdo favored. But he wouldn't be keeping this herd for long. He would sell them quickly. Get them off Circle M grazing land.

That's another thing the hard winter had taught Montana cattlemen. You couldn't overgraze in this country. Not anymore.

"What's your price?" Murdo asked and got ready for the greedy Coloradan's suggestion.

"Whatever you want to pay me."

Murdo set down his cup. He studied Boone but couldn't read the face. That reply made no sense to a rancher like Murdo Maddox.

The rancher shrugged.

Murdo nodded at the bottle, and Boone made the same movement. After splashing his coffee with the Swede's rotgut, he drank down the coffee quickly and set the empty cup on the table.

"For the whole herd?" he asked.

"That's what I'm sellin'," Boone replied. He sighed, and Murdo thought he saw tears in the man's worn-out eyes, but Boone found his loosened bandanna, brought it up, blew his nose, then wiped his face.

When the bandanna dropped onto the table, Murdo knew that the rancher had been crying.

"Laurie died last week," the rancher said. Murdo had only seen Boone's wife three or four times. He couldn't even describe her.

The worn-out man chuckled without any mirth and shook his head. "Now I know why gravediggers are so busy digging holes in the fall. So they don't have to fight frozen ground in the dead of winter."

"I'm sorry to hear that, Carlton," Murdo said.

"No, you ain't. But I am. Never should have brought her up here. Pneumonia. Wish we'd stayed in Colorado."

"Twenty dollars a head," Murdo said. He had planned on going no higher than fifteen and had hoped to get them for twelve. "One of my men and one of yours do the counting."

The rancher shook his head. "I ain't got any hands left, Murdo. Paid 'em off. Them that hadn't already quit. Your boy does the counting. I give you the bill of sale. And your silver and gold gets me away from this miserable world of ice and heartache."

Murdo added more of the busted rancher's whiskey to the empty coffee cup and drank some.

"How about if I just hand over six thousand dollars in greenbacks and gold? That's twenty a head for three hundred head. You can leave. If my man's tally shows more than three hundred head, I'll send you what I owe you. If the count comes up less than three hundred, that's my problem."

The pathetic creature wiped his eyes again.

"I ain't after charity."

"It ain't charity. I'll make a profit on your cattle." He wasn't as confident as he had tried to sound.

"You want to draw up a bill of sale?" Boone asked.

"Swede," Murdo called without taking his eyes off this busted-hearted rancher. He was thinking of Jeannie Ashton, a widow, and her dead husband and those dead children on that hilltop behind her place south of town. "You got any writing paper around? And pen and ink?"

"*Ja. Ja.*" He came off his stool. "Think so. *Ja. Ja.* Think so." He disappeared behind the bar.

"Before you start writing this up, Murdo," Boone began, "or handing over gold pieces, you need to know one thing."

Here it comes, Murdo thought.

"All those cattle—it ain't a lot for a man like you, but I ain't like you." The broken man sighed, shook his head, and leaned closer. "The deal I made with that land speculator, well, those cattle have to be off my land in two weeks. Well, actually, in twelve days now. Signed that contract two days ago. Cattle off the land and in the hands and control of, or on the property of, the buyer. Else they go with that skinflint with my deed and my house and barn and corrals."

"What kind of deal is that?" Murdo demanded.

"The deal I cut with him. Or the deal where he slick-ered me good. Take your pick. But it's the deal. Signed and witnessed."

Boone was reaching for the whiskey bottle, but Murdo snatched it and dragged it away from the fool. He had half a mind to break the bottle over the dunce's head, but the saloon doors opened, and he jerked his head to find Jeannie Ashton in the doorway.

CHAPTER 7

She came to town when the snow started falling. She blamed that on her ankles. How they ached when a big storm came up, and they had been aching all that night. So when she stepped outside to break the ice in the troughs and throw enough grain out for the horses that morning and felt the stinging bite of snow on what little of her face was exposed to the elements, she decided that she was not going to wait out winter alone in her cabin. Not again.

Jeannie Ashton could hire some saloon swamper to come out and take care of her livestock. She could find a room in the hotel—trade a horse if she had to—but she just wasn't made for Montana winters, even if she had lived through more of them than she wanted to remember.

She hitched up the black Percheron she had bought from Abe Killone that fall to her phaeton, figuring the big draft horse would be strong enough to pull the buggy out of any snowbanks she might run into, though it hadn't been snowing that hard and the wind had been just gusty, not a nightmare. Yet.

It turned out to be roughly a hundred times harder than she had figured, and twice Jeannie considered turning back, but the big black was a monster, and it pushed through the wind and snow and finally led her into Basin Creek.

God kept looking after Jeannie Ashton. Lois DeForrest must have been staring out her frosty window when the phaeton passed her house, and she ran outside and shouted Jeannie's name.

Jeannie pulled the horse to a stop and turned around.

"Are you crazy?" Lois demanded. "It's eighteen degrees. And has been snowing since yesterday morning." Her hand pointed to the thermometer hanging on a nail on a log column that held up a roof porch.

"Let me—" Jeannie started, but the seamstress was stepping off her porch and slogging through the snow, past the county sheriff's home and to the side of the road, where she drove her way through knee-deep snow and finally stopped on the right side of the buggy.

"Are you sick?" Lois asked.

"No. I'm just . . ."

"This is no day for a picnic, Jeannie. And it's getting dark."

She sighed, seeing her frosty breath. "All right," she confessed. "The cabin's walls started to close in. I decided I wasn't going to wait out this storm. I'm going to the hotel, and I'm staying there till Percy Willingham kicks me out."

"You're doing no such thing, Jeannie Ashton," Lois told her. "Hand me your grip."

Before Jeannie could voice a suitable rejection, Lois had reached over and jerked the luggage off the seat.

"You're staying with me. As long as you like. As long as you help with the dishes and maybe look after those little devils of our county sheriff."

Jeannie only got her mouth halfway open.

"No argument, woman. Now, I'll let you take your sled to Finnian O'Boyle's, and then you can make your way back here. Are we in agreement?"

Jeannie smiled. "Dare I argue?"

"You won't win if you do. Hurry back. It's getting colder, and the sun will be down before you know it. I don't want to have to come looking for you."

"All right." Jeannie sighed, shrugged her shoulders, and then gave the seamstress a beaming smile.

This was working out much better than she had planned.

Feeling a tad warmer, she called out to the black and covered the distance to the livery stable quickly, slowly only when she passed the saloon run by the Swede. She didn't need to see the brand on the zebra dun stallion's hip to know that was Murdo Maddox's horse, Captain Lewis. What she couldn't fathom was why Murdo would be drinking in that saloon.

Luke Jasper was working at O'Boyle's livery. Jeannie sometimes wondered if that poor boy ever got a day off. She wrote down the instructions, said she did not know how long she would be staying, and asked if he knew of any out-of-work cowhand in town that might be able to take care of her place till the storm passed through.

The kid said he would ask around, and Jeannie told him that she would be staying at Miss DeForrest's cabin till she came back for her horse and buggy.

Which, she thought but did not say, *might be late spring if she didn't thaw out in a hurry.*

The dun was still hitched in front of the saloon when she walked past, and she stopped, then decided to see if there was a horse thief in town or if she might get to see Murdo.

The door she opened almost knocked him down.

Murdo backed up, looked up, and his eyes widened.

"Jeannie!" he shouted.

He wasn't the first person to yell at her for walking into a place like this. Nor would he be the last.

Then they spoke at the same time. "What brings you to—?"

She laughed first. He sort of coughed.

Another figure came from the back of the saloon to the bar. She recognized Carlton Boone and heard him ask the Swede for a bottle to take with him. He slapped a coin on the bar, and the Swede ducked below the bar and brought a bottle up, holding it till he saw the greenback in the rancher's hand.

Boone turned away from the bar and looked past Jeannie at Murdo. "I'm staying at the hotel. Bring the money there sometime tomorrow."

"Percy won't let you take liquor into the hotel, Boone," the Swede warned.

Taking the bottle in his hand, Boone chuckled. "It won't reach the hotel, old man."

He nodded at Jeannie, tipping his hat, and walked past her.

"I'm sorry," Jeannie said softly, "about Laurie, Mr. Boone. She was charming and kind."

"Thank you, ma'am. I surely appreciate hearing that from a lady like you."

She felt the wintry blast as the door opened. Boone had trouble closing the door, but it finally clicked shut, and the saloon felt much colder now than it had when Jeannie had first stepped inside.

"What on earth are you—"

Both of them stopped before finishing the question

they were asking each other. Jeannie smiled. Murdo didn't.

She answered first. "I think they call it cabin fever, Murdo. I'm staying with Lois for a while." Sighing, she shook her head. "I just couldn't take another night alone in that cabin."

Her eyes focused on the floorboards, looking at the bullet holes, ditches carved by spurs, a couple of crushed bugs that had not been swept out since it was warm enough for insects, and what appeared to be dried bloodstains—or so she fathomed.

She felt his fingers underneath her chin before she even saw them, then felt her head being lifted until she stared into those bottomless eyes he had.

"I've offered you a way out of that cabin for some time." He smiled warmly. "Lost count of the times."

"Well . . ." That was all she could think of to say.

He let out a long sigh but did not look away from her.

"Someday . . . maybe." It wasn't a question.

Her head bobbed before she realized she was nodding. But she clarified the gesture.

"Maybe. Someday."

"Buy you some supper?" he asked.

"Oh . . . I think Lois . . ." On most days, she wasn't so uncertain or indecisive. "Is Doris open?"

Doris Caffey owned the café in town.

The Swede answered before Murdo could. "No. She closed. I got nuts. And pickles."

Now both smiled, and that pleased Jeannie immensely.

"Maybe Lois wouldn't mind setting another plate," Murdo said. "I'm not all that fond of pickles and nuts."

The Swede shrugged at the mild rebuke.

"I don't know, Murdo . . ." Jeannie began, but she let

Murdo Maddox take her arm, and she turned with him, and they walked to the door.

Lois, of course, was delighted to have Murdo Maddox join them for supper. And Jeannie had been foresighted enough to have brought a bottle of wine from her cabin.

The biscuits were leftovers from dinner, heated up in the stove, and the sizzling steaks cooked in the cast-iron skillet filled the cabin with a wonderful aroma. Lois refused to let either Jeannie or Murdo do any work.

They ate at the table, drinking wine and listening to Murdo talk about the deal he had struck with that poor rancher, Carlton Boone.

Lois said it sounded like a story right out of a dime novel.

Jeannie, though, was all business.

"How far away is Mr. Boone's ranch? I know it's pretty far south."

"Forty miles," Murdo answered, "or thereabouts."

"Can you get the cattle off there in twelve—well, it'll probably be eleven days now?"

"Most drives we've made to Fort Benton, we average twelve or fourteen miles a day."

"In summer," Jeannie told him.

He nodded. "In summer."

"It's shaping up to be one nasty storm, Murdo," she told him.

"I'm hoping it'll blow itself out." He drank some wine. "It's not the ideal way to do this, but I have some ideas. Call me crazy—"

"You're crazy," Lois said, and chuckled. Jeannie

tried not to roll her eyes. The seamstress was not used to drinking wine.

"The deal as Boone told me is that the cattle have to be off his land and under my control in that time period. His land is three sections. Three hundred head. I think we can do it. And under my control *or* on my property. That's *or*. They'll be under my control."

"But if the storm gets worse," Jeannie said, and left it there.

He shrugged. "Well, if this buyer wants to put up a new town, God be with him. I don't think he wants those Herefords. Maybe I'll have to cut a deal with him, but I think he'll be fine. And I got that herd for a fair price. Fatten them up in the spring. Get them to market by fall. It'll all work out."

"Do you have enough cowboys?"

He finished his glass of wine and refilled it with a generous pour.

"I'll have to hire some men." His face betrayed him.

He would have to hire men. There weren't many cowhands drifting up this way in winter, looking for work. And this was a pretty heavy snow. Jeannie figured that Murdo might have a herd of three hundred cattle frozen to death in snowbanks and in ditches, or caught up against the fences that were taking over this country.

Granted, he could afford the loss. He was a wealthy, wealthy man.

But could he take the bruises to his pride?

She started to say something else when she heard someone knocking on the door.

Lois rose and crossed the room.

"Yes?" she said, starting to open the door. Jeannie rose from her chair.

"Miss Lois—"

Lois jerked the door open before the caller could say another word.

"Eugene Drew, what on earth are you doing out on a night like this? You'll catch your death, son!" She jerked the boy inside, slammed the door shut, and pulled down the locking board.

There was just enough light shining from the cabin outside for Jeannie to notice that the snow was coming down harder now.

"Eugene!" Jeannie sang out. "Does your father know where you are?"

He was the sheriff's oldest child, twelve years old— Jeannie had baked a cake for the party that summer. Napoleon Drew had two other children—Parker, two or three years younger than Eugene, and Mary Ellen, a precocious little girl, maybe six years old. Another child had died shortly after birth earlier that year—just hours after the mother, Rebecca Drew, had died herself.

"Th-th-th-that's just it-t-t-t-t, Miss J-Jeannie," the boy stammered, either from the freezing wind and snow outside—although Napoleon Drew's cabin was not far from Lois's—or from having his arm almost jerked out of its shoulder socket by the seamstress.

"We don't know where Pa is."

Chair legs scraped on the floor as Murdo Maddox rose. Jeannie turned to him. She saw his face twitching as he tried to figure out what to say, what to do, and then he looked into Jeannie's eyes. He sighed and tossed the napkin onto the plate.

"He's not in his office?"

Eugene shook his head, then found his voice. "No, sir. I checked."

"Eugene," Lois scolded. "You went out in this weather dressed like it's spring?"

He wasn't dressed exactly like spring, but he certainly hadn't thought to put on overshoes, gloves, scarves, and a hat.

Murdo asked, "When's the last time you saw your pa, boy?"

Eugene whispered. "He came home for dinner. He didn't say nothing about anything."

"He didn't say that he had to go somewhere?"

The boy shook his head, then remembered his voice. "No, sir."

Murdo grumbled and grabbed his coat and hat.

"I'll walk you back to your cabin, boy," he said. "You need to look after that brother and sister." Then he turned and stared at Jeannie.

"I'll see what I can find out. Check the office. Wake the judge up if I must. See if that boy at the livery knows anything." He walked over to Eugene. "Come along, boy."

Eugene, Jeannie thought, looked like he was walking to the gallows when he left the cabin with Murdo Maddox.

But then, Eugene was a Drew.

CHAPTER 8

On days like these, Napoleon King Drew regretted ever running for the office of Cutthroat County sheriff. He looked at the letter, read it, glanced up at the man who had just delivered it, personally, to the sheriff's office, then reread the letter. Setting the paper on the desk, Napoleon reached for the tin cup of cold coffee near him, took a long swallow, and then stared at Judge Van Gaskin.

"I don't like it any better than you do, son," the judge said. "But this isn't from me. It's not from Helena or the governor. It's from the attorney general of our United States. And Montana is a state now. Remember?"

Napoleon drank more coffee. He would need it to get this job done. "Last I heard, I'm a county law dog. This ought to be a job for a deputy US marshal."

The judge nodded. "Well, consider yourself a deputy US marshal."

The laugh that exploded from Napoleon's lungs held not an ounce of humor. He hooked his thumb toward the two cells in the back of the county sheriff's office.

"You think those can hold Bo Meacham?"

Horace Van Gaskin moved to the potbellied stove, found a towel to grab the handle of the blue-speckled enamel pot, and filled a porcelain mug with what passed for coffee in this cabin. "It's just overnight," he said without looking up from the steaming liquid that splashed into the cup.

Napoleon nodded toward the window.

"If the weather doesn't worsen."

With a shrug, the judge set the pot down and took a sip of the strong brew. "Too early for a big storm, Napoleon," he said. "We usually don't get those till later in the month, and that's just a warm-up for the ones that'll hammer us in February."

"It's snowing pretty good."

Van Gaskin drank more coffee. "It'll stop. Mark my words."

"Mark your words on my tombstone if I don't come back."

"You can deputize as many men as you need."

Napoleon considered that, but it didn't take more than a couple of seconds before he shook his head. "I'd rather not. No need putting any part-time lawmen in harm's way."

"I'd go with you, son," Van Gaskin said, and grimaced. "If not for my rheumatism."

It wasn't a joke. It wasn't an excuse. The cane leaning near the coatrack wasn't a prop Horace Van Gaskin used. It had likely hurt like the devil for him to get from what passed for a courthouse in the new Montana county to the sheriff's office.

So Napoleon just nodded his understanding.

"And I know there's bad blood between Drews and Meachams."

Bad blood. That was more than an understatement. Bloody Bill Drew had lynched Ben Meacham back in 1881, but that had been during the territorial years, when vigilante justice had been needed because the law, regular legal law, seldom got out of the territorial capital. Wealthy ranchers and merchants, or ordinary, hardworking salts of the earth, had to protect their families, their land, their wealth, and their pride. So they had hired men who could do the work that needed to be done. Men who did not care about spilling blood. Men who knew that the only law in Montana Territory was the law of survival.

Napoleon had seen Ben Meacham die. Bloody Bill had told the teenager's mother that it was time Napoleon saw what the world was really like and why his pappy was so hard on him all the time.

He had hated his father for that. But now he saw that maybe there was not madness, but reason, in what now was known as the Strangling Year.

"Who else knows of this?" Napoleon asked.

"As far as I know, me, you, the district marshal, and our state attorney general, Monsieur Haskell. I seriously doubt if Haskell even told Governor Rickards. Like I said, this is a federal matter, not state."

Napoleon grinned, but he lacked any humor at that moment. "Do I get a federal deputy's wage added to my regular salary as a county peace officer?"

Van Gaskin smiled and drank more coffee. "I'll see what I can do. But that's up to how merciful our federal government wants to be."

Napoleon looked back at the letter and reread it. The instructions were simple. Bringing an extra horse, "sufficient armaments" and "no one else," the last part underlined, Napoleon was to ride to the crossroads at Sacagawea Pasture, arriving there by seven this evening and wait for a special stagecoach traveling from Fort Benton to Deer Lodge. The stagecoach would stop, and upon Napoleon producing identification and the code word *Ernest Pressman*, the prisoner, Bo Meacham, would be turned over to the custody of the Cutthroat County sheriff. Pressman was the name of the express agent Meacham had murdered during a train robbery east of Bozeman Pass in 1883, the first known crime committed by the outlaw gang Meacham led. The stagecoach would proceed south. The sheriff would transport the prisoner to the county jail, where, on or about Wednesday, the third of January, but no later than Friday, the fifth of January, four federal deputy marshals and six to ten soldiers from Fort Assiniboine would arrive in Basin Creek. A written order signed by the district marshal with the words "Justice for All" written in the margin in red ink would be produced, and the prisoner would be turned over to the federal posse, which would then take the prisoner to the new town of Havre, where the prisoner would be hanged by the neck until dead on Monday, the eighth of January.

All the newspapers that Napoleon had seen—which amounted to four—had said that Bo Meacham was to be hanged in Deer Lodge on the fifteenth of this month.

"The orders are clear," Napoleon told the judge, "as written." He laid the papers on his desk and pushed his chair back. "Lots of trickery, don't you think?"

"I'm just a little judge. I don't second-guess higher courts." He thought about what he said, then amended his verdict. "I don't verbalize what I think about orders from higher powers."

After pouring the last of the coffee in his cup down his throat, Napoleon rose.

"Guess I ought to get going. Mind if I head to the cabin to tell Eugene that he'll be the man of the house tonight? Let Lois know—"

The judge started shaking his head.

"I'll ride over to your cabin," Van Gaskin said. "After you're out of Basin Creek. Tell Eugene that you got called away, but will be back by morning."

Finding his holster, Napoleon checked the loads in the Remington and eased the revolver back into the holster before bucking the rig around his waist.

"You lie better when you're playing poker, Judge," Napoleon said.

The judge responded with a slight nod. "Well, we can't tell anyone. Not your kids. Certainly not a woman."

"I'll be sure to tell Lois that when I get back—and after Bo Meacham is hanged."

"That's your call. Women ain't voting in this state yet."

Napoleon found the sheepskin coat and pulled it on, then picked the gloves off a bench and began pulling them on.

"Anything you want from me?" Van Gaskin asked.

"Yeah. Tell that farmer who got the drop on Bo Meacham with that scattergun in Sweet Grass that he could have done me and the whole state a favor if he had just blown Meacham's head off when he had the chance."

After tossing some crackers, slices of beef jerky, and an airtight can of peaches in one sack, he filled another sack with coal, both of which he would shove into his saddlebags when he got to the livery. He found his hat, wrapped a woolen scarf around his throat, and grabbed the Winchester repeater from the gun rack. He strapped the spurs onto his boots, grabbed a leather pouch filled with cartridges, shoved those into the coat pocket, walked to the door, and opened it, and just before the slamming door cut him off, he was saying, "And, for the record, you, the district marshal, the state attorney general, and anyone else who signed off on this idea are—"

Napoleon stood outside his office and looked into a town of whiteness. At least the snow falling now was soft, the kind of scene that artists painted. Snow dusted the saddle on the judge's mule, but the animal didn't seem to notice the weather. The storm wasn't letting up, but the wind remained fairly mild by Cutthroat County standards. He could see his breath, a cloudy foam, coming out of his nostrils. He looked over at his cabin, and Lois's, and debated defying the judge's orders, but that wouldn't do him any good. That old man had to be staring through the ice-coated window of his office, just waiting for Sheriff Napoleon King Drew to defy his orders.

Cursing softly, Napoleon turned and walked toward O'Boyle's livery.

"Reckon the sun'll break through those clouds?" Luke Jasper said as he led the brown gelding—Napoleon had bought the horse from Abe Killone back in late October—that Mary Ellen had named Blackie. Napoleon had said she could name the horse whatever she wanted, and she had said, "Blackie." Eugene had started to laugh, but his father's stare nipped that in the bud.

Well, Blackie was a dark brown.

"Won't do us much good, torturing us with sunshine just an hour before it sets," Napoleon said, a bit more cheerful than he felt.

The youngster chuckled.

"Where you off to on such a cold day, Sheriff?"

Drew shrugged. "A sheriff's job is never done. Remember that if you're ever asked to run for office."

Luke chuckled, and Napoleon flipped him a nickel, cutting off the stable boy's protest with a Drew stare, then swung into the saddle and rode back into the world of white. He rode straight back to the office, dismounted, and was untying the reins from the hitch rail when Horace Van Gaskin stepped through the door.

"What the devil are you doin', Napoleon?"

"Getting a mount for Bo Meacham. He won't outrun me on your mule, Horace." Napoleon purposefully did not call the old reprobate Judge or Your Honor.

"I certainly am not *walking* back to my house, Sheriff. Now listen here, young man –"

But Napoleon was already back in the saddle, and turning the horse toward the road, he began leading the mule down the snowy street.

"I said I am not walking to my house!" the judge roared.

"Then crawl," Napoleon said, kicking the gelding into a trot, the mule following without resistance.

At least the rendezvous point had high hills, rocks, and trees to block some of the wind and snow. Napoleon lighted a small fire, dragging over some deadwood that wasn't covered with snow, hoping that the flames would dry the wood enough that it would burn. He didn't care about smoke. The sun was already sinking by the time he had the fire going, and the flames would be hard to see, but they could be seen from the north.

And that's the way the stagecoach would be running. The driver or the messenger would see the flames, and the mud wagon would stop. Then the real job would start once the lawmen had left Bo Meacham in Napoleon's possession.

The coal, he thought after ten minutes of full dark, had been a good idea. But he parceled out the chunks like a miser.

His watch, which kept decent time and which he had wound in the livery stable while waiting for the kid to saddle Blackie, said 7:37—the first error the district marshal had made in his orders. The stagecoach was supposed to have been here more than a half hour ago, but some people never quite understood what winter was like in northwestern Montana.

At eight o'clock, Napoleon readjusted the blanket draped over his head and shoulders and reluctantly added two more coal pieces on the fire. The wood wasn't burning very well, but he figured the smoke blowing into his face and eyes warmed him a bit— maybe even more then the piddling flames.

He ate crackers and jerky, which was tougher to tear with his teeth in this frigid night, but he realized he never should have brought the peaches. He would have to remove his gloves to work the can open, and that wasn't happening on this night. It had to be in the midteens by now, and the snow had started to come down harder, propelled by a northwesterly wind.

The mule snorted, its ears alert, and Blackie stamped his feet.

Drew sat up, breathing hard, aware that he had

almost fallen asleep. Groaning, he rose from the fire and looked north. All he saw at first was the fire-lighted mix of snow and sleet, coming straight into his face, but then he saw something moving, far away, but moving. A light.

Lanterns on the stagecoach. It had to be.

He felt alive again, and he added two more pieces of coal to what had become embers, then leaned over the fire, jerking the bandanna and scarf off his face, and blew till the chunks lighted. He found the driest pieces of wood, and when the coal was burning good, added those.

He picked up the Winchester, wiped it off, and worked the lever slightly, just enough to make sure a fresh cartridge was in the chamber. Napoleon wasn't going to take any chances here. He gave both mule and Blackie some oats, and then he left the warmth of the fire and crossed the road to the other side of Sacagawea Pasture.

Should have waited, he thought, ten minutes later, freezing now, stamping his feet in six inches of snow. Looking down the road, he now saw two bouncing lights. *Yes,* he thought, *it had to be the stagecoach*. He saw that his fire was burning good now, meaning the horse and mule were much more comfortable than he was.

But he wasn't going back. He wasn't taking any chances.

What felt like four winters later, he could hear the clomps of hooves and the jingling of traces. Then a squeaky wheel. Finally, the curses of the driver and then the slowing of the coach. It stopped at the rocks and trees, barely silhouetted by the dying flames of his once-roaring, once-warm fire.

"Sheriff!" a man called from inside the stagecoach.

Napoleon brought the Winchester's stock to his shoulder and slowly pulled back the hammer. He aimed at the driver, the closest target.

"Ernest Pressman!" Napoleon bellowed and watched the messenger and driver turn rapidly toward his voice. But they had been staring at the fire, which wasn't much, but enough to take them longer for their eyes to adjust to the darkness.

"Drew?" That came from the messenger.

"Who's in the coach?" Napoleon said, then quickly but quietly moved ten yards back and twelve feet to his left—in the wind—no protection, but not where he had been.

Just in case.

"Someone you're welcome to, Sheriff." Napoleon waited. "Arvid Persson."

Napoleon let out a sigh of relief. The right answer, according to the letter Judge Van Gaskin had delivered. The second man known to have been murdered by Bo Meacham, a Swedish sodbuster from south of Billings.

"Here I come." Napoleon walked toward the shadow of the stagecoach. He did not dare look at the dying fire or the stagecoach lanterns, just in case he was mistaken.

He wasn't.

The guard and the driver, lighted by the front lanterns on the sides of the rig, kept their eyes on Drew, who could not see anything inside the coach. He moved in front of the mules pulling the mud wagon and came toward the rocks. The door to the coach opened, and two gloved hands showed no weapon, then rose, gripping the top frame, and a tall man in a heavy black coat dropped to the snow.

Slowly, the man pulled back his coat just enough to show the Deputy US Marshal gold shield pinned to the lapel of a woolen vest.

Drew pulled back his coat, letting his sheriff's star show. He also reached his left hand into a coat pocket and pulled out the letter Judge Van Gaskin had given him. He showed that to the deputy, who let out enough air for a company of troopers.

"Sheriff, I have to admit that all this dime-novel stuff sounded like . . . well, dime-novel stuff, but . . . I'll be hanged if it didn't have me sweating in subfreezing temperatures since leaving Fort Benton."

"You won't be hanged, Deputy," a voice said. "But Bo Meacham will be."

Napoleon could not help himself. That was a woman's voice.

"Shut up, you dirty little—"

A thud shut up the voice of Bo Meacham, but just for a few seconds. "You wouldn't do that if I wasn't shackled like a—"

The thud sounded again. Bo Meacham made no more threats.

"I'm glad to get rid of him," the lawman said. "But I still don't know why we couldn't have just dropped him off at your jail. How far is it to town?"

"In this weather?"

"We'd get there a lot faster," the driver interrupted them, "if you'd stop yer gabbin' and make this wagon lighter by two hundred pounds."

They took the hint, and Bo Meacham came out of the mud wagon, rattling like some heavy piece of machinery. He was chained at the ankles, chained at his thighs, chained at the wrists, and had two more chains tight across his forearms and upper arms, wrapped tight around his back.

Another deputy and two soldiers also emerged, stamping their feet to get the blood recirculating.

"There should be a fresh team waiting for you in Basin Creek," Napoleon told him. "Finnian O'Boyle's livery. You should be gone by the time I get there. The kid working there is named Luke. He'll get you all ready for the ride south."

The second deputy nodded at Bo Meacham's back.

"Want us to undo those leg irons and chains so he can ride that mule?" he asked.

Everyone, except Napoleon, looked at the mule.

Napoleon looked at the back of Bo Meacham, then at his Winchester. A second later, he put his gloved hands around the top of the barrel and swung the stock, which caught the murderer with a solid crunch, and the man fell like a timber, face-first into the snow.

"I think," Napoleon started before catching his breath. "I think . . . he'll travel better like this. But I'd be obliged if you could lend me a hand to get him over the mule's back. And give me the keys to those padlocks."

CHAPTER 9

Three more had died that day, including Sokw, whose name meant "sour," though the old woman had been anything but ill-tempered and grumpy—at least not since her husband had died many, many years ago. She was even older than Keme, and Keme had seen many, many winters.

But none like this.

Younger Blackfoot men had helped Keme with the burial, wrapping the old one's body in the robe and using dogs to pull the sleigh that held what had been Sokw. They placed her high in the branches of a tree. Come summer, they would give her remains to the earth.

Come summer, they would return the remains to the Mother Earth of many, many Blackfoot women . . . men . . . babies.

The bluecoats at the soldier-fort had promised to bring food—even the food the white eyes ate would be welcomed in this frigid world of whiteness and death. But the bluecoats had not come.

They had sent Samoset, who loved to walk and climb and run and walk some more, to the soldier-fort. He had been gone for many sunrises—so many that Chogan had said He Walks Over Much must have perished in the blizzards—but this morning Samoset had returned. He was cold, frozen to the bone, but the fires warmed him, and though his teeth pounded together so hard that many feared they would break, Samoset said that the soldiers could not bring the white-man cattle or any of the white-man-food-held-in-metal or bread or rice or anything. They could not even leave their soldier-fort. The snow was too deep. Traveling was too dangerous.

"And why," Chogan said with violent sarcasm, "should a white man risk his life for an Indian?"

Powaw, the medicine man, had told the men of the village that morning of his vision. Keme had told no one what he had heard from the wise counsel, and he knew the other men who had sat in the lodge and smoked the pipe and heard the great man talk, they, too, would keep his words to themselves, but never forget.

The Blackfoot people would endure, as they had since their beginnings. But many would not see spring bloom with the promise of a better world, a better life.

There would be much sadness in his land. Many stomachs would be empty. Many heartbeats would be stilled. Sad songs would be sung. But that is sometimes the way. The cold would worsen. The snows would deepen. The wind would turn unmerciful. Yet in the darkest hours of the Blackfoot, those who had not been taken, they would be saved, to live, to grow stronger, to keep the Blackfoot from disappearing like most of the buffalo. They would be saved by a people who were not of the people but of the people.

"You speak in riddles," Chogan told the village's

oldest, wisest, and most honorable man. "How can a people be not of the people but of the people?"

"My eyes were not strong enough to see that. My ears were not sharp enough to understand what I heard. My heart not strong enough to comprehend and interpret." Powaw paused to smoke the pipe, then passed it to Keme. "But I believed. For a white buffalo never lies."

"You saw a white buffalo in your vision?" Sucki asked.

"He was white, but he was not white. He was a buffalo, yet he was not a buffalo."

Chogan let out a moan of exasperation. "You see things that are but aren't. You hear things that are spoken but aren't. You drive me crazy with your ramblings that make no sense."

The pipe came to Chogan, but he angrily passed it to Keme, who smoked and passed the pipe to the next man, then leaned closer to hear how the medicine man would respond.

"I tell you what I have seen. I tell you what I have heard. I never said any of those visions that came to me, any of those words that were spoken to me, were scenes and sentences that I understood. Yet. But I will know what I have heard and seen in time."

"Maybe when we put your bones in the ground," Chogan said.

"Silence," Keme said, and Chogan bowed his head in shame.

Keme leaned closer to the wise man with great medicine.

"This buffalo that was a buffalo that wasn't and was white, but wasn't. From which direction did he come to visit you, Grandfather?"

The pipe had returned to Powaw, and he pointed with it.

South. Keme nodded. Survival . . . help . . . that would come from the south. A white buffalo that was white, but not, and a buffalo, but not.

Indeed, Powaw's vision was uncertain, but it was something. And Powaw had never been wrong in all the years that Keme could remember. Keme wasn't as old as Powaw, but he had lived a long time.

They left the moderate warmth of the great man's teepee and returned to their lodges in the stinging snow and biting wind.

"Keme!"

He recognized the voice, and with great reluctance, he turned to face Chogan. At least Keme's back was to the wind.

"Do you think his mind is gone?"

Such a question was not worth answering with words when Keme wanted to save his breath for the long walk to his own teepee. His head shook.

"What is south of here? But white men?"

Keme spoke loud enough to be heard in the wind.

"What is south of the white men?" He smiled at the bewilderment he found in Chogan's eyes. "I have seen a white man that was as dark as you. As dark-skinned as I am. He said he was a Mex-i-can. Perhaps a man like him will come to help us. Or perhaps the white men will come. As we helped them."

"When did the white man ever help us? Why would a white man help us now? And, my wise brother, I have seen a Mex-i-can. Some ride for the men who raise the puny cat-tle. I find them no better than the white man."

"You forget," Keme told him, "that I have grandsons

who are white men. White men, but red in their hearts. They have helped us. I have helped them."

"They have never helped me." He shook his head. "The cold freezes my tongue. I go to my lodge."

Keme nodded, turned, and trudged through the numbing cold.

A man who was Indian, but wasn't. Or men who were Indian, but not. A buffalo that wasn't a buffalo, but was. Somehow that strange man and strange animal would come to save this Blackfoot village.

It would be worth seeing. But, yes, Keme could not disregard Chogan's words. Maybe Powaw's mind, and his visions, had been confused by this bitter night.

When he reached his teepee, he felt warm. A grandchild must have walked over and started a fire in the center so that Keme would be warm this night. It was good to live to this age, when young boys and girls were considerate and helpful and respectful. A man like Keme could grow to like being lazy, having no chores to do, and Keme thought he would sleep well that night. Warm with a fire going in the teepee, covered with the skin of a buffalo that he had had since he was a young man with feet that did not hurt and many more teeth than he had now, teeth that could tear into a roasted buffalo rib—or bite the heart of the beast and let the blood run down his throat and stain his chin and cheeks.

But sleep did not come easily, no matter how hard he tried. He twisted and turned. He got too hot. Then not warm enough. He tossed off the robe. He pulled it back over.

He drank water. He stepped outside to urinate.

He added dried beef dung—remembering when dried buffalo dung was everywhere in this country—to the fire. He stared at the smoke rising through the opening above.

In the smoke, he saw a man—a man who was Keme—walking. The smoke was white like the snow that was a foot deep outside and growing in height by the hour. Keme focused on this man in the smoke who was Keme.

The man walked south. It was hard for him to walk. The snow often swallowed him, but each time, he broke through and continued. A bear chased him into a tree, and the great silvertip tried to shake him down out of the tree, then tried to uproot the tree. But the tree was Keme's friend. And the bear grew tired, angry, and roared a final beastly curse up the tree at Keme. Then it walked away.

Keme kept watching.

He found a horse. A white horse in the white snow. At first he thought it was just a white rock that looked like a horse. But it was real. The horse stared at Keme in the smoke, whinnied, and turn around. The white horse in the white snow was saddled with a saddle of a white man and with a bridle of a white man.

But the white-man animal nodded, and whickered, and snorted. And Keme understood because the white horse spoke in the Blackfoot tongue.

Keme walked in the smoke that was wafting through the hole in the lodge and climbed into the saddle on the white horse. And they rode. They rode as if it were spring, and the grass was green, and the skies were clear and blue, and the wind felt warm.

And Keme felt young. But he was hungry. Very

hungry. And, he knew, so were the people of his village that he had left behind.

The white turned green, but Keme knew it was still white. Green but white. Much like a buffalo that wasn't. And a Blackfoot that wasn't. But in the smoke from his fire in this warm lodge, green could be white and white could be green. A man might be a Blackfoot but not a Blackfoot. A buffalo could be a buffalo that was not a buffalo.

Keme rode south. Then he understood.

He was not hungry. His belly felt full. He could taste hot buffalo grease in his mouth. He could feel white-man coffee going down his throat. He could hear—hear the children of his village singing songs of joy, not the songs of mourning for those that were no longer with the Blackfoot people but had returned to the earth that was the mother of all creatures.

The man who was Keme on the horse in the smoke from the fire vanished.

Keme was cold again, and he rolled over, closer to the fire, pulling the robe over his head.

He was cold. And hungry. But now he knew what he had to do. For his people.

Tomorrow, he would go south. He would find the Blackfoot who was not Blackfoot, but was, and the buffalo that was not a buffalo, but was.

That was the way to save these people.

Or maybe Keme was just as crazy as Powaw.

CHAPTER 10

Jeannie Ashton stared at Lois DeForrest and said, "I think—"

Lois was saying the same words at the same time. Both stopped and laughed. Lois grabbed her coat, Jeannie picked up hers, and they pulled their heavy snow boots over their stockings and stepped outside.

They met Murdo Maddox as he was coming out of the Drews' cabin.

His eyes widened—and Jeannie figured she could see the frown underneath the woolen scarf that hid most of his face—but then softened, and he stepped back, and opened the door.

"The little ones are already asleep," Murdo said. "I sent the biggest one to get some more wood to get through the night. Fire was about out when we got here, but I got it going." He nodded down the street. "I'll see what I can find out about the sheriff. Let you know."

"You're not riding back to the Circle M after—" Lois started, but Murdo cut her off.

"Got a room at Sissy's." He pulled down his hat and started into the night. "I'll let you know what I find out."

Lois went inside the Drews' cabin first, and Jeannie held the door open as she watched Murdo Maddox trudge through the snow, head down, wind whipping snow from the northwest. She followed him with her eyes until losing sight of him in the black of the night and the white of the snow.

Closing the door, she pulled off her coat, scarf, cap, and gloves, hanging them on the coatrack, and then climbed up the loft and made sure Parker and Mary Ellen were, indeed, asleep. Climbing down, she had reached the back door and was opening it just as Lois was coming in with an armload of wood.

Eugene came inside, too, coated with snow and carrying his own armload of wood.

"Stack that neatly, Eugene," Jeannie told him. "Then get out of those wet clothes and towel yourself dry and get into your winter pajamas, climb upstairs, and go to bed."

"But we need—"

"Lois and I will get more wood. And kindling."

"There's enough kindling already," the boy protested.

"I'll be the judge of that. Now get—and don't make me come up there to make sure you are dressed properly for the night."

That threat probably scared him enough to do exactly as she had instructed him.

"I'll get another armful," Lois told her after Eugene had climbed into the loft.

"I'll help," Jeannie said.

The woodpile was close to the cabin, and she didn't plan on being out too long. Lois did not protest, and Jeannie was back inside in no more than a couple of minutes. But once she had stacked the wood in the box next to the stone hearth, she told herself that she would never do anything like that again.

She looked at the big tin bucket and decided that Eugene was right. They had enough kindling to last a good while—as long as no one let the fire burn out—and on a night like this, that wasn't about to happen.

"How cold do you think it is?"

"Colder than it has any right to be," Jeannie answered.

After pulling on his long handles, Eugene Drew shoved his pest of a kid brother over on the cot, closer to the wall, which is where he should be. It was colder against the wall, but Parker was the young one. At least Parker had warmed up this side of the bed.

Eugene pulled up the sheets and all the blankets, rested his head on the pillow, and stared at the ceiling. He could hear the fire crackling in the place and the voices and footsteps of the two women.

How long will they be here? He wondered. One of them would stay the whole night. If it was Miss Lois, that would be fine. She would fall asleep. But if the Widow Jeannie decided to wait till their father came home, well, her ears could hear a flea jumping, her nose could smell wet hair, and her eyes, even closed, could see a boy trying to sneak out of the house.

He might have to wait till morning.

That might work just as well, though. Mr. Murdo Maddox had said that he was spending tonight—and maybe another—in the boarding house. Eugene could get his chores done quickly. The best thing about winter was there was no schooling. Well, if Mrs. Jeannie or Miss Lois stayed over, there was bound to be not just chores for Eugene, Parker, and even Mary Ellen—baby chores for her, the lucky brat—but reading, too, and maybe, if they weren't careful about doing everything they were told to do, arithmetic.

That thought almost made Eugene groan—and he knew Mrs. Jeannie wasn't close to falling asleep yet.

He remembered a conversation he had had with his father, probably two or three years back. His father had taken Eugene and Parker to Mr. Killone's spread, where they were serving potatoes and biscuits and brisket to eat, and then they watched cowboys try to ride a wild bronc that Mr. O'Boyle said was impossible to stay on.

Ride that horse to a standstill, the livery man had promised, and the first cowboy to do that would earn fifty dollars in greenbacks.

Now, they had to pay five dollars for a try—and they had to understand that any doctor's bills would be charged to them, not Abe Killone.

When they were riding out to the ranch, Eugene figured the only cowboys competing would be those who rode for Mr. Killone's brand. But that wasn't the way it was. No, sir. Not at all.

There were riders from outfits as far away as Fort Benton to the north and Choteau to the south. Eugene had never seen that many cowboys. Even Circle M riders came with their five-dollar ante.

Twenty-four riders went down quickly, none staying atop that high-kicking, red-eyed devil longer than six seconds. One cowboy for the Rafter 5 came out of the corral with a busted nose, some missing front teeth, a mangled ear, and a dislocated shoulder.

"Was that worth five bucks, Buster?" Brent Garfield, Basin Creek's town marshal, called out.

"Shoot, yeah." The cowboy spit out blood and saliva and pride. "He didn't hurt nothin' but my pride. But I'll get'm next time. I've figured out his tricks."

Ten riders down, they let the horse rest, and Mr. Killone gave the others a chance to withdraw and take their money back.

He offered the same deal after the next ten went into the mud and dirt, hurting more than just their pride and pokes of money.

Forty-one riders tried that horse that afternoon. The longest to stay on was a Blackfoot—one minute and seventeen seconds—before the bronc did a quick stop-and-duck and sent the Indian over the horse's neck and into a couple of cowpunchers standing close to drag any tossed rider away from the widow-making bronc's hooves.

Mr. Killone paid the Indian ten dollars, saying he'd toughed it out the longest and had put on the ride of the day.

"The only man who made more money than Abe Killone," Eugene's father said, "will be Doc Scovil." He laughed then. "This'll probably be the first month he made more money doctoring than cutting hair."

That day, Eugene knew, was the most important day of his life. Even now. Two, three years later. That's when Eugene knew that he did not want to be a lawman like his father. He wanted to be a cowboy.

That kept going through his mind until, five minutes later, he fell asleep.

"I'm freezing to death," Bo Meacham said, adding more than a few insults at Sheriff Napoleon Drew.

"I hear," Napoleon said, "that's a better way to go than hanging."

Meacham cursed the lawman long and hard, but that got old—and cold—quickly. Napoleon welcomed the silence, interrupted only by the howling wind and crunching of snow, which was now reaching Blackie's knees.

There were no stars, no moon, nothing but deep, white snow to mark the trail, and the snow had covered the tracks Blackie and the judge's mule had left when Napoleon had ridden to Sacagawea Pasture, but he knew this trail. He had been riding it pretty much his whole life.

His watch had stopped before he had kicked out the fire at the crossroads, and he wasn't about to pull off his gloves to wind it. Besides, winding might not do any good. The whole piece might have been frozen solid.

He made out the sign, even though it was blasted with snow and ice and unreadable, and let out a long sigh. He could make out where the mud wagon had turned off the trail for Basin Creek, then returned to make that long haul to Deer Lodge. A long haul for being a decoy. Napoleon wished them, and the pregnant woman, luck.

He turned onto the trail, feeling a bit easier knowing that town and a warm home lay ahead.

No. He wouldn't be going home. He couldn't leave Bo Meacham alone in the cell. He'd be spending practically every minute in his office until the soldiers and deputies arrived on Wednesday.

Wednesday, he thought, and let out a mirthless, frigid cough. *That'll take a miracle.* ". . . but no later than Friday, the fifth of January . . ." He wasn't even certain about that now. That relief of four deputies and some soldier boys from Fort Assiniboine might not be able to get to Basin Creek, let alone Deer Lodge, until late spring.

He saw Lois's place and his own home, and he knew it was cold as he rode past and realized that both the Swede's place and the Hangman's Saloon and Gambling Emporium were closed. So much for a brandy warmup.

He stopped at his office, eased out of the saddle, and felt his boots push through snow. Not as much accumulation here as along the main road, but the town was fairly well protected. He did not bother reining Blackie. The horse wasn't going to wander off in this weather, and he reached under Van Gaskin's mule and removed the rope that secured Meacham's manacled hands to his manacled feet.

The killer was snoring, but Napoleon wasn't sure if that was an act. It didn't matter. He grabbed the cold steel between the prisoner's boots and rose, lifting the legs high and then shoving.

Bo Meacham fell off the saddle and into the snow with a roar of profanity.

Then the door to his office opened, and Napoleon dropped to a knee, threw back the tail of his heavy coat, and tried for the Remington on his hip.

"It's me, Drew." Murdo Maddox slowly spread his arms away from his side. The light from the lantern inside might be blinding the lawman, so Murdo added his name.

He heard the sound of Napoleon's revolver clicking, then watched the gun slide into the holster, and the marshal slowly rose.

"What are you doing here?"

Murdo shook his head. *So much for doing a good deed for a Drew in this town. I should have known better.*

"Your oldest boy was worried about you." He could have kept talking, pointing out things like manners and letting people know where you're going, but it was too cold to point out frivolous things.

"Why would Eugene come to you?"

Murdo stepped away from the door, which he left open. "He came to Miss DeForrest's. I was enjoying some supper—with Jeannie Ashton."

He threw Jeannie's name like he would a horseshoe in a pitching contest at the Circle M headquarters. Then regretted it. He was no better than a miserable Drew for saying that—and enjoying the reaction on the sheriff's face.

Change this conversation, he told himself. And nodded at the carcass in the snow.

"What's that?"

Drew holstered his revolver and walked around the mule.

"Bo Meacham."

That caused Murdo to straighten, and he walked in front of the two worn-out animals and stared down. The winter coverings had fallen from Meacham's face, which rested beneath the mule's belly. The man's cold, deadly eyes locked onto Meacham, but he was too cold, and maybe too angry, to say anything.

"You caught Meacham?" Murdo looked up and could not hide the shock and—he couldn't believe it—respect.

"No."

Then Drew added, "It's a long story." He shook his head. He wasn't going to explain. Murdo knew he ought to read newspapers more often. But even his cowhands were telling Bo Meacham stories in the bunkhouse and around campfires.

"And it's too cold to tell it." Drew buttoned his coat, probably more to keep his revolver away from the prisoner than anything else, and bent down and grabbed the chains between the man-killer's boots. He began dragging the prisoner through the snow.

Murdo Maddox said something he never though he'd say to a Drew.

"I'll help you."

DAY TWO

FRIDAY

CHAPTER 11

He had been awake for ten minutes, but John T. Drew had no desire to throw off the blankets and comforter and start the coffeemaker. He was warm and comfortable and had been dreaming of Mary Broadbent. They had been riding horses up to Keme Mesa, but not in January. It had to be July or August. Well, it was warm, anyway. Drew tried to decide what he needed to do first—after the showering, shaving, getting dressed, and having that first cup of coffee.

The snow should have stopped by now, and some of the older Scouts might be shoveling the sidewalks. Was there a merit badge for shoveling snow? There ought to be.

For a moment, he thought he might try to fall back asleep. See if he could pick up that dream right where he had let off. They had reined in their mounts, and Mary was stepping down out of the saddle, looking ever so lovingly at Drew.

But his cell phone buzzed, and he swore.

That wasn't a wake-up call or a belated happy new year wish. After throwing the heaviest covers off, he rolled over and blindly reached for the phone, caught it before he dropped it onto the hardwood floor, saw the caller ID name, and swore as he hit the connect button and said, "Yeah."

"John. Will. Is your jail cell empty?"

Will Ambrose and Drew went back many years, when they would hit the nearest bar after work—Ambrose a trooper for the highway patrol and Drew a deputy for his dad. They'd complain about the size of their paychecks and the egos of their fathers, or, often in Ambrose's case, his uncle, the state attorney general who had not seen the brilliance of Will Ambrose's law-enforcement skills and gotten him a cushy job in Helena.

Well, he had a pretty big job in Helena now, but he still complained. He was a DCI lieutenant for Montana's Department of Criminal Investigation.

And he wanted to know about the Cutthroat County/ Basin Creek Town Jail.

"No. I locked up Colter Norris yesterday."

Ambrose cursed. Drew waited. "Norris. Norris? That's . . . ?"

"Foreman for the Circle M."

There was a long silence. Finally, Ambrose said, "Yeah. He hasn't caused much trouble in a year or more, has he?"

"He made up for it yesterday. Practically knocked the Busted Stirrup off its foundation."

Ambrose repeated that first curse.

Drew waited.

"John . . ."

Drew shook his head and swore softly.

"I need you to kick him out."

"Did you hear what I said? Cindy's bar is a total wreck.

"But Norris is sober now."

"And I'd like to keep him that way."

"John."

"You're asking for a mighty big favor, considering—"

"It's not a favor, John. Kick him out. However you want to do it. Drop the charges."

"I can't do—"

"Then release him on his own recognizance. But the Department of Corrections needs your jail."

Since when did the Department of Corrections go through the Department of Criminal Investigation? John thought.

"What's going on, Will?"

Ambrose swore softly, then louder, then cursed some more.

"Osborne with the Department of Corrections called me ten minutes ago. The pilot flying Rupert Chadwick to Deer Lodge radioed that he was making an emergency landing in Cutthroat County."

Drew had walked barefooted to the kitchen and had just hit the coffeemaker and was walking back to the bedroom when his friend gave him that jolt. He wouldn't need coffee to wake up now.

"I thought he was going by van. That's what—"

"That's what Corrections put out. On purpose. So any friends of the Chadwick gang would be watching the roads from Milk River City and not the airport. They took off at dawn. Probably shouldn't have, considering the weather, but there was supposed to be a clear avenue to get them to Deer Lodge. That avenue closed quickly."

Drew left the bedroom and headed, his feet freezing, to the front door. He opened it, felt the blast of wind and the stinging snow on his face, and saw the thick whiteness all around him, a dark gray sky. He didn't know how the sun had made this world light enough to see.

Swearing, Drew slammed the door. "The weatherman said this storm was supposed to bypass us."

"Yeah, and I don't know what the meteorologist is saying in Great Falls, but in Helena and on the Weather Channel, they are giving all sorts of excuses and reasons that everyone in the country got this wrong."

Ambrose swore again.

"Billy!" Drew roared down the hallway. "Get up. Now!"

Drew turned back into his room, put the phone on speaker, and tossed it onto the bed. He pulled off his T-shirt and boxers and began getting dressed. No time to shave or shower now.

"What about the other two?" he asked as he opened a drawer.

"Baxter and Jones went by van. That was part of the plan. Send them by van, escorted by a half dozen patrol trucks, so any friends or any right-minded Montanan who wanted to kill those sons of—"

Drew looked at the open doorway to his bedroom and yelled, "Billy! Up! Now!"

He pulled on his pants, then started with the thick woolen socks. "Where was the pilot landing?"

"Sacagawea Pasture." Ambrose sighed. "Well, the pilot thought it was Sacagawea Pasture."

"Sacagawea . . ." Drew pulled on yesterday's shirt.

"I know."

"Has he landed yet?"

"Nothing yet reported from the city-county airport in Choteau or Cut Bank–Valier International." Ambrose stopped to talk to someone else in his office. "We'll relay what we know by regular channels as soon as we hear."

"I can contact Choteau and Cut Bank myself."

"Then let me know when you have Chadwick in custody."

Custody. The thought was mirthless.

Drew pulled on his boots.

"Billy!" he roared again.

Standing now, he grabbed the phone. "You know what kind of cells we have, Will."

Ambrose did not speak.

"I wouldn't be surprised if I found it empty already. Colter Norris is not the brightest bulb, but it doesn't take a Houdini to figure out an easy way to get out of *that jail.*"

"Use your deputies."

Swearing again, Drew grabbed the heavy gun belt. Deputies. Plural. Denton Creel would be no match for Chadwick. Mary Broadbent wasn't cleared for anything beyond paperwork.

"All right, Will. You owe me big." He yelled again, "Billy. Get your butt out of bed now!" Finding the keys to his Interceptor, he spoke into the phone. "Do you know if the highway departments are clearing roads?"

"It's not that bad here in Helena. Yet. It's coming down harder now. What they're saying on TV is anyone east of Interstate 15 all the way to the Continental Divide should prepare for the worst. That's from Cut Bank south to Rogers Pass."

Rogers Pass was on State Highway 200 northeast of Lincoln in the Helena National Forest. Basin Creek wasn't that far, as the crow flies, south of Cut Bank—and it was right between I-15 and the Divide.

"John."

He didn't like the way Ambrose said his name.

"Yeah."

"We haven't heard from the van or the security vehicles leading and following Baxter and Jones."

"Which route did they take. Fifteen?" The interstate would be the fastest.

"Afraid not. They cut down to Saint Nicholas and picked up State Highway 76."

Drew sat down on his unmade bed.

"Seventy-six," he said, hoping he had heard wrong.

"Yeah."

Drew swore softly. He felt a billion miles away from that wonderful dream he had been dreaming.

"A winter storm, even a mild winter storm—forget what this storm has turned into—and the Department of Corrections thought that going over the Always Winter range was a good idea?"

"Don't take it out on me, John. But trust me. I gave the deputy director an earful thirty minutes ago."

That didn't help anyone now.

"Well, you had better call the highway department and get some salt and sand and bulldozers up here quick."

"Already done. And I'll have as many officers as I can from my department driving north as soon as they can. As soon as the roads are open north of Augusta."

"Keep me posted." John ended the call.

"Billy!" he roared again as he fiddled with the phone and called another number.

"Yeah?" Mary Broadbent's voice sounded like she was in a thick fog.

"Mary. John. I need you to kick Colter Norris loose

as fast as you can. I'll explain as soon as I can. Just head over to the jail and turn him loose. And the roads are all closed."

"What are you—"

"Look outside and you'll see what I mean."

"John."

"Mary. Listen to me. I don't have time to explain. But we need that jail for the Chadwick gang."

He waited five seconds for that to kick in.

"You with me?"

"Yes, Johnny. What else?"

"Tell Norris he'll have to go to the school gymnasium. We impounded his pickup, right, or did Ashton Maddox—"

"It's at the garage."

"Good. I'll call O'Riley." Dan O'Riley was the county manager. "We'll have to go into the winter weather emergency. Open the gym for any travelers stuck, any residents without heat. Before you kick Norris loose, call Denton. Tell him what's up and have him head up to Sacagawea Pasture. The plane flying Rupert Chadwick to Deer Lodge was supposed to have made an emergency landing. I haven't heard anything yet from the pilot or DCI."

"Ten-four." She was acting like a cop now. A good cop. The best he had, though he wouldn't let Denton Creel know that. He didn't have to. Denton was smart enough to see that for himself.

Drew caught his breath. He debated briefly with himself, then swore.

"Then I need you to call . . ." He couldn't believe he was saying this. "Elison Dempsey."

He thought of the cliché. *Her silence spoke volumes.*

"Tell him I'm swearing in him and five of his C.A.N. men—the best he has available—as special *temporary* deputies. Don't tell him about Chadwick or anything else. Just tell him to get those men to the courthouse jail ASAP."

She was still silent.

"You got that, Mary?"

"Ten-four."

"I don't like this any better than you do, Mary. But I can't think of another option at the moment."

She cleared her throat. Her voice was soft, but he heard her perfectly.

"George Grimes?"

He sighed.

"I'm not that desperate, Mary. Not yet."

"Roger that."

"I love you," he told her and ended the call.

He moved down the hallway, punched Dan O'Riley's name on the CONTACTS on his cell phone, heard the buzzing, and pushed open the door to his son's bedroom.

"John." Dan O'Riley's voice sounded like he had been awake for hours, but he was vacationing a couple of time zones east of Montana.

O'Riley must have heard the roar of profanity as Drew ended the call and raced to the kitchen, bypassing the coffeemaker, and pushed open the door and looked into the garage.

The Interceptor was there. But Billy's Nissan pickup wasn't.

Slamming the door shut, Drew called O'Riley again,

then saw the note held by a magnet on the door of the refrigerator.

> *Dad:*
>
> *I'm heading up to the Always Winter park to practice for tomorrow's big event. Picking up a friend on the way. Don't worry. I've already put chains on the pickup.*
>
> *I just want to be prepared. And get the advantage. I've never won, and I'm sick of third place. This is my year.*
>
> *Imagine some other guys will have the same idea, though. But it should be fun. Snow looks great.*
>
> *It's 6 a.m. Will grab coffee when I fill up the truck before heading up.*
>
> *Should be back before sunset.*
>
> *Promise.*
>
> *Have a rocking day.*
>
> > *Billy*

"John? John? John?"

The note fell slowly, gliding like a parachute, to the floor.

Dully, John looked at the cell phone, turned off the speaker function, and brought it to his face.

"Dan."

"What's the matter, John?"

"You wouldn't believe it, Dan. Trust me. But here goes."

He left out the part about Billy driving an old Nissan

pickup to the Always Winters to practice for a stupid annual event that, the way this storm was shaping up, was not going to happen this year. But he carefully relayed everything the manager needed to know about the storm.

When he was finished, Dan O'Riley said just about every profane word that was going through Drew's mind.

"What do you need from me?" O'Riley asked. "But I don't know what all I can do from the Georgia coast."

"I need you to approve the hiring of special deputies till this mess is over."

"Whatever you need. This *is* a mess."

"You'd better green-light Operation Overlord. D-Day is today." That was the name for the winter emergency plan.

"Already done. I woke up the commissioners after my wife woke me up. She was watching a special bulletin on CNN. Looks like it's a mess out West."

"It's messier than you think." He paused, looked at the note on the floor, and let out a long sigh.

"An airplane is making, or has just made, an emergency landing in Sacagawea Pasture. I'm driving there as soon as I can get on the road. Can you get some emergency vehicles there just in case they are needed?

"How big of a plane?"

"Well, it's no Seven-thirty-seven. Since it flew out of the airport at Milk River City."

That was all Dan O'Riley needed to hear. "You don't mean—"

"That's exactly what I mean, Dan. Rupert Chadwick's plane."

"He was supposed to be—"

"That was to mislead everyone. I just got off the phone with Will Ambrose."

"You better get out there now, John. I'm on it."

Drew ended the call, then punched his son's name.

The phone kept ringing. After picking up his son's note, Drew moved into the garage, hit the door opener, saw no tracks left by Billy's Nissan. The snowfall had already covered those up. He ended the call, hit redial, and stepped into his SUV.

It was cold in the garage. Colder in the Interceptor. The phone kept ringing. He started the engine, put the Ford into gear, in four-wheel drive, and backed out, turning sharply, and then stopping at the dirt road.

He hit the heater button—and the heated seats button—and looked both ways . . . as though anyone might be out in this miserable weather.

The road was covered by at least a foot and a half of snow.

After turning on the emergency lights, Drew drove through a white hell.

By now, he guessed, his son had to be at what passed for a ski resort in Cutthroat County, and there was no cell phone signal there—not even inside the cafeteria and ski-rental shop. But he kept trying Billy until he had passed the Wild Bunch Casino before giving up.

That's when he realized that he had not even poured himself a cup of coffee. But there was no time to stop—and from the looks of the parking lot, the Wild Bunch had not opened this morning.

He made it to Neely Road and saw few signs of any traffic. If the county and state were grading roads, they had not made it to Montana Highway 60 yet. And probably wouldn't be here for days or weeks.

The windshield wipers worked rapidly. He drove slowly north, and then slowed to a crawl and flipped through the names on his cell phone. He cursed softly, then tapped a name. The phone rang and rang, but he did not disconnect.

No voice mail picked up.

He ended the call and redialed.

The voice that answered this time was profane and belligerent.

"Shut up, Grimes. This is John Drew. I need you to do me a favor."

CHAPTER 12

Billy Drew debated paying the astronomical prices for gasoline at the Wantlands Mercantile, but decided that a full tank in the Nissan would give him better traction in the snow. He recalled his grandfather's instructions: "Full tank for snow. But for ice, it's better to lighten the load."

The snow kept coming down pretty good—harder and colder than what had been predicted—and it didn't look like it would warm up today to make ice a danger on the way to the Always Winter range. Seven and a half gallons later, he paid cash and bought a package of doughnuts, a cup of coffee, and what passed for a latte in Basin Creek, then hurried back to the Frontier. The two hot drinks warmed his hands, and the pickup coughed to life, the windshield wipers went to work, and he pulled slowly onto the empty road.

Basin Creek was sleeping in this morning. It might be snowed in before sunset.

He took his first sip of coffee and thought with a smile, *Now what if we got snowed in at the ski basin?*

His twenty-year-old imagination went to work. There were a handful of cabins there that they rented out, but none was occupied when his father and he had been getting everything set up. In fact, he couldn't remember any tourists ever renting out cabins in the winter. Fall sometimes for the leaves, not much action in the spring because Montana's springs often were just an extension of winter at that altitude, but the summers were often popular with tourists escaping the heat of Texas, Arizona, and the Midwest.

If those cabins had kerosene heaters, that would be all right. He could break in. The owner of what was called by some a resort would not complain about replacing a lock in a life-or-death situation. And if the kerosene tanks were empty, well, there were other ways to stay warm.

Weren't there?

Neely Road hadn't been plowed, but the snow wasn't too deep, and Billy had been smart enough to fasten chains on his tires—though he hadn't liked the time it took, fearing his dad would wake up before he put the truck into neutral and let it roll down the driveway to the dirt road. After that had come the agonizing trial of waiting for the motor to catch and then easing down the white road in low gear.

Luckily, his dad had had a full day and hadn't gone to sleep till after four that morning. Sure, Billy had been up late, too, but that's because he was too excited to sleep.

He got up to thirty, and sometimes forty miles per hour on Highway 60, and that was as fast as he dared. The clock on the truck didn't work, but his wristwatch told him he was running late, and in this weather, he wasn't going to be able to make up any time.

Eventually, he saw the sign for the Circle M ranch,

but that did anything but make him relax. He hit the signal, turned left, and parked at the closed gate. The Nissan coughed, but he kept it running. That was one good thing he could say about this pickup. The Japanese knew how to make a really good heater.

Nervously, he glanced at his watch again. Then he found his cell phone. It didn't take long to scroll down recent calls to find Alyson Maddox's name and hit the call button.

She answered with a whisper: "Where are you?"

"At the gate," he told her. "Where are you?"

"Stuck."

Any other day, he might have been able to laugh. But this wasn't funny at all. Not on this day. And not in this weather.

"Where are you?"

"A hundred yards from the gate."

He swore softly, then asked, "I can climb over the gate."

"Don't be ridiculous. That'll set off the alarm in the bunkhouse and in our house. Here's the code."

He couldn't find a pen that would write, and the only paper he had was the mercantile receipt, but when she gave him the number, he laughed. "That's it?"

"Yes. Think you can remember it, jock?"

"I'll do my best."

"Hit the pound key first. And then again after the number."

Shifting the truck into gear, he pulled up to the box, rolled down the window, which was irritatingly slow on this frigid morning, removed the glove, typed the pound key, and then one number: 1.

When he pushed the pound symbol again, the gate

began creaking. After bringing his arm inside, he quickly rolled up the window and shook the snowflakes off his hand. The gate was opening. The truck started toward the opening gate, but he braked before he reached the fence line and swore.

"What's the matter?" Alyson asked.

"It's stuck."

"What's stuck? Not your truck!"

"No. The gate."

"Can you get through?"

"I can," he said, feeling his face flush. "But this truck can't. There's maybe two or three feet."

"All right. You wait. I'll get my gear and head up there."

He didn't like that idea, either, but she ended the call, and he stared at the gate, barely making out the grinding noise from the motor, and that stopped after a minute. The gate had not budged. It didn't even close.

Billy thought for no more than ten seconds before he opened the door, stepped outside, and looked south down the state highway.

Like any fool is driving in this weather!

His father would remind him that Cutthroat County might not be big, but if you leave a vehicle unlocked, you're just asking for trouble. And if you leave it running . . . well, don't be surprised to find your wheels gone.

At the gate, he stopped and tried pushing, but the University of Wyoming football offensive line could not push this gate open. But not even a University of Wyoming football offensive lineman would have been able to push this gate open. Maybe if the motor were running, Billy might be able to help it move, but that would take too much time. He was in a hurry.

So he slipped around the frozen gate and headed down the road.

Alyson was coming up the road at a slow pace, carrying skis and poles, a helmet over her shoulders, the snow in lower places almost to her knees.

That was the first time he thought, *This might not be a good idea.*

But that thought died when he saw her look up and smile.

Billy walked to her, feeling pleased that the snow wasn't deep where she reached him. He took the skis, but she insisted on carrying the poles, and they moved up the road, through the gate. She stopped and hit the code, and the gate groaned, but it kept trying to move forward, not back to lock.

After depositing Alyson's gear in the bed of the truck and closing the gate, he came back.

"Just leave it open," he suggested.

"You're not a rancher."

"And I never want to be one."

She looked at him and he saw her smile. "That's one reason I like you."

"Maybe if I push." He walked past her and slipped through the gate. He stepped into the mountain of snow that had stopped the gate from opening and called out to her, "Okay, Aly, hit it."

When he heard the gate grinding, he pushed against it.

To both of their surprise, the gate started closing. Then Billy had to think fast and move even faster to get through the gate before it shut and locked. He tripped over something and fell forward, breaking his fall with his arms and soft, fluffy mounds of Montana snow.

They were laughing as she helped him up and brushed off some of the snow before they both hurried to the still-running Nissan, wiping off more snow as they went, opening the doors, slamming them when they were in the warmth of the pickup. He handed her the latte and motioned at the doughnuts, which just made her laugh.

Then he backed up the road and turned onto the highway.

His heart raced, but he kept the Nissan running slow.

"Did you check the Weather Channel?" he asked.

"No. I wasn't about to turn the TV on and wake up Daddy." She glanced at the packaged doughnuts, sighed, opened the plastic, fingered one, and held it up to him.

Billy grinned, then took it out of her hand with his teeth.

She ate a different one, sipped the latte, and stared at the wipers as they worked overtime, but the glass began to fog over.

"I'm gonna have to turn on the defroster," he told her. "Before it gets any worse."

The temperature read nineteen degrees.

"Go ahead," she said. "I'm warm enough." She stared out the windshield, finishing that doughnut and sipping her fancy drink. Then her face changed and she looked at him. "How worse can it get?"

He reached for the radio dial, but she stopped him.

"Both hands on the wheel," Alyson ordered. "I'll find some news."

They found a Great Falls news station and listened to national news for what seemed like an eternity. She stared out the window, and he tried to focus on the road and not her.

He remembered meeting her just that summer, broken down in a rented Mustang that had blown a tire—and didn't have a spare—when he had stopped. Then came that psycho killer—whose name Billy had blocked from his mind—and how they had been the first two people the fugitive had taken hostage, stealing Billy's pickup and keeping a gun on Alyson while hiding out in the truck bed. The lawyer for Alyson's daddy had been taken later—not far from where Alyson had gotten her car stuck in the snow—and then came that long, frightening walk up Dead Indian Pony Creek till the ambush by Montana peace officers. And Billy liked to think that his whipping of a river stone at the killer had helped save their lives, too.

They had known each other in high school, but she was two years older and usually dated the sons of other ranchers. He had not paid much attention to her, anyway—or many girls, not in high school, anyway—and she preferred cowboys, even barrel raced for a time. Then she graduated and left Basin Creek and became one of those who left Basin Creek and came back only to visit.

Billy had envied that about her. Then he went to the University of Wyoming, walked on the baseball team, and picked "Outdoor Recreation & Tourism Management" at the Haub School of Environment and Natural Resources. She was an air-traffic controller, and her brains and beauty intimidated him.

Well, so did her father. Billy realized he feared Ashton Maddox more than he feared his own dad.

And, boy, would Mr. Maddox raise Cain when he

learned that his daughter had run up with a Drew to the Always Winter mountain resort on a morning like this.

The meteorologist in Great Falls finally came on just after they had turned onto the road that led up and over the Always Winters. But before she got started, a news reporter broke in.

"Dennis, I hate to interrupt you as I know many ranchers and marijuana growers and everyone else are worried about the strength of this storm that's moving south, but we're getting reports that an airplane out of Milk River City Regional had radioed that it is having to make an emergency landing in Cutthroat County, which is south of Milk River City and north of Choteau and Teton County."

Alyson leaned to look out the side window. Even Billy chanced a few glances before focusing on the road. The twisted and steep grades weren't far away, but this road wasn't the safest or best for traveling in the most perfect of conditions.

The weatherman asked, "Is this because of the weather, Ginger?"

"That's unclear at this time, Dennis," the woman said. "The pilot has radioed that he is making an emergency landing . . ." The coordinates meant nothing to Billy, the weatherman, or the reporter, who said, "But it's not a big county. The county sheriff, we have been told, has been alerted."

"Well, from what's on our radar, Cutthroat County isn't an ideal place for landing or driving or snowshoeing right now."

"We'll have more to report as soon as we learn what kind of plane it is. Unconfirmed reports say it is a Cessna, but we don't know if it is a turboprop or piston, passenger or freight."

"Keep us informed, Ginger."

"I will. But Montana Highway Patrol is urging locals throughout Cutthroat County to stay inside, and do not try to assist emergency personnel. They say the weather is too dangerous right now, and our public servants don't want to have to rescue Good Samaritans and put more lives at risk."

"Good advice, Ginger. You stay home and stay tuned right here. We'll keep you updated on this aircraft situation. And the weather. But first, a few words from our sponsors."

They looked at each other briefly.

"Should we turn back?" Alyson asked.

"Well, that pilot's not going to try to land anywhere on this road. That's for certain." He hooked his thumb toward the truck's bed. "He'd have to try to land it down that way."

"You think on Neely Road?" she asked.

He shrugged. "I'm no pilot, but that's what I'd do." He shrugged again. "Maybe a pasture, but the road would make a safer runway."

"Oh, my." Her voice fell into a whisper. "Oh, my . . . my . . . my . . . my . . . my." She stared at the hard-working wipers, then turned toward Billy again. "If that plane crashes on the highway, that road will be closed for hours."

They were already climbing now.

The commercials ended, and the weatherman came back on the air. What he said did not sound good.

"That's not what they were saying all yesterday." Billy started to grind his teeth.

Alyson sighed. "It's like that corny joke. If you don't like the weather in Montana, it'll change in a minute."

"Yeah." He eased around a curve. The trees were

thickening now as they started the long, winding climb, and that seemed to block some of the snow. Or maybe, Billy tried to think hopefully, the storm was blowing itself out and the weather prognosticators were once again making a mountain out of a molehill.

"Maybe we should turn around." The sentence sounded like it broke Alyson's heart. When Billy shot her a glance, he thought she was sad. Not nervous. Sad. He wanted to stop the truck, lean over, and kiss her.

She was, he had learned on a date in Cheyenne, a most excellent kisser. And he had been scared out of his wits when he'd moved closer to her lips that she would slap him.

"Well," he said, nodding.

The weatherman began saying things like highs in the low twenties and lows below zero this night, and that accumulations were expected to be in feet, not inches. Then he started explaining what had happened to make all those predictions of a fast-moving storm with moderate snowfall just plain wrong.

"My dad's gonna beat the crap out of me," Alyson said.

"My dad hits harder than your dad."

She looked at him and smiled. "Does not."

He laughed and shot her a quick glance with a quicker, "Does too!"

Her laughter drowned out the weatherman, and her smile warmed up the cab of the truck by a good twenty degrees.

"This might be the first year the Downhill Run got canceled since I can remember," he said.

"Well, it was a good idea. It would've been fun."

"How long is your vacation?" he asked.

"I have to fly back Sunday."

He nodded.

"If the airport is open," she said, and looked again at him with that wonderful smile and those mesmerizing eyes.

"Well, that'll give us a few days, anyway. We can find something to do. And I have to report back to campus on Monday. But we'll see what the weather's like."

He had to downshift into a lower gear.

She reached over and covered the top of his hand on the stick shift with her own.

"You're going to turn around?" He heard the hopefulness in her voice.

"Yes." He nodded but did not dare look at her. The snow kept blasting the windshield, and the wipers were moving at top speed. "But I have to wait till I find a place I can turn around."

He wasn't about to risk making something like a twenty-seven-point turn on this part of the road, with hardly any shoulders to speak of and ditches that were hidden by a foot or more of snow. Towering pines lined the right side of the road, while the left was, sometimes, a guardrail—at least underneath the snowfall—and beyond that a long drop down to rocks and Circle M country.

"Okay," she whispered, unable to hide her nervousness. "How far is that?"

He shrugged. "Not too far."

Not too far in good weather. But as best as he could remember, the closest turnout was about two winding, strenuous miles up this mountain.

CHAPTER 13

"You gonna shoot me in the back? Say I was killed trying to escape?" Colter Norris had to yell to be heard over the electric heater, and his voice echoed off the basement walls.

Mary Broadbent opened the cell door wide, taking a few steps back, even though Colter Norris sat on the far wall, the stone one, resting on a blanket with another one around his shoulders. Keeping her eyes on the prisoner, she bent over and pulled hard on the cord. The heater turned silent, but the wind moaned through cracks and pipes.

"No, sir," Mary said, "but I'll shoot you in the mouth if you don't get up and get out of here so I can go back to my coffee."

He must have sobered up a lot because he laughed. He wasn't smoking, so Mary deduced that he was out of cigarettes. The Circle M foreman reached up and grabbed a horizontal bar, and with a grimace and the sounds of joints cracking, he pulled himself to his feet, leaned to his left to stretch his back, then stamped his boots to get the blood circulating again.

"I don't reckon the charges were dropped," he said.

His voice boomed in the basement, even though he wasn't shouting, but at least that made the wind less noticeable.

"Christmas came and went, Colter," Mary told him. "You're being released on your own recognizance. You'll be notified when your hearing is."

He was patting all his pockets. He stopped and chuckled. "That might be a while." He tilted his head. "Sounds like a blizzard out there."

She shrugged. "It's snowing pretty good."

"How do I get back to the Circle M?"

"How'd you get here?"

He shrugged, cursed, and said he didn't have a clue. She knew his truck had been impounded. But just a glance out of the door window before heading into the abyss was enough to know that Colter Norris wouldn't get far. He was a heck of a rider on saddle broncs and in the Fourth of July rodeo, but he had totaled two pickups in the years Mary had been on the Cutthroat County sheriff's force—and those came on clear summer nights.

"They've set up a shelter at the school gym," she told him.

Colter frowned. "I got to spend the night in that ice bucket, listenin' to Californians who come to Montana for the sunshine? Or the pot farmers south of Mack's beaver pond and everywhere else?"

"You can walk back to the Circle M," she told him.

He snorted and started moving toward the open door.

"Cowpunchers don't walk, missy," he told her. "You wouldn't happen to have a cigarette or the makin's, would you?"

"You know I don't smoke, Colter."

"I was hopin' you mighta taken up the habit. Maybe some other bad habits."

"Out." She pointed the nightstick toward the stairs.

He laughed again but that turned into a hacking cough, and he spit phlegm twice on the walls on the stairway leading to the first floor. She followed him up the stairs and to the front door, which he opened and let in that numbing, frightening blast of wind and pounding snow. The wind almost took the door off the hinges.

They stared into a world of white.

He struggled to close the door, and when he straightened as much as he dared, he looked her in the eyes.

"You are tryin' to kill me," Colter Norris said.

But the wind died, or at least changed direction, and Mary saw that the snow wasn't too deep. Except the drifts, like the one building against the front of the building. The school wasn't more than a quarter of a mile away, but Mary had lived in Montana long enough to understand that a quarter mile could be a deadline at any time of the year.

She should have thought to bring a blanket.

Colter Norris shrugged. "You might as well go back inside, missy. No use in you losin' some digits to frostbite. I can make it to the school. If I don't, I will leave you the grullo. He's the worst horse in my string. I call him Mousey."

One job down. But the next one would be harder.

She came back inside the drafty old building and hurried upstairs. She had to look up the phone number in Drew's directory, and when she couldn't get the landline to work, she dialed the number on the cell.

"Citizens Action Network, Cutthroat County Chapter. How may we help you today?" The voice was nothing but nasty sarcasm, which meant C.A.N. had caller ID. Behind that voice came mocking laughter that the adult or adults in that Victorian house were not trying very hard to hold back.

"Elison Dempsey," she said, adding, much to her distaste, "please."

The pause was long. "Who is calling?"

"The Cutthroat County Sheriff's Department."

"It ain't April Fool's Day." The call ended. She hit the redial button.

"Listen," the man at C.A.N. said, "I don't—"

"This is Cutthroat County Sheriff's Deputy Mary Broadbent." She added some of her favorite curses she had learned in the Marine Corps, and then she told that fool who had answered the phone what she would do to him—in front of his C.A.N. pards—if he didn't hand the phone to Dempsey right then.

"My apologies," Dempsey said a few moments later, and Mary could picture Dempsey grinning at his hoodlums. "It is hard to find good workers in this county, Deputy Broadbent."

"That's too bad," Mary told him, "because Sheriff Drew asked me to call you because he needs five good workers. Now."

"Is this about that airplane about to crash near here?" Dempsey wasn't mocking her now. "The one we just heard about on the radio?"

That made sense to him now. "Partly. I need you, Dempsey, and five men, the best five you have—"

"Where's the airplane landing?"

"You're not going to the landing site," she told him. "The sheriff wants you here. At the courthouse. He's hiring you and five men as guards."

"Guards," he sang out. "I am qualified for CPR. And . . ."

His brain might have started working. She took advantage of his silence.

"You're being hired as special deputies. This is temporary only. But you need to be here, at the courthouse, in fifteen minutes."

"It's the Chadwick gang, isn't it?"

"Just get over here now. You'll be sworn in by the sheriff. Be here in fifteen or I'm calling Fergie Trent." She ended the call. Ferguson Trent was the game warden. And she wished he was coming over as a special deputy rather than Dempsey and his so-called friends.

She had already called Denton Creel, telling him about the airplane hauling a prisoner who at some point would get pricked by a needle and die for his crimes that was about to crash-land in a pretty big whiteout just a few miles from Basin Creek. That would wake anyone up.

The messages had piled up by the time she was back on the second floor and at her desk.

US Highway 103, which basically formed Cutthroat County's southern border, was closed from Clark Colony in Pondera County to Bear Basin in Flathead County. State Highways 60 and 76 were closed, too, in Cutthroat County.

"We're completely cut off," she whispered. The two state highways and the US route were closed. The only other roads in the county were not paved, and some of those practically all but impassable in the best of weather. And the National Weather Service was already declaring much of northwestern Montana, but specifically

Cutthroat County, underneath an extreme winter weather advisory.

She heard Denton Creel's voice on the radio.

"John, I'm on my way."

"Hold on," John Drew called over almost immediately. "Where are you, Denton?"

"Just pulling out of the carport, John."

"All right. I'm on my way. Be safe."

Mary turned up the volume and sat down, rigid, her body so tight she felt her heart pounding against her rib cage.

She cursed when the telephone rang again, but drew in a deep breath and let it out quickly before she answered.

"At the time, the temperature will be too cold!" Giggles followed. The call ended.

"Stupid kids!" Mary yelled. If things weren't going haywire, she could find the caller and scare the dickens out of those punks. Sounded like fourth graders.

"Mary?" Drew asked over the radio.

"Copy, John," she said. Or thought she said.

"Change of plans. Send Dempsey and his boys over to Sacagawea Pasture. For the time being."

"Ten-four."

"Over and out."

The door opened, and she jerked up, fending off a gasp, but there was no doubting that the man who opened the door saw the shock on her face—and Mary Broadbent didn't like that. She had never cared for being caught unawares.

But to be caught by—?

"Colter Norris!" she barked. "Why aren't you at the gym?"

"Nobody was there, honey chil'," the foreman said. "Door was locked. And I almost caught my death comin' all the way back here." He shivered. His clothes were damp from melted snow, and he looked frozen to the bone.

Finding her cane, she pushed herself to her feet and limped over to the prisoner-parolee-prisoner again. She pulled a jacket off the lost-and-found pile and tossed it to him. It wasn't the warmest of coverings, but people in this country held on to wool and sheepskin and thick blankets and anything winterproof. What Colter Norris had was a hundred-dollar windbreaker made overseas but sold at national park gift stores for a two hundred percent profit. Colter Norris started to say something, but she stopped him with a cold stare.

She grabbed her phone, called Elison Dempsey, and told him about the crash. That excited him more than being a part-time guard. The news media, if anyone could get here, would certainly cover a plane crash. Then she glared at Colter Norris.

"What do you mean closed?" She didn't give the cowhand time to answer, because the telephone was rattling her brains again, and she answered it before the third ring.

"Cutthroat County Sheriff's . . ." She hit the RECORD button, grabbed a notebook, and motioned at Colter Norris to find a chair and wait.

"Yes, Missus Auchter." The mother of Polly Poe, a waitress at the Wild Bunch Casino, was good for a phone call at least every other weekday and two or three times a night on Saturdays. She must have slept before and after church on Sundays.

Once she was certain the seventy-eight-year-old

widow was in a warm, safe place and as in control of her faculties as best as any widow in northern Montana at that age, she began half-listening to Poe's mother and waiting for any words from Denton Creel or John Drew.

"Someone's been on this road already," Creel said.

"Yeah, Denton. Billy."

"You're joking, Sheriff."

"Nope."

Creel swore.

"There's a man gliding on a snowflake, floating toward the beaver pond." That was new from Maeve Auchter.

"John. That looks like smoke."

"Copy that, Denton." John Drew swore softly. "Hold on, I've got another call coming in." He cursed. "It's Grimes. Denton, call Bobby Ward. I'll call you back as soon as I can."

Creel cursed, then muttered a short prayer.

Denton moved to a channel that Mary could still hear.

"This is Cutthroat County Sheriff's Office calling Basin Creek Volunteer Firehouse. Come in, Bobby."

"Watchya got, Denton, ol' boy?"

Mrs. Auchter rambled on about roman candles.

"We have trouble, Bobby. We have an airplane down in Sacagawea Pasture. It's burning badly."

"You got a visual."

"Black smoke. Lots of flames. I'm about ten miles shy of the old Foster border."

Mary bowed her head. She wasn't sorry that a killer like Rupert Chadwick had been involved in this plane crash, but she did feel sorry for the pilot. And the men who'd been guarding him.

"How much medical assistance do you anticipate?"

"I'm not close enough yet, but from here it sure looks

like a job for George." George J. White was the county coroner, but he wouldn't be able to get out of Havre till this storm broke and the highway departments got their act together, which was, thankfully, usually like a Marine Corps drill. "But we better get this fire put out as fast as we can."

"Ten-four."

Now Mrs. Auchter said there were two crazy fools hang gliding on snowflakes. "Don't they need permits to do that?"

John Drew came back on the audio.

"Grimes confirms the crash. It must have just happened. He says he's just a mile or two from the Circle M road. Mary's calling Dempsey, and he'll be at the site with five men."

Mary said, "John. Confirmed. Dempsey is on his way to Sacagawea Pasture."

"Mary," he said, "I need you to put in a call to George White and Will Ambrose. Tell him that the plane is down, burning, survivors are unlikely and . . ."

And two hang gliders were using snowflakes to drift down onto Mrs. Auchter's property.

"John!" she shouted. "No one's in that plane. The pilot and Chadwick parachuted out. They're about to land near Maeve Auchter's and Polly Poe's place."

CHAPTER 14

George Grimes had been nursing a Jack Daniel's hangover and freezing his rear end off in this frigid patch of the fiery pit, so the last thing he needed was for some ignorant telephone solicitor to cut an early nap short. He had tried letting the caller get the message and hang up, but the phone just made his right temple push toward his left and his brains try to squeeze his eyeballs out of their sockets. Maybe he should invest in that voicemail option the evil phone company had tried to force him to buy.

With a roar of profanity, he sat up on the couch, lunged for the phone, grabbed it, and swore as vilely as he could even before he got it to his mouth so that the imbecile could really hear him loud, strong, and clear.

"Shut up, Grimes. This is John Drew. I need you to do me a favor."

That kept his favorite curse in his mouth. He tried to swallow, looked for something, and found a beer can with probably just saliva in it, but that did a decent enough job.

"Is it a payin' favor, pardner?"

"It pays. But I'm not your partner."

Grimes started to laugh, but that just made his brain implode.

"What's up, hoss?" he finally said.

"I have a stupid kid."

"Like father, like son."

He figured that would get a rise out of the sheriff, but Drew said something that sounded like *That's about the size of it.*

He found the pack of cigarettes, tapped one out, and was lighting it as he asked, "So, what's the boy done? Knocked up some teen? Bought a bottle of Mad Dog Twenty-Twenty with a fake ID?"

"He's heading up to the ski basin in the Always Winters to practice."

"That's a bad thing? Sheesh, and I thought my old man was a Nazi."

"Have you looked outside this morning?"

He didn't think he wanted to, but the cord on the phone was long enough for him to move from the third-hand sofa to the window, and he pulled back the curtain.

"Hold on, hoss, the lousy window is iced over like a woman's foo-foo drink." He opened the door and quickly closed it, cursing the wind.

"Is it always like this in January, pardner?"

"February is usually the bad month. Do you know how to get to the ski basin?"

"Drive north on Neely Road to run into Highway Seventy-Six. We ain't got many ski resorts in the great state of Texas. Those snow freaks usually would drive up to Red River or someplace in New Mexico. I never cared to go, though. They grade them roads, don't they?"

"When they can."

"How long has the boy been gone?"

"Early morning, I guess. I didn't hear him leave. There's a fair to middling chance that he didn't get all the way to the basin. Snow's coming down harder than predicted, and that truck of his has four-wheel drive, and from what I see from the driveway, he was smart enough to put chains on. He left a note. Said he was picking up a friend."

"Give a name?" Grimes looked for a notepad and pen, but found just empty beer cans, wadded-up newspapers, and some dirty clothes that he ought to throw in a pile.

"No. I don't know who would be fool enough to go with him."

Now Grimes laughed out loud. Daddies could be as dumb as their kids sometimes.

"What's so funny?"

"Nothin', hoss." But Grimes had already pegged that wannabe Yogi Berra as having eyes for Ashton Maddox's hot little daughter since that deal with that high-priced hit man and the late Garland Foster. Smart kid. Smarter than his dad. That gal was a looker, and her daddy had lots, lots more money and property than a county sheriff could earn in forty thousand years.

"I'll get my truck warmed up and see if I can round him up."

"I appreciate it."

"We'll see if you say that when I hand you my bill. Texas Rangers don't come cheap." He hung up the phone and started putting on some warm duds. Then he hurried outside, into the Dodge, which he cranked up and let run as he returned to his apartment and finished dressing, finding a pack of cigarettes that might keep him halfway sane as he chased down some stupid lawman's stupid kid. But it beat spending the day when there wasn't even a decent football game on the tube, and he always wondered what it would be like to drive up a mountain in a snowstorm. They didn't get many blizzards in South Texas, but it sure could get cold in that Big Bend Country way down in far West Texas.

He figured he had some tools—shovel, hatchet, chains, ropes, things like that—in the toolbox on the back of his truck, so he gathered a few other essentials and his Colt revolver and .300 Winchester Magnum bolt-action rifle in case he got attacked by a grizzly or abominable snow monster. And a six-pack of Coors.

Pulling on his Resistol hat, Grimes left his apartment, locking it up, and climbed into the truck, depositing the rifle and blankets behind the front seats and the six-pack on the passenger seat, within easy reach.

He backed out without hitting any of his neighbors' cars, shifted into drive, and eased out of the apartment complex to the dirt road, then drove to the main road that led to the north-south county highway.

He decided to make a quick stop at the Wild Bunch Casino, getting a big cup of coffee, a couple packs of cigarettes, and a pack of saltines in case the kids he rescued got hungry. He also got a fifth of Jack and had Chuckie Corvallis put it on his tab. Chuckie was a good fellow. Those who enjoyed killing their lungs always stuck together.

Well, there hadn't been much traffic on any road, and the county or the state highway boys had not done a thing as far as grading was concerned. He wasn't sure what kind of track a truck with tires with chains made, but what he saw heading north on what the locals called Neely Road but the sign said was MONTANA 60 sure looked like a puny little Japanese truck with chains on the tires. But those tracks were filling up pretty fast with snow.

He smiled when he saw where the truck had turned onto the road that led to the Circle M, and he eased the Ram to the left side of the road but didn't turn down the path. Yes, sirree, ol' George Grimes was one super-smart detective. He rolled down the window for a better look, noticing footprints that led to the gate and back.

So Miss Smarty Pants, who could land planes at DIA, had met him at the gate. Walked with him to the tin truck, and they had headed north.

Grimes had gone just a couple of miles north when he heard the drone of some motor. Leaning against the steering wheel and taking his foot off the accelerator, he tried looking left and right and into the colorless sky. The Dodge slowed to a crawl of fifteen miles an hour, then ten, then five.

It had to be that airplane. The one he had heard some-thing about on the news. But he couldn't see anything but his windshield wipers working overtime and the snow covering just about everything.

Then came the explosion, something so hard that it shook his hands off the steering wheel, and he made the mistake, from instinct, of slamming on the brakes. The Dodge slipped, turning right, then sliding on ice or whatever, and he could see the firebomb of orange and black and yellow off toward the east, but then the truck was spinning, and he just held his breath until the Ram finally stopped.

He was still on the road. The engine had stalled, but the snow did not hide the massive fire about two hun-dred yards off the road.

Grimes found the cell phone and prayed he had a signal.

"Grimes?"

He breathed easier. It was John T. Drew.

"Buddy, your plane just landed in a firebomb."

"Where are you?"

"How the devil do I know? I can't see a blasted thing but white. And now orange and black."

The sheriff said nothing, just waiting, and Grimes looked out left and right. "I guess I'm a mile, don't think two, from the Circle M entrance." He leaned forward and shook his head at what he saw.

"Survivors?"

"Sonny, I ain't no pilot, never wanted to be one, but I could land a plane better than that. I heard that whining, like a missile headed straight for me. Then there was a whoosh and a roar and a bomb blasting, and I'm lucky I didn't flip over my ride and slide all the way to that windmill farm up the road."

"Hang on. I'll be back in a minute."

The call ended, and Grimes shook his head. At least he had a front-row seat. It was like watching a movie.

Yeah, Grimes decided, he was in a drive-in, taking in the show. So he reached over to pull a beer can out of the plastic holder, popped it open, and took a healthy slug.

He had finished the beer when his phone buzzed.

"Still burnin', pardner. Though it don't make this rig any warmer."

"I've got the fire department and Denton Creel on the way."

"Want me to stay here and help 'em out?"

He waited, smiling, knowing the sheriff was trying to

sort out what was the right thing to do. Grimes could have told him, and Grimes wasn't a daddy. Well, he wasn't a daddy that he knowed of, anyhow.

"You still up for driving to the ski basin?"

"That's why I'm here." He figured he might as well fill the daddy/sheriff in. "There's not much in the way of tracks, but I saw some that probably came from your kid's toy truck." He considered letting the sheriff know that his boy had a sweet-looking young thing riding with him now, but decided that the lawman had enough on his plate already. "Headin' north. I can still make out the tracks, but they'll be covered before too long if this storm don't stop dumpin' on me."

"All right. But take it easy. And if you don't think you can make it up that mountain road, don't try it. We've lost some hikers, skiers, and more than a couple of drivers on that road. Some of them we didn't find till summer. Two we never found."

"Your confidence inspires me, Sheriff."

"Just be careful."

"Ain't I always?" he said softly, adding, "Sheriff?"

"Yeah."

"I think you like me." Laughing, he hit the button on the side of the phone and tossed it next to the five beers.

After taking one final look at the fireball surrounded by a white sheet, he started up the Dodge, put it in gear, and headed north, following the trail made by a kid and a pretty girl in a little pickup.

Highway 76 started out all right. He found it peculiar that it didn't appear to be snowing as hard as he gained elevation, but then decided that would change. When he was creeping up at a snail's pace, leaning forward, scarcely breathing, and making sure he was keeping his rig as close to the mountain and as far away from the guardrails on the left-hand side as possible, he wondered if maybe he ought to stop and head back home. Catch a football game on the tube in the casino. Or get drunk at the . . .

No . . . that fool of a ranch foreman had shuttered the Busted Stirrup till spring.

The snow wasn't coming down hard, but the temperature was dropping like a stone. Twelve degrees.

Grimes had no idea how high he had driven, and if he had passed any mile markers telling him how far he had to go to the tourist trap or the next galaxy; the snow had covered up all the signs.

He rounded a hairpin and caught sight of what appeared to be a brake light. The distance was a good bit away, but it was darker up here, with trees and mountains and, of course, those monster snow clouds blocking out any sun.

Or maybe it was the hazard lights. No. Brake lights. Red. On and off. On and off. On and off.

A driver would wear out the brake pads doing that. Stupid kid. Stupid *kids*. Stupid truck.

Then that cop's sense came to him, and he hit his brake pedal, but he didn't tap it. He stopped the Ram and shifted into park, then pulled up the emergency brake.

He focused on the brake lights about two-tenths of a mile up the mountain road.

Red-red-red. Red. Red. Red. Red-red-red.

Red-red-red. Red. Red. Red. Red-red-red.

Red-red-red. Red. Red. Red. Red-red-red.

"Son of a . . ." Grimes reached for the .45 revolver and brought it closer.

Red-red-red. Red. Red. Red. Red-red-red.

Morse code. That Billy boy wasn't the dumb jock Grimes had taken him for. If that was Billy Drew.

He was tapping the brakes, sending out a distress signal: Red-red-red. Red. Red. Red. Red-red-red.

SOS.

CHAPTER 15

There probably wasn't enough coffee on the entire Circle M ranch, all 149,000 acres, including the bunkhouse and line shacks, to keep Ashton Maddox in on this morning, but he poured his first cup and downed it quickly. The hot shower had helped some, but it was coffee that he needed. He stood in the kitchen, wondering why he put up with Colter Norris. When he was sober, there wasn't a better cowhand in all of Montana. But when that SOB went into one of his funks, well, how much would it cost to fix up the Busted Stirrup?

Was it worth it?

In a year, maybe two, if Cutthroat County got lucky, Norris would go on a tear again.

He was yawning when someone tapped on the door.

Ashton let out a soft curse and topped off his coffee. He had glanced out the bedroom window when he had awakened from a poor sleep, and he knew the weather forecasters had blown another prediction. That someone was knocking on his door at this time of morning—it certainly wasn't UPS delivering some package—meant bad news.

"It's open," he yelled.

Mateo Balcázar, wearing a sheepskin coat and winter skullcap, came inside. His eyes remained red-rimmed and the plaster over his nose made him look ridiculous, but he somehow was standing up—and straight, too. He would have made a good hand, but Ashton could not blame him for coming in to collect his pay and move off to find a better outfit that didn't have the Colter Norris factor.

"Pour yourself a coffee, Mateo." Ashton nodded at the pot and Alyson's cup.

"*Gracias*, but no." He shuffled uncomfortably in his snow-covered boots.

"If you're quitting, I understand. I'll pay you a full month's wages—"

"*Patrón*, it is not that." The little man shook his head, wetted his lips, and sighed. His eyes met Ashton's.

"It is your daughter."

Maddox turned so fast, coffee spilled onto the floor. "Alyson!" he shouted upstairs. "Alyson!" Then he spun back to look at the Mexican, who had pulled off his cap and was twisting it in his leathery hands.

"Señor Cooper found her car at the main road."

Homer Cooper had been riding for the Circle M for several years now. The gutless wonder had sent the new man to break the news. Ashton would deal with that gutless wonder in good time.

"Alyson!" He ran up the stairs and pushed open the door to her bedroom, then swore, flinging the coffee cup against the wall. He turned and moved to the balustrade, staring down at the little Mexican, yelling, "What do you mean Cooper found Alyson's car?"

"It was parked on the road, behind the gate."

He hadn't heard her showering or anything, but when

he had finally fallen asleep, it had been a hard, hard sleep.

He came downstairs and looked for a note—anything—then realized that kids these days didn't believe in notes. He had turned off his cell phone when he got home after the Basin Creek ruckus. He looked for it near his billfold and car keys, then remembered the parka hanging in the coatroom. Sure enough, it was in the pocket, cold as the dead. It seemed to take forever for it to come on, and then he had to fumble with the keys before he got his password right and saw the messages.

He skipped the business ones till he found Alyson's name.

> Going up w/a friend to the Always Winter resort—yeah, right—to take advantage of fresh powder. Home before dark.

Signed with a stupid little heart emoji.

He exhaled heavily.

"She left her car?" he said, staring at the battered hired hand. He wanted to make sure he had heard the Mexican right.

"Sí, Patrón."

"All right. Go back to the bunkhouse. And tell Homer Cooper he had better be dressed by the time I get there. And he better remember everything he saw before we head to Neely Road. I want you to get the Expedition warmed up. Load it with blankets, tow chains, anything we might need. Have Yukon fix some sandwiches and fill as many thermoses as he can with coffee."

"Sí."

"Cooper say anything else?"

"No, Patrón."

"Well, he better tell me everything by the time we get to Neely Road."

When Maddox was fully dressed, he gathered what he figured he would need and pulled on his parka. The last thing he remembered was the half-filled bottle of Blanton's Single Barrel. It was too early for a bracer this morning, but he knew he would need one before this day was over.

The exhaust pipe of the old ranch truck was smoking, the ice melting off the windows. Someone had already scraped as much snow as they could off, and the wipers were moving. Ashton trudged through wind and about a foot of snow to the bunkhouse, opened the door, and saw Yukon Hearst filling a gunnysack with food.

Then he found Homer Cooper.

"You want to keep earning a check from this outfit, Cooper, you might remember that I don't like second-hand information. You see something, you tell me. Don't send someone else just because you think I won't like what you're telling me."

"Yes, sir." Well, at least Cooper remembered that Ashton Maddox wanted a man to look into his eyes when they were talking. "I'll remember."

"She left her car at the gate?" he asked.

"Near it. Then she walked. I guess they couldn't get the gate open all the way. A couple of feet was all it would open. Two sets of footprints. Hers and someone."

"Man or girl?"

"Man, by my guess. Maybe my size. Chains on his wheels. Guessing a truck, but not a big one."

The cook brought Ashton a cup of coffee, which he accepted without thanks. It was strong, bitter, cowboy coffee. Since Alyson had arrived from Denver, he had been drinking coffee with flavors like maple pecan and pumpkin spice. He thought this morning's cup had been at least something simple like hazelnut. This was just black and bitter.

"She had her skis," Cooper said.

He nodded. "Yeah. She left me a text that she was going with a friend into the Always Winter range. That piece of crap that they try to call a ski resort."

"That highway won't be graded for some time," Yukon Hearst said, nodding at the big flat-screen TV that was showing a nasty looking radar map of northern Montana.

"No, it won't."

"You want me to call Search and Rescue?" Hearst asked.

"No." This was Maddox business. Ashton didn't want John T. Drew or any of those town boys to know that Ashton Maddox's daughter could be as clueless and stupid as those fools in town—if anyone really thought Basin Creek was a town.

He looked at his hired men. They would gladly go with him to bring back Alyson—and maybe hang the punk who took her into those freezing mountains.

"You'd better take some grain to the winter pastures. Bring a sledgehammer to break ice in the water tanks." He looked back at the cook. "They say anything about when this storm might let up?"

"Severe warning in effect till five this afternoon. For now. It was noon an hour ago. Roads are closed throughout the county. Everyone is advised to stay home."

"Yeah. Too bad everyone doesn't listen."

The heavy-duty Ford was warmed up when Ashton got behind the steering wheel.

"I'll bring Alyson back," he told Yukon Hearst. "But I'm not sure about her *friend*."

Turning the wheel, he put the big truck into reverse, then shifted and let the Ford grind through the snow, following the tracks of the puny little SUV Alyson had rented in Great Falls until he saw it, stuck. Maddox slowed just a tad and steered the big Ford around it, dipping in what passed for a ditch and, when he had cleared the piece of crap his daughter had rented, back onto the road. By now her footprints had been covered with snowfall.

It pleased him that his daughter had to walk about the length of a football field to get to the gate. That would teach her a lesson—*maybe*, she was a Maddox after all—about being sneaky with her old man.

He hit the remote, and the gate opened to exactly where it had stopped when Alyson had tried opening it. Shifting the truck into park, he swore.

"Let's shovel some snow out of the way," he told himself, and he wondered why he hadn't brought one of his cowhands along.

He cursed the thermometer in the Ford.

At least most of the snow wasn't ice, making it somewhat easier to shovel. But the wind and the stinging flakes didn't make this task easy.

He focused on getting to that spot near the top of the Always Winter range where fools played in the snow and thought that was fun.

Something caught his attention. A noise. Not another truck on the state highway. He sank the shovel blade into the snow and tried to listen.

"Snow plow?" he thought aloud.

No. The noise was above. Ashton looked up, shielding his eyes with one hand and wishing he had thought to bring snow goggles or something. At least the snow was pelting the sides and back of his head.

It was a single-prop airplane. Fair sized. Painted blue on the bottom. Dark blue. Navy. White, or perhaps silver, on the top. He saw no smoke, and the engine appeared to be running. But it was coming down hard and fast. Ashton couldn't look away.

The plane hit in some of the oldest land that belonged to the Circle M, and the fireball caused Ashton to close his eyes tightly and turn his head. The concussion that followed was deafening.

When he turned back to the sight and the ringing stopped in his ears, he saw the flames and thick, black smoke.

He started working harder, faster, at a furious pace, shoveling, then gave up. Emergency vehicles would be at the scene as soon and as fast as possible. The roads would be shut down. He climbed into the Expedition, shifted into first, and rammed through the gate that had cost him a small fortune.

He stopped, briefly, and saw the flames and smoke. No one could survive a crash like that. The pilot and any passengers he might have been carrying were dead, and probably it would take a forensics team days or even weeks to identify any bodies or put the body parts together.

There was nothing anyone could do for the pilot and—if any—crew and passengers. But Ashton did not want to be here and answering questions and telling

John T. Drew and the Federal Aviation Administration flunkies what he had seen. He wanted to be on the road to the Always Winters before those pesky cops and investigators showed up.

No such luck.

By the time he had the gate opened and had pulled the big truck past the gate, he saw the flashing lights of a Sheriff's Department SUV.

At least it wasn't the sheriff's rig.

Denton Creel, the deputy, stepped out and ran to the driver's side of the Ford. Reluctantly, Maddox put the truck in park and rolled down the window.

"Mr. Maddox, did you see that?" Creel asked stupidly.

"I didn't see much, Denton. I was trying to get the gate open. Any idea what that plane was doing here?"

The deputy's mouth opened, then closed. He knew something. But he wasn't saying anything.

He looked up, as if trying to find parachutes or something. His face soon disappeared in a fog of frozen vapor. He was breathing that hard.

"I need to put on snowshoes. Get out there. See if . . ." Creel shook his head. There had not been an airplane crash in Cutthroat County in . . . in . . . in . . . Well, as far as Maddox knew, this was the first. Which meant more TV crews and newspaper reporters. And all those federal, state, and county agents.

The deputy hurried to his county rig, opening the hatch. Ashton put the truck into drive and eased onto the road. He did not look at Creel. He just focused on the road, following the tracks left by whoever had put his daughter in harm's way and whoever had passed the

Circle M gate before the airplane had crashed in the fabled Sacagawea Pasture.

He did glance in the rearview mirror to see Denton Creel slogging toward the inferno in his snowshoes. He pitied the deputy.

CHAPTER 16

Twice the old Nissan got stuck, but both times—and Billy thanked the Lord—the truck managed to find some patch of something that wasn't icy, which gave the old pickup enough traction to push ahead and up the slope. By now, all Billy wanted to do was reach those cabins. They could wait out the storm there. That had to be a whole lot safer than trying to turn around and head back downhill.

Downhill, on this road, in this weather, on this particular day—and with a passenger like Alyson Maddox, with her life in his hands—could turn out to be a disaster.

He slowed to a turtle's pace, trying to control his breathing, not daring to glance at white-faced Alyson Maddox, who sat with her hands clasped and her face paling. If he could have found a place to pull off onto the side of the road, he would have parked the pickup there, and they could have hiked, using their skis, the rest of the distance to the cabins. Even that shed they used for concessions would have provided something that might keep them alive. Billy even considered the stands he and his dad had been working on—when was that? Just yesterday morning?—and thought that, in a worst-case scenario, they could make a snow cave underneath the stands.

He took a glance in the rearview mirror. Had that been headlights he had seen a while back? Or just a rare glimpse of the sun somewhere in the east?

Alyson's lips were mouthing something. A prayer, Billy guessed. Well, they were having a quiet duet. Billy kept praying, too.

A quick glance at the odometer made his heart beat faster. They ought to be there by now. Had he passed it?

He slowed even more and leaned forward, looking through the windshield off to the right-hand side of the road.

Suddenly, Alyson gasped. Billy straightened. Her eyes were focused up the road, and Billy looked straight ahead.

They weren't the only fools on this mother of all winter days. Somebody else had been on the road— someone heading over the pass from the northwestern side of the Always Winters. Well, they had to be twenty million times dumber than Billy Drew had been. That side of the pass was a whole lot worse than over this way.

His heart felt like it was about to slow down. Then he thought he saw something again in the rearview mirror. But whatever that was, it disappeared in an instant. It might have been his imagination.

"Oh, my God!" Alyson brought her hands up to her face. Her eyes stared ahead, wide, like a deer in the proverbial headlights.

Billy looked ahead.

That's when he saw the guns.

Which was almost exactly the same time that the truck's right front wheel found the ditch.

John Drew stopped the Interceptor. He ran Mary Broadbent's words through his mind, then said, "Come again, Mary?"

"No one's in that plane, Johnny. It's a trick." She had a few choice adjectives about what kind of trick it was.

"Don't yell, Mary. Get a hold of yourself. Now, what do you mean?"

"John," she said, her voice rattling but at least now a few decibels lower. "Maeve Auchter called. She said she was watching two hang gliders on parachutes. Coming right down near her house."

He started to roll his eyes, but then he understood what Mary was saying.

"You think Rupert Chadwick bailed out?"

She answered with her own question.

"Do you think any pilot would attempt an emergency landing in Sacagawea Pasture when there are miles of straightaway roads—some actually paved—around here?"

Like the one Denton Creel was driving on now.

"There had to be guards. Not just a pilot and a prisoner," he said, more just to hear him speak. Sounding out the theory usually was a good idea, his dad had told him. He had rarely seen eye-to-eye with his dad, but the old man did know a few things, having been a cop for almost all of his adult life.

"And how long will it take them to identify the remains?" she said.

He changed the radio setting so that both Denton Creel and Mary Broadbent could hear.

"Denton, I'm going to investigate a situation at crazy old Auchter's place. You stick by the plane wreckage. And keep a sharp lookout. We might be dealing with the Chadwick gang."

The reply took longer than normal.

"Copy that, John . . . I think."

"Keep your service weapon handy, Denton . . . Mary?"

"Yes, John."

"Is Dempsey on his way to the crash site?"

"Ten-four. According to Dempsey. With five men. I don't know how long it will take him to get there."

"He's probably listening on this frequency. Elison. To the plane site. I see you near the Auchter place, you'll be in the same cell with Rupert Chadwick."

This is like . . . He tried to think of the author's name. He had read a ton of his books as a kid. Thrillers. English guy. Had some of his novels turned into movies. Well, the name didn't matter. It wasn't important.

He turned onto the road that led to the cabin where Mrs. Auchter lived with her daughter.

"Mary?"

"I'm here, John."

"Put in a call to Will Ambrose. Tell him what's going on, or what we think might be going on."

"Roger that. Any message?"

"Tell him he might ought to radio the van carrying Chadwick's psycho relatives and accomplices. If he can reach them. If he can't, then he might think about asking the governor to send in the National Guard."

"Copy. Anything else, John?"

"Keep this line open."

"Ten-four."

"And stay put, Mary. Stay put."

"Holy . . ."

Mary was speed-dialing another number before Homer Cooper finished his curse.

Will Ambrose listened to Mary's concise report of everything that was going on. She heard him asking someone to call the FAA and someone else to get in touch with the director of prisons.

"How bad is the weather up your way, Deputy Broadbent?" he asked.

"It . . . it isn't good."

"Visibility?"

"On the ground, it was all right, but that depends on which way you're facing. At any altitude, I would say it is extremely low."

"What kind of backup do you have?"

She sighed. "John asked for Elison Dempsey and four men. No five men. Six including Dempsey." She was getting flustered, and Marines do not get flustered. "And there's me."

She had put him on the speakerphone and was taking notes.

"So a plane is down. Possibly two survivors parachuted out. No crash landing attempted. That right?"

"According to Deputy Creel, yes, sir, Captain."

"Denton's at the crash site. John . . . the sheriff is heading to investigate the possible landing of two airplane survivors at . . ." She had to find the address that someone who didn't live in Cutthroat County could find.

"Anybody else there John can deputize?"

She gave Norris a quick glance, stopped herself from rolling her eyes and said, "Unless I find someone stranded at the Wild Bunch or taking shelter in the school gym . . ."

"You can't even find that blessed barn of a gym," Norris said, and spit into the trash can.

"There's nobody."

"Well . . ." She heard Ambrose breathe in deeply and slowly exhale. Like he was using what Mary had been taught to deal with anxiety attacks. Breathe in slowly through your mouth. Think good thoughts. Count to three and a half. Breathe out all bad thoughts, all stressful situations, every person that got on your nerves, through your open mouth. Over and over again.

If Mary tried that, she would be breathing in and out twenty-four seven.

"Maybe that was the pilot and a guard who bailed out of that Cessna."

Mary didn't see any reason to acknowledge that.

"Tell the sheriff that I'm on it. There's not much I can do from Helena. We're starting to get hammered with some wind and snow now ourselves. But I'll see what I can do. Tell John to hang on. The cavalry's on its way. I'll be in touch. Stay close, Deputy. I'm doing everything that I can."

"Roger. Over and out."

"Over and out."

She pushed away from the radios and communications center and looked up at the Circle M foreman.

"I ain't got no cigarettes," Colter Norris said.

"I don't smoke," Mary told him.

"I know that. I'm just tellin' you that I ain't got no cigarettes."

Mary looked at the locked gun cabinet. Then she looked up at the battered old cowboy.

"You want to earn some smokes, Colter?" she asked.

The battered old faced looked about twenty years younger. Colter Norris leaned forward. "Throw in a fifth of rye whiskey?"

Alyson clasped her hands together. The Nissan was struck, though Billy was trying his best to rock the old pickup out of its predicament. The three men ran closer, though ran was not the correct verb. They staggered, slipped, and flailed about, at least until they stood by the truck.

"Billy," she pleaded. "Stop it!" The last command was a loud order. Those three men were aiming massive weapons at both of them. She could almost see the windshield shattering as bullets tore through her body.

But they did not fire their weapons.

"Stop!" one of the men yelled. "Stop! Stop! Stop now or we will kill you both!"

"Billy." She cursed him. And he looked up, saw the rifles, and let off the accelerator.

He nodded slowly at the middle man. Alyson had seen his photo in newspapers, even in the *Post* in Denver, and she tried to remember the name.

Uncle Hemingway Jones. One of Rupert Chadwick's relatives—and a cold-blooded killer.

Slowly, Billy cranked down the window with his left hand. Alyson could not feel the cold blast of winter. She already felt like a dead person.

"Can you get this piece of Japanese junk out of that hole, bucko?" the killer asked.

Billy gave Alyson a sideways glance.

"Maybe," he told the short, but deadly, little old man. "Can you three push?"

The second man had to be another one of Rupert Chadwick's "Killing Kinfolk," as the *New York Post* had labeled them. Lyle Baxter.

But the third man. He kept a distance. And she realized that he wore the uniform of a Montana officer. She wanted to spit on that man's face before she died.

"Step back and I'll—"

"No." Hemingway Jones smiled. "Don't be so hasty, boy." He looked through the window and nodded at Alyson.

"Let the little lady out. We wouldn't want to see you lose control and go over the edge, taking that fine lookin' piece of summer with you. Now would we?" The accent was faked, sugary and Southern.

"Get out," he told her, losing the saccharine and pointing an automatic rifle at her. "Now."

Billy's hands tightened against the wheel, and his face paled rapidly.

But Alyson knew she had to obey. Before Billy Drew did something rash and stupid—and got them both killed.

She had to force the truck door open, as there wasn't much room and the snow on this side of the road was thick and icy and high. No one tried to help her, even when she fell into the ditch. She grabbed the front wheel, found another handle, and came up and to the front of the pickup.

Lyle Baxter started toward her, but Hemingway Jones

told him not to lay a hand on her. The law officer did not move. That was fine with Alyson. She stood there in front of the truck and tried to stamp the snow off her boots and pants legs.

It had been in the twenties when she had left the Circle M—and that was early morning. It had to be late morning, maybe even noon, by now, but the thermometer in the Frontier said it was three degrees.

That was without any wind chill.

She slowly moved to the back of the truck, stepping toward the middle of the road.

When the turncoat guard started toward her, Jones snapped at him, "Buck. She'll keep. You and Lyle get in the front . . . and push. And you boy." He smiled a murderous grin at Billy. "You better be as good at getting out of sticky places as you is as getting stuck."

"All right," she heard Billy say. "Let me straighten the wheels." He looked over at Alyson. "Aly. Get back behind me. Kind of guide me out. And if I lose control, run toward the right-hand side of the road."

"You lose control," Hemingway Jones said, "and you both die an unnatural death. But it'll be quicker than freezing to death."

She moved according to Billy's instructions. He started turning the ignition, but the old Nissan was slow to catch. And then she noticed the brake lights. She drew in a breath and held it.

The SOS command of Morse code.

Alyson started to look behind her, but stopped, fearful that she might give away the signal.

But who, she wondered . . . who was back there?

Who did Billy think he was signaling? Up there. Near

the top of the mountains. More than eleven thousand feet high.

Who could see those lights?

John Drew stopped the Interceptor about fifty yards from the turnoff to Mrs. Auchter's cabin. He zipped up his coat, but not before removing the service revolver and shoving it into his coat pocket. He also took the twelve-gauge pump shotgun.

For some reason, shotguns, he had learned over the years, scared most men who knew guns more than AK-47s or .44 Magnums.

He locked the unit with a click on the chain, shoved the keys deep into his pants pocket, and took off toward the white-covered dome of a rural mailbox, then jogged down the quarter-mile path to the cabin. He didn't hear the voices until he had turned into the empty lane that led to the house.

The noise came from the back. Raising the shotgun to his shoulder and easing the safety off but keeping his forefinger outside the trigger guard, he moved slowly to the corner of the house, raising the barrel upward, then peering around the corner.

Two men stood on the ground next to the steps to the kitchen door.

"Lady . . ." one of the men said. "Please put down that rifle. See this, lady? Put the rifle down. My automatic is in my holster. And this . . . ? This is my ID. I'm a duly appointed . . ."

While the man was talking, the other man was reaching behind his back, and even with the snow falling pretty

good, John Drew could see the flash of nickel before
a gloved hand took hold of a revolver.

Then Drew came around the corner, brought the
shotgun level, and called out, "This is Sheriff John Drew,
mister! You move one more inch and I'm blowing your
head off, Rupert Chadwick!"

The cold-blooded killer froze. His accomplice started
to turn, but stopped when he heard Mrs. Auchter.

"I can blow your head off just as quick, you snowflake
hang-gliding alien from outer space."

1894

JANUARY

CHAPTER 17

Murdo Maddox threw the quilt off himself as soon as the first hint of daylight shined through the window as he swung his tired legs over the bed, and somehow managed to make it to the dresser, where he dunked his hands into the washbasin and grimaced from the shock of cold water. Well, the room was so cold it was a miracle he had not bruised his knuckles on a block of ice.

He felt wide awake after he splashed icy water across his face and quickly toweled himself dry. Only then did he move to the wall lamp and turn it up so that he could see better. The lamps in the boarding house had been converted to gas a year and a half ago.

Basin Creek wasn't as backwoods as most folks thought. If Cutthroat County wasn't careful, before long they would even have electricity and those newfangled telephone contraptions.

Having slept in his clothes, he just needed to pull the boots over his socks, pull on his vest—after checking his watch for the time—wrap the scarf around his neck, buckle on his gun belt, and grab his hat and his heavy coat. He sat down long enough to pull up his socks and then stuff his little feet into the boots he had handmade by a cobbler down in Helena three years ago. The boots looked thirty years old, but they were broken in, with just one patch over a tear in the left one.

His spurs had remained on, and they sang a cold song as he walked to the window and tried to look out. But all he could see, especially at this time of morning, was the white block of frost on the outside.

Or, he thought, *maybe on the inside.*

Last night, after helping the county sheriff drag the heavy carcass of one of the most ruthless cutthroats in Montana history—and that was saying a lot—he had walked back to tell Jeannie Ashton that Napoleon Drew was all right, that he had been called away to bring in a prisoner.

"And stay away from the sheriff's office," he had told her. "He's got Bo Meacham locked up."

That was enough to put the fear of the Lord—or the fear of the Meacham gang—into anyone's heart.

He had also stopped at the sheriff's cabin and told the boy that his dad was all right, had to go bring in a prisoner, and that the man was locked up in the jail. "Stay away from your pa's office," he had told the kid. "Keep your brother and sister away from there, too. Your pa will be all right. But he says you're the man of the house till he gets rid of that prisoner. Shouldn't be more than a couple of days, but, hopefully, sooner."

Now that he was looking into an ice block, he thought a couple of days was way beyond an understatement. If the storm didn't let up, it might be a couple of months before anyone got this far north. He wondered if the Great Northern was running.

He wondered, *How in heaven's name can I get those*

*Herefords off Carlton Boone's place—and keep my own
cattle alive?*

Murdo could back out of that deal. No papers had
been signed. Yeah, he had given his word, but his word
could not best nature's wrath.

He left the room, hat in hand, heavy coat hanging
over his arm, and followed the smell of bacon, eggs, and
hot coffee. *God bless Sissy's heart.* Murdo was her only
guest. He wouldn't let Jeannie Ashton know, but Sissy
White cooked the best meal in Basin Creek. He would
tell that cantankerous old lout who cooked for the boys
at the Circle M that she was a better cook than he'd ever
be, but ol' Neb Jones would point out that Miss Sissy
couldn't drive a team of mules or put up with thirty-a-
month-and-found cowpokes eight days a week.

She smiled when he walked into the dining area,
holding a cup of coffee in her hand and pointing at a
mound of food.

"It's all yours, Murdo," she said.

"I couldn't eat that much in a month of Sundays," he
said, hanging the coat over the back of an empty chair
and resting his hat on the seat, before sitting next to
Sissy.

"Sleep well?" she asked.

"Well enough," he said, and filled his own cup from
the coffeepot in front of him. "Maybe not warm enough,
but well enough."

He found his plate and spooned some eggs, pulled
some thick slices of bacon, and added a couple of biscuits
to his plate. There was enough food left that, even if
Murdo had seconds and thirds—which he wouldn't—
there would be enough food left to feed an army.

"You expecting company, Sissy?" he asked with a smile.

"Just call me Florence Nightingale," she said.

He forked some eggs into his mouth, swallowed, and looked at the woman.

"Who's that?"

She shook her head. "Ever heard of the Crimean War, Murdo?"

"Heard of it. Didn't fight in it." He sipped coffee and found a knife and butter dish to doctor up his biscuits.

"That figures. You read anything other than cattle brands?"

He laughed, drank more coffee. "I've heard of Florence Nightingale and the Crimean War, Sissy. She was that nurse. The war . . . well . . . it wasn't the Rebellion or our Revolution. Russians against France, England, the Ottoman Empire."

She grinned over her coffee cup. "You do read more than beef prices."

"Don't let anyone know that." He devoured the first biscuit. "You taking all this food to the sick and wounded?"

"The out of work." She helped herself to a piece of bacon.

"You'll go broke doing business that way."

"With a clear conscience."

He smiled, then shook his head, gobbled down the scrambled eggs, chasing them down with greasy but delicious, thick bacon, and then wiped his fingers on the napkin and reached for the biscuit. But he stopped before it hit his mouth.

"Who in Basin Creek doesn't have work?"

"Oh, it's not an epidemic. If it was, I probably wouldn't have such a big heart. I'd be stingy."

He dipped the biscuit in coffee and took a bite.

"I ran into a good ol' boy at the livery. O'Boyle was renting him a stall."

She nodded. "He has some saddle pards with him. And there's a family that Judge Van Gaskin said could stay in our lovely courthouse for the winter if they'd keep the place clean and give it a good whitewashing inside before they left come the first thaw."

After finishing the biscuit, he ate the last piece of bacon on his plate. He started to reach for another, but stopped. He could be a Good Samaritan, too. Leave it for the indigent. Wasn't that the word he had seen in a Helena newspaper a while back?

"A painter?" he asked.

"Well, the judge said he said he could paint. He worked for the railroad. The Great Northern."

Oh. Murdo didn't have much use for railroad men. They had a habit of thinking they were better than cattle-men. And cowboys.

"Lost an arm in a railroad accident."

He nodded, but had no comment.

"Working in a cattle car."

Murdo was about to stand, but that sentence caused him to stare at Sissy for a long while, then he refilled his cup with coffee and topped off Sissy's—to her surprise.

"Why, thank you, Mr. Maddox," she said, and gave a slight bow, though she remained seated.

"He's staying at the meeting house?"

That's what most folks in Cutthroat County called the courthouse. The oldest part of the cabin, if you believed what the old-timers said, had been the cabin

Eb Maddox and Benjamin Franklin Drew built when they had arrived in this far corner of the world in the 1820s, years after they had signed on with Lewis and Clark.

How much of that was true, Murdo couldn't say. But if this man had worked in the cattle cars, that meant he knew cattle. If he had one arm, he could still ride a horse. And trailing cattle was a whole lot easier—though not without its hazards—than being stuck in a cattle car with a bunch of mean, irritable steers heading to the slaughterhouse.

A cowboy could bail off a horse that was about to roll. A cowboy could get out of the way of a stampeding herd if he had good sense. A cowboy could shuck his boots, his gun rig, and anything else that might cause him to drown while crossing a swollen stream. A cowboy could take off his spurs and anything metal to reduce the risk of being struck by lightning during a thunderstorm. Cowboying was a dangerous job, but you were out in the open, breathing God's air, and on the back of a horse. It was a mighty good way of life.

And you weren't at the mercy of an engineer or a fireman—like the cowpunchers that worked the railroad cars. You weren't trapped in a box of wood and iron that was speeding across the West as long as the iron wheels kept a good grip on iron rails.

Two—no three—men had worked on the Circle M with only one good hand. And he had at least a couple working for him this past spring, summer, and into the fall who were missing fingers from roping accidents.

He didn't have enough cowboys back at the Circle M to get a herd from Carlton Boone's place to his ranch and keep enough men at his ranch to keep his beef from freezing to death. But if he could hire some out-of-work men here in town . . . ?

Maybe he could pull off this deal after all.

"That railroader," he said, as he reached into his vest pocket for a coin. "You know his name?"

Sissy shook her head. "I didn't ask. He didn't give it."

He showed her the coin and placed it next to his cleaned-off plate of breakfast.

"That's why I like you, Sissy." He rose. "You know the rules of the West. Don't ask a fellow his name. He'll tell you if he wants you to know. And he's at the meeting house?"

"He was," she said. "I don't think he would have gone anywhere last night." Her eyes turned curious. "You hiring men? This time of year?"

"A deal came up. Carlton Boone."

She studied him, but must not have heard about Boone's decisions or his hard luck. And Murdo Maddox was too much of a Westerner to tell her. She could find out from someone else, but he doubted if she would ask.

He pulled on his coat, buttoned it, and then picked up his hat.

"You set a fine table, Sissy." He grinned at her. "I'll be seeing you." She started to rise, but he waved her back down. "I can let myself out. And you'll need all the strength you have to get that food over to those boys. If you feed them vagrants at O'Boyle's livery, tell Charley Bandanna that I might have a job for him and his out-of-work pards. And tell that railroader squatting at the meeting house the same thing."

She was standing when he reached the front door, but he turned before opening it and stared down the shotgun setup.

"Oh, I know your heart is as big as the territory—the state . . ." He chuckled. "I'll never get used to that. The *state* of Montana. But stay away from the sheriff's office. I mean it. Our sheriff has locked up a mess of trouble. Don't go near that cabin. You might be Cutthroat County's Florence Nightingale, but Bo Meacham isn't worth any charity."

She stiffened and gripped the back of the chair.

"Bo Meacham?" Her voice was just a whisper.

"That's right. Our sheriff has him locked up, waiting for some higher law dogs to come fetch him to his own hanging." He waited, staring at her, making sure she understood.

"I mean it, Sissy," he told her. "Helping cowboys and maimed railroaders is one thing. But you don't—"

Sissy cut him off. "I want absolutely nothing to do with Bo Meacham, Murdo."

"Good girl," he said. "Thanks for the hospitality. See you next time I'm in town—though that might not be till spring."

He tugged on his hat, opened the door, and stepped into a cold, white, foggy morning.

CHAPTER 18

Keme had been walking since before the sun rose. He'd left the camp when only a few dogs and horses were awake. It was still snowing then, snowing hard. He had to leave the camp because if he waited, the elders, his uncles, his aunts—his parents were no more of this earth—and his siblings would do all they could to talk him out of going.

And if the elders spoke, if they said that he must not do what he knew he had to do, then he would have to obey them.

By now, the Siksikaitsitapi, which was the name the Blackfoot-Speaking Real People called themselves, in the small camp that Keme had left would know that he was gone. They might think that he had walked into the land of white and death and cold so that there would be more food for the elders, for his granddaughter who was sick with fever and child, for many, many others. That he had sacrificed himself. And maybe that was what he was doing.

But he thought that he walked for another purpose.

He did not think that Powaw or any of the elders would send young men after him. Powaw, especially, knew that Keme listened to his own voice and to the voices that spoke to him but no one else. They might find Keme's bones in the spring. They might never find any sign of Keme. Life—and death—could be a great mystery.

A buffalo that was white but was not white. And was a buffalo but was not a buffalo.

That was what would save Keme's people.

It made no sense.

And it was very, very cold.

He scooped snow into his hands, which were wrapped in animal skins, and put the snow in his mouth. The water that the snow became hurt his teeth and his tongue and felt as though it left his throat and windpipe frostbitten, but it kept him going.

Many footsteps later, too many for Keme to count, and by then he was not sure where he was because the snow, while not driving and blinding and confusing, fell in giant flakes, but the country looked different. There was no sun, no stars, no moon to guide him. Besides, he did not know where he was going. He kept following his spirit, his heart.

Maybe his mind was gone.

Whiteness covered everything. He had lived all his life in this country, except for that time many winters ago when the Great White Father—who, it turns out, was not so great—had invited Keme and others to visit his house.

He came to a crack in the rocks, but he did not remember this place. Yet his right foot took a step toward it and his left followed. And he walked between the rocks. Here, there was not as much snow to walk through, and the wind blew over his head. It was darker, yes, but

not as cold, and he felt that this must be the right path.
He moved fast because he had never liked being in any
canyons, pinned in by great walls. And he felt relief
when he stepped out of the rocks and felt the snow
stinging his face and the wind chilling his entire body.

Then he heard the scream.

He turned, but the wild and savage cry seemed to
be coming from all directions, and it was not until he
looked up that he saw a massive shape falling from the
top of the rocks toward him.

There was no time for him to grab his knife. He barely
realized what was happening, and only his instinct—or
perhaps it was just his fear—caused him to raise his
arms above his head and meet the falling animal.

The wild man was heavy, and the force of his weight
drove Keme backward. Yet somehow he managed to
push this great beast away from him, to Keme's left, and
he fell hard into a mound of ice and snow, though his
head cracked against something hard.

A rock, he figured. It opened a wound above and
behind his right ear. But the blood froze almost immediately.

He felt dizzy. Hungry. Cold. Almost ready to die.

But the beast who had fallen from above and had
almost driven him into the ground was singing. Not
words of the Siksikaitsitapi. But of the Shoshone. This
was a song he had not heard in years.

Keme rose quickly. So did the Shoshone who had
attacked him from high above.

Snowflakes danced in the air between them.

The Shoshone came closer, moving his knife. He was
hard to see, but Keme kept his eyes on the knife. A
trader's knife. Probably traded for one of the white-man

cabins that were few in these days. There had not been many when Keme was young, but many or few, they offered not much for Siksikaitsitapi. Except the whiskey to make young Blackfoot men crazy and stupid. And Shoshone men, as well. And Crow. And the Lakota. The Cheyenne. All the nations. Even the white men that sold this bad, cruel water that burned the throat and killed the mind.

But this Shoshone was hard to see.

And then Keme knew why. He wore a heavy coat made of buffalo, but not just any buffalo. This buffalo had been white. Keme had only heard of such magnificent, beautiful, powerful, and holy beasts. Never had he seen one. He had known of no one in his village who had seen one. One or two, including Powaw, had heard of them. But never had they seen one. And only Powaw had ever seen the skin of one of those beasts of magnificent power.

The Shoshone sang, and as he sang, Keme looked skyward. He had to find the sun. Mother sun would tell him what he needed to know. But he could not keep his eyes off the Shoshone because that would mean that Keme would be killed, and killed quickly. And then his people would starve to death, or freeze to death, or just vanish and never be remembered.

They danced in circles, the Shoshone singing his song of battle, while Keme kept silent, thinking, looking, and then . . .

There. He caught just enough of a ray of sunlight. The sun rose in the east. That meant the Shoshone with the knife came from . . .

South of here.

He thanked the Great Spirit for sending him this

message. This was the buffalo that was white, and now Keme understood something else.

As the Shoshone danced around, more snow fell off the heavy robe that kept him warm.

It was not a rare albino—as he had heard a white man call those animals. It was just an ordinary buffalo skin. Brown. Shaggy. Covered with snow and ice. Made to look white. The vision became clearer.

"This buffalo that was a buffalo that wasn't and was white, but wasn't."

To survive, Keme had thought for some time now, meant he had to travel south. But to survive now meant that he had to beat this Shoshone. And the warrior held a knife in his hand. Keme's hands clenched only cold air and snow that melted in his hands that were wrapped by wolf skins.

No, that was not a knife. Not the knife of a Shoshone, anyway. It was a long knife—the heavy blades carried by the white-faced pony soldiers. The Shoshone yelled and moved his left arm—so he was left-handed—and Keme leaped back to avoid being gutted by that vicious weapon.

The Shoshone almost spun around and fell. That's how hard he had swung the blade. Keme thought about charging the enemy then, but he had waited too long.

He remembered his father's lessons.

Do not think. If you think too much, you will die. Attack. You may die, anyway. But at least you will die as a Blackfoot and not as a coward.

"Let us talk," Keme said, knowing the Shoshone would think him a coward. But Keme had always been a peacemaker. Or had tried to be. He had helped bring a peace between his people and the white men and now white women who had taken the Blackfoot land south of them. Sometimes he regretted this. Most times, in fact, he regretted this. But he had made friends among those strange men with pale skin and bad habits. But the Siksikaitsitapi still lived. And they lived in the country that had always been theirs. Maybe not as much of the country as they once had. But it was still in the land of the Siksikaitsitapi.

The massive blade came closer to his belly this time, but Keme leaped back, feeling the whoosh. Again, the Shoshone almost fell over, but he was strong, agile, and younger than Keme. He righted himself before Keme could charge in.

"You came to me in a vision," Keme said, speaking in what he knew of the Shoshone tongue. "You can help me. You can tell—"

He dodged the vicious blade again.

The Shoshone was getting better with the long knife.

Keme still tried to find a way. "We can talk in peace. I have matches—fire sticks—that I traded beads for. Traded with a pale eye. We can be warm." He nodded at the canyon that had brought him here . . . to near death.

"We can wait till this snow moves on."

The blade swung at him again. Keme leaped back, knowing that this would not end well for either the Shoshone or Keme.

The Shoshone was wild, maybe had lost his mind. Keme was sent here for a purpose. A white buffalo that was white, but not, and a buffalo, but not.

This Shoshone held the answer.

And Keme did not have enough strength to keep this going. The Shoshone was just wearing him down.

So Keme made sure he had a good grip on the handle of his knife.

"Where must I go?" he called out to both the man who was bent on killing him and to the fathers and grandfathers and elders who came before him. "Where will I save my people?"

The Shoshone let out a whoop of savagery. Keme stepped toward him. He saw the long knife rise above his enemy's head. Keme kept coming, and the blade sliced down as the warrior let out a wild cry. His eyes, Keme thought, said that the Shoshone was victorious.

But the blade went over Keme's scalp, taking perhaps a few black hairs but nothing more. The force of the swing turned the young man around, and Keme came up and drove his knife into the man's back.

He hated to do this, but what choice had he? He was here to save his people. And a Shoshone was trying to stop him.

Keme's blade twisted. The long knife fell and disappeared in the white ground. Keme twisted again, driving the blade deeper, then pulled it out and brought it up, over the warrior's head, then pressed the blade against the throat.

"You fought well," Keme told him. And dragged the blade across the young warrior's throat. "I wish you would tell me where I am to go."

He stepped back, and the Shoshone fell, leaving a trail of crimson in the snow.

Keme tried to catch his breath without freezing his lungs. He dropped to his knees and thanked the spirits for his success, for keeping him alive. It would have been better if the dead Shoshone had food, but Keme would not complain.

The Shoshone had been a brave man. A good warrior. Maybe crazy, but who wouldn't be in a storm like this. Keme would take no scalp. Besides, the bluecoats at the fort who were supposed to guard and protect the Blackfoot did not like to hear of Indians scalping Indians these days.

Keme might not have an answer, but he had a buffalo robe. It was white but was not white, and it would keep Keme warm in the miles he had to travel. He had thought he should travel south, but now he was not sure. The spirits had not answered him.

Then the dead Shoshone moved.

Keme brought his knife closer. He had been about to reach for the buffalo robe, but stopped when he heard the noise.

The Shoshone lay still. Snow was already beginning to cover the spray of blood that came from his throat.

Keme waited till his breathing had returned to normal, and only then did he pick up the buffalo robe and bring it up and over his shoulders, not caring about the snow that melted quickly from the inside of the robe. Keme would begin to feel warm soon enough. In fact, he no longer felt as though he were frozen like the world around him.

He knelt by the dead Shoshone and gathered his sack—a sack traded for or stolen from some bluecoat soldier—and peered inside it to find that the man did have food—what the white eyes called hardtack and beef jerky, even some ready-made cigarettes.

That would help. Maybe it would keep him alive.

Keme rose and nodded at the brave, if somewhat crazy, warrior. But he still was not sure of where he should go.

Then he saw the dead man's right hand. It lay stretching out, beginning to be covered with falling snow. Three fingers clenched along with the thumb, but the first finger pointing.

That was the direction. Keme thanked the spirits and the dead Shoshone. He could not tell the direction he was walking, but he knew it had to be the way to the white-eye settlement. That's where he thought he should be going, but he needed confirmation from the wise spirits of the Blackfoot.

He started walking toward what the white eyes called Sacagawea Pasture. And beyond that the ugly town with the ugly people—and his grandsons, though they were white, not Siksikaitsitapi. Yet they were Siksikaitsitapi.

Just like he had been told that he would find his way from the buffalo that was not a buffalo and was white but was not white.

He started down the long, brutal trail to the place the white eyes called Basin Creek.

CHAPTER 19

He heard Finnian O'Boyle's loud Irish brogue, even though Murdo Maddox was a good two and a half blocks from the livery. The Irish, he noted, sure have a way with profanity. A few women stood in front of the butcher's shop, shaking their heads and whispering to one another. The girls playing in the snow put fingers in their ears. The boys just grinned, probably trying to remember those words for future use—when they were out of earshot of their folks.

At least O'Boyle had to stop to catch his breath when Murdo walked into the livery.

"Morning," Murdo greeted him and walked to the coffeepot on the stove. He was full of coffee, but he poured that thick black brew in a dirty cup and brought it toward Finnian, the stall, and Charley Bandanna.

The latter sat, covered with straw, about as dirty a person as Murdo had seen in months. O'Boyle seemed to be dumbstruck by the appearance of the rancher, but Murdo wasn't interested in the livery man. He knelt and extended the cup toward the old cowhand.

"How you been, Charley?"

The green-eyed, thick-mustached man stared at

Murdo for a long while, then slowly took the cup, for which Murdo was grateful. The coffee was mighty hot, even on a morning like this one.

"Passable." Charley Bandanna blew on the steaming coffee and brought it to his mouth, but he kept it there without tasting it, letting it cool to something that wouldn't burn a hole in his tongue. His head tilted slightly as a thanks. "You?"

"Fair." Murdo looked up at the livery owner. "Miss Sissy been here this morning?"

"No." O'Boyle seemed perplexed. "She needin' a rig to rent?"

Murdo shook his head and returned his attention to the cowhand. "I thought you had some bunkmates."

"He did," O'Boyle answered. "I run them out of here this morn. Let them sleep in the stall because I'm a generous man, but they can't while away the hours all day. This is a business."

"Fetch them back here, Finnian," Murdo ordered.

"Why in bloody—"

Murdo cut him off. "Fetch them."

That was all it took. The Irishman drew in a deep breath, let it out, and buttoned up his coat as he walked to the open doors.

Charley Bandanna cocked his head. Then he took a tentative sip of the potent coffee.

"I got a job for you, Charley," Murdo said.

"Doin' what?"

"I'm buying the Herefords Carlton Boone was running on his spread south of here. Three hundred head. I need to round them up and get them at least to Sacagawea Pasture in, let's say, ten days."

The man lowered the cup. "You turned loco?"

"I'm a cattleman. I don't have to *turn* loco. It comes naturally."

The cowhand considered that but did not smile. He did sip more coffee now that it had cooled a mite.

"Way this winter's goin'," Bandanna said, "you'll have three hundred dead Herefords to burn on Sacagawea Pasture come spring. If we could even get them there."

"I don't intend to keep them there long," Murdo said. "And if they freeze to death, that's my problem. I just need some cowhands to bring them from Boone's spread to mine."

Bandanna drank more coffee. "You got your own waddies."

"They'll be busy keeping my Black Angus from freezing to death."

The weathered old man considered that and took a healthy swallow of O'Boyle's brew.

"Three hundred head?"

"That's right. You'll ramrod the outfit. You hire the men you need. I'm guessing your two bunkmates will be willing to earn some money. Find a cook. You'll probably be shorthanded, but this isn't a drive from Texas."

Murdo smiled.

"Like the ones you made with my pa back in '80 and '82. All you have to do is get them to Sacagawea Pasture. In ten days."

Bandanna pointed his cup toward the open doors.

"The weather ain't what I'd call favorable."

Murdo managed a short shrug of his shoulders. "It isn't snowing now. Maybe the storm blew itself out last night."

Charley finished the coffee, handed the cup back to Murdo, and began searching for the makings of a smoke. "It ain't. My rheumatism tells me that."

"There's a hundred dollars in it for you."

That got Bandanna's attention.

"Seventy-five for the cook you'll hire," Murdo continued. "And fifty for the cowhands. For ten days of work. Thirty for a cook's louse. He'll likely need a helper, and the louse can handle the remuda. I'm thinking two extra horses per cowhand. We might even be able to tie those on behind the wagon. Not the best way to work a drive, but this isn't the best drive I can think of."

"You ain't comin' along?" Bandanna asked.

"If I were, I wouldn't need a top cowhand like you to be the ramrod."

Bandanna rubbed the thick mustache that covered his upper mouth and dropped down past his chin and the graying stubble that covered the rest of his face.

"It's gonna be hard to find many cowpunchers in Basin Creek or anywhere in this county," he said.

"There's your two bunkies."

He nodded. "But that leaves me two hands short."

"That's your job. And a cook. Unless you want to go without one. I might have another cowboy for you, though. I'm going to find him as soon as I'm done here."

Those green eyes turned cold. "I hire my own men, Mr. Maddox."

"That's fine by me. But if he's willing and able, I'll be sending him over. If you like him, hire him. If you don't, well, I've seen a bunch of schoolboys playing in the snow." He pulled a twenty-dollar gold piece out of his vest pocket.

"This is an advance. I'll pay you the rest when the job's done."

"What if I don't get those beeves here in ten days?"

"You will." Murdo tossed him the coin, then turned and walked away. "Because you'll be riding for the Circle M. Don't spend that money on liquor. I want you riding to the Boone spread come first light tomorrow."

From the livery, Murdo made his way to the meeting house. The county officials kept saying that Cutthroat County would get its own courthouse soon, but that had not happened. Murdo had not been in the meeting house since 1891, and that was on the first day of Cutthroat County's official existence, just after Napoleon Drew, on his first day as the new county's sheriff, had gunned down Frankie Maddox, Murdo's cousin, and a quick inquest had been held. No bill of indictment had been issued against the sheriff, and though Murdo had fumed with hatred—just as all Maddoxes had despised all Drews for decades—he had known that his cousin got exactly what he deserved.

Now folks were talking about turning the meeting house into some kind of monument, a park or something, because this, they liked to say, was where Cutthroat County was born.

Until then, though, Murdo figured folks guessed that it was all right to let any vagrant have a free place to spend the winter—providing he could paint it up real pretty come spring.

He saw the kids having a snowball fight outside, but they stopped when they saw Murdo and hurried inside.

Murdo walked to the rectangular log building, removed his hat, knocked on the door, then opened it.

At least it was warm inside. He smelled wood smoke

from the fireplace and saw the melting snow that the children had tracked inside. He could hear their excited voices, then footsteps, and a big man stepped out of what was typically the judge's chambers during a trial or hearing. His left sleeve was pinned up to the shoulder, but his right arm was huge.

The man towered over Murdo, and his right hand rested near an old Navy Colt that was stuck in the waist-band.

"Morning." Murdo nodded at the man.

The thick-bearded man stared and nodded back.

"My name is—"

"I know who you are. You be Murdo Maddox."

Murdo nodded. "That's right."

He waited, but the man did not give his name. And he did not move his hand from the .36's butt.

"Miss Sissy told me about you. You and your family." He looked at the walls, then nodded as though approving. "Nice place. But I'm wondering if you might want a job. Ten days. Fourteen at the most. Though if I like the way you work and if you like the way I run an outfit, we might talk about a job, permanent-like, come spring."

The man moved his hand from the Colt.

"What kind of job you be talkin' 'bout?"

Murdo told him. The man cocked his head as if trying to figure out the joke.

"I'm paying fifty dollars."

The man's black eyes widened.

"If you're interested, you'll find the ramrod I've hired, goes by the name Charley Bandanna, at the livery stable. If you're not . . ." He smiled as he shrugged. "Well, I wouldn't blame you. You've got a nice place to wait out the winter. And a wife and kids to keep you company. I'm offering you a chance to get frostbite or maybe freeze to death. But if you freeze to death on the job, I'll see that your wife gets that fifty dollars."

He waited as the man studied him.

"This ain't no joke?"

Murdo shook his head. "It better not be. If it is, then the joke's on me, and they'll be finding pieces of Carlton Boone's remains around these parts for the next thirty or forty years."

He heard the whispers of the man's kids and what he guessed was his wife, trying to shush them.

With a nod, Murdo put his hat back on and turned to the door. "Talk it over with the missus. And if you're game, you best hurry over to O'Boyle's livery and tell him that you talked to me and you're signing on. I'll supply the horses—"

"I got my own."

Murdo turned back to him. "All right. But I'll have a couple other mounts for you. This won't be a picnic."

"No, sir, it'll be plenty hard." He grinned, and that surprised Murdo, who did not surprise easily. "But I likes a good challenge."

Murdo nodded again, then turned back to the door and walked outside into the frigid morning.

He stopped, straightened, and rested his gloved hand on his holstered revolver. A man on a dun horse waited in the trees that ran along the banks of Basin Creek. Just sitting on his horse, not looking at the old meeting house, but at the town. Another movement turned his head, about twenty or thirty yards farther.

So there were two of them.

No. Three. He spotted a horse's tail swishing a few yards past the second man.

People in town sometimes got water from the creek. In spring and summer, sometimes fall, kids would fish for trout. But not many travelers came to town that way. And this was not a day meant for leisurely traveling. Or waiting in the woods.

He caught a quick movement from the first rider he had spotted, and Murdo moved his hand from the revolver and buttoned his coat. There was no law against sitting on your horse by the creek. Murdo made like he had seen nothing. It had been just luck that he had seen any of them.

Pulling his hat down low, he tried to whistle as he walked to the corner of the long cabin, but it was too cold to whistle, so he stopped and rounded the corner, walking in his boot prints back toward the center of Basin Creek.

Yet he half expected to feel a bullet rip through his back at any moment. And he had to fight the urge not to look over his shoulder at the three riders.

He thought he saw Sissy heading toward O'Boyle's place, but it could have been any woman. At the corner of the Hangman's Saloon and Gambling Emporium, he stopped and stepped up onto the wooden porch. The place wasn't open. It typically didn't open till afternoon, but here he couldn't be seen by those three riders. Slowly, he peered around the corner. Nothing. No dun horse. No two men on darker horses.

Had he imagined this? No, Murdo knew he did not have that much imagination. But those could be any three riders. Maybe from Killone's place. Maybe from some of the smaller spreads, looking for strays. Those strays would have wandered a long way.

He sighed, cursed his imagination, and walked down the wooden planks to the main entrance of the gaming house, then turned, stepped down, and walked past the hitch rails and to the main street.

Most of the children had been called in by their mamas. Another mother was yelling at her sons to get back inside before they froze to death, that she had made hot chocolate and doughnuts for them and was going to throw them out for the buzzards if they didn't get in and not to track any snow inside.

He glanced down the street toward the seamstress's place and then the other way toward O'Boyle's. No sign of the one-armed man, but maybe he would show up. He looked at the cabin in front of him, thought about going back for his horse or maybe to Swede's place. He could use a morning bracer.

Instead, he walked to the door and rapped on it hard.

He saw the curtain to his left open just a bit, then heard footsteps inside. The bar was lifted, leaned against the inside wall, and the door pulled open a crack.

Murdo could see Napoleon Drew's eye and a revolver through the crack.

"I just saw three riders at the creek," Murdo told him, and he wondered why he was telling a Drew this. "Just sitting on their horses in the woods. Watching the town."

The door opened, and the sheriff looked over Napoleon's shoulder.

"They're gone," Murdo told him. "I couldn't see much. Too far, and the snow was half-blinding me, anyway. A dun horse. Two darker ones. Figured you ought to know." He stepped back. The lawman nodded his thanks.

"Luck to you," Murdo said, and then mentally cursed himself for saying that.

"Thanks."

The door closed, and as Murdo walked away, he heard the heavy oaken bar returning to secure the door.

CHAPTER 20

Eugene had been awake for some time, but only when he heard bacon sizzling in a skillet did he toss off the quilt and start getting dressed. His brother and sister slept soundly. Eugene had spent half the night thinking about what he needed to do. Well, the first thing was to get out of the house. And that would not be easy with the Widow Jeannie Ashton cooking breakfast below.

Once he was dressed, he quietly came down the ladder, wet his lips, and walked to the winter kitchen. The aroma of fresh bread, butter, and frying bacon made his stomach pinch. He cleared his throat, and Jeannie Ashton turned around.

"Well, good morning, Eugene," she said with a pleasing smile. "You're up early today."

"Yes, ma'am."

"Hungry?" She turned back to flip the bacon over.

"Are you making some breakfast for Pa?" he asked.

She turned again, wiping her hands on the apron she wore and stepping away from the fireplace where his mother had cooked their meals before God called her home. Eugene wasn't sure how he felt about Mrs.

Jeannie Ashton cooking for Eugene and his brother and sister. But he could not help but like her.

"Your father left clear instructions that we were not to go near his office." Her voice was stern and her eyes hard. She must have read his mind. He had planned to volunteer to take Pa breakfast.

"Yes, ma'am," he said.

Her head bobbed once. "I asked if you were hungry?"

He was famished. His mouth watered at the smell of bacon. His pa had claimed that Eugene could go through a pound of bacon in one sitting, and Eugene figured that was just about right.

"I'll just take some toast with jelly." He saw the pitcher. "And some milk."

The widow had been busy this morning. She had even gone out and milked the cow. But that made him curious. He shot a glance toward the window, but couldn't see a blessed thing through the frosted panes.

"Is it still snowing?"

"It wasn't when I went outside earlier." She spoke with her back to him. "But the clouds haven't moved much, and it's bitterly cold."

She moved the skillet out of the fireplace. Pa kept saying they would get one of those stoves out of the Montgomery Ward & Company catalog before too long. Most of the kids Eugene's age said that they had stoves and that the Drews must be dirt poor to have meals cooked in their fireplace, but Eugene liked that. His ma could make wonders in the stone fireplace.

He made himself stop thinking about his mother, gone now three years and some months.

The widow had piled some toast smothered in cherry jelly. Nothing tasted better than jelly made from cherries from the Flathead. It was said that folks would kill for cherries from Flathead Lake, about a four-day hard ride southeast of Basin Creek. Pa kept saying that they'd go there one summer, on vacation, catch trout and eat cherries till they were sick.

But Eugene didn't figure they'd ever get out of Cut-throat County.

"Are Parker and Mary Ellen awake?" the widow asked as she slid a plate and glass down the hearth. Then she removed the skillet, set it on the far side of the hearth, and stepped back, wiping her face with the end of the apron, then finding her cup of coffee she had set on the table.

"No, ma'am," Eugene told her. He moved toward the food and devoured it.

He felt like a glutton, but he chugged down the milk and wiped his mouth with the napkin.

"My," Mrs. Ashton said. "Did you taste anything?"

"Yes'm. Yes, ma'am, I mean. It was mighty filling. And real good. You cook just fine, Mrs. Ashton."

Her eyes gleamed. "Thank you, Master Drew."

He looked around, then looked up at her.

"Yes?"

She must have been expecting this since she saw him downstairs at this time of the morning when there was no school and it wasn't a Sunday.

"Well, ma'am, I gots to go see somebody." He wet his lips.

"It's a little cold to be having a snowball fight. And some folks might still be sleeping."

"Yes, ma'am. No, ma'am. Yes, ma'am." He stopped, breathed in, then out, and tried again. "I want to go down to Mr. O'Boyle's livery."

That caught her by surprise. He could see that in her eyes, and, besides, she also spilled some coffee, which she hurriedly wiped up, then stared at him again. "Well?"

"It's about a job, ma'am."

"A job?"

"Yes, ma'am."

"At Mr. O'Boyle's livery?"

He nodded. Mr. Maddox was hiring for that cattle drive. It wasn't a lie. Well, not exactly a lie, anyhow.

"Is Mr. O'Boyle busy enough to need someone other than that poor young Luke Jasper . . . at this time of year?"

"He might be."

She eyed him with skepticism.

"When does school resume?"

He shrugged. "Whenever Miss Hunter says it's warm enough to start up again."

Last year, that had been in late February, but that was because of that warm spell that took all of Cutthroat County by surprise. Usually, it was the first of March. Though all the students were expected to study their Readers and write a few words about their winter. Then Miss Hunter would hammer arithmetic and boring stuff into their heads.

"Does your father know about your winter plans?"

He nodded. "Yes, ma'am. He surely does." Now he could speak with authority and a wee bit of accuracy. "Just the other day he was telling me and Parker—I mean, Parker and me—that I was getting old enough to start thinking about what I might want to do when I was all growed. And that I did not have to be like him. Like Pa, I mean. That there was a lot to be said for being a lawman, but there was a heck of a lot—Papa didn't say heck, though—of better jobs out there than pinning a badge to your chest."

"So you want to work at a livery stable?"

He had to think about that. "I don't think so, ma'am. But I want to know about horses."

She frowned, and Eugene knew why. Finnian O'Boyle tolerated horses and mules, and the only reason he tolerated them was because horses and mules— or, rather, the owners of horses and mules—kept him supplied with enough coins to spend at the Swede's saloon drinking Irish whiskey.

"And Luke Jasper . . . he knows lots about horses. Why, two weeks ago he saved the life of a colt that was having a hard time getting birthed by this mare."

That was true, too. He bet Mrs. Ashton had read about that in the Basin Creek newspaper. Pa had read the story to them over supper.

She sighed, then shrugged. "Wash your plate and glass, Eugene, and dry them off. Then find your coat and mittens and a scarf and hat. Stay out of deep snow. And be back here as soon as you can."

"Yes'm. Thank you, ma'am."

He did not think he had dressed that fast in all his years, and he stepped outside into a freezing blast of Arctic wind, lowered his head, and let the wind whip him toward the livery stable on the far side of Basin Creek.

He ducked as he ran past his father's office, even though he doubted if, holding a wild demon like Bo Meacham in jail, his father was watching the streets to see if his son was doing something crazy. And Eugene knew what he was doing was crazy. But he liked horses. And he liked cattle. And maybe, since cowboys were scarce this time of year in this frigid country, he might luck out and get a paying gig. His father sure wouldn't frown at Eugene bringing in a good bit of money to the household.

When he saw the livery stable clearly, he slowed down. He remembered hearing one cowboy tell another that you don't ever want to look like you need the job, you want the boss man to know that you can take this job or ride on till you find something you might like to do. Well, he still walked pretty fast, even when he was in the middle of the snowy street. Because he did not want to have gone all the way to Finnian O'Boyle's livery and find out that the jobs had all filled up.

When he stepped out of the biting wind and into the damp, dark livery, he drew in a sharp breath. Two men who were obvious cowboys sat on hay bales drinking coffee as a slim, wiry man with a thick mustache that Eugene's daddy could not grow in ten years was scratching a pencil across a small notebook.

Luke Jasper stood in front of the seated man.

"All right," the slim, leathery man said. "Ross and Grubstake, you're hired. Fifty bucks when the job's done. Get your traps. I'd like to pull out this afternoon, but that's only if we get a crew hired."

One of the men—two fingers were missing from his left hand—cleared his throat.

"You got a full crew already?"

The man with the mustache frowned. "I got you two. And I got me."

That made Eugene feel a bit better, though he still thought the nerves that were suddenly attacking him would make him throw up Mrs. Ashton's toast.

The cowboy who had just been hired took a step back.

"How many men you plan on hirin', Charley?"

The leathery man just stared.

"Three hundred head?" the cowboy added.

"It ain't the twenty-five hundred I brought from Uvalde, now, is it?"

"It ain't late spring, neither."

"All you gots to do, Ross, is walk out. And kiss your fifty bucks goodbye."

The cowboy named Grubstake looked up at Ross, who must have been his saddle pard. "It's just pushing red and white cattle from south of here to Sacagawea Pasture . . . for fifty bucks. Quit thinkin', Ross. That's the trouble with you. You think."

"I've been thinkin' for the both of us these past five years, pard." Ross sighed and spit tobacco juice onto the ground. "But I'll ride with you. Give me something to tell the chippies 'bout next time I'm someplace warm." He reached down, and the mustached man let him sign on.

"Make your mark or sign your name," he said and then stared at Luke Jasper.

O'Boyle's stable hand stuttered but finally got control of his nerves and let this "Mr. Bandanna" know that he wanted one of those jobs, too.

"You ain't shoein' no hoss, boy, or forkin' hay over the stalls. This'll be most likely eighteen hours in a saddle. For a week. Day and night. And it ain't gonna get no warmer."

Luke Jasper's head bobbed. "I know that, sir."

"Don't sir, me. My name's Charley. Charley Bandanna. The only person you need to sir is your daddy and Murdo Maddox—because he's the dumb ox that's payin' your wages for this dang-fool scheme he's latched hisself to."

Luke Jasper opened his mouth, closed it, and nodded his head.

"That's better. You ride good?"

"Yes, sir."

"Ever been bucked off?"

Luke opened his mouth, then closed it, and nodded after letting out a long sigh.

"How many times?"

"More than I can count," Luke whispered.

Charley Bandanna laughed. "Give him that notebook when you've remembered how to spell your name, Grubstake."

And then this Charley Bandanna stared at Eugene.

"What do you want, kid?"

Eugene answered, but he realized he had just whispered. He tried to draw in a deep breath, but the cold almost froze his lungs. Fighting through the pain, he swallowed and said, "I'd like to hire on with you."

"Maybe I'm full up," Bandanna said.

"You need four cowboys," Eugene told him. "You have three."

"Nah. It's four."

Eugene turned around and saw a towering man lugging a saddle, a blanket, and reins, wearing a well-used mackinaw that stood out because the left sleeve was pinned up just below the shoulder and decorated with beaded fringe.

"Well, I'll be. Eli Hazzard. I ain't see you since that ruction in Cut Bank five years back."

"Five years of blessed peacefulness," the towering man said.

"Northern Railway cut you loose?"

He nodded. "Said I ain't much good with just one arm."

"They's a bunch of fools."

"That's what I told them. After I broke one loud-mouth's jaw and knocked the other all the way to Boise."

Charley Bandanna laughed and looked down at Eugene.

"Sorry, boy, but now I got my four cowhands. Come back in ten years. When you've growed to my size."

Eugene fought to dam the tears. Charley Bandanna's size. He would be past him in two years the way he kept growing.

He did not cry, though, and he said, "But, sir . . . you . . ."

"Boy, I got my four cowboys. Now you run along and find someone to build a snowman with. This is a man's job. And I ain't hirin'—"

"I hear you need a cook, Charley Bandanna."

Everyone, including Eugene, turned, and everyone, including Eugene, gasped.

She stepped inside, dressed not in one of her fine dresses, but in duck trousers and a plaid shirt, the mackinaw unbuttoned, with a sheepskin jacket and tall cowboy boots, and she wore a battered hat with a scarf tied over the crown, which flattened the brim against her hair and ears.

"Golly," Luke Jasper said. "Miss Sissy."

"The one and only."

"This ain't no boardin' house, Miss Sissy," Charley Bandanna said as he rose and removed his hat.

"And," Grubstake said, "ain't no woman goin' on no trail drive, even if it ain't a fer piece."

"Buster," Miss Sissy said as she crossed the stable until she stood by Eugene, turning him around so that he and she stared at the little cowpuncher with the big mustache, but then Sissy looked at Grubstake. "Women have been drivin' cattle since before you were born. They've gone up the Shawnee, Chisholm, and Western Trails, and the Goodnight Trail, too. I know a few come all the way to Montana. I know that for a fact. And I know that one of them was me."

Charley Bandanna nodded and let his hat fall to his side. "That may be so, Miss Sissy, and this might not be as fer of a drive as them to Kansas and even up here. But it ain't what I'd call the best of seasons and weather to be pushin' beeves."

"Murdo said you need a cook. Am I right?"

When Bandanna did not answer, Sissy gave him another blast. "And he said a cook's louse would be a good hire."

Bandanna scratched the side of his head with his hand that did not hold his hat.

"You been talkin' to Mr. Maddox?"

"He was a guest of mine last night."

The cowboy wet his lips. Briefly, he stared at Luke Jasper, as though the stable hand could give him some advice, and then he sighed again and shook his head. "It don't make no sense, Miss Sissy, and I just can't—"

She steered Eugene ahead and stopped just a foot from the small, leathery, stinking cowboy.

"Do you know who Sheriff Drew has locked up in his jail right now, Charley?"

He nodded. "Yes'm. The judge was in his cups and . . .

well . . . well . . . ever'body in Basin Creek knows by now. It's Bo Meacham."

"That's right. And that's why I think it's a good time for me to get out of Basin Creek."

Eugene tried to make sense out of that.

"I want to be safe. And I'd like this boy to be safe, too." Though now Eugene wondered why Bo Meacham, even if he were a bad man, would want to hurt Miss Sissy. And if Bo Meacham was that bad of a man, perhaps Eugene ought to stay in Basin Creek in case his father needed help. Suddenly, a trail drive in the dead of winter did not sound like an adventure.

"He'll be a lot safer on a cattle drive than anywhere near Bo Meacham, Charley," she told him. "And most certainly so will I."

CHAPTER 21

As soon as Murdo Maddox was gone, Napoleon Drew returned to the coffeepot and poured his third cup of the morning. Keep this up, he knew, and he would have to go to the store for more beans. And with three strangers sitting on horses along Basin Creek near the courthouse—or what was supposed to be a courthouse—he didn't like that idea. He didn't like the idea of having someone bring meals. Maybe he could just wait here, drinking water and eating stale crackers, till the deputies arrived to take the man-killing fiend in Napoleon's jail down to Deer Lodge to hang.

After finishing that cup—his last of the day, Napoleon promised himself—he thought about who he could hire as a special deputy. Or who would be crazy enough—and good enough—to take the job. Napoleon had not slept much at all that night, leaning back against the wall, shotgun and rifle near him, the Remington revolver in his right hand.

Who was he trying to kid? He had not slept at all, except for a few long seconds, maybe a full minute if he got lucky, then his eyes would pop open at the moan of the wind or the creak of the log walls. Now, after three cups of hot coffee and some hardtack soaked in the bitter, black brew until it softened enough not to break his teeth, he summoned up enough courage to rise and walk to the washbasin. He dipped his hands into the freezing water, fought back a curse, and then splashed his face.

Once was enough. He toweled off his face and found another cup of coffee, one that he had poured some hours ago. That cup he brought with him as he crossed the room and opened the door to the jail cells. It was colder in here than it was in his office.

There were two large cells, one on the left, the other on the right. North-south. The county had approved a measure to divide the two cells in half, making four cells, but the county had yet to find the money to . . . what was it they called it? Remodel. Yeah. Remodel the jail cells.

That struck Napoleon as funny.

There was one window, maybe ten inches tall by twenty inches wide, on the east wall, running along just below the roof. Iron bars crossed the glass vertically, as though some prisoner could slip through if the glass had been broken. Bo Meacham couldn't fit through that even if he dropped a hundred pounds. It did provide a bit of light, but this morning the glass was frosted over. But Napoleon could not see his own breath, so he decided it was warm enough.

And Bo Meacham was alive. He hadn't frozen to death during the night.

What a shame, Napoleon thought. *That would have saved us a lot of trouble.*

Meacham sat on the floor, atop one blanket in the corner, with another, thinner blanket pulled over his chest and shoulders. He glared at the lawman but said not a word.

Kneeling, Napoleon put the cup on the floor in the cell, stood, and pushed the coffee closer to the prisoner with his boot.

"Here's your breakfast," he said, stepping back until his back rested against the other iron bars to the other cage.

The blanket fell off, and Meacham slid across the hard stone floor and let his fingers touch the cup. His brutal eyes shot up and locked on Napoleon.

"This is cold," Meacham said.

Napoleon nodded. "I didn't want hot coffee thrown in my face."

The killer cursed, then waved his hand around the cell. "There ain't no chamber pot in here, neither."

Napoleon nodded. "I didn't want that thrown in my face, either."

He moved back to the door and opened it.

"Walk around some if you want. You might catch your death sitting on that cold floor."

The curses rang out, echoing in the cold room, but when Napoleon was back in his office, the roar of that evil man was no louder than the wind outside. That's one thing the carpenters had done a good job on. There was a semblance of peace and quiet in the sheriff's office in Basin Creek. The wall separating that from the jail was mighty thick. And there was a potbellied stove in the main office, too.

Napoleon moved toward it, extending his hands and soaking up the warmth. When he felt half human, he set his cup on the stove, grabbed a heavy towel to pick up the well-used, deeply blackened pot, and topped off his coffee.

Then he grabbed his coat off the rack, put it on, and opened the door to see what this morning looked like.

He guessed a foot and a half, maybe two feet of accumulation. Some drifts reached four or five feet. And some walls of homes and businesses had snow banked up all the way to the roof. Some kids were taking advantage of that, climbing onto the roofs and sliding down in their makeshift sleds. Well, that was just like children in this day and age. The winters he remembered were spent shoveling snow, splitting wood, filling a bucket with kindling, and practically freezing to death.

What, he wondered, were his children doing right now? Sleeping, most likely. He couldn't remember a morning when he hadn't been dressed and doing chores or studying or getting ready for church—that was his mama's doings—from the time he was five years old till he was old enough to walk out of the house. Eugene? He shook his head but found himself smiling. That boy would sleep all the way to Easter if anyone would let him.

That thought had Napoleon straightening and reconsidering. *I wish to Sam Hill I could sleep until Easter.*

He saw men shoveling paths to the sidewalk. He smelled wood smoke and the aroma of food. Turning, he looked over toward his house, but saw just smoke rising from the chimney. He doubted if the kids were awake yet. He wanted to go see them, but he wasn't about to leave Bo Meacham alone. After failing to stifle a yawn, Meacham saw a boy pushing his sister down the main street in a real sled.

He recognized them as the son and daughter of Carlton Tate, Basin Creek's mayor.

After taking a sip of hot coffee, Napoleon thought he might have some luck after all. When the boy—the names of both children escaped Napoleon, but most Drews never were very good at remembering names—and the smaller girl, both redheaded like their mama, came even with the sheriff's office, he yelled, "Hey, kids!"

The boy stopped, straightened, and stood trembling, not from the cold—they wore enough duds they could have survived a week at the North Pole—but giving Napoleon that look that every schoolkid gave him. The *Am I about to get in big trouble?* look of sheer terror.

"Can you do me a favor?"

The boy glanced at his younger sister, but she couldn't take her eyes off Napoleon. So when he looked back in Napoleon's direction, the sheriff tried to smile.

"You know where Mr. Miles Seabrook lives?"

The girl's eyes showed terror. The boy glanced down the street toward the cabin closest to Napoleon's.

Seabrook was the primary card dealer at the Hangman's Saloon and Gambling Emporium. As far as Napoleon knew, he was that rare house dealer who did not cheat the customers. He always had his nose in books when he wasn't playing faro or poker, and he spoke like a well-educated man—maybe the only well-educated man in this part of Montana, or even all of Montana. He won more than he lost, but then he was a professional—and he wasn't playing with his own money. He was also the second-best man with a gun in Cutthroat County.

It was the girl, though, who answered.

"Papa says we aren't supposed to go anywhere near that house," she called out.

"And your papa is a real smart man, a good daddy. I don't let my kids go near his house, either."

He didn't have to. They always saw Seabrook sitting on the porch, reading. Most kids in Basin Creek wouldn't go near a book. For that matter, most adults here avoided a book like they would yellow fever.

"But," Napoleon said, "this is official business. All I need is for you to go over to Mr. Seabrook's cabin and tell him that I need to see him as quick as he can get to the sheriff's office."

He could see in their faces that a request from a sheriff wasn't going to be enough.

"Of course," he said, putting his hands on his hips, "that means I'll have to deputize you. Make it official."

"Deputize?" the girl asked.

"Make you a special deputy. Sheriff's deputy. For Cutthroat County."

"Honest?" both boy and girl asked simultaneously.

He unpinned the star on his vest. "You can carry this to his place, show it to him, tell him if he would come to the office, I'd appreciate it. And I'd appreciate you two for helping Cutthroat County. And me."

The girl started to rise from the sled, but the boy pushed her down, and then lunged through a smaller drift, almost lost his footing when he stepped on an icy spot. The girl came up and called her brother all sorts of names and tried to stand, but she slipped, too.

She was up, screaming at him and wishing she were an only child, when he stopped in front of Napoleon.

He held the badge toward the boy, but when he reached for it, Napoleon covered it with his fingers.

"You must promise me that you'll let your sister wear it, too. And not to stick her with the pin."

Frowning, he shuffled his feet, staring at those big shoes, before sighing and saying, "All right. If you say so."

The girl had stopped making a fuss.

Napoleon looked up, stepped back, and held out the badge for the kid to take.

"All right," he said, "now both of you raise your right hands . . ."

He made up the oath as best as he could remember it and told the children to bring the badge back after they had done their duty, and he would see if he had some deputy badges they both could have. That excited them, and they took off, the boy running in the middle of the street, the girl dragging the sled.

The deputy badges must have been a big enticement, because they were back before he had managed to refill his cup of coffee, check on the prisoner, and open the drawer. The door burst open, and that would have startled him had he not heard the girl's screams and the brother's taunts a full minute before they were back in the office, letting in the cold and a lot of snow that fell off their shoes and the sled that the girl pulled in behind her.

"That was fast," he said, and he wasn't joking.

"He was chopping wood on the side of the house," the boy said. "But he still was wearing his hogleg."

"He said he would be over in a few minutes."

"Well, you're right handy as deputy sheriffs." He found a couple dented old badges, both of them tin, probably made by the tinsmith before Cutthroat County had officially been formed. But it wasn't like he would have need of these, so he laid the two badges on the edge of the desk and held out his hand for the one the boy had pinned on his coat.

"I can't keep this one?" he said softly.

"After you're elected sheriff," Napoleon said with a smile. The boy frowned until he saw the tarnished badges. Then he fumbled in his excitement to remove the badge, handed it to Napoleon, and grabbed the worst-looking badge.

"Look, April!" he called out to his sister. "See this dent. I bet that was made by a .44 slug."

The girl glanced at the badge, then looked at her brother as though he might be the dumbest kid in the United States. But the boy was already running outside, grabbing the sled, and saying something about how the last one to the schoolhouse was a rotten egg. She took her own badge, which had no similar dents, but at least she thanked the sheriff—though she called him a marshal—and raced after her brother, calling out to him, "Wait, Toby. How do I pin this on?"

Neither of them thought to shut the door, so Drew walked toward it, but then he stopped and held it open for Miles Seabrook.

"Mighty young deputies you're hiring," the gambler said after removing his hat and gloves.

"They'll do in a pinch." Napoleon closed the door. "But I'm hoping to hire one a little older, a lot stronger, and a pretty good man with a gun. Or guns."

Seabrook had two nickel-plated .45-caliber Colts stuck in his sash, though he wasn't dressed in his usual brocade vest and black coat, string tie, and trousers. He wore work boots, thick woolen trousers of red, brown, and green plaid, a woolen scarf, and a furry hat that covered his ears. He was removing his gloves, then shoving them into his coat pocket.

"You're up early," Napoleon told him.

"Went to bed early. Not much business at the faro

layouts this time of year. And I figured I'll need a lot more wood for the stove before spring comes."

He took the cup of coffee Napoleon handed him and sipped it but made no face.

Napoleon hooked a thumb toward the door behind him.

"I've got Bo Meacham locked up in there."

The cup came away from the gambler's face quickly. "You catch him?"

Drew shook his head and briefly explained that Meacham had been captured by a farmer in Sweet Grass.

"Well, we've been short on newspapers in Basin Creek for a while," Seabrook said. "I'm having to read the tripe that would-be journalist puts in what he calls a newspaper, but what I say is better suited for the business needed in a privy."

"It's a long story. Meacham is supposed to hang in Deer Lodge. The marshal of the federal district was afraid that Meacham's kinfolk and gang members . . ."

When he was finished with the story, Drew found the coffeepot and filled both cups. Seabrook was sitting down now, contemplating what he had just been told.

"I guess it's not likely that a gang would be able to get far in this weather." He looked out the window. "Though it has stopped snowing . . . for now."

Napoleon took a sip from his cup and gave a slight nod.

"It's also not likely that a stagecoach or jail wagon or a posse would be here in a day or two to take that man-killer to Deer Lodge."

Seabrook shook his head and sighed. He pulled a derringer out from a pocket and laid it on the closest table. "How much do I get paid?"

"Five dollars a day."

"I'll need more than this, most likely. Can I go back and get my twelve-gauge Greener?"

"I surely hope you would."

"You got any other deputies," Seabrook said, "other than those two that you sent to fetch me?" He had not lost his sense of humor—yet.

Trying to keep that good mood going, Napoleon shook his head, drank more coffee, and said, "And those two deputies just quit."

Seabrook chuckled and pushed himself to his feet. "Those two deputies have pretty good sense. It would be a whole lot simpler, and much safer for us, if we just took that man-killing, woman-raping son of Satan out to the nearest hanging tree and strung him up."

He found his furry hat, his gloves, and his thick coat and began pulling them on before he moved to the door. He started to open it, but then stopped and looked back at Napoleon.

The lawman was staring at the floor. Sensing Seabrook's actions, he looked up and into the gambler's clear eyes.

"That story of a hanging tree seems to remind me of something I heard over drinks and cards."

"Yeah." Napoleon nodded. "It's a popular tale in these parts."

"There are too many tales in this wild land." Seabrook walked outside.

1881

MARCH

CHAPTER 22

"You want to do what, boy?"

I'm not a boy, Murdo Maddox thought. *I am seventeen years old.* But he knew better than to backtalk his father. Cap Maddox still wielded a powerful backhand.

"Bring cattle up here," he said.

"Cattle!" The old man scoffed and found his jug.

"From Texas."

Shaking his head, Cap Maddox lifted the jug and shook it next to his cauliflower right ear, then moved it to his left ear and shook it again. "Don't sound like you gotten into my corn liquor, boy. I'd hate to have to whup you like I done when you was ten."

He had not whipped him that time. Murdo remembered that much. He had made him drink about half the jug, though, and would have made him finish it if Murdo's mother hadn't berated the old man as a brute and a vindictive, evil man. "You'll kill him!" she yelled.

And Murdo sure was sick the rest of the day and much of the following week, puking out his guts till he wished his father *had* killed him.

The old man took a healthy slug, then wiped his mouth with the sleeve of his buckskin shirt.

"Texas cattle. And just what would you do with a bunch of stinkin' beeves?"

"Sell them."

"You want to be a butcher?"

Murdo shook his head. "A rancher."

The old man laughed and drank again. "Ranchin'. In this country. There ain't more'n thirty folks within three hundred miles of here. And only half of them be white."

"The railroad's coming."

Now the old man let out a belly laugh. He shook his head again, took another dose of liquor, and called out to Maël Desrosiers, who had been partnering with Cap Maddox for as long as Murdo could remember.

"You ever heard of such a notion?"

Desrosiers shrugged and went back to his book-keeping.

"What about you, Frankie?"

Murdo tensed. That was just like his father. To ask Murdo's cousin, a hothead and a fool.

"You're the one that brings in that newspaper from Bozeman, Uncle," Frankie said. "My pa says nothin' good comes from readin'. Murdo musta read about 'em cows that 'em no-'count Texians keep bringin' to the railroad in Kansas."

Cap laughed. "That what you wanna do, boy?" He studied his son, then took a final pull from the jug before slamming the cork in. "Drive 'em cattle down to Kansas."

But Murdo wasn't about to cave in to the old man's bullying.

"There's the Northern."

Now his cousin and his father howled in delight, and even Desrosiers shook his head.

"Reckon all that readin' didn't learn you nothin', boy. You're as silly as your ma was. That railroad ain't goin' nowhere. Ain't you heard about the Panic since Jay Cooke lost his hide and brains? All 'em railroaders is busted. They ain't buildin' nothin'." He looked at Frankie. "Where was they when they stopped? Fargo?"

Frankie shrugged, but Desrosiers said, "Edwinton. Maybe a few miles west of there."

"Edwinton." The old man found his pipe and tobacco. "You gonna take cows to Edwinton. What's that? Seven hundred miles from here?"

Frankie gave another shrug. This time even the Frenchman shook his head, saying, "*Je ne sais pas.*"

But Murdo knew. "Eight hundred and fifty. Maybe nine hundred."

Even Desrosiers found humor in that, but he just shook his head and smiled. Frankie and Murdo's father roared with laughter.

"You'd herd your cows that far to make a nickel?" his father said.

"If I have to," Murdo answered. "But the railroad will be closer. This panic won't last forever. And by the time the railroad got here, I'd have a good-size herd. Eating free grass."

That was like talking back to his old man, and Cap Maddox rose, his cheeks reddening above the thick black beard and his brow knotting.

"That grass ain't free, buster. Me and the Maddoxes that come afore me paid dearly for that grass. And I still pay my bills the way Maddoxes have been doin' it since they come to this godforsaken country. Your grandpa Ezekiel and afore him Ebenezer Maddox knowed how to make money." He walked closer, towering over Murdo, but Murdo did not back down.

"And none of 'em ever had nothin' to do with no mangy milch cows."

But Desrosiers, who always looked after Murdo, came to his rescue. "Nelson Story has done all right down Virginia City way."

Story, who had made a fortune in mines and trading goods, had traveled to Texas, bought a herd of longhorn cattle, and herded them up Bozeman's Trail to Virginia City back in 1866.

Cap turned, tossing his jug to Frankie, and leaning down over the scrivener. "Sometimes, Frenchie, I like you a whole lot better when you talk in your native tongue." Straightening, he cast a sideways glance at his son.

"What's Virginia City now? Nothin'. It won't even be the territorial capital five years from now. Probably sooner. It'll be forgotten like Bannack."

And you, Murdo thought.

A horse whinnied outside. They had been talking so loudly, no one had heard the clopping of iron hooves on the ground outside the trading post that was slowly growing into something resembling a settlement. Four new cabins had gone up in the past five years, and two more settlers were trying to farm potatoes at Sacagawea Pasture.

Frankie started to pull the Navy Colt from his hip, but Cap said, "Shod hooves, boy. That mean it's a white man."

"White man can be a renegade, Uncle." Frankie did not holster the .36.

"Renegade wouldn't let us hear him comin', boy." But Murdo's father walked to the wall and pulled the Dragoon .44 from a holster hanging on a peg before he went to the door.

"I'll be a son of . . ."

He stepped outside.

Maël Desrosiers glanced out the window, then went back to his figuring. Frankie and Murdo looked at each other, then followed Cap Maddox outside. Murdo had no weapon. Frankie still did not lower the hammer on his pistol, and he started to raise it when he saw the big man sitting on a black horse. But Murdo grabbed his cousin's right arm and brought the gun back down, pointing it at the ground.

But it was a renegade, Murdo thought, when he saw not one, but two riders. The lead rider sat straight in the saddle, cradling a Henry repeating rifle across his thighs. Behind rode a younger man, thin, and he pulled a horse behind him.

The two men rode dark horses, but the trailing horse was a buckskin, and draped over the saddle was a dead man. Of course, dead men were common in this country. That's why Murdo's father had led a bunch of wolfers and other traders into Canada a month or two earlier.

Cap Maddox had asked Murdo if he wanted to come along, get some injun scalps, become a man at last. Murdo had not wanted to go with his father, but it was his mother who answered for him.

"You're not taking him away from me," she said,

struggling for breath and wringing her hands. "You let him be. Go to Canada if you want. But you won't take my only son to show him how much Satan himself lives inside your wretched soul."

His father had laughed.

Cap Maddox wasn't laughing now. And Murdo's mother was buried in Sacagawea Pasture, her lungs finally giving out after thirty-six years. She had married—if that's what they called it in northwestern Montana—when she was thirteen. Murdo had been born a bit over a year later. But his mother had always looked ancient, for as long as Murdo could remember.

Murdo, his father, and his cousin stared at the bay.

"Easy," Cap Maddox said to Frankie, who started again to raise the Navy Colt.

The riders reined in.

"Well?" Cap Maddox demanded.

"Your wolfer got killed," Bloody Bill Drew said.

"You have reason to kill my man?"

"Probably." The old man's badge reflected sunlight. Badge. But no one had elected him. He had appointed himself law of the land, and most people in the settlement south of Sacagawea Pasture had accepted that. Some kid had hammered out a badge of tin for the king of Basin Creek.

Well, Billy Drew might be king, but Cap Maddox was the pope. Even if he didn't believe in God. He worshiped only himself.

"But I didn't kill him."

Cap Maddox's eyes moved to the rider pulling the horse.

"Napoleon didn't kill him, either." He laughed. "My

boy don't take to gunplay, though he's a fair to middlin' shot."

Cap Maddox waited.

"We found him where he'd set up camp. Probably had a good bit of wolf pelts for you. But they got stole with your hider's life. But the man who kilt your man, he was in a hurry. Because he knowed I was comin' after him. You boy lived long enough to tell me it was Ben Meacham."

Murdo and Frankie straightened at that name. But Cap Maddox just spit in the dirt.

"You didn't have to come by to tell me. Reckon you're lettin' Meacham go. So I'll take care of Meacham from here. 'Preciate you bringin' word and McFarland here. We'll bury him. Then we'll bury Ben Meacham."

The law of Basin Creek shifted in his saddle and pushed up the brim of his black hat.

"You'll need me to ride along with you."

"I don't reckon a Maddox will ever need a Drew for nothin'. Except killin'."

Bloody Bill Drew shook his head.

"You'll need me. Meacham's in Canada by now."

"You ain't got no jurisdiction in Canada, Bill."

He let out a mirthless laugh. "Clark, I ain't got no jurisdiction here or anywhere else, if you ask the lawyers and governor and other high muck-a-mucks in Virginia City. But if you cross the border into them North-West Territories, well, I think them Canadians formed that newfangled North-West Mounted Police just to catch you—after what you done at Cypress Hills."

Cap turned his head just to spit.

"I ain't ashamed of nothin' I done."

The big man shook his head, and the saddle leather

creaked as he leaned forward against the horn. His smile showed no mercy. "How many Indians did you kill up there? Twenty? Fifty?"

"Steal my wolf pelts, that's what you reap."

Bloody Bill laughed. "Those babies, little kids, the pretty girls . . . how you reckon they got all the way down to Basin Creek to take your wolf pelts?"

"How you reckon you never managed to catch one of those thieves, you bein' the law, or at least callin' yourself the law, in these here parts?"

Bloody Bill Drew's smile vanished.

He pulled the brim of his hat low, and without turning to look back at his son, gave him the order. "Drop the lead rope, Napoleon, and let these stinking hiders bury their own. We'll go catch Ben Meacham ourselves."

Cap Maddox did nothing till the two Drews had ridden out of sight, disappearing in the valley northeast of the compound that folks called Fort Maddox.

"Frenchie," Cap called without looking through the doorway they had left open. He did not wait for any acknowledgment. "Get a couple squaws to fix up McFarland for buryin', and get the two Huns to dig a grave. Tell the squaws to take half of what they want from McFarland's poke, only half. You tally up what's left, and if you think they cheated us, let 'em feel the lash. And them Huns better dig that grave deep. If I hear coyotes diggin' up that grave or get a whiff of that rottin' Portuguese guy, I'll leave their backs sliced to ribbons from the lash."

He turned around and looked at Murdo and Frankie.

"Saddle up, boys. And saddle Midnight for me."

"We ridin' with that vigilante to kill Meacham?" Frankie asked.

"'Course not. We'll foller'm. Maybe Ben will kill that hard rock. Then we can kill Ben. But if Bloody Bill gets him, he won't bring him back to this territory to hang. We'll take care of that ourselves." He chuckled. "And maybe hang ourselves a Drew, too."

CHAPTER 23

"Go ahead," Bloody Bill Drew called out to his son as they climbed another hill. "Say it."

Napoleon was drinking water from his canteen. Swallowing, barely avoid sending the brackish water down the wrong pipe, he coughed a bit and corked the container, then wrapped the strap around the saddle horn.

"Say what?"

"Whatever the devil's botherin' you, boy."

What's bothering me, Napoleon thought, *is you. You're the devil that's been bothering me all my life.*

He wiped his wet lips and chin with his shirtsleeve and looked over his shoulder, but saw only grass waving in the breeze, then looked at his father's ramrod back.

"Well, I don't see why we rode all the way to Fort Maddox and—"

"Don't call that pigsty a fort, boy. Didn't you smell the stink? Especially don't give it the Maddox name. It's a wonder old Zeke didn't name that patch of grass Maddox Pasture instead of Sacagawea Pasture, the lout." He laughed. "I bet he's cussin' me up a storm down in the fiery pit right about now. Me. Callin' him Zeke. He always insisted on being called *EEEEE-zek-ee-al*. What a horse's . . ."

"Well," Napoleon tried again, "but cutting all the way to that place, Ben Meacham will be farther away from us. And he has a string of horses he stole. We won't catch up with him before he's in Canada."

"That's a fact."

"I don't know all the laws, but I don't think a lawman can just take a prisoner out of Canada without the permission of the government of at least the North-West Territories."

"That's a fact, too. Your ma done quite well readin' to you from them books and such."

Napoleon felt himself grinding his teeth. He didn't care much for his father at all, but he despised that miserable rabid wolf when he spoke of Napoleon's mother.

They rode another four hundred yards in silence.

"Well?" Bloody Bill asked his son.

Napoleon was at a loss. *Well . . . what?* He took a glance behind him, and guessing his father's meaning, said, "I don't see any sign of us being followed, Pa."

The old man grunted and spit to the side.

"Oh, we're bein' followed, boy. Cap . . . he's such a mule-headed scoundrel, he'll follow us all the way through them Cypress Hills. Even though ever' Assiniboine still livin' up there, man, woman, child, horse, and dog, would kill him on sight and stuff his scalp down his throat, because takin' a scalp and keepin' it from a man like that—if any dumb oaf would call Cap Maddox a man—would be a disgrace to the entire Assiniboine nation."

Napoleon shrugged and fell silent.

"You ain't got nothin' else to say?"

Napoleon sighed. "I don't know what you want, Pa." His voice cracked, and that angered him so much his young face flushed. "What do you want me to say?"

"I don't want you to say nothin', boy. What I want is you to buck up and be a man. That's why I took you along with me." He chuckled while shaking his head. "I sure didn't bring you along for no stimulatin' conversation. That's certain sure."

Two miles later, Bloody Bill reined in his horse atop a hill and waved his hand, but did not look back, signaling Napoleon to rein in alongside him. Napoleon obeyed. They could see forever, it seemed, atop this hill.

It was beautiful country. Like the Garden of Eden. But the serpent was sitting in the saddle, letting his horse catch its breath, so close that Napoleon could hear the old man's heart beating, see the sweat on his forehead and the lack of humanity in his eyes.

"Canada's maybe thirty miles from here," Bloody Bill said. "If we had a right powerful telescope, we might be able to spot Ben Meacham down yonder."

"Maybe," Napoleon tried, "we could spot the . . ." He managed to stop himself before he said the prohibited, profane word, *Maddox*, and managed to say "hide vermin." How he came up with *vermin* was beyond him.

"No need." The big man turned and stared with his hard eyes at his son. "If you know you're bein' trailed, that's good enough. And if you know it's gonna come to a fight, then you pick where you want to fight. That's something you ought to file away in that soft noggin of yourn. Let them think you're runnin'. Let them think that you don't know they're behind you. And when you find the best place for a trap, that's where you spring it.

Then kill 'em all before they kill you. That's the law of the West, boy. You reckon you can remember that?"

"Yes, sir."

He laughed without humor, turned away, and spit in the grass. "Yeah. I bet." He turned to the sun, nodded, and kicked the horse down the slope.

"We can make ten more miles, I reckon. There's a good crick where them trees are. Looks closer than ten miles, but it ain't. Grass is usually high and soft this time of year. No snakes to speak of. You might be able to scoop a trout or two out of the water for supper. Or we might just eat hardtack and jerky. Then we can ride into Canada sometime tomorrow and finish this job maybe the next afternoon."

And sometime in the early afternoon, the next day they crossed into Canada—which looked no different than Montana Territory to Napoleon. Maybe if they had taken a road, it would have looked different, but they rode far away from travelers. Napoleon wondered how his father knew the trail, and the man of iron explained a while later, laughing at some old memory.

"This is the way we came," he said, "when those Assiniboine got massacred."

Napoleon shot his father a curious glance. "*You* were with them?"

"Did I say we? I'm gettin' senile in my old age. Nah. I was back several miles, protecting the rear in case the Canadians or other Indians decided to take a hand."

"But you rode with . . . a Maddox?"

"I rode with some tough hombres from Basin Creek, boy. And I wasn't nowhere near that village when the butchery started." This time, he turned around and looked at his son. For most of his life, Napoleon rarely recalled his father staring him in the eye when they talked—or when he talked.

"A Drew don't never ride with no Maddox, boy. If you remember one thing I've told you, you keep that in your head. Never. They can't be trusted."

"Why?"

The big man stared like he was looking at the dumbest rock on the earth.

"Maddoxes kilt your great-grandpa, boy. Kilt him deader than dirt." He spat in the wind and swore. "Ezekiel Maddox. Got into a row with my pa. And Ben Franklin Drew, who hired on with captains Clark and Lewis, he tried to break up this row between my daddy, your grandpa, and this miserable Maddox cur dog who run the tradin' post. Ben Franklin Drew died in the dirt. Pump broke. Broken heart, some say, but I say it was murder, foul murder. Because of a Maddox."

Then the big man laughed. "But I'll fix one Maddox's flint before I'm back in Sacagawea Pasture. That's certain sure."

Napoleon had heard stories before, but never that particular one. And he wondered how a heart attack could be murder.

He was still trying to figure that out when Bloody Bill reined in his gelding. Napoleon looked up, saw a man sitting on his horse atop a grassy knoll, and he had to neck-rein his horse to the right to keep from running right into his father's horse. Then he pulled his mount to a stop.

"That's . . ." Napoleon started.

He stopped because Ben Meacham had put his horse into a trot, covering the distance in good time, riding straight toward the man whom some called the king of

Basin Creek—those, at least, who did not cotton to the Maddox family.

Bloody Bill grinned and held up his right hand. He even kept his left away from the small Manhattan revolver he kept in his coat pocket.

A few yards in front of the two, Meacham stopped his horse and nodded at the king of Basin Creek.

"You took your good sweet time," Meacham said.

"You in some hurry, Ben?"

"Did you get the money to my wife?"

Bloody Bill Drew breathed in deeply, then slowly exhaled. He leaned forward in the saddle and said, "I told you I would. Didn't I?"

Meacham straightened. "Meant no offense, Bill. But . . ." He grinned. "I'm a careful man."

"Yeah." Bloody Bill nodded at Napoleon. "This is my boy, Napoleon King Drew. Named him after the emperor." He let out a mirthless chuckle. "He ain't conquered much, though, but, well, so far he ain't met his match at Waterloo."

Ben Meacham had no idea what the king of Basin Creek was talking about.

"You sure this will work, Bill?"

The old man chuckled. "Reckon we'll find out." He turned to his son. "You got them manacles in your saddle-bag, boy?"

Napoleon turned and began working the strap and buckle, and moments later held the iron bracelets out for his father.

"Nah." Bloody Bill sat straight in the saddle. "Let's see what kind of deputy you might make. Light down. Put that iron on our prisoner's wrists. Tight. But not so his hands'll rot off before we get back to Montana Territory."

To Napoleon's surprise, Ben Meacham slipped out of his saddle. He was unbuckling his gun rig and then tossing it about halfway between his horse and the mounts of Bloody Bill and Napoleon.

Slowly, cautiously, Napoleon covered the fifteen yards, the chains rattling, the wind blowing, the sun baking. He glanced at the thief and killer's Remington .44, and a moment later, stood in front of the man they had trailed into Canada to bring back to Montana.

Or, Napoleon began to think, had they trailed him at all? He didn't remember his father looking for sign since they had left Basin Creek.

The iron bracelets went on without any fight, and with his hands cuffed in front of him, Meacham turned to remount his horse.

"Boy," Bloody Bill called out. "Ain't you got a lick of sense? That's Ben Meacham. Notorious scoundrel. He might have a pepperbox pistol hidden on his body and be plannin' to shoot us both in our backs."

Ben Meacham laughed. "I wouldn't use a pepperbox on you, law dog. But there's a stiletto in my boot. And a jackknife in my left pocket."

He wasn't lying. After Napoleon collected the weapons, Meacham remounted his horse, and Napoleon carried the iron back to his father, who motioned toward the saddle bag. Napoleon stuck the contraband there.

"This better work, Bill," Meacham said.

The three rode south.

Two hours later, Bloody Bill Drew laughed and reined in his horse, holding up his hand so that the prisoner and Napoleon stopped their mounts.

"Would you give me a weapon, Bill?" Ben Meacham said. "Just in case."

"Relax, prisoner. I ain't never lost nobody, even the lowest cur alive, to some mob. Any man I got hung, I hung myself."

Cap Maddox was leading about a half-dozen men, including his son, toward them.

Bloody Bill Drew found the makings and sat easy in the saddle, but he looked off to the east and waited. While he rolled his cigarette, he said softly to Napoleon.

"See where the sun is, boy?" his father asked.

Napoleon looked east. "Yes, sir."

"Draw your revolver. Let that nice nickel catch the rays. Be a nice, quiet little reflection toward that grove of trees yonder. Don't make it obvious. Just four-five good reflections. Then raise that hogleg, uncocked, so that Cap and his scoundrels will see that we's ready, but ain't hankering for no fight."

He lighted his smoke. "Get busy, boy. And jus' look natural."

Napoleon thought he had a couple of good flashes, but he wasn't sure anyone was in those woods, and if they were, he couldn't tell if anyone had seen him. He didn't even know who would be there.

"That's enough. Now raise that hogleg. And keep it pointed up toward God. But keep your finger on the trigger and your thumb on the hammer. And if this don't turn out like I planned, shoot slow. Take good aim. And put the man you be aimin' at down. Permanent. 'Cause they'll sure as the devil be tryin' to send you to meet Lucifer."

The Remington shook in his hand no matter how hard he tried to keep the weapon still. The riders slowed, fanning out, and stopped in front of them. Maybe twenty yards separated them. Napoleon's heart pounded. The Remington felt like the anchor of a sloop.

Cap Maddox cradled an old Hawken in his arms. His nephew, Frankie, put his hand on a big Colt. Cap's son had a Spencer. All eyes were on Ben Meacham.

"We'll be takin' him from you, Bill," Cap Maddox said. "Unless you want to die tryin' to keep him for yourself."

Bloody Bill Drew nodded. "That a fact?"

"That's a fact. I don't want to kill you, Bill. But I will."

Napoleon heard his father cackle. "You been wantin' to kill me since you was five years old. Same as I've been lookin' for a chance to put you under. Let's not beat around the bush."

"Well," the wolf man said. "I'll let you start the ball. But I'll finish it."

"Pa."

That was from Murdo. His father stopped, but would not take his eyes off Bloody Bill Drew.

Napoleon did. He looked east, saw the dust, and made out at least twenty, maybe thirty, riders loping from that copse of trees, down the slope, and across the flats.

"Cap?" one of the riders said, then spoke in fast French.

Only then did Cap Maddox look to the east. Napoleon did not see fear in the man's eyes, but hatred, especially when the hide man looked back at Bloody Bill Drew.

"You low-down son of—"

"Careful now, Cap. You might give yourself a heart attack." Deliberately, he turned in the saddle, even stood in his stirrups, and whistled. "By grab, 'em riders must be that newfangled North-West Mounted Police. They sure dress purty and look finer than my grandma on her weddin' day."

"Your grandma wasn't nothin' more than a Black-foot—"

Cap Maddox laughed when he stared down the barrel of Bloody Bill Drew's revolver.

"Marshal Drew!" one of the riders yelled as the North-West Mounted Policemen slowed their horses and fanned about until they had circled the riders of Cap Maddox as well as Napoleon, his father, and their prisoner.

"Frenchy," Bloody Bill said as he lowered the hammer and let his revolver return to the holster. "I gots the honor of presentin' you my prisoner, Cap Maddox. That ain't his real name, but I reckon it sounds a mite tougher than Cap."

The officer and three other riders walked their horses forward.

"In the name of the Queen," the officer said, staring directly at Cap Maddox, "I arrest you for leading the slaughter of twenty-three Assiniboine men, women, and children, committing rapine and other atrocities, at the Cypress Hills near Battle Creek on the first of June in the Year of Our Lord Eighteen and Seventy-Three, and for illegally and without permission of the sovereign nation of Canada bringing an armed force of mercenaries into our country."

Cap Maddox's malevolent eyes locked on Bloody Bill Drew's, but then he turned to the Canadian commander and said, "My son here, he had nothin' to do with what happened to them Indians. You got that on my word of honor." He seemed to have trouble swallowing. "I'll take your punishment. But ask you to spare these men. None of 'em was here in June. But I was." He nodded. "And I was glad to be here doin' what we done."

Murdo Maddox might not have taken part in the massacre, Napoleon thought, but Cap Maddox was undoubtedly lying about some of these raiders with him. He could see one scalp lock hanging from a rider's buckskin vest.

But the commander of the North-West Mounted Police did not want to start another battle, and he nodded.

"You are who we want, sir. But we will promise you a better, at least more civilized, form of justice than what you gave that Assiniboine village."

Cap Maddox made no response.

"Pa," Murdo called out.

"Ride away, boy. I'm caught. Tell Frenchie . . . aw . . . just get out of my sight."

So Maddox's men and his son and Bloody Bill and his prisoner and Bloody Bill's son rode south. They rode hard, maybe fearing that the North-West peace officers—or other Canadian settlers—would reconsider and disobey their commanding officer's orders.

By afternoon, they had crossed the border and followed Bloody Bill Drew to a dead tree atop a slope. There, the vigilante leader reined in his horse, removed his lariat, and tossed one end over a limb.

"Pierre," he called out to one of Cap Maddox's hide hunters. "Swing on that rope a spell. Let's see if that limb is sturdy enough for some Montana justice."

Napoleon drew in a sharp breath and twisted in the saddle to look at Ben Meacham, who stiffened in the saddle, but otherwise tried to hold his emotions in check. The teenager was still looking at the shackled thief and, presumably, murderer when a French accent cried out, "Why this tree could hang ten men before that limb gives way, Billy."

Then Bloody Bill Drew slid from the saddle, handing the reins of his mount to one of the pardoned Maddox riders, and walked toward Ben Meacham. Maddox's son stared, his face paling and his hands holding the saddle horn as tight as he could.

"Well, Ben," the vigilante said, "this is as far as you go."

"I'll see you in hell, Bill."

"Most likely. But you'll be fried to a crisp by then."

"You're a double-crossing bas—"

"Watch your language, boy. You're about to meet your maker." Drew kept his eyes on the condemned man—a man condemned by one man, not a jury, not a judge, just a man who could take the law in his own hands and declare it Montana justice. "Fix a good noose, boys. We wouldn't want a fine outlaw like Ben Meacham to choke to death."

But Ben Meacham did choke to death when they led his horse away from the branch of the dead tree.

Somehow, Napoleon Drew managed not to throw up. Two wolfers did, but Murdo Maddox just stared, long and hard, steady and cold as a rock. Napoleon watched his father scratch a note on a piece of paper, and one of Cap Maddox's men, still in his saddle, rode toward the body that twisted in the wind and stuck the piece of paper into the dead Ben Meacham's vest pocket.

Napoleon never saw the parchment, so he had no idea what it said, but legend said that it read:

**This be a lesson
to lawbreakers
in Montana Territory
3-7-77**

Three for three feet wide.
Seven for seven feet deep.
Seventy-seven for six feet, five inches long.
The dimensions of a man's grave.

DAY TWO

FRIDAY

CHAPTER 24

It took a good twenty minutes to get the Nissan Frontier back on the road, and then Billy Drew hit the brakes too hard and the truck spun. His first thought was, *I didn't buckle my seat belt.* Which would have been a crazy last thought. Like a seat belt would save his life when this piece of tin dropped, oh, four or five hundred feet into granite and then a few thousand more. Billy might have heard Alyson scream, but then he realized that it probably had been him shrieking. The truck slid toward the edge, and he undoubtedly would have gone over if not for a couple of trees that stopped him. But he didn't think he hit the trunks hard enough to warrant a trip to the body shop. Not as old as this truck was. And not with the crappy insurance that his father had taken out on the truck.

His heart pounded against his ribs. The Frontier had stalled, and he was reaching for the key what seemed like a hundred years later when the driver's door was jerked open and a big brute grabbed Billy by the collar of his coat and pulled him out and threw him into a snowbank.

"You fool." That had to be Hemingway Jones.

The other killer, Lyle Baxter, said, "You were the one who let him stay behind the steering wheel."

"Shut up." Jones climbed into the truck and turned the ignition. But the motor would not catch. He tried it again, with the same result, and slammed the palm of his hand against the top of the wheel. "Fool kid!"

"Let me . . ." Billy started but stopped when he stared down the barrel of a giant revolver.

"You got us stuck here. Well, you're gonna pay . . ."

"It's his truck, Jonesy," Lyle Baxter said. "Let him give it a try."

Jones glared past Billy at the killer's companion, but a moment later, he lowered the pistol and stepped out of the truck. "All right. But you put that piece of junk into gear and I'll decorate the interior of that truck with your brains."

After swapping places, Billy whispered a prayer. He patted the top of the wheel and looked through the windshield. The cop or guard or whatever he was stood next to Alyson, holding a revolver against her ribs. She wasn't breaking down, though, but stood there trembling from the cold and staring hopefully at Billy.

Like I can do anything to get us out of this mess.

He wet his lips.

"Get that thing runnin', boy!" Hemingway Jones roared.

Billy, unable to hold the fury in him, barked right back at the killer. "You want me to flood it? Is that what you want, you sick little—"

Jones leveled the pistol, but Lyle Baxter said, "Nissans have really good heaters, Jonesy. Let's see if he can get that thing running and we can warm ourselves up . . . And I'd rather not ride down this hill with my pants soaking up that boy's brains."

Jones's pistol lowered. "Get to it," he said.

Once the truck was running, Billy thought, Alyson and he would be worthless. The men would kill them both and take the truck down Neely Road. He was trying to think of how he could run them over, but he sighed.

I couldn't even turn my own truck around without losing control.

He pressed the accelerator just a bit and turned the key. This time, the Frontier coughed a couple of times but then fired up.

Billy turned back toward Hemingway Jones, expecting to see the muzzle flash and then see nothing at all but eternal blackness. But he didn't see Jones at all. Lyle Baxter had stepped between the truck and Jones. He nodded at the boy, then motioned him out.

"Just stay right by the front wheel," Baxter said, and he stepped up into the truck, reached over, and opened the glove box. A baseball rolled out and bounced off the passenger seat and onto the floorboard. Like a highway patrolman, Baxter removed the plastic container that held the vehicle registration and insurance card. The killer looked at it, then turned to Billy.

"You're William Drew?" he asked.

"Yes . . ." He didn't want to say anything else, but he did want to stay alive. "Sir."

Baxter cocked his head to the left. "Let me see your driver's license."

Billy pointed at the front visor. "My wallet's up there," he said.

And Baxter found the wallet, flipped it open, and first

removed a twenty and three ones and stuck them in his pants pocket, then he took the gas credit card and the Visa his dad told him to use only in emergencies. After that, he looked at the license.

He laughed. "You got your hair cut and shaved that fuzz off your chin."

"That was taken when I was eighteen," he explained. "Coach doesn't like hair touching the collar or facial hair."

"Stupid jock," Hemingway Jones said.

Baxter pressed the gas pedal briefly before glancing out the passenger sideview mirror. Turning back toward Billy, he said, "Get behind and push if you have to." He nodded at Jones. Billy figured that was the secret command for Jones to gun Billy down as soon as the truck was on the snowy road.

But Billy did what he was told. He might get shot if he helped push the truck. But he certainly would be murdered if he refused to obey.

As it turned out, he only had to give the Frontier a short shove, then Lyle Baxter drove the truck over a fallen log and slowed down, stopping next to Alyson and the turncoat cop. The condemned murderer stepped out of the truck and looked at the cop.

"Reynolds," he said, "in the back seat. With the boy on your right and the girl on your left."

The cop waved his gun at Alyson, and she slowly walked toward the pickup.

"What's in the bed?" Baxter asked Billy.

"Skis, poles, snowshoes. Ski boots. Some food."

"Liquor?" Hemingway Jones called out.

Billy shook his head.

"Worthless punk."

Baxter kept his eyes on Billy. "How far down till we hit Highway 60?"

Billy answered.

"Then we turn left to get to Basin Creek," Baxter said.

"No. You turn right. And you know that."

That brought a wicked grin to the murderer's face.

"You're pretty smart," he said, "for a jock." Leaving the engine running, he stepped out and pulled the seat forward.

Billy decided that Lyle Baxter was the brains of the gang and maybe not as cold-blooded as Jones. He certainly wasn't a turncoat like that cop. Baxter was holding the door open and the seat forward to let Alyson slide into the back, which she did easily. The cop stepped to the door but stopped.

The 2008 pickup was a two-door model—not an extended cab with four doors—and had only four seats.

The cop looked up. "I don't know how all five of us will fit in here," he said. "Maybe we should lock one of the kids in the bed."

Baxter shook his head. "That's too cold. I'd hate for us to have a frozen corpse in case we need a hostage."

The cop stared and shook his head. "You want me to ride in the bed?" He turned to look at Billy. "Are there any blankets and such back there, boy?"

Billy nodded. He had lived in Cutthroat County all his life. His dad was the sheriff. There was one rule that everyone lived by up here in this remote part of the world.

Be prepared . . . for anything and everything.

Of course, who could have prepared for being taken

hostage by two fleeing felons on the FBI's Most Wanted list?

The cop grimaced, and Billy could not blame him. Nobody would want to ride those harrowing miles downhill in the pickup bed. No matter how thick his blankets were, it would be a brutal and terribly frigid ride down.

"Maybe." The cop smiled and looked back at Hemingway Jones. Quickly, he turned to Lyle Baxter. "Listen, the state police and FBI are going to be looking hard for you two. Maybe it would be a good idea for one of you to ride back there. Don't you think?"

Actually, Billy thought, the best thing to do would be to have Lyle Baxter and Hemingway Jones ride in the bed. Billy recalled the past summer, when that psycho killer had made Alyson ride in the bed with the murdering fiend through roadblocks and all the way to the Circle M ranch. Then, when Ms. Taisie Neal had shown up, they had taken Billy's truck to one of the pastures on the ranch. That time, Billy had ridden in the bed with Alyson. The bruises both of them had earned on that brutal ride took months before they faded away.

Suddenly, Billy thought that he might be wise to trade this old truck in for something newer. He was getting sick and tired of being held captive in his own ride.

"What do you think?" the traitorous cop named Reynolds asked.

Lyle Baxter nodded. "That's not a bad idea. But I got a better one."

He shot the cop in the face.

Alyson screamed. Billy gasped. Hemingway Jones chuckled as he bent over to relieve the corpse of his service weapon, and Lyle Baxter looked at Billy.

"You got any ideas?"

Billy shook his head and stepped into the back seat next to Alyson. He did that quickly. Before Lyle Baxter, who wasn't such a decent guy after all, decided to blow Billy's head off.

CHAPTER 25

"Sheriff," Rupert Chadwick said pleasantly, with his arms extended as John T. Drew walked slowly toward him.

Drew stared down the barrel of his Bushmaster Model M4-A2 Patrolman's Carbine. The .223-caliber semiautomatic did not waver as Drew moved slowly.

"Mrs. Auchter," he said, though his focus remained on the two men. Drew took a few steps to his left, and when he had both men in his vision, with just a small adjustment needed to shoot them both dead, he finished his sentence.

"If that man you're pointing your pistol at makes one move that I don't tell him to make—and that includes a sneeze—pull the trigger and keep pulling it till you're empty." He focused on Chadwick. "I'll be doing the same with this rattlesnake."

Chadwick sighed. "You're making a mistake, Sheriff."

"I've made them before."

Like when I ran for office.

"But it could be your last."

"You won't be alive to know if it is."

The snow crunched underneath his Ariat waterproof boots. He stopped, not close enough for Chadwick to make a move to knock the rifle away, and he still had both men in his line of fire. The mic attached to his bulletproof vest was still on, and the earbuds underneath his skull cap allowed him to hear Mary Broadbent's heavy breathing back at the sheriff's office.

"Mary," he said.

"Yes, John."

Her voice made him breathe easier.

"Good job."

He could picture her smiling, but he knew she wasn't. She wouldn't relax till these two killers were locked away—and not in the pathetic jail at the courthouse. Put away in Deer Lodge. Or strapped on the table ready for the lethal injection.

Drew didn't think he would relax, either.

"Any report from Denton?" he asked.

"Nothing yet." She waited. Then asked, "Do you need assistance?"

"A fifth of Maker's Mark."

He heard her laugh.

"I might have some in my apartment."

"Don't make me lose my focus here. Radio Denton as soon as I have these two perps cuffed. As soon as . . ." He knew he was stressed. He couldn't think of the C.A.N. man's name. "As soon as . . . as soon as . . . Dempsey." He felt better. "As soon as Dempsey is on the scene at that crash, tell Denton to get over here to assist me. I don't want these two prairie rats in the same unit. Tell him I need him here ASAP."

He didn't want either of these two perps in his jail, either, but he saw no way around that now. Unless he executed them right here and now. Well, that was a thought. Maeve Auchter would likely pull a trigger herself and find a pickax and backhoe to dig the graves.

He waved the barrel of the carbine at both men. "Keep your hands behind your neck and drop to your knees."

When both obeyed, he asked, not focusing on either man, "What happened to the rest of the crew . . . and guards?"

Chadwick offered a slight shrug of his shoulders. "I would hope they bailed out." He nodded at the other man. "Keith couldn't land. So he ordered us all out. We jumped first." Sighing, he shook his head. "Those fine public servants. I sure hope they made it out."

Yeah, Drew thought, they were probably dead before they realized what was happening. The pilot flew the Cessna here, circled, then Keith—if that was his real name—programmed the automatic pilot for a steep dive into Sacagawea Pasture and he and Chadwick bailed out.

Some emergency landing.

While emergency crews were surrounding the crash site, Rupert Chadwick would have planned to travel the backroads back north, sneak into Canada, use his contacts, and disappear for a while. And his kinfolk? Chadwick was a ruthless and cold-blooded murderer, but he seemed to be loyal to his family—like those Wild West outlaws of the late 1800s.

Wild West days? More than a century ago? Not hardly. Here was living proof of that. The Wild West hadn't died with the turning of the century. Nineteenth to twentieth and now twentieth to twenty-first.

"Mary," Drew said.

"I read you, John."

"Get on the horn to Will Ambrose. See if they've made any verbal contact with the van or vans or whatever they were using. Just see if they have found out where the devil Rupert's accomplices are."

"Ten-four."

He waved the .223's barrel at both men.

"On your bellies," he ordered. "Face down, and I mean in the snow."

"I might have to sue you for cruel and unusual punishment," Chadwick said with a sinister grin. "If my nose gets frostbite—"

"It'll warm up where you're going."

He waved the barrel again. "I won't tell you two again."

When they were down, Drew said, "Put your hands behind your back and your wrists close together."

Only when they were lying face down in ten inches of snow did Drew hit the safety of the carbine and lean it against a picnic bench in Mrs. Auchter's backyard. He drew the nine-millimeter Glock Model 17 from the holster and pulled out a pair of handcuffs.

"Mrs. Auchter," he said as he walked behind Chadwick, "if that other feller lifts his head or wiggles his fingers or coughs, put a bullet in his crack."

"John," Mary said over the radio.

"I'm a tad busy, Deputy," he said.

"Ten-four. Denton's on his way."

"Roger. Over and out."

He knew she was still listening. "You're an angel, by the way."

He wanted to picture her smiling, but he could not let anything distract him right now. Drew had been in some pickles in his life, but nothing like this one.

Drew hit the Glock's safety and shoved the weapon in his waistband. Then he took one pair of handcuffs by the ring. "Back of your right hand facing your back," he ordered, "and palms out." When Chadwick obeyed, he double-locked the cuff and repeated the process with the left wrist. He did a thorough search, finding a switchblade and a wallet filled with twenties and tens and a Canadian driver's license and a California driver's license with Chadwick's photo but the name Ronald Preston Marcum.

He rolled the prisoner over, but did not brush the snow off the murder's face. "Let the sun dry you off," he said, "but move, even sneeze, and you die."

Drew went to work on whom he assumed was the pilot, finding a wallet filled with hundred-dollar bills, what he assumed was a fake driver's license, and a waterproof Montana highway map. No weapon. And no directions drawn on the map.

Once the pilot was handcuffed, Drew rolled him over, stood up, and backed up to Mrs. Auchter.

"You can lower your weapon, ma'am," he said, "and put it away."

"I'll put it away when these two rats are off my property, young man," she told him.

"I will need a statement from you, Mrs. Auchter, but I want to get these two felons in custody first." He felt the weight of ten Brahman bulls lift when he heard the siren wailing and the tires of Denton Creel's unit crunching as he drove down the two-track and then onto the bumpy road to the Auchter cabin.

"John." Mary's voice came through his earbuds.

"Two suspects in custody, Mary," he told her. "And Denton just pulled up."

"Copy that. Will Ambrose was busy, but Lieutenant Killius said they've had no communication with the van that was taking Chadwick's two accomplices to Deer Lodge."

"I thought they were being escorted by a posse of guards!" He realized he was shouting.

"In the snow, with little visibility, the van disappeared in the mountains," Mary told him. "And, yeah, Will Ambrose had the same reaction you had."

Shaking his head, Drew swore again.

"They think they turned off on Highway Seventy-Six," Mary said.

"Tell me they are pursuing."

"Not yet," she said. "Visibility is practically non-existent at elevations over eight thousand feet, and the Always Winters are getting dumped on."

Billy. Drew let out a heavy sigh. *What the devil were you thinking, son?*

"Sit up," he told the prisoners. Then he looked over the hills and could make out the black smoke that the falling snow and clouds tried, but failed, to hide.

A summer crash like that, as dry as some summers had been lately, could have turned all of Cutthroat County into a tinderbox. He tried to be thankful that this had happened in one of the worst winter storms of recent memory. But he wasn't feeling thankful for anything.

He had no way of telling how many dead men, maybe even a woman guard or two, were burning in the wreckage of Sacagawea Pasture. He had one of the FBI's most wanted criminals handcuffed in the snow that he would have to hold in the sorriest excuse of a jail cell in the entire Rocky Mountain West. He had a stupid jock of a son who thought he could drive up to the ski area in this weather, and Drew himself had come up with the absolutely terrible idea of sending a hard-drinking, fly-off-the-handle ex-Texas Ranger to the mountains to get that boy back to safety. What Texan ever knew how to drive in conditions like this?

He had a deputy—who happened to be his lover—who still wasn't cleared for anything other than radio duty.

And he knew that the phone lines to the sheriff's office would be buzzing about the smoke that folks were seeing in Sacagawea Pasture, not to mention the rescues that always had to be performed in weather like this. Fetching people in the county whose power grid had shorted out before they froze to death. Rescuing stranded travelers who had about as much common sense as his idiotic son. He needed more help. But who the devil could . . . ?

Who the devil . . . ?

Denton Creel was churning his way through the mountains of snow that had drifted up against the fence to the Auchter-Poe garden and shrubs.

"All right," Drew said. "Both of you stand up, and be still. And then both of you sidestep your way till you are fifteen yards away from each other. Then plant your roots there because if one of you moves, both of you die."

Denton got the message. He waited till both men were separated by enough snow.

"Want me to search them again, John?" Denton Creel asked.

"That would be a good idea, Denton. A thorough

search." They would do an even tougher search when they got to the county courthouse and jail.

He watched until Denton Creel had the pants and long underwear on the pilot pulled down to his ankles.

He saw Rupert Chadwick's face redden, not from the frigid temperature and snow, but the humiliation he was about to endure as soon as Creel was finished searching his accomplice.

But Drew was not thinking about the prisoners. He was thinking about how he and his deputies were going to get out of this mess alive. This storm wasn't moving fast. No helicopters would be flying in. No National Guardsmen parachuting to the rescue. They were going to be stuck here for at least another day. Alone. And two of Chadwick's vermin-like relatives were still unaccounted for. With luck, they might be dead in the Always Winter range.

But Drew did not want to think about that possibility. Because he knew his son could very well be frozen to death up there, too.

Chapter 26

George Grimes cursed his poor luck. Or maybe it was his stupidity. He kept getting careless in his old age. But he would still point the finger at that backwoods, hayseed sheriff in Basin Creek. John T. Drew had sent him up into these frigid, miserable, impossible-to-see-much-of-anything mountains.

The snow had died down for a while, but now it was picking up. Bigger, heavier flakes. He glanced at the dashboard thermometer and cursed the temperature. Fifteen degrees in the Big Bend. That's as cold as the weather could get there, he thought. The stupid thermometer here said it was five. No, negative five. That couldn't be right. It couldn't get that cold except in outer space.

Then again, he was practically in outer space. He was breathing in and out as if he had just run ten marathons. And he was freezing.

Those SOS signals must have stopped, as Grimes had not seen much of anything for the past ten minutes or so. Well, there wasn't much a person could see but cursed snow.

He had forgotten to bring binoculars, but the sheriff hadn't given him much time to be prepared. But Grimes did have something he could use. Somehow, he managed to turn around in the seat and reached behind him, feeling around until he touched the cold but comforting barrel of his bold-action rifle. Carefully, he pulled the .300-caliber Winchester Magnum into the front seat. He wasn't going hunting, but that rifle's telescope might come in handy.

Problem was, even his Dodge Ram wasn't big enough for him to level the rifle in the cab—at least not without breaking the windshield. That meant he would have to step outside because there was no way he was going to take the scope off the Winchester. It had taken him hours upon hours to get the telescope sighted in the way he wanted.

He found a cigarette, punched in the lighter, waited, then lighted the smoke, enjoying it and hoping the snow would blow on out of here before he stepped outside to see if he could see anything.

No luck. So he crushed out what remained of his smoke in the ashtray, then zipped up the heavy coat he had been forced to buy at the Wantlands Mercantile back in October—early October at that—pulled on the woolen cap, which he had also been forced to buy, and stepped outside, though he kept as close to the Dodge as possible.

Aiming the rifle at the last position he had seen the flashing brake lights, he saw only a blur. Nothing but white and dark shapes. And the lenses fogged over—or maybe that was ice forming—so he climbed back into the pickup, found a Kleenex that was in halfway decent shape, and tried cleaning both ends of the telescopic rifle sight.

Nothing.

He would have to get closer. But he could not risk driving the Ram up the mountain. If those were bad guys, and he had to think they were, they would hear the diesel engine of his truck. He guessed at the distance the SOS lights had come from.

"All right, Ranger," he told himself, then coughed and spit phlegm onto the floorboard on the passenger side. "Stay on the right. Count your steps. A hundred yards. No more. Then you're turnin' back. Count your steps back. Get in the truck. And warm your sorry behind back up."

He cursed himself again. George Grimes had such a big heart, and everybody in Montana took advantage of him.

His boots were Tony Lamas. Cowboy boots. Nothing fancy. Thirteen inches high, tanned goat leather, pretty scuffed from kicking some butts in honky-tonks and back alleys for the past three or four years he had been wearing them. Of course, that moneygrubbing kid at Wantlands Mercantile had tried to get him to buy a pair of boots for the winter. Ariats, maybe, or a good Justin work boot. He'd need them come winter.

Son of a gun, the boy had been right.

Grimes stepped out of the truck and prayed that he wouldn't slip on some ice or trip over a snow-covered rock and break his legs.

Snowflakes stung his face as he moved, rifle in hand. He stopped a bit later and worked the bolt, just enough to make sure he had a live round ready to fire. Just in case things got exciting.

"You dumb peckerwood," he said hoarsely and stopped. He turned back and saw the Dodge. That looked like fifteen paces. Heavy as he was, his tracks would take some time to fill, but just in case. Fifteen steps.

He turned back and began creeping up the road.

Sixteen.

Seventeen.

Eighteen.

Nineteen.

He had to stop to breathe, and breathing in frigid air felt like he was giving himself instant pneumonia. Grimes forgot how many steps he had counted off already. He thought about looking at the truck again, but shook his head.

And he thought about that February night when he was searching for that slippery coyote cheating them poor Mexicans who wanted to slip over the border in the Big Bend. Fifteen degrees, and that wasn't including wind chill, and the wind was howling at fifty-mile-an-hour gusts. And George Grimes had thought that was as cold as a body could get.

Montana, he was learning, ain't no place for sissies.

Five below zero. Probably even colder now.

Crud. The road was curving again. He stopped and looked back, but he couldn't see his pickup now, and he hated the surveyors who'd made all these winding roads. The Winchester felt like a Navy destroyer's anchor, and he kept flexing his gloved fingers just to make sure they didn't freeze and break off. Once he rounded the hill, the world darkened, and he realized it was because of the towering cliffs and trees high above him. But it also meant it wasn't snowing quite as hard here, and the road ahead, while snowy and gray and white, was a bit easier to see.

Something metallic sang out. A door slamming shut. Grimes slid back against the cold granite mass, brought the rifle up, and peered through the scope. Something blurry appeared. Steadying the rifle against a protruding arm of gray rock, he slowed his breathing as best he could.

He recognized the truck. That puny little Toyota or whatever the brand name was. Well, it was Billy Drew's rig. Stuck in a snowbank. He looked through the scope again. The truck came out of the snowbank, and snow plummeted from the branches of pine trees above as men scattered, and the pickup stopped.

The lens was freezing or fogging up again, but he had seen enough to know that the sheriff's son was still alive. Maybe some strangers had helped him get that pickup unstuck. Maybe there were Good Samaritans in this country after all. Maybe Grimes could get down from this wretched, frozen rock and crank the heat up in his apartment—*three cheers for global warming*—and drink enough Jack Daniel's to take him back to Texas in the summer.

Instead, he wiped the glass, front and back, on the scope, and brought the rifle back up. This time he found a face, and he focused on that image for maybe three seconds, no more, before the man turned.

"Good Samaritans my . . ." He moved the rifle till he found another person, but that man's back was to him. The rifle moved again, and he saw the back of the girl. That had to be the Maddox chick—a fine-looking little dish even if she didn't have enough meat on her bones—and finally found the second face he had hoped to see.

Well, no, hope wasn't the right word.

But now he was sure. The Drew boy and the Maddox dish were in deep trouble. They were with Lyle Baxter and Hemingway Jones. There was a third man who wore a uniform, but he had either stolen it or, most likely, bought it off those filthy rich Mafia boys or drug dealers or whatever they were. Criminals. Scum of the earth. The kind of men George Grimes didn't mind putting down permanently.

He thought about that plane crash that seemed to have happened a million years ago.

This was all organized. The airplane that was carrying Rupert Chadwick to the Montana pen down south. And the vehicles that were supposed to be carrying Chadwick's uncles the long way to prison. The rich swine who hired the Chadwick gang to do whatever they needed done had paid for a brilliant escape—or would have been brilliant had Mother Nature not stuck her finger in the pudding.

His fingers and toes were starting to feel numb, but Grimes made himself lift the rifle and check out the enemy and hostages once more. The gunshot almost made him slip and fall into the icy wasteland. He blinked, refocused, then swung the rifle left and right, up and down.

He let out a breath of frosty air when he saw the girl. His heart slowed when he found the sheriff's kid. There was Jones. And he saw the back of Lyle Baxter, who was addressing the two hostages, or so it seemed. So . . . the uniform.

Lowering the rifle, he scanned the ground. Near the toy pickup the Drew boy drove, he saw the body.

"When you sup with the devil," he whispered. It hurt

to breathe now, but he peered through the telescopic sight. They were leaving the body, but at the rate the snow was falling, no one would discover the dead man till late spring. The girl was getting into the back of the truck.

Grimes didn't have to see anything else.

He lowered the Winchester, turned around, and ran. His toes felt like they might break off, and the rifle turned heavier than a load of bricks. He didn't count his steps. Grimes just tried not to fall on his face. His lungs burned, and he cursed his daddy for not whipping the tar out of him after catching him smoking one of the old man's hand-rolleds that first time.

Then he his feet hit ice, or something, and Grimes went flying, landing hard on the snow, but at least it was a thick mound near the shoulder. He tasted snow, spit it out, pushed himself up, grabbed the rifle—which he finally got a good enough grip on—and used the rifle to push himself back to his feet.

He spotted the Dodge then, and lungs heaving, heart about to burst into a million pieces, he reached the front, literally slid to the door, and jerked it open. After tossing the rifle over on the passenger side—figuring in a worst-case scenario, he might have need of that .300—he pulled himself into the seat, slammed the door, and turned the key while pressing down on the accelerator.

The lights were on, shining ahead. He quickly turned them off, then put the Ram into gear and tried a three-point turn. The truck was too big and the road too narrow, so it took three extra turns, but he was heading down hill.

A glance at the rearview mirror showed him nothing

because the back window was like a white curtain. The side mirrors didn't help much, either, but then he was around a curve.

Now he had to remember. Where the devil was that turnoff he had passed on the way up? It was a dirt track that went up to some hiking area or campground or whatever. It would be on his left. He wasn't running, he told himself, but he was giving that boy and girl a chance at living. At least living a little bit longer.

He could pull up there. Pray that Hemingway Jones and Lyle Baxter did not see the Ram's big tracks. Let the toy truck zip on past. Then Grimes could follow the kidnappers and killers at a safe distance. Blow their heads off when he got a chance.

There had to be a reward on those miserable, lowlife, murdering thugs.

The Ram survived another hairpin turn, and Grimes slowed down just a bit as he came to another curve.

When he rounded that one, he stared into the bright headlights of a big truck that was hogging both lanes. Just like George Grimes's Dodge Ram was doing, too.

CHAPTER 27

The headlights came out of nowhere, and Ashton Maddox swore, jerking the big Expedition's wheel to the right. That way he would at least hit the trees and rocks on the side of the mountain and not go off it.

Problem was, the driver of whatever train was coming right for him must have had the same idea.

Metal crunched, glass broke, and the airbag hit him like the proverbial ton of bricks. A tire must have blown. Or maybe the driver of the rig was shooting at him. Or maybe Maddox was just dreaming about all of this. There was another numbing jolt. He felt as though the bed of the truck was lifting, maybe about to flip the rig over, but then it was falling. More glass exploded. The horn began to blare. It all sounded like some of the music the younger ranch hands listened to these days.

Whatever happened to the Statler Brothers? he thought.

Then he thought of absolutely nothing. There was blackness before him, behind him, above him, below him, to his left, to his right. The blackness, unlike the white world he was remembering, felt warm, comfort-

ing. It was a bottomless pool, eternal, and he could float
in its warmth and comfort forever.

Eternity, however, did not last long.

His eyes shot open, and pain seemed everywhere. He
tasted blood. He breathed in blood. He coughed, spit,
and leaned forward, but the seat belt and shoulder harness almost tore him in half. The airbag was deflating.
He was trapped in a giant spiderweb.

No. That was the cracks of the windshield and the
glass window of the driver's door. Steam hissed. He spit
out more blood and fumbled with the seat belt. Eventually,
the shoulder harness and belt gave way to his stubborn-
ness, and he could breathe deeply.

The pain almost knocked him out.

He wouldn't breathe like that ever again. The blaring
of horns and groaning of motorized parts screamed all
around him. Grabbing the door handle, he leaned
against the side and shoved, but that did nothing but
send spasms of pain up and down his left side, from hip
to head. He saw the door lock, button, pushed it, and
tried again. The door did not move, but the pain again
came close to blinding him. This time he gritted his
teeth, let out a curse, and shoved again with the weight
of his body.

The door did not open, but glass from the window
showered down, inside and outside.

Cold air, for once, felt rejuvenating, for a few seconds. He heard hissing steam, or maybe the tires of his
Expedition deflating. The strong scent of gasoline and
oil increased his determination to get out of the SUV.
Twisting again, he reached up, out of the window, locking his bare hands on the long roof rack, and pulled
himself, screaming at the pain but never losing focus,

determination, or consciousness. The frigid air and numbing snow fueled his determination, though shards of glass tore through his jeans and into the flesh of his thighs and buttocks. But he was out—at least partially.

He felt like a contortionist as he pulled both legs up, standing on the driver's seat now, bending a knee, the left one, placing it on the twisted metal and more glass, then his right.

Both legs kicked free, but this time he felt no new pains. He dropped to the ground, slipped, and fell hard onto snow and bits and pieces of either the Expedition or whatever the heck had totaled his really expensive SUV.

The snow cooled his face and hands. When he managed to push himself up, he saw the splotches of dark crimson.

A moment later, he was on his knees, and he scooped up more snow and pressed a handful against his nose. His tongue ran around his mouth. Somehow, he hadn't lost any teeth that the dentist had not already pulled. He applied more snow to his lips, and then he found the cleanest handful he could locate, and that he put in his mouth and over his tongue and let it melt in his mouth.

Swallowing hurt, but standing would make that seem like a mosquito bite.

He let the dizziness pass and leaned against the warm wreckage. After shaking his head gently to try to recover enough of his faculties, he looked at the tracks in the snow and saw where whatever had rammed him had gone to the right.

"Oh," he managed to say.

He started to stagger to the road. Here, there was no guardrail. Nothing had stopped the big, speeding—it had looked like a Massey Ferguson tractor from going over the edge.

"That poor, stupid son of a . . ."

The curse died in his throat, and he turned to look up the hill, at the turn that he had not reached. Slipping on ice and tripping over what had been the side mirror, he fell against his crumpled front bumper.

It was a small truck, and it braked quickly as it rounded. Ashton started to wave his hands, hoping, praying they would stop and give him—and maybe the poor, crazy driver who had come close to killing him—some assistance.

The truck began to spin, but the driver was smart enough to turn into the skid, and Ashton had enough brainpower to move toward the far side of his SUV.

Because the muzzle of a gun stuck out of the driver's side door window, which he had rolled down.

Ashton dived behind the ruins of his SUV as a machine pistol opened up. Bullets whined off the ruined Ford. Other rounds churned into the granite rock, scarring the face and splintering the bullets into ricocheting fragments that seemed to hit everything—timbers, rocks, gravel, rubber, parts of his SUV, and the pavement, and one knocked off the heel of Ashton's boot.

But nothing struck his body.

He expected another round, and there was a burst that went underneath the rig, but Ashton, by pure dumb luck, had come up to sit behind the mangled front tire. One ricochet popped metal a half inch from his left ear, and another tugged at his collar.

The engine roared. A door started to open. Ashton tried to find a place to hide, but there was nothing. His pistol, a snub-nose .38, was in the glove box. Ashton would never get to it in time. He doubted if the passenger-side door would open any easier than the driver-side door had.

Another noise sounded.

"Hey, you piece of dirt" The voice was gravelly, and a curse followed, and then a boom from a gun that was a lot louder than a Colt .38.

"Get in!" An automatic sprayed bullets, but none at Ashton, who moved now, jerking on the handle of passenger-side front door but getting nowhere. He lost his grip and fell on his side, rolled over, and flattened himself in case he was shot at again.

He heard another fast round, the roar of an engine, and saw the little pickup with chains on the wheels digging up snow. No one fired shots after the fleeing vehicle.

Get the license plate . . .

Ashton dismissed that thought. The truck was out of sight. And, slowly, he pictured the pickup. A Nissan. The little rig that Billy Drew—the county sheriff's son—drove.

More profanity came from the road, and Ashton looked underneath what had been his SUV. He saw jeans and cowboy boots. Cowboy boots. Not even good ones. In snow that was a foot and a half or more deep.

The wearer of those boots cursed again. And Ashton Maddox pushed himself onto all fours. He knew that voice. The voice of the stupid Texas peckerwood who had come charging down the mountain road like he was drag racing.

Ashton stopped. It hurt to move. He couldn't even get to his feet. He couldn't even make it to his knees.

He thought he was going to pass out when strong hands gripped his shoulder.

"Easy, buddy."

Easy? The man jerked him to his feet and leaned him, before Ashton doubled over, against what was left of his Expedition.

"Oh, crapola." The man let go of Ashton. "You gonna live?"

Ashton blinked. George Grimes took a step back.

Live? That remained to be seen.

"What the—"

"Easy, hoss." The Ranger—ex-Ranger, Ashton corrected himself—had a big gash over his forehead, and his right eye was blackening. His coat had been ripped, and his knuckles were a bloody mess. Two fingers were either broken or dislocated on his left hand. He turned and spat out blood.

While blood poured out of Maddox's nostrils.

"What were you doing, driving in the—" His mind cleared. He practically shouted, "Where is my daughter?"

"She's in that truck, pardner." The Texan tilted his big head down the road.

"That—"

"That ain't the sheriff's boy's doings, Mannix," he said, using the wrong name, Ashton knew, intentionally. The Ranger thought he was funny, but he wasn't. And never would be.

"Clear your head," the big brute said. "The men driving that puny little truck are Hemingway Jones and Lyle Baxter. You know them names, pardner."

Ashton's eyes must have been readable.

"They got your girl. They got the sheriff's son. And they left a dead accomplice in the snow up yonder."

Blinking, Ashton tried to make sense of what the Texas idiot was saying.

"I don't . . ." He stopped to wipe his nose.

"First things first, pardner." The Texan turned to spit more blood from his mouth. "Your rig ain't goin' nowhere. If the van the marshals were using was any good, I gotta figure them two killers would still be usin' it. So you know this country a lot better than me. So you tell me where the devil we can find something—I don't care if it's a snowmobile or them stupid ski poles. It's five below nothin' here. So we gotta find a way off this mountain before we freeze to death. And then, maybe, just maybe, we can save your daughter's life—and Sheriff John Drew's punk of a son."

For one moment, Ashton's head cleared. He understood everything. And he suddenly felt a cold that went beyond the thermometer's readings, that was starting to settle all around them.

Alyson was in the hands of two cutthroat butchers. He could blame Billy Drew all he wanted, but his own daughter had come up here on her own volition. She hadn't been kidnapped. But now she was being kidnapped. By a couple of professional killers. His mind recalled the plane crash. And he remembered hearing on the news that Rupert Chadwick was being flown to Deer Lodge prison.

Nothing made sense. Maybe it never would. But he felt the bite of the wind, and he knew one thing was certain.

Ashton and Grimes had to get off this mountain. But quick.

He took a step away from the ruined SUV, spit again, and nodded.

"There are sheds." He had to stop to catch his breath. "Half a mile. Maybe less."

He staggered a bit, managed to right himself, and started walking.

"A shed. We don't need no shed, pardner."

Actually, they might need a shed—just to survive. It could be a long time before anyone came up this road. The snow and wind started driving harder.

"What we need," the Texan whined, "is a—"

"Shut up. Save your breath. And follow me."

CHAPTER 28

Stopping the Interceptor in front of the courthouse, where the wind was whipping the snow high against the old walls, John T. Drew looked in the rearview mirror to see Rupert Chadwick smiling while the pilot looked ashen. The radio buzzed, and leaving the engine running, John answered the call.

"Yeah, Bobby, what can you tell me?"

Bobby Ward, the volunteer fire chief, caught his breath.

"She's burning too hot right now, John. We can't get close enough to do anything."

"Any danger to . . . ?" He stopped as Denton Creel's unit pulled up alongside John's.

"If we're going to have a plane crash—the first in county history—this is the time to do it. I'll need to secure the area for the FAA boys. They'll know what to look for."

"Survivors?" John saw Chadwick's smiling face in the rearview mirror.

"Not if they were in the plane when it hit. There's a crater I don't know how deep."

"Are Dempsey and his volunteers there?"

"They're here, but it's not like there's much anyone

can do. The snow's helping, I guess. I just wish the wind wasn't so fierce."

John paused, thought about ending the call, but sighed. "Do you need Dempsey there?"

"Well . . ." Bobby Ward took a lengthy pause.

That was enough of an answer. "If you don't need them, send them over to the jail. I have two prisoners here and . . ."

"You're desperate."

The laugh held no mirth. "Reckon I am, Bobby."

"He's got one good man, former hotshot from Idaho. Mind if I keep him . . . just in case?"

"He's all yours. Send the others back here."

"Ten-four." He turned to give instructions to one of his volunteer firefighters, then spoke into the walkie-talkie. "We'll keep our eyes open, John. I've radioed Choteau, asked for them to put out an emergency warning throughout the county asking residents to stay inside and do not come to assist or gawk at the crash site."

"Copy." Though even as curious as some residents might be, most of them—probably all of them—had sense enough not to leave their house in this storm. Which grew worse every minute.

"I'm staying here with Freddie, Cutch, and Bobby Black. And Dempsey's boy. I've sent the rest of my crew home. They'll spell us at dawn, but they know they're on emergency call in case something happens. I don't think there's much chance of that, but . . ." He paused again to talk to another volunteer, then came back to update Drew.

"We're a good distance from most of the wreckage, but the heat from the flames is most welcome. This was no crash landing, though, unless the pilot was a moron. The plane nose-dived."

"Ten-four. The pilot I have here. He bailed out. With Rupert Chadwick. I got him, too."

The pause was lengthy. But that bit of shocking news came hard for anyone to comprehend.

"That double-crossing, miserable mother . . ." Bobby Ward bit off whatever he was going to say. "Bring those two men here, John, and we can invite them to a barbecue. See how those flames feel when they're the ones cooking."

That, Drew thought, was not a bad idea. But the man in the back seat still just smiled that cocky grin.

"When do you think we can get the FAA in here?" Drew asked. "And the National Guard if needed? Or at least DCI and state police?"

Ward sighed. "Every airport from Great Falls to Salt Lake is shut down, John. And south to Denver. DIA is open, but they don't know for how long. They're just starting to catch some snow. The good news is that the worst seems to be settling over just one area. The bad news is . . . we're right in the heart of it."

Drew swore softly, then said, "I've got two men to lock up, Bobby. Keep me posted if anything changes."

"Ten-four."

"Good luck, Bobby. Over and out."

Drew looked again in the rearview mirror, then glanced out of the driver's door window, but could not see Denton Creel or the Cessna pilot.

He cradled the radio and found his cell phone, pressed a button, and brought the phone to his head.

* * *

"Johnny," Mary Broadbent said.

"Any word from Grimes?" Drew's voice sounded like he had aged a hundred years. That made her head hurt, and she had just taken those potent pain pills the doctors insisted she would never become addicted to.

"Nothing. Where are you?"

"Out front."

"Denton?" she asked.

"He's parked next to me."

She wet her lips. "You need me down there?"

The pause was agonizing. "Dempsey is bringing some men from the crash site now." She heard him swallow. "You ought to go home. It's snowing hard now."

She waited. He said nothing. Then, "You kick Colter Norris loose?"

"I tried to. But he's sitting up here with me."

"Great."

"Well, he's sober now."

"Any word from . . . Grimes?"

She closed her eyes and held her breath. Her heart ached now worse than her head. Johnny had already asked that question, and she had answered.

"He hasn't checked in, Johnny, but you know what it's like trying to find a signal up there."

"He can make an emergency 9-1-1 call."

Maybe, she thought. But George Grimes didn't have the brains to figure out how to use the emergency call on his cell phone.

"Go home, Mary. Get some sleep. Be back here at dawn."

"Johnny?"

"No argument, sweetheart."

That endearment made her feel better, but she spoke evenly. "Colter and I came up with some ideas."

His chuckle sounded mirthless.

"He went to Rudy Pierce's and borrowed some tow chains and padlocks. Heavy duty. And brought them to the basement. We put them around the door. Lock them and don't leave much slack in the chains, and that door won't open."

The silence went on forever. Then the call ended.

John Drew glanced in the rearview mirror, saw the blank face of Chadwick, and ended the call. Then he stepped outside. When Denton Creel started to open the door, Drew waved him back inside, and he hurried through the stinging snow and bitter wind until he stepped into the alcove and redialed Mary's cell.

"You're not halfway downstairs are you?" Drew tried to sound jovial.

"Don't be a jerk."

"I didn't want Chadwick to hear what you were saying."

"You can take the call off speaker, you know." It wasn't a question.

"Yeah, but Chadwick might hear something. Go on. Tell me about the chains."

She paused. Then cursed. Then started talking, though he could tell she was mad at his lack of manners. "The door won't open. Norris also climbed a ladder and secured one of the other bars to the ceiling. It's not going anywhere. Well, it might, but it'll likely bring down the wall behind them. And that big block in the center? Well, Colter rigged up a chain so that you can pin one of them to that. He won't be able to get within three feet of any of the cell bars."

"Go on."

"There's another place. We hung . . ."

"We?"

"I was watching . . . mostly."

"All right." *Mostly!* He shook his head.

"One chain's padlocked around the rafter. Another chain is slipped through it, and that goes down to the floor. We handcuff the prisoner to the end of that chain, and he can walk around a bit, but he can't get close to the other prisoner, and he can't get to the bars, either."

"Are you sure about that?"

"We tried both of these on Colter himself."

"Do you think they'll hold?"

"Well." She sighed. "They'll hold better than those weak bars will. And it's only for a day or two. Right?"

"I don't know. This storm isn't helping matters."

"It's not helping the basement here, either. Walls are leaking like a funnel."

"Yeah," Drew said, staring at the mountain of white piled up against the outer walls of the courthouse, almost halfway up the first floor.

He saw the lights of two vans and sighed. "Send Colter down, Mary." He shook his head and cursed. "Oh, both of you come down. Show us how these things work. Elison Dempsey and our special deputies just arrived."

The man named Lyle Baxter rarely took his eyes off Alyson Maddox.

He sat in the passenger seat while studying Billy

Drew's cell phone, but always looking up, making sure Alyson and Billy were seated, buckled in the back seat of the tiny pickup. He also had Billy's billfold, and he studied the driver's license. Then without a word, he rolled down the window and pitched the phone into the snowy world.

Now he went to work on Alyson's phone.

She had a password, but somehow he either figured it out or worked around it. Then he began scrolling, and that made her look away, out the window, at the falling snow. The driver had slowed down, a good thing, because the road was getting worse, though they had only a few miles to go before they would reach the intersection with Cutthroat County's other state highway.

She thought about seeing her father, hearing her scream as the driver, Hemingway Jones, had rolled down the window and let his machine-gun pistol send bursts of shots into her dad's Ford Expedition. Her father had dived behind the SUV, and the man shot again. But she didn't think her father had been hit, though how he had wrecked his pride and joy of a ride remained a mystery. It had been snowing too hard, and the exchange had happened so fast. But she had kept screaming until Lyle Baxter tossed cold coffee into her face.

Then he had aimed his weapon at Billy Drew's forehead.

"I can kill both of you," Baxter said. "Will kill both of you. If I have to. Remember that. And keep quiet."

Jones had chuckled.

"Just drive, you stupid twerp," Baxter had said. "And slow down. It's a miracle we've come this far."

She saw the smoke. Baxter must have seen her face change, because he turned and looked out the window.

"Looks like Rupert got out according to plan," Jones said with a chuckle.

"Of course he did," Baxter said. "He's God, after all."

The driver snorted. "Well, he thinks he is. Treats us like he is."

"We'd be on our way to Deer Lodge, pardner," Baxter said. "If not for our nephew. Remember that."

He looked back at Alyson, smiled, and held up her phone.

"Should I hit the CALL DAD button, girlie?"

Her face tightened.

"It's a good thing we didn't kill these two kids, Hemingway," Baxter told the driver. "They have value to us."

"Maybe the girl," Hemingway Jones said. "But I don't know about the boy."

"Oh, I do. We have esteemed passengers. The boy, apparently, is the son of John Drew. As Rupert told us. That's the county sheriff. And the girl." He looked back at Alyson and blew her a fake kiss. "Her dad is Ashton Maddox. A big rancher. The biggest. In Montana and a lot of the big West."

"You wanting him to fry you up a steak?" Jones turned up the wipers to the max. "Damn blizzard."

"Slow down, and watch the bloody road."

Baxter smiled at Alyson and then at Billy.

"If things get ticklish," he said to the driver, "we have a couple of hostages we can use."

"I'd rather kill them. Hostages can turn on you. Remember what happened in Boise three years ago."

Baxter shrugged.

"Where are we supposed to pick up Rupert?" Hemingway Jones asked.

Baxter shook his head. "No signal yet. When we have one, we'll ring our godlike nephew." He looked at the dashboard. "But maybe we're far enough down the mountain to have a decent radio signal." At last, he turned around, but he still looked into Alyson's eyes through the rearview mirror.

"If you move, I kill you both. So enjoy the ride. And let's hear what the news of the day is."

He turned the radio on, twisting the dial, getting mostly static, and finally found an all-news channel out of Great Falls.

It was all weather and some politics out of Washington. Some actor had died that Alyson had never heard of. Then more weather. And then . . .

"Kenneth, I hate to interrupt you, but we just got major breaking news from Cutthroat County."

The driver let off the accelerator and braked to a stop. Alyson could see smoke in the distance.

"All right," the radio announcer said, "what's going on, Rachel?"

"Thank you, Kenneth. I just got off the telephone with Elison Dempsey, the head of the citizen's committee— C.A.N.—out of Basin Creek. That reported airplane crash is a lot more serious than expected. According to Dempsey—and I must stress that these reports are unconfirmed. We're trying to get the attorney general, FAA, and Cutthroat County Sheriff John Drew, but no luck.

"According to Dempsey, the plane that crashed was flying convicted murderer Rupert Chadwick to Deer

Lodge—the reports of Chadwick being transported by
van were just a ruse—although another van was bringing
Chadwick's accomplices, Hemingway Jones and Lyle—
oh, I've forgotten his last name."

Jones laughed. Baxter called the reporter a foul name.

"That van was bound for Deer Lodge but somehow
took a wrong turn. No communication has been reported. And the plane carrying Chadwick was trying to
make a forced emergency landing in Cutthroat County."

The weatherman, Kenneth, at the station broke in.
"We've had reports of a plane crash or some explosion
in Cutthroat County."

"That's right, Kenneth. But Dempsey says that the
pilot of the plane bailed out with Chadwick."

"My God!" another radio broadcaster exclaimed.
"This is like an action movie."

"Unfortunately, this is no movie," the woman said.
"However, according to Dempsey, the pilot and Chadwick were captured by the county sheriff. Dempsey and
his C.A.N. contingent are diligently assisting the
county sheriff, who is shorthanded, in holding Chadwick
in the county lockup until Montana prison authorities,
marshals, and perhaps other agencies can come to their
assistance."

"How certain is Dempsey?" Kenneth said. "This is
just so . . . insane."

"Dempsey swears this is going on. He says C.A.N.
can handle this, but reinforcements will be welcomed.
And a call to the Department of Criminal Investigation
in Helena ended with—quote—We have no comment
on any of those allegations at this time—end quote."

"With this weather," Kenneth, now back in his area
of expertise, said, "is there any chance of getting more

law enforcement and emergency personnel into Basin Creek?"

"Well, Kenneth, the National Guard is ready, I am told, but the governor has not asked for their help. Apparently, even the governor has had no contact with anyone from Cutthroat County. The bigger problem is the shutdown of all airports in the general area, and as far away as Denver and Salt Lake City."

"Well, Rachel, I'm looking at our radar map, and things are looking even worse in Cutthroat County. It's the smallest county in our state, but that's where this wicked and powerful winter storm is settled over right now. And this storm is moving at a snail's pace, but it is dropping temperatures well below freezing, with gale-force winds and more snow than I've seen in eleven years."

1894

⛰

JANUARY

CHAPTER 29

Murdo Maddox went looking for Jeannie Ashton at Napoleon Drew's cabin. The other boy, the younger kid, opened the door and sang out, "Happy New Year."

Talking to kids was never something Murdo had mastered, but he took his hat off and said, "Yeah." There wasn't much happiness so far.

The boy pouted. "You're supposed to say 'Happy New Year,' too."

Now he was being bossed around by a five-year old. Or maybe the kid was six or seven. Criminy, what did he know about boys—what would he ever know? Jeannie Ashton kept putting off his marriage proposals, but he thought he might be wearing her down.

"Is . . ." He gave up. "Happy New Year, kid. Is Mrs. Ashton here?"

His head wagged, and he pulled the door open wider, and as soon as Murdo was inside, he peered out. "Shucks, it ain't snowin'," the boy complained.

"Sun's out," Murdo said, looking around. "For now."

"Aww, shucks. I like snow."

"It's not going anywhere for a while, boy." He didn't see anyone in the cabin, even when he glanced up at the loft. The door closed, and Murdo looked back at the boy, who shoved his hands into his pockets. "You're . . . Peter, right?"

"Noooo! I'm Parker."

Parker. That was right, though Murdo doubted if he would remember it. "Where is Mrs. Ashton?"

The kid nodded. "Outside. With Miss Lois and my sister."

Murdo turned for the door.

"Mary Ellen's my sister. She's six."

"Happy birthday to Mary Ellen."

"It ain't her birthday."

Murdo was out the door, letting it swing shut and rounding the house, where he saw Jeannie, the seamstress, and the little girl, all bundled up, filling a basin with snow from the tin roof of a shed.

"Look!" The girl, wearing a coat, a hood, and mittens, held up a handful of dirty snow.

"That's fine," Jeannie told her, "but we'll get the snow off the roof, not out of the ground." Then she looked over and saw Murdo.

"Hello, Murdo, we're about to make snow cream for the children. Care to join us?"

The seamstress knelt and shook the snow out of the kid's hand, then scooped her up and gave Murdo a warm smile.

"Ummm." The last thing Murdo Maddox wanted on a freezing day like this one was to put anything cold, especially snow cream—whatever that was—in his mouth. His teeth hurt enough already from chattering.

"No, but thank you," he said, and he remembered his manners and hurried forward, taking the basin from Jeannie's hands. Parker tagged along beside him and yelled out, "He thought it was Mary Ellen's birthday!" He laughed.

"Come along," Lois DeForrest told the children. "Unless you want this snow to melt before we can make some delicious snow cream." She smiled as she passed Murdo, who turned sideways to avoid being trampled by the boy and girl.

Then he was alone with Jeannie Ashton.

"How was Sissy?" she asked.

"Who? Oh. Fine." He turned to walk beside her.

"Did you find some men to drive your cattle?"

"Maybe. Charley Bandanna I hired as trail boss."

She stopped and stared up at him. "I thought you would be bossing the herd."

"Yeah. I did, too. But Charley's a good hand, a top hand. He can get the job done better than . . . well, he can get the job done, anyway. It's not like we're coming up the Western Trail with two thousand head from Texas."

Jeannie did not seem to accept that.

"No. But it is January. And there's a foot of snow on the ground." She looked at the sky. "You think this will hold? Think the storm is done?"

He shook his head. "I doubt it. But Montana weather is rarely predictable."

As they approached the front of the cabin, Murdo glanced down the street, as he kept walking.

"What's the matter, Murdo?"

He stopped, realizing that Jeannie had stopped behind him. Turning, he frowned and walked to her.

"Probably nothing," he told her. "I might just be getting touched in my old age." Old age. He was thirty. Jeannie was older, but the rancher didn't know that.

She didn't laugh. Did not even crack a smile.

"I saw three riders in the woods around Basin Creek." He gave a vague wave in the general direction. "When I went to the meeting house to see if this fellow might want to hire on."

"You didn't want those three riders?"

He opened his mouth, but shut it. "I'd like you to stay away from the sheriff's office. Keep those kids away from—"

"Those kids," she told him, her face a stone monument, "happen to be the sheriff's children." Her head turned quickly toward the cabin door, then she stared down the street. "Have you seen Eugene?"

It took him a moment to realize that Eugene was the sheriff's oldest boy.

He looked down the street, too, but there were few children out now. Not many adults, either, except those chopping wood or bringing wood inside.

"Oh . . . well . . . I thought I saw him earlier today. But . . ." He shrugged. "Probably playing with some pals of his."

"Eugene doesn't play enough for a boy his age."

She turned toward the cabin, stopped, and looked back at Murdo.

"What about those three riders?" she asked.

He let out a heavy sigh. "It's probably nothing. But the sheriff has Bo Meacham locked up."

"Everybody in Basin Creek knows that now." Her eyes did not blink. "Bo Meacham had a father, too."

He breathed in cold air, held it, let it out. "Yeah. He did."

"You were there, weren't you." It was not a question.

"I was there. But I wasn't with Pa at that Indian village. And Pa paid for what he did, though I know many a man who did something worse back in those wilder years, and they didn't spend seven years in a Canadian dungeon."

His exhale felt like a dragon's breath, and his heart pounded, and he realized his fingers had balled into fists and both arms shook.

A mirthless laugh escaped from Jeannie's throat. "Murdo, sometimes I don't know who the devil you are. Who the devil . . ." She laughed again, a painful laugh. "Who the *devil*. Maybe that's the key word there. *Devil*. Do you think those three men you saw at the creek are some of Meacham's men?"

"It's just a possibility."

"A possibility." She shook her head. "You're one hard rock, Murdo." She walked toward the cabin.

"I told the sheriff what I saw," he called out to her. "Warned him."

"Bully for you." She did not look back. "Just go back to your ranch and take care of your cows, Murdo. Or ride down to Carlton Boone's spread and bring your new herd back here. Maybe there'll be a town still standing. Maybe Basin Creek won't be another Fletcher City."

She was at the door, opening it, then closing it hard.

He figured she pulled the latch string in, too.

How long he stood there, he could not recall. It couldn't have been long, though. Jeannie Ashton always tried to make him forget his last name was Maddox. But Jeannie hadn't been there to see Ben Meacham lynched by Napoleon Drew's father. Jeannie had not seen how that vigilante had tricked Murdo's father, led the old man right into the hands of those Mounties. When his father got out of prison, out of Canada, and back to

Montana, he was a broken man. He lived only seventeen months longer, and till his dying day he railed in that worn-out, cracking voice of his that the Maddox line would die with Murdo. The poor excuse of a Maddox hadn't married, probably never would, and likely couldn't even get a son birthed out of wedlock.

The Maddox line would die out. Well, Cap Maddox's line would end. *And God*, the old man often said, *help us all if we have to depend on any sons to come out of Frankie Maddox's loins.*

Murdo turned away from the cabin. He had to walk past the sheriff's office, and he did without slowing down. He kept walking till he reached the boarding house, hoping to find Sissy, but there was a note on the door.

> *HELP YOURSELF, MURDO.*
> *Don't come looking.*
> *I'm Gone To Texas.*

He pulled the parchment from the nail.

Everybody in Basin Creek is mad as a hatter, he thought. The door remained unlocked, so he went in, walked to the room he had let, and once inside, packed up his gear. He tossed some bank notes on the bed. Maybe Sissy would regain her good sense and come back. He couldn't figure out what had gotten into her.

Once he had his gear wrapped in his bedroll and grip, he left the boarding house and started for the stable, but Charley Bandanna stopped him with a hail.

He was waving some men along. The one-armed man was among them and so were . . . Murdo shook his head.

He recognized Luke Jasper. The other two men he had seen loafing for most of the winter, and those were some sorry cowboys. Too lazy to ride south to find an honest day's work. Too lazy to work through a Montana winter.

Bandanna waved the men on, saying he would catch up with them before they were far down the main road. He loped his horse over to the piecemeal boardwalk and reined in.

"Boss," he said, and leaned forward in the saddle.

"That your crew?"

"Most of it. Got a cook." He laughed. "And a louse. You want to look 'em over?"

"It's your crew. You hired them. Just get that herd to Sacagawea Pasture."

Bandanna nodded and sat straighter in the saddle, lifting his head toward the sky. "Might just be able to do that. If this weather don't change."

"Fat chance."

Bandanna shrugged. "What can I say, boss? I'm a dreamer." With a nod, he turned the horse and kicked it into a lope.

They were out of sight in a few minutes, and Murdo turned toward O'Boyle's livery. He took four steps, then stopped, cursed himself, and turned around.

He walked straight to the sheriff's office, dropped his gear by the log wall, and knocked hard on the door.

The tiny peep door opened, closed, the bar was removed, and the door opened.

Napoleon Drew held the big Remington in his right hand as he pulled the door opened, looking past Murdo and up and down the street.

"Yeah?"

Murdo considered picking up his gear and heading to O'Boyle's. But he would have to ride right past the Maddox and DeForrest cabins. Right past Jeannie Ashton.

"You don't have to deputize me," Murdo said. "But I'm coming in to help."

Napoleon Drew did not even blink. The door cracked just a few inches, and he said, "Why?"

Murdo frowned. Again, all he had to do was turn around and leave. Instead, he said, "Fletcher City."

CHAPTER 30

Once Murdo Maddox stepped into the office, Napoleon Drew went outside, scanning the street, his cabin, and the town east and west. The town looked dead, but it usually did this time of year —and quite often throughout most of the other seasons, except on payday at the area ranches. From here, he couldn't see much of the creek, and he didn't want to look into the whiteness for too long. A case of snow blindness was the last thing he needed right now. It wasn't snowing, but off to the northwest he saw those ominous clouds.

"You make an inviting target," Miles Seabrook called out to him. "More importantly, you're letting a lot of cold air inside."

Drew tried to smile, but his lips did not cooperate, and he backed into the cabin, closing the door and finding the wooden bar to make it harder for anyone to bust in.

Murdo had deposited his gear atop Napoleon's messy desk and had helped himself to the coffeepot.

The gambler turned to the rancher, "I guess you didn't think to bring some grub with you."

Murdo returned the coffeepot to the stove and held

out the cup he had filled to cool. "I had a right hearty breakfast at Sissy White's." He blew on the tin cup and smiled. "You should have joined us."

With a chuckle, Seabrook turned his attention to the game of solitaire he was playing, but he stopped after either bad cards or boredom and shot a glance toward Napoleon.

"Fletcher City," he said. "I seem to recall hearing that name, but the details aren't coming back to me."

Napoleon frowned before he looked at the rancher, who set his cup down and began moving his coat, gloves, scarf, and hat from the sheriff's desk and hanging them on the rack next to the door that led to the jail cells. *This freezing air must have frozen my brain,* the lawman thought. On the other hand, he likely would need every gun he could get.

When Murdo Maddox turned around, he stared at Napoleon. "You gonna tell him?" he asked.

"You were there," Napoleon said.

The rancher nodded, picked up his coffee cup, and walked to the fireplace.

"I didn't get there till Meacham and his gang were gone," he said. He moved to the side of the hearth and sat down, took a sip of coffee, and looked at Seabrook.

"Five years back," he said. "Late summer. Fletcher City was a town, chartered by the Great Northern Railway, northeast of here."

The gambler looked skeptical. "I took the Great Northern to Cut Bank. I don't recall any place called Fletcher City."

Napoleon answered that one. "You got here in '90, when Cut Bank was just going up and Basin Creek was a few months away from being christened as Cutthroat County seat. Fletcher City was gone by then."

"Thanks," Murdo said, "to Bo Meacham and his gang." He took another sip of coffee. "You might have passed the ruins, though."

The gambler nodded, and Murdo continued:

"The Great Northern had big plans for Fletcher City. Got its name from an engineer who had died while hauling supplies to the end-of-tracks. He died getting away from Bo Meacham's gang, but he saved the railroad a lot of money and supplies. So the town was going up, before the tracks even reached there, and the leaders decided it would be a good place to put some shipping pens. They asked me to come plan the best place for the yards. My uncle went up with some designs I had put together, though I was pretty much borrowing from what I had seen on trips south to Ogallala, Dodge City, and Wichita. When the pens were going up, my uncle sent a rider down here and said I ought to come up and make sure everything looked all right.

"But before I got there, two of Meacham's owlhoots got caught by the law in these parts." He stopped.

"That would be my daddy," Napoleon said. "Though he was coughing his lungs out from consumption and pneumonia by then."

"Wouldn't live out the year," Murdo said.

"But he outlived Meacham's men," Napoleon said.

Murdo nodded. "Hanged them both. Well, he ordered the hanging. It was my uncle who slapped the horses from underneath those two outlaws."

"No trial?" the gambler asked.

Both Murdo and Napoleon shrugged.

"They were guilty," Napoleon said.

Murdo nodded. "No doubt about it."

Miles Seabrook shook his head.

"Bo Meacham couldn't let two of his boys be lynched—strung up by the same man who executed Meacham's pa—even if that sick old scoundrel was in a sanitorium in Deer Lodge County."

"Deer Lodge County!" Seabrook sang out.

Murdo's head moved up and down. "Talk about power. Here was a sick old man, oh, almost three hundred miles south of there, but he still controlled the western half of Montana."

"I'd say," Napoleon interrupted, "that Cap Maddox, sick as he was, too, controlled his share of Montana."

Murdo shrugged. "Well, my father was broken after a long prison sentence in Canada by then. His brother, my uncle, was trying to run things in Fletcher City with his son. But Frankie, my cousin . . ." He stopped long enough to study Napoleon, as though the sheriff had forgotten that he had shot Frankie Maddox dead—in a killing ruled justified—back in 1891. "He got drunk, as he was prone to do, and rode up the tracks to the end-of-track to drink whiskey, play cards, and have a whirl with the painted ladies."

It seemed as though Murdo would stop the story there, but when Seabrook cleared his throat, Murdo finished his coffee, wiped his lips with the back of his hand, and looked at Napoleon while he spoke.

"So Bo Meacham rode into town. I didn't get there till most of it was all over. Saw the black smoke and spurred my horse. By the time I got to Fletcher City—or what was left of Fletcher City—I could only fire a few shots at some of the riders as they rode away. Folks were beating at the flames with whatever they had left.

Coats. Shirts. Brooms. Most of them had run toward the coulee, took shelter there. Some men said they held off the Meacham gang with rifle fire. Maybe they did. But I didn't see any empty casings in that coulee. And didn't hear any shots when I was galloping toward town."

He shook his head.

"They burned the town," Miles Seabrook said in a hoarse whisper.

Murdo nodded. "Burned everything. The buildings. The privies. The sheds. Everything but those cattle pens. Which got taken apart and hauled to Cut Bank the next year. Everything else was either burned out or burning down when I rode into Fletcher City. Except there was one other structure the Meacham gang left standing."

He looked up and stared at the gambler.

"The gallows. They didn't burn the gallows. Though they did take down the bodies of the two gang members Bloody Bill Drew had ordered executed from way down in Deer Lodge County. And left two men swinging in their place."

Knowing what he would see if he closed his eyes, Murdo rose from the hearth. He busied himself—stretching, bending over, rubbing his backside. Even with his eyes open, he could picture what he had seen, the cries he had heard. The crackling remnants of the fire reminded him of the heat and roaring inferno from what once had been a promised city of wealth and railroads. Fletcher City. Which now was nothing more than a water stop, the remnants of a graveyard, maybe some charred timbers and the ruins of chimneys surrounded by deep Montana snow.

"One was the jailer," Murdo heard himself say, and he turned to grab the poker and began stirring the fire to get more heat and scatter the coals. "Sorry to say I don't recall that brave man's name. He was an old man, lost an eye fighting for the Union during the rebellion."

He sighed. "You hear all these songs about dead outlaws. Murdering fiends. All across Montana. All across the West. When they ought to be singing songs about heroic jailers."

He returned the poker to the other tools on the other side of the hearth, then turned around to look at the gambler and the lawman.

"The other man swinging," Murdo said, "was my uncle."

A long silence chilled the room, even as Murdo Maddox found a couple of logs to add to the fire.

"Is that why you're here?" Napoleon asked.

Murdo brushed his hands on his pants, picked up the coffee cup, and walked to the stove.

"I'm here," he said, "because of Jeannie Ashton."

CHAPTER 31

"Have you seen Eugene?" Jeannie Ashton asked Lois DeForrest.

"Not since this morning," the seamstress answered. She was stitching a hem, letting Mary Ellen pretend to help. *That woman had the patience of an oyster,* Jeannie thought. Lois looked up and smiled, "Maybe he found a job. He was looking for one, you know."

"Yes, but it's not like him to—"

Someone knocked on the door. Lois started to stand, but Jeannie waved her back down. As long as Mary Ellen was occupied doing something and the two boys were out of the cabin, peace settled over here—and Jeannie needed as much peace as she could get.

She crossed the room and opened the door, feeling the cold air that wasn't quite as cold as it had been earlier this morning. There were even some blue skies to be seen off to the north.

"Oh . . . Mrs. Ashton." Finnian O'Boyle removed his winter cap. "I was looking for Miss DeForrest, but . . ." He pulled out an envelope that he had tucked inside his filthy coat. "Well, this one's for her." He held it out, and she took it, staring at the fine cursive handwriting of Sissy White. She blinked, confused, then looked back up at the liveryman and started to ask him a question, but he was fumbling inside his coat.

Another envelope—the same type as the one she moved to her left hand—had fallen between O'Boyle's boots, and he was hurrying to catch it before a wind gust sent it all the way to Wyoming.

When he straightened, he held out the envelope. "But this one's for you, ma'am."

That one wasn't from Sissy. She saw Eugene's scrawl, which wasn't much better than Mary Ellen's—or their father's.

She moved the note for Lois to her left hand, took Eugene's in her right. The seal was faint, so she opened it easily, and when O'Boyle excused himself and stepped toward the road, she said sharply, "Wait a moment, sir, if you will."

The wind caught the envelope and sent it sailing as she pulled out the single piece of paper. She made no attempt to catch the flying envelope, but she did look up to make sure Finnian O'Boyle remained planted in front of her.

"Who is it, Jeannie?" Lois called.

"It's for me," she answered and let the door close.

"I might send a reply through you, Mr. O'Boyle," she said. It was the only thing she could think of. She bowed her head and read.

Deer Pa
& Ms Ashton
& mis lois

   I am hirred on to help Mr Madux fech
cattel up frum a ranch S of here it pays
good am goin to be a cowboy for aweek
thats how long it shood tayk says mr
Maddux dont wurre Ill be al rite
   wil be fine got my wintR coat & boots
   they wil be fedin us
   tell pa
   see you in a week or 2

                    yors trule
                    Eugene Drew

She would have a long talk with that schoolteacher
the parents were paying for the subscription school.
After she had a longer chat with Eugene Drew.

"Mr. O'Boyle," she said, and reread the letter.

"Yes'm."

"Those men Mr. Maddox hired to round up Mr. . . ."
She let out a breath of exasperation. She could not recall
the man's name. "Boone. Carlton Boone." At least her
mind had not been completely obliterated. "How long
have they been gone?"

O'Boyle found his watch in a vest pocket. "I'd say
two, three hours. Charley Bandanna hired four, five—"

"Including Sheriff Drew's oldest son?"

"I didn't know about—" She held out the letter and
his eyes squinted. "Son of a . . ."

"Profanity will get you nowhere, sir."

He reached for the letter, but she pulled it back.

After shuffling his feet, he cleared his throat. "I know that Mr. Maddox hired that waddie Bandanna to hire some hands." He let out a heavy sigh. "He even took Luke Jasper from me. Luke, who's been working for me for better than three years."

"When he should have been in school," she told him.

He pretended not to hear her condemnation. "You want me to take that note to Sheriff Drew, ma'am?" He was reaching for it, but she pulled it away, stuck it in her apron pocket, and ripped open the letter from Sissy.

She had steeled herself for Eugene's letter, but she let out a heavy sigh when she read Sissy's. O'Boyle had started back toward his livery, but she called out his name, and he stopped.

When he turned around, she had finished Sissy's note, and let her eyes bore into the Irishman.

"Did you know about this?" she said, waving the note.

He shrugged. "Some of the boys Charley Bandanna hired was talking about it, ma'am." He shoved his hands into his pockets. "I don't reckon nobody else knows that Mr. Maddox hired that girl to cook for them boys."

That caught her by surprise. She stiffened. "Mur . . . Mr. Maddox knew Sissy was going with those boys in this weather to round up those Hereford cattle?"

He thought about the words before he answered. "I can't say for certain, Mrs. Ashton. But, well, I just don't think nothing happens on the Circle M that Murdo Maddox don't know about."

That, she thought, was about the smartest thing she had heard all day.

"Thank you, sir." She swallowed and chanced a glance at the sheriff's office. "Please get to someplace warm. You'll catch cold."

He thanked her and turned down the street.

She was inside the cabin seconds later, and Lois saw the look in her eyes and moved toward her. "Jeannie—" she began, but stopped when she was handed the note.

"That . . . this . . ." She didn't drop the paper, but her hand fell to her side, and she stared in disbelief at Jeannie.

"She took Eugene . . . in this . . . on . . . to . . . I mean . . ." She didn't know what she meant, and she tried to shake some sense into her head. After breathing in deeply and then letting it out, she glanced at Parker and Mary Ellen before she looked again at Jeannie.

"Why would she do this?"

The letter gave no answers.

"I don't know."

"Well . . . it's warmer. The sun's out. Maybe the storm . . ."

Lois did not finish. And Jeannie had been outside. She had seen those clouds over the Always Winter range—dark, low, foreboding. The sun would set, the storm would move in, more snow would fall. Jeannie had been in cattle country long enough to know that nothing ever came easy in that business.

"Look after the children, will you?" She found a heavier coat and a good hat to keep her warm. "I have to go tell Napoleon. And see what Murdo knows."

* * *

Napoleon Drew opened the door just a crack, but Jeannie saw the anger in his eyes.

"Jeannie, I told you not to come—" But she thrust his son's letter toward the door. His eyes turned down, and his mouth hardened. The door opened, and she stepped inside.

The sheriff had thrust the letter out toward Murdo, who was standing by the fireplace.

"Did you know about this?" Napoleon roared about a second before Jeannie could ask the same question.

After a quick glance at the letter, Murdo looked up with a face she had never seen on him.

"I . . ." He turned from Drew and looked Jeannie in the eyes. "Charley Bandanna had a free hand in hiring whoever he could get. I didn't think he'd be stupid enough to hire a kid."

"He hired more than that, Murdo," Jeannie said. "He hired Sissy White as his cook."

Murdo took a step back toward the fire. "That's impossible."

"She wrote Lois a note," Jeannie told him.

Napoleon moved toward the coatrack.

"She left a note for me, too," Murdo said. "At the boarding house." His eyes followed the sheriff for just a moment, then he looked back at Jeannie. "I couldn't make sense of it. Said I could help myself to . . . well . . . she didn't say what. But she said she was going to Texas."

"Those cattle are at the Boone spread," Maddox said.

"Well, I am sure some people in town—even kids playing in the snow—saw who rode out today. I don't know what's going on here, but . . ." Jeannie stopped.

She was shaking. She wanted Murdo to come to her, to put his arms around her.

But Murdo had turned to Napoleon.

"I'll go after them," he said. "I'll bring your boy back."

Drew was already pulling on gloves.

"You didn't deputize me, Sheriff. I'll go. I can ride better than you can on the best of days. And those are my men."

Drew reached for the nearest Winchester.

Murdo let out a loud curse and slammed his fist on the sheriff's desk.

"You can't leave Bo Meacham with this cardsharper and me, Sheriff!" Murdo bellowed.

Napoleon was headed toward the door. "Try and stop me," he said.

"Sheriff," the gambler from Hangman's Saloon said softly. "Have you already forgotten about Fletcher City?"

The door was opening, letting in frigid air. Jeannie watched Napoleon's back.

"You think Bo Meacham won't turn Basin Creek into another Fletcher City?" the gambler asked.

The door shut.

Jeannie felt her heart beating again.

"What I've heard of this Charley Bandanna," Miles Seabrook said, "is that he's about as good of a hand as you'll find from Texas to the Canadian border."

Jeannie added, "Sissy, in her note to Lois, said she'll keep Eugene close. He's what they call a . . . cook's louse."

Napoleon nodded. "Cook's helper." He chuckled. "That was my first job on a trail drive. I was eleven."

But his face hardened. "But I wasn't driving cattle in a blizzard."

"It stopped snowing," Murdo said.

"For how long?" the sheriff roared, but that was all that was left in him. He dropped the carbine on the floor and barely made it to the nearest chair before he collapsed onto it, rested his elbows on his thighs, and buried his head in his hands.

But only for ten, maybe fifteen seconds.

"Sissy wrote that she was going to Texas," Murdo said. "Why would she say that? When she's going just, what, a day's ride from here."

"A day's ride," Napoleon said, "in good weather. Maybe. Where'd you find that note?" He looked up.

"Tacked to the front door of her place," Murdo said.

"Where," the gambler whispered, "anyone could have seen it."

"Listen." Jeannie was taking charge again. "You three need to stay right here. I'll see if I can find some men at the Hangman's Saloon."

"Carberry's a good man," the gambler said, "if he's tending bar. And Virtanen, the swamper, he's Finnish— or so he says—so his blood is used to this weather."

Jeannie thanked him, and Napoleon rose again and moved to the door, but this time he opened it for Jeannie. She stopped, reached up with her left hand, and placed it on his stubbled cheek.

"They'll be all right," she whispered. "Now . . . you be all right."

The smile was forced, but he nodded. "I'm a Drew," he said. "Don't fret over me. Or . . . Eugene."

She stepped outside and heard the door close behind her, followed by the wooden bar. Turning, she made her way toward the Hangman's Saloon and Gambling Emporium, hoping that those two men Seabrook had mentioned would be working there and praying that she had just imagined a snowflake stinging her cheek.

The Hangman's wasn't crowded, but a man was leaning against the hitch rail, and he shoved away from it, pulled his coat collar up, walked down the shoveled path, and raised his gloved right hand to tip the brim of his hat as she passed.

She gave him a nod.

The next thing she knew, the fur-lined sleeve of the man's coat was around her chest, crushing her arms against her side. She hadn't realized just how big the man was. She started to scream, but the man said, "Shhhhhhhh."

And the sharp blade of a knife rested on her throat to give more authority than the big man's whisper.

"Ain't nothin' gonna happen to you, lady," the man whispered. "Unless you scream, shout, bite, or don't do what I tell you to do. Then you bleed out like a deer carcass." He twisted her around and shoved her off toward the meeting house. Or the creek.

"C'mon. Pelletier wants to hear what you gots to say."

"Who's Pelletier?"

"Him and me, and a few others, ride with Bo Meacham. That's all."

"Well, I have nothing to say to him."

"Fair enough, lady. But if you don't change your mind in about ten, twelve minutes, then you'll be dead."

DAY TWO

FRIDAY

CHAPTER 32

Ashton Maddox stopped. He had lived in this county for years, and while he never had been much for skiing, he had been up this high before. His contributions had helped make this ski area, and here he was, freezing his butt off and hardly able to catch his breath. He sounded like that fat slob of a Texan who finally caught up with Maddox. Grimes wheezed like some cartoon character.

"Well . . . ?" the Texan managed to say.

Maddox didn't answer. Finally, he said, more to himself than to Grimes, "It's around here somewhere."

"What's 'round here?"

Grimes's lungs worked overtime. He pointed. "There's one."

Turning, Maddox looked where the Texan was pointing. "That's not it," he said in disgust. That was a lean-to with a bench underneath, though the snow was up to the seat. For people to sit down. George Grimes looked like he needed to sit down. Actually, he looked like he was about to keel over and drop dead from exhaustion.

"It's big. Like a carriage stable. Painted yellow. Or was. Last time I was up here. Green doors."

The Texan wheezed, then managed to swallow and pointed, saying, "Think . . . I . . . saw it . . . maybe . . . there."

Maddox stared and softly swore. "Why didn't . . . ?" He stopped. "Let's go."

It was about two hundred yards, but at least they were going downhill now, into the wind and pounding snow, but now Maddox was moving with a purpose. That was the shed. He must have been blind to have missed it. He should thank that Ranger, who might have saved his life, but thanking a Texan wasn't something a Montanan was going to do.

"What's in . . . that big S . . . OB?" Grimes managed to say.

"The cavalry to the rescue," Maddox said.

They had to walk up the wide, snow-covered gravel path and stood before the big barn-like structure. The two wide doors were chained and padlocked shut.

"You . . . got . . . a key?" Grimes asked.

"No." Maddox looked around. "But I know where it's hidden."

The Ranger laughed, or maybe he had just coughed. "I got . . . to keep . . . tellin' . . . myself . . . This ain't . . . Houston . . . or . . . Dallas." He swore and laughed again. "It ain't . . . even . . . Marfa."

"There's a yellow rock," Maddox said. "At the foot of a tree."

Grimes coughed, spit, and swore. "That rock's . . . covered . . . with two . . . feet . . . of snow, pardner."

Maddox didn't answer. He was looking for the tree. It took him only four minutes to find it.

He had scraped the bark away with the Barlow knife his father had given him for his eighteenth birthday. It had been his grandfather's knife. Then he had carved the heart and the initials.

A M
+
P C

For once, that blowhard redneck ex-cop didn't say a word.

Maddox thought about his wife briefly, remembering how he had brought her up here when they were both seventeen. And now she was gone. Running off with some cowhand or lawyer or who the devil knew? Leaving a note on the dining room table with her wedding ring on top. She had done a real good job of disappearing. Four, no, five private detectives hadn't located her. Patricia hadn't even tried to contact Alyson, if he were to believe his daughter. And he did.

Releasing a sigh, Maddox began kicking the snow away. Grimes joined in, and they dug down till they saw the yellow rock. Grimes moved it out of the way, and Maddox found the Band-Aid box wrapped in the plastic bag. He ripped open the bag, then had to pull off his gloves to get the lid opened as the keys rattled inside. He was also careful not to let the keys drop into the snow when the lid finally released.

He took the smaller key and gave it to Grimes.

"Open the door," he ordered, and Grimes kicked snow away until he was at the door, then began fiddling with the lock.

It took both of them to pull both doors wide open. At

least the wind blew toward them, and the drifts were piling up behind the structure.

Grimes stared into the dark cavern of the shed.

Then the idiot starting singing, or rather panting, Townes Van Zandt's "White Freight Liner Blues."

CHAPTER 33

"This is cruel and unusual punishment," Rupert Chadwick said.

The airplane pilot, already chained in the ramshackle cell, sat on the floor, his face ashen and tears welling in his eyes.

One of Elison Dempsey's C.A.N. hoods laughed, but the others stood, white-faced, as John T. Drew, Denton Creel, and the brainchild of this new method of incarceration, Colter Norris, locked the murderer in the cell.

"My lawyer," Chadwick said after the men stepped away, "will sue you for all you and this poor excuse for a county are worth."

"Go ahead," Drew said. "You described Cutthroat to a *T*. Poor." He held the rickety door open for his deputy and the Circle M foreman, then closed it. Then Mary Broadbent wrapped a smaller chain to secure the door and clicked the old Master Lock securely.

Drew pointed at two of Dempsey's men. "You two. You have first watch. You don't talk to the prisoners. Not one word. You stay six feet from the cell at all times. If you have to answer nature's call, there's the bucket. You don't sleep. You don't read. You turn off your cell phones and give them to your boss." He took the handheld walkie-talkie that he had handed Dempsey and handed it to the red-bearded man. "Use this to report to me every half hour." He pointed. "That's the panic button. Hit that if anything happens."

He started for the stairs, stopped, and turned back.

"And if you don't obey those orders to a T, you'll be locked up like they are."

The third man was sent to the top of the stairs on the ground floor. Drew sent the fourth to the front doorway. He started wishing he hadn't let Bobby Ward talk him out of leaving that hotshot who had joined C.A.N. stay at Sacagawea Pasture, then realized that was probably for the best. He would rather just deal with four C.A.N. freaks and Dempsey.

"Colter," he said softly. "Go home."

The battered old ranch hand shook his head. "Reckon not. I'd get stuck in some snowbank."

"Then why don't you wait out the storm at the Busted . . ." Drew almost smiled. Colter Norris did. Mary Broadbent even chuckled.

"There's an old story," Denton Creel said, "that when an early saloon got burned down back in the late eighteen hundreds, the people of Basin Creek built a schoolhouse in its place."

"I heard it was a church," Norris said.

"It wasn't the saloon that got burned down," Drew said. "It was the sheriff's office. They moved the sheriff's office here before this Old Bailey Building and Loan got put up in its place. And it was the sheriff's office that they replaced with a new saloon." He turned to Dempsey. "I want you to run up into Dan O'Riley's office. Look out the window. And keep looking out there. In case they come in from the back."

The county manager was vacationing somewhere in the South near some beach. Hilton Head. Savannah. Daytona. Someplace like that. Drew stopped trying to remember. The window in Dan's office faced the south side. So did the sheriff's office, but there was no window in Drew's. The jail was on the north side, and those walls were taking a pounding, and as bad as the heat was in the basement, that stinker Rupert Chadwick had to be freezing his fingers off. Drew almost pitied the guards he had left down there, even if they were a bunch of gun-loving idiots.

Dempsey frowned but said nothing. He just moved his assault rifle off his shoulder.

"Dan's got better coffee," Drew said, and watched Dempsey hurry toward the stairs.

He looked back at the Circle M foreman.

"Why don't you run over to the Wild Bunch Casino?"

"It's closed," Denton Creel said. "So is the Wantlands Mercantile. Everything's shut down, John, because of the storm."

After a soft curse that was drawn out for several seconds, Drew shook his head. He couldn't just turn the old cowpuncher out. In this weather, Norris couldn't make it back to the Circle M, and Drew wasn't about to give him the keys to his house. He might be safe here. But would anyone else be if that wiry little fellow got in one of his kick-some-butt moods?

"All right, Colter. Come on upstairs with us."

* * *

"John." Will Ambrose's voice crackled on the sheriff's cell phone, which he had put on speaker. "The governor's made the call on the National Guard. As soon as there's a break in the weather, they're coming in by the buttload in helicopters. What's it like out there?"

Mary Broadbent ground her teeth, which made her head hurt, and fought the urge to tell that DCI lieutenant a thing or two, while John Drew just stared down at his phone. No one had to go find a window and look outside. This ramshackle old building was so dilapidated that the walls and ceilings creaked from savage winds, and the cold settled in all over them. She glanced at the thermometer on the far wall.

Inside: Sixty-five.

Outside: Thirteen.

Nope, inside dropped to sixty-three. But it felt a whole lot colder.

The sheriff had answered Ambrose's question, though Mary had not been paying attention. She knew what the weather was like outside. The locals called these hard winters, but *hard* didn't come close to describing this one.

It was the kind of snow that hurt when it hit.

It was the kind of cold that killed.

It was the kind of wind that cut like a knife.

It was brutal, merciless. It refused to let up. She started to understand all those accounts of early settlers driven mad in the winter. The wind's moans and howls and icy breath reached inside the Cutthroat County Courthouse/Basin Creek Municipal Building.

She pulled out the little device the Missoula doctors had given her, slipped her pointer finger on her left hand into the opening, and tapped the button. It was small, quiet, its case fit right into any pocket, and it did not take long to display the results of her oxygen level and her pulse rate.

The oxygen level was 91. It almost always ranged between 90 and 93.

Her pulse rate was 107. She could feel it pounding against her chest. Her at-rest rate was typically in the low 70s, and she was sitting in a chair, with a bottle of mineral water. She had taken her pills. She was fairly comfortable. But that heart banged against her ribs so hard, it seemed, that she felt a tightness between her breasts. No pain, just tightness.

Anxiety was what her doctors called it. They had even suggested that she find something a little less stressful than working in law enforcement. But she had told them that, honestly, most days on the job in Cutthroat County weren't a whole lot different than Mayberry, North Carolina. That had gone right over the doctor's head—and Mary Broadbent was too young to have seen *The Andy Griffith Show* except on TV reruns at John Drew's house.

She was doing absolutely nothing strenuous, but the pressure of the storm and the killers and all she had been through was taking its toll.

The pulse rate jumped to 111.

Mary ripped the little thing off her finger, pushed it in the little case, and shoved it back into her pocket.

Remembering her instructions by her therapist, she began that exercise. Breathe in through your nose slowly and think of peaceful thoughts.

My cat when it wants to play. Mama's poached eggs

on toast. A hike in June through the wildflowers. A night with Johnny Drew.

And breathe out all the negativity.

This job. The most vicious killer down in the basement. A winter that won't end. The chance that this might be my last night on earth.

"Will," she heard John say, "I've got to go. Billy's calling me."

Mary turned, found herself praying that the boy was all right.

She saw John bring the cell phone to his ear, turning off the speaker, and heard him say softly, hopefully, "Billy."

Then his face tightened. Mary whispered a quick prayer.

John put his left hand against the desk, as if for support, and his face paled, and he bit his lower lip. Slowly, he moved the phone away from his ear, hit the speaker function, and laid the phone atop papers and magazines.

The voice that came out of the phone was not Billy Drew's.

"Sheriff John T. Drew?"

"Yeah," John said.

"You recognized your son's voice, I presume."

"Yeah." His hands tightened into shaking fists.

"Well, here's another voice you might recognize."

There was a short pause, and in the background came the noise of an engine, maybe even tires crunching packed snow. Then . . .

"Sheriff . . ."

That was a young woman's voice, a very frightened young woman. Denton Creel straightened. Colter Norris stepped closer to hear better. John Drew's face turned into something Mary Broadbent had never seen.

"I'm sorry, Sheriff. It's me . . . Alyson."

"It's not your fault, honey," Drew said. "Don't worry. Are you all right?"

"Of course, she's all right, Sheriff." The man's voice came on again, and Mary heard someone else croak out a hideous laugh.

"Do you know who I am, Sheriff?" the voice asked.

"Hemingway Jones or that other soon-to-be-dead . . ." Mary had never heard John use that profane word before.

The voice laughed. "Careful, Sheriff. You might provoke me into doing something that would break your heart."

"What do you want, Baxter?" John said, his voice steeled, his clenched fists white and shaking.

"I assume that Rupert is in your custody."

"With enough trigger-happy guards to cut him into ribbons."

"Which, Sheriff, we would be happy to reciprocate by turning a pretty young girl and a stupid-looking punk into something that the coroner might mistake for airplane crash victims."

The pause stretched for what felt like hours.

"Have you ever seen the movie *Rio Bravo*?" the voice on the phone asked.

"Yeah."

"Rupert will be Slim Pickens. Your son will be Dean Martin. You send Rupert out. We send Dean Martin walking to you. Unlike in the movie, Dino doesn't beat up Slim Pickens, but runs into his daddy's arms. Rupert steps into . . . I don't think we want to take this crappy little tin can for our escape vehicle, but you can have your SUV running for us, with the heater on high, please. We get Rupert. You get your son. All's well that ends well."

A sound of wind, followed by a muffled curse, and then another curse came, followed by the roar of a pistol shot.

"Billy?" Drew screamed into the phone and picked it up, his face now white. "Alyson?"

"We're . . . all right, Daddy." Billy's voice trembled and was barely audible over a loud roaring. "He just rolled down the window and shot outside."

Only parts of another voice came through. "Roll . . . ing window . . . before we free—"

The sound of wind stopped, and the other voice came in calm and collective. "I believe I have made my point, Sheriff."

Mary realized her hands had balled into fists and were shaking at her side.

"Now, do we have an agreement?"

"What about Alyson?" Drew asked. He was also shaking.

"We keep her but just as far as the county line."

No one in the office believed that would happen.

"I can't let you do that, Baxter. You know I can't. Maybe you release Alyson and . . ." He was having trouble just making that suggestion.

"Oh, no, no, no, Sheriff. I have learned that young, beautiful women make much better bargaining tools than stupid jocks and sons of cops. But don't worry, Sheriff, you can keep the pilot." The man laughed. "Fair enough? He should be happy to stay with you. He never would have made it out of Montana alive with us, you know."

Drew stared at Mary as if seeking help.

"Sheriff," Lyle Baxter said over the speaker, "in a few minutes we will be parked in front of your courthouse. Where you will be waiting for us outside. We'll let you get a good view of your son and his hot little number and make the exchange and be on our way. Or, if no one's out there, waiting and looking peaceful, we will simply keep on driving and leave what's left of your boy somewhere in this cold, wretched, and downright worthless county."

"Listen—"

But the call ended, and John Drew smashed his balled fist into the closest file cabinet, leaving a huge dent and driving the drawer halfway open.

1894

January

CHAPTER 34

The tapping on the door to the sheriff's office had Murdo Maddox jumping out of the chair. In frustration, he kicked at it, sending it sliding a few feet, and moved for the door.

"Hold it!" Napoleon Drew's voice carried an authority that Murdo wasn't used to, and he turned, dropping his hand toward his revolver, but stopping.

The sheriff made a beeline across the room. His pal the faro dealer just sat, staring across the darkening room, his hands cradling a Greener double-barrel.

"That's . . ." Murdo began.

"Not her knock." Napoleon was at the door now, and he slowly pulled the Remington out of the holster. The thumb pulled back the hammer slowly as well, and he coughed and cleared his throat to hide the metallic clicks as the .44 came to full cock.

"Yeah."

"Sheriff?" came a man's voice from the other side of the door.

"Yeah."

"I gots a message fer ya." He waited and, hearing no

reply, added, "It's from that sweet little widder woman. You know, who was stayin' with yer neighbor."

Murdo started to pull his own revolver.

"You want to hear this message or donchya?"

The sheriff glanced at Murdo, then quickly turned toward Seabrook and gave him a nod. Gripping the Greener, the gambler rose and moved toward the door that led to the jails. He leaned the shotgun on the wall, removed the wooden bar, put it on the floor, and opened the door. Then he picked up the shotgun, thumbed back both barrels, and shouldered the weapon, aiming the twelve-gauge at Bo Meacham.

"All the way inside, Miles," Napoleon whispered, and the gambler disappeared into the dark walkway between the cells.

"Speak your piece," Napoleon said as he moved closer to the door.

A few curses sounded from outside. "For God's sake, Sheriff, it's bitter cold out here, and the snow's comin' down again. Comin' down hard. I got a message. And I got bona fides to boot. This won't take more'n a minute. So canchya open that door?"

Napoleon looked at the rancher, who shrugged.

"If I see anything I don't like," Napoleon spoke to the door, "or if I hear a hammer cocking, or if I even sneeze, your boss will be catching two barrels of buckshot, and while we might be dead, you, if you aren't killed, will be scraping your boss off the wall for a long, long time till you've got enough of him to bury."

"Fair 'nough. But I'm freezin' my . . ."

Murdo stepped forward, lowering the hammer of his revolver, which he holstered, and removed the wooden bar. Once that was on the floor, he filled his right hand with the pistol and stepped softly to the side. When the sheriff opened the door, Murdo would be hidden behind it, out of view, while Murdo could look through the crack to see if anybody was with the messenger.

It was snowing. Hard. And the sun was starting to dip behind the trees. The man was hard to see, wrapped as he was in the skins of various animals, some pelts wrapped around his boots from the toes to the shins. His chaps were woolies, and his coat sheepskin. A woolen scarf pulled the brim of his hat over his ears and then wrapped around his throat like a muffler. A bandanna was pulled up over his mouth and nose, and Napoleon could make out ice crystals around the cloth over his mouth and nose.

"Here be my bona fides," the man said. His hand dipped into the sheepskin's pocket, and Napoleon let him see the Remington's barrel, which was close enough to blow a mighty big hole in his front and a bigger one when the bullet exited through his back.

"It ain't nothin' but a purty girl's purty hair."

And he held out a lock that Napoleon knew had been cut from Jeannie Ashton.

His eyes moved up to lock on what little he could see of the outlaw's face.

"Oliver says he'll swap her fer Bo." He laughed, and then his teeth chattered, and he cleared his throat and stamped both feet to keep the blood from freezing. "At the liv'ry." He held out the lock, and when Napoleon made no move to take it, his fingers rose, and the wind took Jeannie's hair away.

"Frenchie's givin' ya ten minutes. If he can't see ya walkin' down the street by then, he's gonna do some mighty unpleasant things to that real purty widder wom'n." The face was mostly hidden, but Napoleon knew the man was smiling beneath all that winter protection.

Napoleon stalled. "I'll need more than ten minutes."

"Take as much time as ya needs, Sheriff." The man laughed again. "But fer ever' minute after 'em ten is up, Frenchie says, the uglier that purty gal is gonna get." He backed away from the cabin. "An' then we start burnin' this town till it's ashes an' corpses—just like we done at Fletcher City.

"Ten minutes. An' we'd better be seein' you, Bo, an' that saloon feller who's been actin' as yer depitty."

Bloody Bill Drew would have shot the louse when he was walking away, but Napoleon just shut the door.

"Miles," he called out, then turned to Murdo. "You hear?" he whispered.

Murdo just nodded.

Miles stepped out of the room of jails and closed the door, but did not return the bar.

"He doesn't know I'm here," Murdo said.

Napoleon nodded.

"What did he say?" Seabrook asked.

Napoleon ran his hand over his stubbled face, then answered Seabrook quickly and turned to Murdo.

"I reckon," he said, "you're gonna have to be Bo Meacham."

The rancher nodded. "We're thinking alike."

Which his father would have hated to hear any Maddox say to a Drew.

There weren't as many in the Meacham gang as there had been. In early 1880s, when Ben Meacham and his brother had formed the gang, the numbers ran in the high teens to low twenties, though most of the newspapers upped those numbers to the forties and fifties. Well, Napoleon thought, they had done enough damage, stolen enough cattle, horses, and payrolls, and killed, maimed, and terrified enough citizens for forty or fifty men. But over the years, as more people settled in western Montana, the gang had lost several to vigilantes and regular lawmen. A few likely got their fill of the life of an outlaw and turned peaceful—in some place far away from Montana.

But Meacham had a handful of men left.

Six minutes had passed when Napoleon Drew stepped out onto the street. It had taken about three minutes to enter Bo Meacham's cell, knock him out, gag him, and leave him on the cold floor with his ankles shackled and his hands cuffed behind his back.

Snow stung his face as he stared down the street, though he couldn't see clearly any farther than the Swede's place. But he did make out a man standing on the corner, and when Miles Seabrook came out of the cabin with Murdo Maddox hunched over and covered with a buffalo robe, the man stepped away from the saloon and waved his hat over his head, signaling the men at O'Boyle's livery.

Maddox walked to the street, turned, and started toward the stable.

"Hold it, Meacham!" Napoleon bellowed, and he brought the Winchester to his shoulder. "You walk when I tell you to walk."

"And stop," Seabrook said as he came to Napoleon's side. "When we say stop."

Murdo remained still. Snow stuck to the robe. It stung

the faces of Napoleon and the gambler, who slowly pulled their bandannas up over mouths and noses.

"You reckon that thespian stuff was necessary?" Seabrook asked in a voice just loud enough for Napoleon to hear. "The way the wind's howling, I doubt if anyone heard a word we said."

Napoleon answered with a shrug. "Saw an opera once in Helena. Couldn't tell you what anyone said or sung. But I figured out the story all right." He hooked a thumb behind him. "And they are sure to have a couple of men behind us—don't look. We'll have the advantage. The snow will be blowing in their faces, but you might be able to see them if they get close enough." He nodded at the shotgun. "Make your shots count."

"I always do," the gambler whispered. "What about us? The snow's blowing in our faces."

The lawman nodded. "Yeah. So they'll have that advantage over us. Let's go."

Buildings, such as they were, on the lots blocked some of the snow, but out in the street, there was no obstruction. Napoleon walked slowly, listening, wiping the snow away with his left hand, keeping his right on the Winchester, his finger and thumb pressing and pulling, keeping the hammer moving up and down. The last thing he would need was the hammer locking up, frozen, in a gunfight.

Murdo moved, stumbling, and Napoleon knew that wasn't acting on the rancher's part. The buffalo robe weighed twenty-eight pounds, and the snow that quickly covered the dark skin added to that.

They passed the Swede's saloon—the man who had been stationed there was walking ahead, glancing over his shoulder. Another man came out of a hiding place on the left, and he, too, walked in front of them. Next, the three Cutthroat County men passed the next street, where Sissy White's boarding house was. Napoleon brushed the show out of his face, still working the hammer and trigger. Every breath burned his throat and chilled his insides. The wind whistled through the trees, sounding like a steer moaning.

Seventy yards and they would be at the livery. The two men at the point stopped, turned, and moved a few paces to their right. Three figures emerged from the open doorway to the livery. Napoleon looked into the loft. He couldn't see anyone up there, but the door was open, and Finnian O'Boyle was too much a miser to let the hay up there rot from getting wet with snow.

That would be about right, Napoleon thought. Two men in the loft. Two out front. Two standing in the livery. Two, maybe three, walking behind the Basin Creek lawmen. Frenchie would wait till the last minute. Maybe with one more man. Then they would bring Jeannie out.

Ten men. Twelve at the most.

"That's far enough, Meacham!" Napoleon bellowed. The two men who had been around Swede's place were about ten feet in front of them, snow whipping their faces, the wind turning the brims of their hats flat against the icy crowns.

Murdo stopped.

"Let's see the woman, Frenchie!" Napoleon yelled.

A fat man in a Hudson's Bay coat came out of the livery, holding the end of a rope in a gloved left hand, a revolver in his right, and pulled Jeannie Ashton out of the barn. She was wearing just a dress. No hat. No scarf.

No coat. She looked all right, but she wouldn't be if she didn't get out of this weather in a hurry.

The man stopped a few yards behind the two men at the corners.

"Send Bo first," the man cried out. "We'll let the woman go when Bo's even with me."

Murdo took a couple of steps, but stopped when Napoleon called out Meacham's name.

"You go when I tell you to go," Napoleon said. "Or you won't go anywhere else, but straight to the devil."

"Frenchie!" Napoleon laughed. "Bo isn't in the same class as his pa, but he sure has more guts than you. Neither Ben Meacham nor Bo would hide in a livery while their men stayed out in the open. There's just two of us. Come on out and show your face, you gutless little coward."

That worked.

A slim figure in woolen pants, a sheepskin coat, and a beaver fur hat that covered his head and ears came through the opening. He held a repeating rifle, too, and he walked through the snow until he stood next to Jeannie.

"Let her go," Napoleon said.

"Let me see Bo," the Frenchman said.

"Go see your lieutenant, Meacham," Napoleon said. "But stop if I tell you to."

Murdo began walking slowly.

"Shun that robe, Bo!" Frenchie yelled and raised his revolver halfway.

"I'll shed it when I'm out of this weather," Murdo called out, lowering his voice into what sounded like a hacking cough from the gravelly sounding killer.

One of the men laughed. Murdo must have made a

passable impression. But Frenchie brought the gun up level.

"Let me see you, Bo!" he yelled. "I . . ."

He stopped and looked beyond Napoleon.

"Holy . . ." one of the men on the left said.

By then, Napoleon caught a glimpse of movement to the north. More men. A lot of them. Had he under-estimated the size of this band of outlaws?

Miles Seabrook took a quick look behind him, then turned back, started to say something, but suddenly spun back around.

"My God!" he yelled.

A finger pointed from one of the mob moving toward the livery.

"By grab, they're burnin' down the sheriff's office!"

That voice. Napoleon blinked. That wasn't one of the Meacham gang. That was the voice of Judge Van Gaskin.

Seabrook had spun back around.

"They're trying to turn Basin Creek into another Fletcher City!" That sounded like Finnian O'Boyle.

"Howell!" Frenchie bellowed. "Not yet you . . ."

A shot rang out. Frenchie dropped to a knee and raised his revolver.

"Start the ball," someone yelled.

But the ball had already started.

CHAPTER 35

Murdo Maddox used the shotgun to raise the buffalo skin over his head. He saw the Frenchman bringing a gun around, then ducking as a shot took his hat off his head. Then he found Jeannie, dropping to her knees in the snow. He tried to yell at her to drop all the way to the ground, but wasn't sure she heard him—wasn't even certain he had managed to say anything. Somehow, he flung the heavy robe. Jeannie was raising her head when part of the skin knocked her face down into the white street.

The Frenchman turned, thumbing back his pistol, dropping to a knee, and swinging his revolver away from Jeannie and at Murdo. The rancher saw bellowing flame and smoke from the revolver. Murdo stood just four feet from the gunman, but the bullet missed.

Murdo touched one of the triggers. He didn't miss. But he did not hit Frenchie, either.

One of the gunmen happened to step right into the blast of buckshot, catching the full load into his side, and he was shoveled against the outlaw gang leader, knocking him down next to Jeannie, who struggled to toss the heavy hide off her upper body.

There was a shadow—at least it looked like a shadow, though there was no sun to cast one. Murdo turned, saw a man fumbling with a Colt but having trouble pushing a heavy gloved finger into the trigger guard. Then his face burst into crimson and bone, and down he went, though Murdo had not fired the last barrel of the Greener. He looked back, saw Frenchie coming up to a knee.

Then down went the killer, a bullet smashing into him plumb center and another ripping a gash across his throat. He dropped his weapon and fell forward into a crimson lake that melted some of the snow before it froze.

Murdo turned, but his boot slipped, and he fell to the ground. A bullet singed his hair as he dropped. He saw smoke and giant flames from the sheriff's office. He saw another man aiming a gun at him. The man dropped to both knees, and his left hand went to clasp the gushing hole in his thigh, but his right kept the pistol.

This time Murdo hit this target, and the man was catapulted back, lying spread-eagled in red-splotched snow.

Dropping the empty twelve-gauge, Murdo came up and palmed his revolver. He tried to find a target, but there was none. Napoleon Drew had dropped one man, who was dragging himself toward the livery. But the sheriff grabbed the man by the back of his vest, jerked him halfway up, and slammed the barrel of his Remington into the man's skull. Then he let him fall in the snow next to Jeannie.

Jeannie.

Murdo glanced around. Two men held their hands straight up and were quickly surrounded by a score of men, including O'Boyle and Judge Van Gaskin. He looked down the street and saw men chasing one man who was galloping his horse toward the main road. They would never catch him, but Murdo would hate to be that fellow, riding a horse that hard in this weather, heading into the oblivion of a Montana winter.

More townsmen ran toward the burning sheriff's office.

"Get the fire engine!" someone yelled.

But what good would that do? All the water was frozen.

Women joined the men at the sheriff's cabin, scooping up handfuls of snow and tossing them into the rabid flames.

"Where's Bo?" said one of the outlaws, a kid who didn't look old enough to be riding with these cutthroats. "Where's Bo?"

Miles Seabrook pointed the barrel of one of his pistols at the jail.

"There. You boys burned your boss alive."

"Oh," the kid said, and he dropped to his knees, burying his head in his hands. "Oh my God. Oh my God. Oh my God." He started sobbing. Bawling over a no-good murdering fiend. Or maybe he was crying because he thought he might be tossed into the fire, too. Or strung up and left to twist in the wind and snow.

Murdo looked at the punk, thinking, *And ten years ago, if Bloody Bill Drew were still ramrodding the law in this country, you likely would be dead.*

At least this way, the boy would stand trial.

"Forget the jail!" Judge Van Gaskin was walking down

the street, a single-shot rifle in his left hand. "Throw snow on the roofs of the nearby buildings!"

"Murdo."

He turned to find Jeannie on the buffalo robe, shivering. Dropping his revolver in the snow, Murdo rushed to her, pulled her up, and wrapped his arms around her.

"Get that robe," he shouted, and Finnian O'Boyle picked it up.

"No." Jeannie shook her head. "I don't want that stinking thing on me. It weighs a ton. Just . . ." She placed her head against his chest. "Just hold me, Murdo. Just hold me tight."

"Come on." He would take her to the seamstress's cabin, but he stopped when he had gone no more than twenty yards.

It was one of his riders. Ben Penny. Who should have been at the Circle M. He had his horse at a gallop and didn't even seem to notice the dead men, the wounded, the armed citizens of the town, or even the inferno that had been the sheriff's office and jail.

"Mr. Maddox! Mr. Maddox!" People scattered out of the rider's path, and he jerked hard on the reins and pulled his roan into a sliding stop, then dismounted, still holding the reins and not even slipping on the icy blood or wet snow.

He pointed. "It's that old injun, Mr. Maddox. Your grandpa or whatever. You know, the Blackfoot." He pointed down the street, and Murdo saw a wagon. He couldn't make out the driver, but his hired man said, "Deke Weems is bringin' him in. He was practically froze when I found him. The injun. Not Deke."

Hearing that, the sheriff ran down the street, passing

his burning office without a glance, tripping and sliding his way toward the wagon.

Murdo turned, stared at Jeannie.

"I'm coming with you," she said, and he put his arm around her, and they walked as fast as they could through the carnage, the dead, the wounded, the good men and bad, and the mounds of snow.

Karl Scovil was the closest thing Basin Creek had to a doctor. Usually, he cut men's hair or gave them a shave. The old Indian, Napoleon Drew's grandfather—and Murdo Maddox's, too—lay in the fancy chair Scovil had had shipped in from St. Louis. Keme was covered with blankets. His teeth chattered.

"How is he?" Jeannie Ashton asked.

"He's alive." Scovil had been rubbing whiskey all over Keme's body, but now he took a pull from a new bottle for himself. Then he lifted the old Blackfoot's head and let some whiskey trickle into the Indian's throat.

Keme coughed and resisted when the barber brought the bottle to the old man's mouth again, but he was too weak, and more rye went down. "It's good for you, chief," Scovil said. "It'll warm you up."

The Indian mumbled something, and his teeth chattered. "I need . . . my . . . grandsons," he whispered.

Scovil looked at Napoleon Drew. He shook his head. "He said he walked all the way from the reservation."

Napoleon nodded.

"He said his people are starving. They need food. He came for help."

"Help!" someone standing on the boardwalk yelled. "Why would we help a bunch of red savages?"

Napoleon's brow furrowed, and his fingers tightened into a fist.

"He's new to Cutthroat County," Judge Van Gaskin whispered. "Don't pay Willie no mind, Sheriff."

The old man's eyes closed, and the barber went to check on him. He nodded at Napoleon, then at Murdo Maddox, and said, "He's sleeping. That's a good thing. He needs lots and lots of sleep."

Napoleon let out a heavy sigh. "I don't know how we can get any help to that village. In this weather."

"I do." Murdo Maddox stepped forward. He turned around and looked at the men, and a few women, who had crowded into the barbershop. "I have three hundred Hereford on Carlton Boone's spread. Being pushed to the Circle M." Then he stared at Napoleon. "I reckon we'll be driving those cattle all the way to the reservation."

"In this storm!" the Swede yelled. "You'll be deader than Bo Meacham if you try that. You, your horses, your men, and all those cattle."

"Maybe," Napoleon said. "But we owe him that much." He nodded at the sleeping Blackfoot elder. "We all do."

1846

▲

OCTOBER

CHAPTER 36

Though wrapped in a bearskin, Keme still shivered as the wind blew ice and snow across the hills. He waited until Cody Drew collapsed the glass that could see far, then turned and slogged his way through deep snow to where Keme remained mounted on his black-and-white pinto, holding the hackamore to Cody's blue roan.

"I cannot tell what the fool is doing," Cody spoke in the language of the Blackfoot-Speaking Real People, "but he will be dead soon. One less white man to bother our people."

Keme nodded, but he said, "Maybe," and this he spoke in English.

Cody stared at the warrior.

"You want to go down and help that crazy white man?"

The Blackfoot stared down at Cody. "Why would he be riding north? In this weather?" He nodded south. "When he is on the trail that would have led him right through—"

"Sacagawea Pasture," Cody said in English. He spat out the words like he would bad liquor. His father, dead

now for two winters, had always called that country
"Linda's Land."

"It is what they call it. The pale eyes."

Pale eyes. Cody Drew's eyes were pale, too, but he
no longer considered himself white. He was Blackfoot.
And those men, and a few women, who had listened to
the lies of the trader, they were fools. They had believed
that wretched white man who had lured those following
what pale eyes called the Oregon Trail to this country,
far north of that trail. He had promised them a Garden
of Eden. Well, the garden would become their graveyard. Maybe Ezekiel Maddox would die, too. That
would please Cody Drew. After all, Cody blamed
Maddox for the death of Cody's father, Ben Franklin
Drew, who had partnered with Ezekiel's father for many
years.

Their fathers had been white men back in the states.
But they had traveled up the river with two government
men named Lewis and Clark. And this wonderful country had captured their hearts and souls. They had stayed
here, befriending most of the red-skinned tribes. Eventually, they had even made friends among the Blackfoot, after the diseases they brought with them killed so
many of the Siksikaitsitapi that the songs of mourning
became as common as the screeches of eagles and the
caws of the ravens.

Keme straightened on his pony, keeping his eyes on
the traveler below, and Cody turned. The man had fallen
off his horse, and the horse had stopped and turned
around but stayed near the white man.

"Ha!" Cody laughed, but he frowned when Keme
kicked his horse into a walk and began going down
the hill.

"His scalp is not worth taking!" Cody cried out.

"I am not taking it," Keme said.

Cody frowned. He kicked at a rock that rose from the snow. His horse snorted, and Cody muttered a pale-eye curse, mounted the roan, and trotted after the tall Blackfoot.

No one was following the pale eye. Cody was sure of that. Still, he drew the knife from the buckskin sheath and kicked his horse ahead of Keme. The horse that had brought the white man to this place began following its hoofprints back south.

That horse, Keme thought, *is the only one showing any brains.*

He pulled the roan to a stop and frowned when he twisted around to see Keme pushing his horse after the fallen white man's. Cody stopped the curse that was coming up his throat and ground his teeth as Keme trotted up and caught the reins in one hand and turned around, bringing the pale eye's horse with him.

The white man breathed, though he wouldn't for long if he stayed in the snow, and Cody knew that Keme would want to see the man's face. So he knelt and grabbed the man's shoulder and hip and rolled him over.

A curse he had not said in a year came like a breath of air, and he rose, reaching instinctively for the knife, but not drawing it. The man was unconscious. He was pale. And thin. So thin. Cody did not remember ever seeing him that puny and sickly. Usually, he was red-faced from drinking too much liquor in his trading post and too fat from all the profits he made out of cheating the Blackfoot and other tribes that traded at his post. He also cheated other pale eyes.

Cody thought about spitting in the man's face, but the

wind would freeze that and carry it away before it even struck this man, Cody's enemy.

By then, Keme was mounted and staring down at the trader.

"That is the man called Ezekiel Maddox."

"Zeke," Cody said deliberately, recalling how Maddox despised being called that.

"He is not dead," Keme said.

"Not yet," Cody said.

As if hearing those words, the man's eyes fluttered and stared. He drew in a ragged breath at the sight of Keme towering above him, but then the eyes moved and eventually focused on Cody.

His mouth opened and formed a word, but Cody could not hear any voice, just a whisper that sounded like "You . . ."

He would be so easy to kill. But his scalp would not be worth taking.

Keme leaned down to get a better look at Ezekiel Maddox.

"Why do you travel from your village? In the Hunter's Moon." Though this Hunter's Moon felt like the Snow Moon.

"They're . . ." His voice was like the last groan a man makes before his spirit leaves the body. ". . . starvin' . . ."

But to Cody's regret, the man did not die.

Keme nodded.

Cody spoke. "We told you this would be a hard winter. We told you that it would come early." He waved his arm around the white world. "And it did. We told you to stock yourself with food to last you six moons. We told you everything you needed to know.

But . . ." He shook his head. ". . . Like all pale eyes, you heard nothing."

He looked up at Keme.

"Everything I said," Cody whispered, "is true."

Keme nodded, but his eyes bore into Cody, who flinched, choking back the pale-eyes curse he wanted to fling into the tall Blackfoot's face. "They brought this upon themselves." He pointed northwest. "Our own village will have a hard winter, and we are prepared."

Keme nodded again.

"Why do you want to help these fools? They take and take and take. That is all they know how to do." He tapped his chest. "I know this. In my heart. I have always known this. I know this because once . . . I was one of them. But now I am . . ."

He could not reach that tall fool. Bowing his head, Cody waited until he could speak without Keme seeing the tears in his eyes.

"Why should we help them?" he asked.

Keme did not answer. He would not answer. Until Cody raised his head and their eyes met and held.

"One day," Keme said, "they will help us when we need help."

Cody shook his head. "They will never help us, Keme. They will only rub us out. That is all they know how to do."

"But when we are rubbed out," Keme said as he slipped off the back of his horse and knelt over the wretched white man. "We will still have our honor."

1894

⛰

JANUARY

CHAPTER 37

Jeannie drove a covered wagon, snow stinging what little of her face wasn't covered with winter clothing. The wind wailed. A white Hades stretched out before her.

We'll never make it, she thought.

Yet she raised the whip and lashed out as best she could in the wind, the blizzard, the nightmare.

Three hundred cattle were behind her, and perhaps half the town of Basin Creek. She couldn't hear the cattle or the horses, the cowboys and townsmen who had made themselves into cowboys. She couldn't even hear the wheels of the wagon turning or the noise of the harnesses and traces.

Worst, she could hardly see the trail before her.

Then she gasped as a gray figure appeared out of nowhere, just to her left, and she pulled hard on the leather lines and reached for the brake.

The rider stopped his horse.

"Who are you?" she yelled.

She couldn't make out his face.

"Who are you?"

The well-covered hands moved the reins, and the horse came closer.

"Who are you?"

He pulled the scarves and wrappings off his face.

"We're here to help!"

It was Abe Killone, a rancher north of Basin Creek. He pulled the wrappings back over his face. He might have said something, but she couldn't understand. Twisting in the saddle, he waved. No one could see. Not in this storm. Another rider came close, and Killone turned to talk to him, mostly using his gloved hands. The rider rode on, and again Killone pulled down the wrappings and yelled.

"That's Buck." She barely heard that. "He'll spell you." Then the horse took the rider past the covered wagon.

She gasped at another sound and looked through the opening in the canvas. A man was crawling over the kegs and boxes and bags and coats and blankets—hand-me-downs from just about every family in Basin Creek and food from their cellars and the stores, whatever they had that they could spare.

The figure cursed, apologized, and then looked from between the muffler around his face and the hat pulled down low.

"Call me Buck, ma'am." He climbed through the opening and onto the bench, brushing away what snow and ice he could. He reached over and took the leather, which was almost frozen stiff, from her hands.

"Giddyap," he said, and reached over to take the whip.

* * *

"How did you know?" Jeannie managed to say without cracking her teeth into myriad pieces. They had probably traveled a mile before she thought to speak.

"Know what most everyone in Basin Creek was doing?" she said. "To bring whatever we could to those poor Blackfoot men, women, and children?"

"We didn't know exactly," Buck said. "Line rider. Chuckie Comfort. He see'd some Indian walkin' like a loco. Rode to the Boss Abe's house. I thought Chuckie's brain had froze, that he was halu . . . haluci . . . seein' things. Boss Abe cussed him up good for lettin' anyone, even an Indian, freeze to death in this storm. So Abe and me, we come a-lookin'. Rode into Sheriff Drew and Maddox. They told us what was a-happenin', and Boss Abe says we'd be helpin'. Comfort was with us—that's what he calls hisself, ma'am, Chuckie Comfort, ain't no tellin' what his real handle is, but Buck's my name. Writ down in the Bible. Buck Callahan."

"It's a pleasure to know you, Mr. Callahan."

His head bobbed. "Likewise." He cleared his throat and went back to his story.

"Boss sent Chuckie back to the ranch. He'll be bringin' ever'thing we can spare from the cookshack and any of the bedrolls we don't need no more. In a wagon with a few other boys."

"My," Jeannie said, shaking her head. "My, oh, my."

She chanced a look behind her, leaning over and realizing this was a much better view than staring into a blizzard.

She could see the Herefords, which were easy to spot at this time of day, in this world of white. Beside them were other wagons. She shook her head.

Judge Gaskin drove one of them. And that old

stagecoach from a line that went belly-up way back in '89. Finnian O'Boyle was driving that one, and inside was the preacher and the priest and Lois DeForrest, who had gathered up all her heavy woolens and flannels.

And there were more. These people had traveled south first, joining up with the Circle M hires—including Eugene Drew—who had ridden south to Carlton Boone's spread, gathered the herd, and started north.

Percy Willingham, clerk at the hotel, drove a wagon with Doris Caffey, who had cleaned out as much food as she could spare from her restaurant. Even Sarah Doolittle, that shameless harlot, and her butler were in a wagon bringing food and supplies to some starving Indians.

"I still ain't got no notion as to what we're doin'. Ain't this the army's job, ma'am, to keep them Blackfoot from freezin' and starvin'? Yet here we be, freezin' our a— Our . . . our fingers and noses off," Buck Callahan continued. "Don't make no sense to me, ma'am, but I ride for the brand."

He flicked the leather lines and shot a glance at Jeannie, who, though the cowboy couldn't see through all the protection she had over her face, smiled a bright, summery smile.

"You know why this is so confounded important to all these folks?" the cowboy asked.

She did. Though she had just heard the stories. Most of the original settlers who thought they could farm this country had given up and skedaddled by 1850. Sacagawea Pasture never became a town. She would have to ask Murdo whatever happened to Ezekiel Maddox, but she suspected that the near disaster of the winter of 1846 and 1847 had broken him.

That first winter had been too much for everyone at that failed settlement. She shook her head, wondering what those survivors would have thought of this winter storm of 1894. But some of the people had stayed. And, eventually, Basin Creek grew up into what it was, which wasn't much to most people but a paradise to many, today.

"We're repaying a debt, Buck," she said. "Repaying a debt." Her smile widened. "One that was long overdue."

Jeannie Ashton found Sissy at the campfire, alone, passing an empty coffee cup from one hand to another. She knelt on the other side of the warm fire and looked at her, but minutes passed before Sissy realized she had company.

"Oh . . ." The cup stayed in one hand now. "How long have you been here?"

Shrugging, Jeannie answered, "Not long."

Their eyes held.

"This is a long way from Texas, you know."

It took a long while before Sissy shrugged. The cup moved to her right hand. She stared into the flames. "I didn't want him to find me."

"Meacham?" Jeannie asked.

Sissy's head bobbed.

Jeannie could have scolded her for taking Eugene along as a cook's louse—both of them could have frozen to death—but she realized the woman was troubled. So she stayed where she was, adding a log to the fire, and waited.

"He swore he would kill me," Sissy said, but maybe not to Jeannie. "And he would have." Her eyes looked up now, reflecting the hungry yellow flames. "So I did what I always did. I ran away. Just like in Fletcher City."

"It's all right," Jeannie whispered. "He can't hurt you anymore."

"I guess so. He can't hurt anybody anymore, can he?"

"No." She pushed herself to her feet. "If you ever feel the need to talk, you know where I am." Though Jeannie had a pretty good idea. Lover? Brother? Husband? It didn't matter. She wasn't one to pry, and right then, Sissy wasn't in any mood to relive horror stories to anyone. Jeannie was walking away when she heard Sissy's voice again.

Turning, she saw the woman still staring at the fire— maybe thinking about Bo Meacham burning to death in the Basin Creek jail. Maybe reliving the tragedy at Fletcher City.

"You're a good friend, Jeannie," Sissy said.

"You know where I live," Jeannie said. "And you're welcome any time."

The woman's face changed. She smiled brightly. "I know where you live now," she said, almost sounding like the Sissy White Jeannie had known for several years. Then she was looking past her. "And I might know where you'll be living sometime soon." Then the face became solemn, and she was back wherever her mind took her, staring at the crackling fire.

When Jeannie turned, she had to catch her breath. She knew what Sissy had meant.

Murdo Maddox was walking toward her.

* * *

On the second night, Napoleon Drew took a bowl of chili that Jeannie Ashton served him and the coffee poured by Lois DeForrest, and turned from the cook fire to find another fire.

He stopped and looked down, waiting for the bundled-up human to turn and look up.

"Join you?" Napoleon asked.

"Sure, Pa." Eugene slid over, away from the fire.

"Eugene."

The boy looked up.

"You can sit closest to the fire."

"No, Pa. I been saving that spot for you. Ground's good and warm now."

"Thank you," he whispered, then squatted.

The coffee was better than anything he could make, and he had to credit the cook for the Circle M. Nebuchadnezzar was how he introduced himself, but most of the cowpunchers called him Nebraska Jones. Whatever handle he went by, he served up hot, filling, and ice-thawing grub.

"You mad at me, Pa?"

Napoleon lowered the steaming cup.

"Well." He shook his head. "Next time, just let me know. Face-to-face. What you're planning. Or what you want to do. You're too old for a spanking."

"No, I ain't. Corey Hill got spanked by his pappy two weeks ago, and he's three years older than me."

Napoleon nodded. "Well, maybe you're too big for a spanking."

"Corey's bigger'n me, too."

He sighed, lowered the mug, and looked at his oldest son. "Well, come to me first, next time. Don't run off. Don't . . ."

Don't run away like I did. Join the cavalry. Find out that your pa was dead in a letter. Come back north to this piece of paradise that often turned into hell. Or maybe it was a hell that every once in a while showed the promise of paradise. For some reason, this country drew a man to it—especially a Drew—and wouldn't, couldn't, let him go. Maybe that's why old Benjamin Franklin Drew came back all those years ago.

"I didn't know it was going to be this cold, Pa."

He handed the cup of coffee to his son. "This will warm you up, Eugene."

But it wouldn't last. He stared up at the night sky. Not a star to be seen. No moon. Nothing. A white world surrounded them, with snow two feet deep in most places. Four wagons were filled with grain and hay, but it was sixty-five miles to the Blackfoot reservation. And this day, by their best guess, they had traveled five.

If the weather didn't break, they'd have to turn back. They probably should have turned back already. Keme was in the back of one of those wagons, too sick, too old, to do anything but sing prayers to the gods that looked after the Blackfoot-Speaking Real People and the land they now shared with white men.

And if they turned back, gave up—with good reason— Keme would die.

"You ain't mad at me?" the boy begged.

Napoleon stared at the chili, then reached down and took his cup from the boy's hand. "If you're not gonna drink that, don't let it go cold." He took the cup and drained it, then set it near the fire.

"I'm not mad at you, Eugene," he said, and put his hand on the boy's shoulder. "Fact is, I'm right proud of you."

Which was something Napoleon's father had never told him.

He focused on eating. All his years in this country, he knew he had to eat, even if he had no appetite, even if the wind and ice turned the food cold quickly. So he ate, not tasting the food, not enjoying anything—even the coffee. Staring at the flames, thinking of his children, and praying—yes, praying—for Keme to live, he lost track of time.

"Pa."

Eugene's voice was just a whisper.

"Yeah, son?"

A piece of wood in the fire popped, sending sparks up like the fireworks he had seen once on the Fourth of July. He couldn't even remember where that had been.

"I think it has stopped snowing."

He remembered those songs of mourning. Back when his father had sent him away from the ranch, the empire, the old man was building. "Time you learnt somethin' that'll help you—somethin' better'n 'em books your ma thinks'll make a man out of you."

Three days later, Keme had shown up. How he knew, Murdo Maddox never figured out. Had the old Blackfoot and Murdo's father conspired? Or had Keme, as had often been the case, just known where and when he was needed. Or maybe it was just coincidence. A year or two earlier, Napoleon Drew had arrived in the Blackfoot village. He had stayed with them for a year. Murdo figured he could take it for three weeks, maybe.

But he had not expected to hear a song of mourning for his grandmother. He stood outside the lodge and watched the medicine man as Keme brought an Appaloosa stud, from the dam of a stallion stolen from the Nez Perce, and handed the hackamore to the old man, who nodded, grunted some words that Murdo had forgotten, and led the horse away.

Napoleon remembered glaring at the holy man and then looking up at Keme with disgust.

"You are troubled?" Keme had asked.

"He didn't keep your wife alive. Why pay him a horse?"

"Because I promised him a horse if he would help. He helped. It is not his fault that she is no longer with us."

He remembered Keme tearing down the lodge and burning it so the ghost could not haunt this place of death. And the women slashing their legs and arms, mourning for Keme's wife—Murdo's grandmother, whom he had not seen since he had been sent to the Blackfoot village as a child. At that time, Napoleon Drew had been with him. The women had cut off their braids, as had Keme. Murdo had thought they would make him cut his own hair or carve his arms and thighs with those knives. But they hadn't.

Now he looked at the coffins the undertaker had brought. In the old days, the dead were wrapped in robe or blanket and placed in a tree. Now they carried the pine boxes up to a hill, covering them with stones as best as they could. He remembered Keme telling him, but a few years earlier, "You trap the spirit when you cover him with Mother Earth."

But on that day, when Murdo's grandmother had died, she was wrapped up and put in a tree. Later, when her spirit began the journey to the Sand Hills, the bones were buried.

Murdo frowned when he saw the riders, coming in in their winter blue coats. He walked away from the lodge, leaving Keme with his people, his dead wife, and did not stop until he joined Napoleon Drew, Doc Scovil, and Judge Van Gaskin, the welcoming party for the soldiers in charge of looking after the Blackfoot people here.

The captain raised his right hand, and the handful of soldiers halted behind him. He looked at the sheriff, the barber/doctor, and the judge, and then spotted Murdo, who walked and stood next to Van Gaskin, away from the sheriff.

"Mr. Maddox," the captain said, "I heard you brought a bunch of your cattle up here."

"I did." He coughed, cleared his throat, and corrected himself. "*We* did."

"My compliments, Mr. Maddox. That was some trip. We haven't had a snow like that in many a year. That's what the old-timers tell me, anyhow."

Murdo pointed at the hill. "Lot of those old-timers are gone."

The captain turned, looked up the hill, and swallowed. Then he looked back.

"Shame. Downright tragedy." He shifted uncomfortably in his saddle. "Well, Mr. Maddox, we've been on short rations all through this storm. Eating mush the last week. When my scout saw those cattle, well, we were hoping your generosity would . . . well . . . I was hoping you'd allow us to cut out some of those cattle."

The captain started to look toward the sheriff, but stopped.

"You'd have to check with Keme, Captain," Murdo said. "Those cattle were delivered to him." He saw the anger in the soldier's eyes. He heard footsteps behind him. This, he thought, could easily turn into another Wounded Knee, even if the soldiers had only rifles and sidearms and numbered just a few.

But that's not why he drew in a deep breath. That's not why he let out a heavy sigh. He figured that Napoleon Drew would be cussing him for a coward and that the young Blackfoot men would drive him out of camp, maybe even kill him.

Yet he pointed up the hill.

"What's left of what made it up from Basin Creek are on the other side, Captain. Cut out fifteen head or so. Make it twenty. That ought to keep your bellies full till your next supply train comes in." It was more than enough for that small detachment.

The soldier's shoulders slumped, and he let out a sigh of relief.

"Send us a bill, sir."

Murdo shook his head. "That's a gift, Captain. From Keme and his people."

He watched them ride.

Judge Van Gaskin spit and kicked snow with his boot. "Those soldiers steal from these poor people, and you give them fifteen, twenty cows. Those soldiers could have helped these Indians, but they didn't even come out to look, to see, to help. You're a rich man, Maddox, but I—"

"I'm a poor man," Murdo said. "And I know it. But I remember what Keme taught me when I was a kid."

He turned and headed back to pay his respects to his grandmother one last time.

But he could hear Van Gaskin swearing. "Poor man . . . That feller's richer than God. What's he mean, what that Indian taught him when he was just a boy?"

It was Napoleon Drew who answered.

"He remembered what I had forgotten. That for these people, wealth isn't measured by horses or gold or even cattle. It's by generosity."

"What do you mean?"

"You've never been to a giveaway ceremony, Judge." The lawman waited a few seconds, then went on. "The richest of the men arrange their teepees in a circle. Then talk about how they got this and that. And then they would all take everything that had won, stolen, bought, and found, and pile them in the center. And let the needy come and get what they needed."

Murdo stopped and turned around. Napoleon Drew was removing his great coat and laying it on the ground. Then he pulled off his gloves and tossed them atop the winter coat. He found his pouch, jingled it—not that it held much—and tossed it down, and finally pulled off the woolen scarf around his neck. Judge Van Gaskin watched as the barber found his coin purse and a hand-kerchief, and tossed them atop the sheriff's coat. Even Van Gaskin, who had been holding a shotgun and as a Southerner who had served under Robert E. Lee himself must have been ready to do battle with the bluecoats again, laid the double-barrel on the pile and added to that his cigar case.

Murdo turned and walked back, pulling off his coat. He had given the Blackfoot roughly two hundred and twenty head of cattle, having lost quite a few on the hard drive north.

But he had more that he could give. More that he would give.

Keme, he realized, had taught him much. The sheriff was tossing his watch onto the pile.

Keme, Murdo knew, had taught both of them so much.

DAY TWO

FRIDAY

CHAPTER 38

"Get on the phone to Will Ambrose," Drew told Mary. "Tell him exactly what's going on, and tell him to keep this off all channels. Those sons of the devil likely have a police scanner with them. I don't know how they plan on getting out of Montana, but they'll have to have another pilot, another plane somewhere. Choteau? Conrad? Shelby? I don't know."

"Why didn't they just fly that plane to Canada?" Mary asked.

Drew shrugged. "Chadwick's loyal. And Jones and Baxter are kin." He was putting on his winter coat and now spoke to Creel. "Run down to Dan's office, let Dempsey know what's going on. Then you two head downstairs, position yourself at the library window. Tell that C.A.N. man at the doorway to get all the way back to the other side of the building. And nobody fires a shot. *Nobody!*"

He reached into his pants pocket and pulled out the keys. "I'll get my SUV started, leave it running. Then run back inside."

Turning to Colter Norris, he swore. "You can probably get out the rear exit and—"

"You'll need me, Sheriff, to get that prisoner out of all 'em chains."

Before Drew could say another word, the old cowboy headed for the door. Drew had to rush after him, but at the door, he stopped and looked at Mary. "When you're done with Will, you and Colter get out of here."

He left before she could make any argument and caught up with Norris at the stairs.

The two rent-a-cops took off up the stairs as soon as Drew told them what was going on, and Colter Norris took the keys and had the first chain off the cell door in a matter of seconds. It took a lot longer to get the chains off Rupert Chadwick, and as soon as he was free, Norris backed away.

Grinning, Chadwick took one of the heavy chains and swung it around.

"What about me?" the pilot bellowed from the other side of the pen. "Rupert. You can't leave me here . . ."

"Chadwick," Drew said, "we have to go now."

The killer, glaring at the Circle M foreman, made no reply to Drew, but turned and walked to the pilot.

"Get the keys," the pilot yelled. "And—"

He screamed. Drew reached for his Glock and had it drawn, but the chain was already coming down, striking the chained pilot hard in the face. Blood sprayed across the cell floor, and then Chadwick swung the chain again, crushing the other side of the dead man's head. He let the chain fall atop the man's body and turned, ignoring the pistol aimed at his chest, and smiled at Colter Norris.

"Be a good boy, cowpoke," he said, "and mop up this mess."

He walked through the open door, cool as anyone Drew had ever seen.

"If you're gonna kill me, Sheriff, now's your chance."

Drew heard and felt the howling wind.

"Start walking," he said, waving the Glock's barrel.

"I might come back one of these days, cowboy," Chadwick said as his walked across the cold floor. "And let you feel chains on your body—but not as briefly as that Red Baron over there got to feel them."

By the time Mary Broadbent got off the phone with Will Ambrose and had run downstairs, John Drew and Rupert Chadwick were walking past the information kiosk and toward Denton Creel, who had taken the place of the C.A.N. man at the door. Creel turned briefly, saw Drew and the murderer, and then looked back.

"I see headlights, John," he said, and stepped out of the doorway. "I think. The Interceptor's running."

Drew hurried toward the library wing, where Elison Dempsey stood shivering. Maybe it was just the poor lighting in the Old Bailey Building and Loan, but the C.A.N. leader looked paler than a ghost.

"I hope it's at eighty-one degrees and the radio is playing classic rock," Rupert Chadwick said calmly. He stopped at the door. "Aren't you going to open it for me, Sheriff?" he asked with a soft laugh.

"Open it before I blow you through it," Drew told him.

The killer laughed and pushed the door open. John Drew followed him into the darkness, where the street lamps barely illuminated the snow.

Mary Broadbent moved fast but quietly toward the

two C.A.N. guards, kept her Glock in the holster, and slid up beside the nearest one.

"That's a M27, isn't it?" she asked.

The holder of the machine gun looked like he was barely old enough to hold a cap pistol, but he grinned broadly at Mary and said, "You know your guns, lady."

"And I know you can't own that weapon, so hand it over."

"Listen . . ." No flirting now. The boy's face reddened.

"Give it to me. Before this Marine takes it from you."

She jerked the machine gun out of his hands, then glared at the man next to him.

"You two. Get around the corner, and stay out of sight."

Then she leaned against the wall and peered through the frosty glass.

The Nissan Frontier slid in the ice, but the driver, Hemingway Jones, managed to stop the skid and eased Billy's truck to a sliding stop on the far side of the street. Billy looked out the window, but he could hardly see anything but white. Snow had banked high against the walls of the courthouse.

"Son of a gun," Lyle Baxter said. "There's our stupid nephew, and I guess that's the sheriff right next to him. That your daddy, pipsqueak?"

Billy sighed. He couldn't make out faces, or even much about the clothes, but the man behind the man in the orange jumpsuit wore a hat just like Billy's father's and had what folks in Cutthroat County called "the Drew Stance."

Like a granite wall.

Lyle Baxter stepped out of the Frontier, slamming the door behind him.

Billy couldn't hear what was being said. The radio was still spitting out news and winter storm reports from Great Falls, and the wind howled like the worst norther in weather history.

The door opened, and Baxter looked at Alyson.

"In or out, Lyle," Hemingway Jones said.

"Shut up." Baxter kept his eyes on Alyson. "The sheriff wants to see what he's trading for." He waved his pistol in her face. "Both of you, step out, take ten steps forward, and stop—or I kill you both." He turned to his partner.

"Shut this thing off. You head over and get the cop SUV. Back it up, so that we're headed out of this Podunk patch of frozen nothing."

The seat was pushed forward, and Billy squeezed out, turned, and helped Alyson out. The wind and cold were like nothing he had ever felt. He took Alyson's hand and squeezed it.

"Recognize these people, Sheriff?" Baxter yelled.

"All right," his father said.

"Hemingway's coming for your SUV. Nobody goes anywhere till he's got it in the street heading out of town."

"Come ahead."

Alyson thought if she didn't get out of this storm in the next ten minutes, she'd be dead. Then she thought that at least she would die in her hometown.

She was shivering, trying not to cry, sludging her way through the deep snow. The SUV backed out, struggling even in four-wheel drive, and stopped. The top lights began flashing, but the siren remained off, and Hemingway Jones must have tapped on the horn. He was having a high time.

"Stupid little . . ." The wind took away most of Baxter's curse.

She and Billy passed the front of Sheriff Drew's Ford. Red, yellow, and blue lights reflected off the snow.

"Stop." Baxter pressed the barrel of his pistol against Alyson's spine. She almost slipped when she stopped.

"Send our nephew over, Sheriff," Baxter ordered.

She saw the man in the jumpsuit step out of the alcove and began bulldozing his way through the snow.

"I'm sending the boy, Sheriff," Baxter said. "As long as nobody does something stupid, maybe we'll all get out of here alive."

The man in the jumpsuit wasn't moving fast. Billy hadn't even started at all. The man kept slipping, and the wind was blowing right at him, just as it kept pushing Billy forward. He had to watch where he put his feet, not wanting to slip on an icy patch, but he kept thinking, *I can't let these murdering maniacs take Alyson out of town.*

"Move, boy!" Baxter turned.

Billy turned, too, staring at the man's face, what little he could see, and then he saw it clearly. Brightly. And heard a strange noise behind him. The killer's eyes widened.

Billy and the killer and even Alyson turned, and all three seemed to be screaming, "What the—"

* * *

George Grimes thought he was ready. He had two pistols beside him and his Winchester in his arms. That's because he had made Ashton Maddox stop the big Freightliner dump truck when they came down the mountain road to the ruins of his Dodge Ram. But he wasn't ready for this as the truck sped past the school-house and Killone Memorial Park and came barreling toward what passed for a Podunk courthouse in this Podunk town.

Grimes felt like a sissy when he heard himself scream-ing, "What the—"

The Freightliner was roaring down Basin Creek's main drag at forty-three miles an hour, and to George Grimes it felt like four hundred miles per hour.

"Hit the brakes!" Grimes roared at Ashton Maddox.

"Move out of the way, honey," Ashton whispered, hands gripping the big wheel, eyes staring into the bedlam.

Grimes could barely make it all out. The dump truck was headed straight for the sheriff's SUV, which was in the middle of the snow-covered street. A boy and a girl were walking slowly, a man holding what had to be a weapon at the back of the girl's head.

Now the man was spinning around, bringing up the pistol, spreading his legs apart.

The police unit began backing up.

"Hold on, Ranger!" Ashton Maddox screamed.

The girl and boy were . . .

"Holy—" Grimes started.

CHAPTER 39

Ashton Maddox would remember it all, when most people could only pick out bits and pieces, for everything happened so fast. But to the Circle M rancher, everything was clear—the big rig's lights were on high beam.

Alyson—just like a Maddox—turned first to see the Freightliner. Then she bolted, grabbing Billy Drew's hands and slogging through the snow, then diving over a drift that had formed between two other parked police rigs—Mary Broadbent's and Denton Creel's, at least as reported in Carl Lorimer's *Basin River Weekly Item* the following Thursday.

A man in a bright orange jumpsuit stopped, turned, then slipped on ice and disappeared in the snow.

The man with the gun in the middle of the street looked one way, then turned toward Alyson and the boy, bringing his pistol toward them as they dived behind the mound of snow.

Grimes recovered and started to roll down the window, gave up, and grabbed one of his revolvers, smashed out the glass, and started firing.

The sheriff's SUV tried to back up, but the rear

wheels slammed into a thick drift, and the Ford just sat there, tires spinning.

Maddox could see the driver working furiously to get out of his seat belt and shoulder harness.

"Holy Mother of God," Mary Broadbent whispered, then rushed through the door with the assault rifle braced against her shoulder. She aimed at the giant truck—a dump truck—but realized quickly that the driver wasn't one of Rupert Chadwick's gang—or one of the stupid Citizens Action Network goons.

She heard a pistol shot and saw Baxter running out of the way, then falling. She took a quick aim and began pressing her finger on the trigger, but quickly took it off.

John Drew came out of nowhere, lowered his shoulder, and crashed into Baxter. Both men disappeared in a snowbank.

The next thing Mary saw was the big dump truck slamming head-on into the sheriff's SUV, driving it back.

She slipped herself, managed to recover, then felt someone knock her aside. She broke her fall with the butt of the machine gun and saw something orange run back into the building.

Mary got up quickly. She could see the brake lights and outline of the dump truck. And what was left of the Ford Interceptor. The following Thursday's newspaper said that the criminal inside was splattered like . . . well, the writer had a rather graphic description for a weekly Montana rag.

Denton Creel was running to assist Drew. A door

swung open in the dump truck. George Grimes, she thought, practically dived out of the front and into snow.

Mary was up, turning, keeping the M27 ready, running into the main area on the ground floor.

John Drew saw the lights, heard the roaring diesel engine, and quickly realized that this was not part of the Chadwick gang's plan.

He found his Glock and leaped into the storm.

Rupert Chadwick screamed. Billy and Alyson were running toward the Old Bailey Building and Loan, diving. Baxter snapped a shot, then he fled and fell. John's SUV backed up.

The dump truck smashed the Interceptor in a shower of sparks and a deafening crunch of metal on metal.

Baxter was pushing himself out of the snow, coming up to his knees, when Drew lowered his shoulder and hit the killer with the full force of his body—like a dump truck, he thought, turning a Ford Interceptor into just a hunk of rubble.

And Rupert Chadwick rushed past Mary and into the old courthouse. Mary went after him.

"Where did he go?" Mary roared once she was in the building.

"Down the stairs!" Elison Dempsey pointed. The man was shaking in his boots. Denton Creel, Glock in his hand, raced past her toward the door. Maybe he hadn't seen Chadwick. Or maybe he was worried about his boss.

Well, Mary was, too, but Rupert Chadwick had to be stopped.

She ran to the stairwell and pressed against the wall, listening and easing down the stairs.

It was freezing outside. But it felt colder as she eased down one step at a time, the Marine machine gun ready, just like she had been trained.

There was a scream below, and she gasped, remembering Colter Norris heading to the ancient jail cells to free Chadwick. Maybe the old cowboy was still down there.

She crept down faster, but kept remembering all her training in the police academy and as a United States Marine.

And for the first time in recent memory, she felt no pain in her head where she had been shot and almost killed. Oh, she didn't need to stick that thing on her finger to know that her heart was racing, but she was calm, breathing steadily.

She came to the last stair.

She put the barrel out, came around, moved toward the stairs.

There was another loud mixture of metal clinging and something crunching.

If that was Rupert Chadwick attacking Colter Norris, she had to move fast. She flipped off the safety and raced into the cell, aimed at the figure standing, saw the body on the floor—and caught a glimpse of another man, still chained, also on the floor of the cell.

Colter Norris looked up. Mary lowered the barrel and stared at the bloody mess of a man lying on the floor.

The chain that the Circle M foreman held in his hand dropped into the quickly freezing blood flowing from a corpse.

"Feller run into a chain, ma'am," the cowhand said softly, and walked toward the stairs.

"One . . . more . . . thing," Drew said, punctuating every word with a ruthless punch into Lyle Baxter's face. "Slim . . . Pickens . . . wasn't . . . in . . . *Rio . . . Bravo.*" He brought back his fist once more, but felt a hard grip on his forearm. Slowly, Drew blinked and jerked around savagely to see Denton Creel behind him.

"Easy, John. He's had enough."

Not yet, Drew thought, *not until he gets that lethal injection.* Yet the rage in him vanished, and he let his deputy help Baxter to his feet. Drew was hot. Almost sweating. He wondered when he had last felt this way. Certainly not in a few days.

Baxter groaned, and Drew looked down at the battered face of the killer. Then Mary Broadbent came into his view, holding a rifle that was not from the Cutthroat County Sheriff's Department. She stepped toward the moaning assassin. Her right leg lifted, and she slammed her boot right into Baxter's groin.

"It was Claude Akins," she said, finishing what John Drew planned to inform the thug. "You stupid son of a . . ."

DAY FIVE

MONDAY

CHAPTER 40

National Guard teams of men and women roamed about in jeeps and on foot, two helicopters sat in the snow-covered Killone Memorial Park, and, once again, newspaper, TV, and radio reporters ran about downtown Basin Creek.

DCI Lieutenant Will Ambrose walked out of the county courthouse with John Drew and stopped by Mary Broadbent's Interceptor, where she sat inside, talking on the radio to Bobby Ward. The fire at the plane crash had been out for two days now, and federal authorities were still planting markers and taking measurements and notes.

Mary opened the door and stepped outside. It was twenty-nine degrees—and felt like summer.

"Let me get this straight, John," Ambrose said. "The wall of the jail collapsed. And crushed Rupert Chadwick to death."

Drew nodded at the orange pylons forming a semi-circle around that part of the old building, orange tape and plastic covering the lower quarter of the ancient courthouse. DO NOT ENTER warnings posted everywhere.

And National Guardsmen standing like statues, making sure everyone could read.

"You see how much snow is piled up against those walls—and that's after about three feet melted away," Drew told him.

"Lucky," Ambrose said, and turned toward Mary. "You were the first down there?"

"That's right," she said. "I pulled Colter Norris out. Couldn't see anything but Chadwick's feet."

She wasn't lying. When they came downstairs that night, Colter Norris might not have been partially buried with rubble and snow, but the walls had collapsed, covering the corpse of Rupert Chadwick, and when Ashton Maddox joined them, they had decided that keeping Colter Norris out of the news as much as possible would be good for everyone.

"I don't want Colter to grow up to be another George Grimes," Ashton had said.

Just as Mary thought about that, George Grimes himself appeared, wiping off the makeup an assistant had put on his face before he stepped up to talk again about the dump-truck-to-the-rescue story—again—for CNN.

"Well," Ambrose said, shoving his hands into the pockets of his parka. "Baxter gave us the ranch where the other plane was waiting. You were right, John. They had one on the Seven-Triangle-T east of Conrad. Got the pilot and his assistant. Though I'm not sure, considering the storm that hit, that Chadwick and his thugs ever would have made it that far."

"Case closed?" Mary asked.

Ambrose shrugged. "I need to talk to Ashton Maddox to clear up a few details. And his daughter. Guess since they've graded the road, I can make it to his ranch. Talk to them."

"Oh," Grimes said as he found his pack of cigarettes. "That sexy little daughter of his ain't at the ranch. I saw her"—he nodded down the street—"at the Wild Bunch Casino. Dancin' with some tall drink of water."

Ambrose shot a sideways glance at Drew, and a smile slowly appeared beneath a day and a half of beard stubble on the DCI investigator's face. "I don't want to interrupt any budding romance. The girl can wait. But I better find Maddox before he lawyers up."

"Oh, hoss," the Ranger said, "you're too late for that. I saw that lawyer of his, Miz Neal, drivin' toward the Circle M earlier today. I bet he's lawyerin' up real fine, since I hear she was mad at him for not givin' her no attention the past week or so."

Ambrose stared hard at Grimes, shook his head in wonderment, shoved his hands in his pockets, looked at Drew, and sighed. "You look beat."

Drew shrugged.

"All right. I've got to give a briefing with Major Westlake. Then I'll drive out to the Circle M." He stared longer at Drew. "We'll talk again later."

"You bet."

They watched Ambrose get about fifteen feet before he was surrounded by the press.

"I could use a drink," George Grimes said.

Drew slid his coat sleeve up and looked at his watch. "Five-nineteen. I could use one myself."

They both turned toward Mary, who shrugged.

"If you're not allergic to cats, I've got half a bottle of Maker's in my apartment."

"Sounds good to me," Drew said, and he took Mary

by the arm and turned her toward her sheriff's unit. "But you'll have to drive."

Grimes spit in the snow. "You ain't got no Jack Daniel's?" he asked.

"Afraid not." But it was John Drew, not Mary Broadbent, who answered.

The Texan fired up his smoke, took a long pull, and exhaled. "Well, that's all right. I gots a bottle in my apartment. And since me and Mary is neighbors in the Basin Creek Apartments complex, I'll just fetch mine and be right over. You two look like y'all might need a chaperone."

Mary Broadbent slipped her arm around Drew's waist. And George Grimes cackled when she gave the Ranger the middle finger.

TWO MONTHS LATER

SATURDAY

CHAPTER 41

"Has the Always Winter Downhill Run ever been held this late in the season?" Paula Schraeder asked.

"You've been up here enough by now to know," County Manager Dan O'Riley said with a smile, "that Cutthroat County has its own calendar. And after the winter we had, we wanted something about this season to remember that was just good old-fashioned plain fun."

Even though her left hand, covered with a Christmas-colored mitten, held a tape recorder underneath her slim reporter's notebook, she scribbled that down with her pen.

"You should have come up and joined us," he told her.

"I would have," she said, "but I-90 and every other road was closed."

"You missed a good story."

"Well, between you and me, Mr. O'Riley . . ." She waited until he looked away from the youthful snow-shoers. "I'm glad I wasn't here."

"Tell you the truth," he said, "I was right pleased to be on Kiawah Island at the time."

She shivered. It could get seriously cold in Billings, which didn't have the Always Winter range to take most of the snowfall, and the wind's howl could chill a person to the bone, but the temperature was in the upper twenties here, with spring just around the corner, and she would be glad to get enough quotes and facts for another Cutthroat County story for *Big Sky Monthly Magazine* and be back in what she considered civilization.

She excused herself and walked to John T. Drew.

"Miss Schraeder," he said as he helped a young girl, maybe four years old, to her feet, brushed the snow off her coat, and helped her onto the plastic sled. "Grab the steering wheel, Patsy," he said.

The girl giggled and reached for the red rope.

"It's not a wheel," she told him. "It's a piggin' string."

"Well, don't knock your mama down. See her?"

"Uh-huh."

"Ready?"

"Uh-huh."

"Here you go."

He shoved the sled down the slope, and the girl screamed with delight.

The sheriff straightened, brushed the snow off his colorful winter pants, and laughed himself as he turned to the reporter. He looked different out of uniform and with a woolie beanie covering his head instead of a cowboy hat.

"Miss Schraeder," he said. "You might think about getting a second home up here."

They shook hands. "Your son couldn't make it?" she asked.

He shook his head. "Baseball."

"But it's spring break."

He nodded. "And they're playing teams in Arizona. Where, unlike in Wyoming, baseball should be played."

"Well, this is supposed to be a fun story—for a change. But how are things with you?"

"Today . . ." He kept watching the girl on the sled until she reached her mother and leaped off, screaming with delight. "Today . . ." He turned back and smiled wider. "Things couldn't be better."

"Maybe Cutthroat County will settle down."

He waved her to walk with him as he moved to another youngster having trouble getting his skis off his boot.

"What happened in January, you know, was not our doing," he said, and then dropped by the boy. "Hung up, Vincent?" That was obvious, but Schraeder had never heard a rodeo term applied to a wannabe skier. She wrote that in her notebook.

The state attorney general, the FBI, and the Montana Department of Corrections had all launched independent investigations into how those dead killers had managed to infiltrate the department and almost allow three cold-blooded killers to escape justice.

"How's Deputy Broadbent?"

Freed of the ski, the kid hauled the equipment back to the shed that served as a ski-rental shop, being run as a fundraiser for the local 4-H club.

"Improving every day," Drew said.

She wanted more, but she didn't want to irritate the sheriff. He had been a reliable source, and she liked the guy.

Ashton Maddox? Well, that was another subject altogether. He'd hung up on her when she called and then called her editor in Billings and complained that Paula was harassing his daughter with phone calls late at night and even at work.

Well, it was almost impossible to get a phone call into the control tower at DIA, and she had phoned Alyson once at home, gotten some good quotes for the March issue. They had hit it off so well, Alyson said she would stop at Billings if she ever decided to drive to Basin Creek instead of flying to Great Falls and renting a car to cover the rest of the trip.

Maddox wasn't here. She didn't expect him to be. She was glad he wasn't because that man just did not like any reporters—and *Big Sky Monthly Magazine* wasn't, she kept having to remind people in this crazy county, the *Washington Post*.

She stared at the food truck, blinked, and made sure her eyes weren't being affected by snow blindness or that the freezing temperatures hadn't fried her brain.

"Anything else, Miss Schraeder?" the sheriff asked.

"No." She shook her head, then turned and smiled. "Well, maybe. I mean." She waved her hand around. "This cost a great deal of money, and I've seen Cutthroat County's budget. Can you tell me—even if it's off the record —who paid for this?"

He looked at her and smiled that smile of his.

"You ever heard of a Blackfoot giveaway ceremony, Miss Schraeder?"

"No."

"You're looking at one. Be safe on your way home, ma'am." He tugged on the winter cap like he was tipping his hat, then moved to the next kid in trouble.

She started to pursue him, then decided against it. She might need him for another story down the road, and Cutthroat County seemed to have endless stories for the smallest county in the state. She moved toward the food stand and cursed the photographer for not being here to get a photo of this.

George Grimes, that obnoxious, obtuse orangutan, and a big Blackfoot Indian named Hassun were bringing bowls of oatmeal to two little boys sitting at a table underneath a large tent—the ski basin's restaurant.

Grimes used a spent cigarette to light the one he had just pulled out of his jacket pocket, then dropped the butt into the snow and stamped on it with one of his army boots.

When he saw her, he sighed.

"You're not supposed to smoke here," she told him, "and especially not around six-year-olds."

The big Indian smiled at her and kept walking to the hungry kids.

George Grimes pulled hard on the cigarette, held the smoke in, and breathed out of his nose. Then he removed the cigarette and said, "I don't see no No Smoking signs anywhere. Do you?"

She shook her head in exasperation, but he took it as her agreeing with him.

"I can't believe you're doing something . . . for the community," she said. "Serving food." She almost laughed. "Giving kids lung cancer aside, what brought you up here?"

He shrugged. "Could be I wanted to see what the fuss was about. Could be the sheriff asked if I'd help out. Most of the ranchers is busy, especially after that hard winter, and you might not have noticed this, sexy little dish, but there ain't a whole lot of help to be found in Cutthroat County."

She scribbled that—omitting "sexy little dish"—on a new page.

"Do you ever plan on leaving Montana and returning to Texas?"

He started to answer, but tossed the half-smoked cigarette into his footprint in the snow. He was looking up the hill, and Schraeder turned to see Sheriff John Drew talking into his walkie-talkie, then sliding that back into the slot on his belt.

"What's up, hoss?"

"Wreck on the road up here."

"Bad?"

"I don't know. Mary was relaying a 9-1-1 call."

He turned onto the trail that led to the parking lot.

"Well, let her handle it. No reason to keep her cooped up—"

"She's still not cleared. And Creel's running the ski lift."

"You need any help, pardner?"

"No. It's just a wreck. I can handle that."

"You sure, pardner?"

The sheriff barked with finality.

They watched him disappear behind tall pines.

The ex-Ranger looked at Schraeder. "You ain't goin' to see that wreck, put that in your story."

Her head shook. "It's just a traffic accident."

He shrugged, sniffed, coughed, and spit into the snow, then began walking down the trail after the sheriff.

"Where are you going?" she called after him, though she knew the answer.

"To help Sheriff Drew." For an out-of-shape smokestack who had trouble breathing down in Basin Creek, he was moving pretty fast for eleven thousand feet.

She was walking down the path, too, wondering if a wreck might be something to liven up this stupid feel-good story. She would text her photographer.

"He said he didn't want your help," Schraeder called out after him.

"Kitten," he said, wheezing, without looking back. "He never means *no* when he's talkin' to *me*."

"Ranger Grimes," she yelled. "Can I ride with you?"

"Come along, gal. I'll try to keep my hands off you, but no promises."

She could handle that fat old man with no problem. But she wondered if that arrogant blowhard knew anything about a Blackfoot giveaway ceremony.

Luke's pretty shaken up by what he's seen but decides
to stay the night, get some rest, and grab some grub.
The town marshal agrees to lock up Luke's prisoner
while Luke heads to a local saloon, Mac's Place.
According to the pub's owner—a former chuckwagon
cook named Dewey "Mac" McKenzie—
the whole stinking town is run by corrupt cattle baron
Ezra Hannigan. An excellent cook,
Mac's also got a ferocious appetite
for justice—and a fearsome new friend in
Luke Jensen. Together, they could end
Hannigan's reign of terror.
But when Hannigan calls in his hired guns,
they might be. . . dancing . . . from the end of a rope.

National Bestselling Authors
William W. Johnstone
and J.A. Johnstone

BEANS, BOURBON, AND BLOOD
A Luke Jensen–Dewey McKenzie Western

On sale now, wherever Pinnacle Books are sold.

Live Free. Read Hard.
www.williamjohnstone.net
Visit us at www.kensingtonbooks.com

CHAPTER 1

Luke Jensen reined his horse to a halt and looked up at the hanged man. The corpse swung back and forth in the cold wind sweeping across the Wyoming plains.

From behind Luke, Ethan Stallings said, "I don't like the looks of that. No, sir, I don't like it one bit."

"Shut up, Stallings," Luke said without taking his gaze off the dead man dangling from a hangrope attached to the crossbar of a sturdy-looking gallows. "In case you haven't figured it out already, I don't care what you like."

Luke rested both hands on his saddle horn and leaned forward to ease muscles made weary by the long ride to the town of Hannigan's Hill. He had never been here before, but he'd heard that the place was sometimes called Hangman's Hill. He could see why. Not every settlement had a gallows on a hill overlooking it just outside of town.

And not every gallows had a corpse hanging from it that looked to have been there for at least a week, based on the amount of damage buzzards had done to it. This poor varmint's eyes were gone, and not much remained of his nose and lips and ears, either. Buzzards went for the easiest bits first.

Luke was a middle-aged man who still had an air of vitality about him despite his years and the rough life he had led. His face was too craggy to be called handsome, but the features held a rugged appeal. The thick, dark hair under his black hat was threaded with gray, as was the mustache under his prominent nose. His boots, trousers, and shirt were black to match his hat. He wore a sheepskin jacket to ward off the chill of the gray autumn day.

He rode a rangy buckskin horse, as unlovely but as strong as its rider. A rope stretched back from the saddle to the bridle of the other horse, a chestnut gelding, so that it had to follow. The hands of the man riding that horse were tied to the saddle horn.

He sat with his narrow shoulders hunched against the cold. The brown tweed suit he wore wasn't heavy enough to keep him warm. His face under the brim of a bowler hat was thin, fox-like. Thick, reddish-brown side whiskers crept down to the angular line of his jaw.

"I'm not sure we should stay here," he said. "Doesn't appear to be a very welcoming place."

"It has a jail and a telegraph office," Luke said. "That'll serve our purposes."

"Your purposes," Ethan Stallings said. "Not mine."

"Yours don't matter anymore. Haven't since you became my prisoner."

Stallings sighed. A great deal of dejection was packed into the sound.

Luke frowned as he studied the hanged man more closely. The man wore town clothes: wool trousers, a white shirt, a simple vest. His hands were tied behind his back. As bad a shape as he was in, it was hard to make an accurate guess about his age, other than the fact that he hadn't been old. His hair was a little thin but still sandy brown with no sign of gray or white.

Luke had witnessed quite a few hangings. Most fellows who wound up dancing on air were sent to eternity with black hoods over their heads. Usually, the hoods were left in place until after the corpse had been cut down and carted off to the undertaker. Most people enjoyed the spectacle of a hanging, but they didn't necessarily want to see the end result.

The fact that this man no longer wore a hood—if, in fact, he ever had—and was still here on the gallows a week later could mean only one thing.

Whoever had strung him up wanted folks to be able to see him. Wanted to send a message with that grisly sight.

Stallings couldn't keep from talking for very long. He had been that way ever since Luke had captured him. He said, "This is sure making me nervous."

"No reason for it to. You're just a con artist, Stallings. You're not a killer or a rustler or a horse thief. The chances of you winding up on a gallows are pretty slim. You'll just spend the next few years behind bars, that's all."

Stallings muttered something Luke couldn't make out, then said in a louder, more excited voice, "Look! Somebody's coming."

The town of Hannigan's Hill was about half a mile away, a decent-sized settlement with a main street three blocks long lined by businesses and close to a hundred houses total on the side streets. The railroad hadn't come through here, but as Luke had mentioned, there was a telegraph line. East, south, and north—the direction he and Stallings had come from—lay rangeland. Some low but rugged mountains bulked to the west. The town owed its existence mostly to the ranches that surrounded it on three sides, but Luke knew there was some mining in the mountains, too.

A group of riders had just left the settlement and were heading toward the hill. Bunched up the way they were, Luke couldn't tell exactly how many. Six or eight, he estimated. They moved at a brisk pace as if they didn't want to waste any time.

On a raw, bleak day like today, nobody could blame them for feeling that way.

Something about one of them struck Luke as odd, and as they came closer, he figured out what it was. Two men rode slightly ahead of the others, and one of them had his arms pulled behind him. His hands had to be tied together behind his back. His head hung forward as he rode as if he lacked the strength or the spirit to lift it.

Stallings had seen the same thing. "Oh, hell," the confidence man said. His voice held a hollow note. "They're bringing somebody else up here to hang him."

That certainly appeared to be the case. Luke spotted a badge pinned to the shirt of the other man in the lead, under his open coat. More than likely, that was the local sheriff or marshal.

"Whatever they're doing, it's none of our business," Luke said.

"They shouldn't have left that other fella dangling there like that. It . . . it's inhumane!"

Luke couldn't argue with that sentiment, but again, it was none of his affair how they handled their lawbreakers here in Hannigan's Hill. Or Hangman's Hill, as some people called it, he reminded himself.

"You don't have to worry about that," he told Stallings again. "All I'm going to do is lock you up and send a wire to Senator Creed to find out what he wants me to do with you. I expect he'll tell me to take you on to Laramie or Cheyenne and turn you over to the law there. Eventually, you'll wind up on a train back to Ohio to stand trial for swindling the senator, and you'll go to jail. It's not the end of the world."

"For you it's not."

The riders were a couple of hundred yards away now. The lawman in the lead made a curt motion with his hand. Two of the other men spurred their horses ahead, swung around the lawman and the prisoner, and headed toward Luke and Stallings at a faster pace.

"They've seen us," Stallings said.

"Take it easy. We haven't done anything wrong. Well, I haven't, anyway. You're the one who decided it would be a good idea to swindle a United States Senator out of ten thousand dollars."

The two riders pounded up the slope and reined in about twenty feet away. They looked hard at Luke and Stallings, and one of them asked in a harsh voice, "What's your business here?"

Luke had been a bounty hunter for a lot of years. He recognized hard cases when he saw them. But these two men wore deputy badges. That wasn't all that unusual. This was the frontier. Plenty of lawmen had ridden the owlhoot trail at one time or another in their lives. The reverse was true, too.

Luke turned his head and gestured toward Stallings with his chin. "Got a prisoner back there, and I'm looking for a place to lock him up, probably for no more than a day or two. That's my only business here, friend."

"I don't see no badge. You a bounty hunter?"

"That's right. Name's Jensen."

The name didn't appear to mean anything to the men. If Luke had said that his brother was Smoke Jensen, the famous gunfighter who was now a successful rancher down in Colorado, that would have drawn more notice. Most folks west of the Mississippi had heard of Smoke. Plenty east of the big river had, too. But Luke never traded on family connections. In fact, for a lot of years, for a variety of reasons, he had called himself Luke Smith instead of using the Jensen name.

The two deputies still seemed suspicious. "You don't know that hombre Marshal Bowen is bringin' up here?"

"I don't even know Marshal Bowen," Luke answered honestly. "I never set eyes on any of you boys until today."

"The marshal told us to make sure you wasn't plannin' on interferin'. This here is a legal hangin' we're fixin' to carry out."

Luke gave a little wave of his left hand. "Go right ahead. I always cooperate with the law."

That wasn't strictly true—he'd been known to bend the law from time to time when he thought it was the right thing to do—but these deputies didn't need to know that.

The other deputy spoke up for the first time. "Who's your prisoner?"

"Name's Ethan Stallings. Strictly small-time. Nobody who'd interest you fellas."

"That's right," Stallings muttered. "I'm nobody."

The rest of the group was close now. The marshal

raised his left hand in a signal for them to stop. As they reined in, Luke looked the men over and judged them to be cut from the same cloth as the first two deputies. They wore law badges, but they were no better than they had to be.

The prisoner was young, maybe twenty-five, a stocky redhead who wore range clothes. He didn't look like a forty-a-month-and-found puncher. Maybe a little better than that. He might own a small spread of his own, a greasy sack outfit he worked with little or no help.

When he finally raised his head, he looked absolutely terrified, too. He looked straight at Luke and said, "For God's sake, mister, you've got to help me. They're gonna hang me, and I didn't do anything wrong. I swear it!"

CHAPTER 2

The marshal turned in his saddle, leaned over, and swung a backhanded blow that cracked viciously across the prisoner's face. The man might have toppled off his horse if one of the other deputies hadn't ridden up beside him and grasped his arm to steady him.

"Shut up, Crawford," the lawman said. "Nobody wants to listen to your lies. Take what you've got coming and leave these strangers out of it."

The prisoner's face flamed red where the marshal had struck it. He started to cry, letting out wrenching sobs full of terror and desperation.

Even without knowing the facts of the case, Luke felt a pang of sympathy for the young man. He didn't particularly want to, but he felt it anyway.

"I'm Verne Bowen. Marshal of Hannigan's Hill. We're about to carry out a legally rendered sentence on this man. You have any objection?"

Luke shook his head. "Like I told your deputies, Marshal, this is none of my business, and I don't have the faintest idea what's going on here. So I'm not going to interfere."

Bowen jerked his head in a nod and said, "Good."

He was about the same age as Luke, a thick-bodied man with graying fair hair under a pushed-back brown hat. He had a drooping mustache and a close-cropped beard. He wore a brown suit over a fancy vest and a butternut shirt with no cravat. A pair of walnut-butted revolvers rode in holsters on his hips. He looked plenty tough and probably was.

Bowen waved a hand at the deputies and ordered, "Get on with it."

Two of them dismounted and moved in on either side of the prisoner, Crawford. He continued to sob as they pulled him off his horse and marched him toward the gallows steps, one on either side of him.

"Just out of curiosity," Luke asked, "what did this hombre do?"

Bowen glared at him. "You said that was none of your business."

"And it's not. Just curious, that's all."

"It doesn't pay to be too curious around here, mister . . . ?"

"Jensen. Luke Jensen."

Bowen nodded toward Stallings. "I see you have a prisoner, too. You a bounty hunter?"

"That's right. I was hoping you'd allow me to stash him in your jail for a day or two."

"Badman, is he?"

"A foolish man," Luke said, "who made some bad choices. But he didn't do anything around here." Luke allowed his voice to harden slightly. "Not in your jurisdiction."

Bowen looked levelly at him for a couple of seconds, then nodded. "Fair enough."

By now the deputies were forcing Crawford up the

steps. He twisted and jerked and writhed, but their grips were too strong for him to pull free. It wouldn't have done him any good if he had. He would have just fallen down the steps and they would have picked him up again.

Bowen said, "I don't suppose it'll hurt anything to satisfy your curiosity, Jensen. Just don't get in the habit of poking your nose in where it's not wanted. Crawford there is a murderer. He got drunk and killed a soiled dove."

"That's not true!" Crawford cried. "I never hurt that girl. Somebody slipped me something that knocked me out. I never even laid eyes on the girl until I came to in her room and she was . . . was layin' there with her eyes bugged out and her tongue sticking out and those terrible bruises on her throat—"

"Choked her to death, the little weasel did," Bowen interrupted. "Claims he doesn't remember it, but he's a lying, no-account killer."

The deputies and the prisoner had reached the top of the steps. The deputies wrestled Crawford out onto the platform. Another star packer trotted up the steps after them, moving with a jaunty bounce, and pulled a knife from a sheath at his waist. He reached out, grasped the man's belt, and pulled him close enough that he could reach up and cut the rope. When he let go, the body fell through the open trap and landed with a soggy thud on the ground below. Even from where Luke was, he could smell the stench that rose from it. He didn't envy whoever got the job of burying the man.

"How about him? What did he do?"

"A thief," Bowen said. "Embezzled some money from the man he worked for, one of our leading citizens."

Luke frowned. "You hang a man for embezzlement around here?"

"When he was caught, he went loco and tried to shoot his way out of it," Bowen replied with a shrug. "He could have killed somebody. That's attempted murder. The judge decided to make an example of him. I don't hand down the sentences, Jensen. I just carry 'em out."

"I suppose leaving him up here to rot was part of making an example."

Bowen leaned forward, glared, and said, "For somebody who keeps claiming this is none of his business, you are taking an almighty keen interest in all of this, mister. You might want to take your prisoner and ride on down to town. Ask anybody, they can tell you where my office and the jail are. I'll be down directly, and we can lock that fella up." The marshal paused, then added, "Got a good bounty on him, does he?"

"Good enough," Luke said. He was beginning to get the impression that instead of waiting, he ought to ride on with Stallings and not stop over in Hannigan's Hill at all. Bowen and those hardcase deputies might have their eyes on the reward Senator Jonas Creed had offered for Stallings' capture.

But their horses were just about played out and really needed a night's rest. They were low on provisions, too. It would be difficult to push on to Laramie without replenishing their supplies here.

As soon as he had Stallings locked up, he would send a wire to Senator Creed. Once he'd established that he was the one who had captured the fugitive, Bowen wouldn't be able to claim the reward for himself. Luke figured he could stay alive long enough to do that.

He sure as blazes wasn't going to let his guard down while he was in these parts, though.

He reached back to tug on the lead rope attached to Stallings' horse. "Come on."

The deputies had closed the trapdoor on the gallows and positioned Crawford on it. One of them tossed a new hangrope over the crossbar. Another deputy caught it and closed in to fit the noose over the prisoner's head.

"Reckon we ought to tie his feet together?" one of the men asked.

"Naw," another answered with a grin. "If it so happens that his neck don't break right off, it'll be a heap more entertainin' if he can kick good while he's chokin' to death."

"Please, mister, please!" Crawford cried. "Don't just ride off and let them do this to me! I never killed that whore. They did it and framed me for it! They're only doing this because Ezra Hannigan wants my ranch!"

That claim made Luke pause. Bowen must have noticed Luke's reaction because he snapped at the deputies, "Shut him up. I'm not gonna stand by and let him spew those filthy lies about Mr. Hannigan."

"Please—" Crawford started to shriek, but then one of the deputies stepped behind him and slammed a gun butt against the back of his head. Crawford sagged forward, only half-conscious as the other deputies held him up by the arms.

Luke glanced at the four deputies who were still mounted nearby. Each rested a hand on the butt of a holstered revolver. Luke knew gun-wolves like that wouldn't hesitate to yank their hoglegs out and start blasting. He had faced long odds plenty of times in his life and wasn't afraid, but he didn't feel like getting shot to doll rags today, either, and likely that was what would happen if he tried to interfere.

With a sour taste in his mouth, he lifted his reins, nudged the buckskin into motion, and turned the horse to ride around the group of lawmen toward the settlement. He heard the prisoner groan from the gallows, but Crawford had been knocked too senseless to protest coherently anymore.

A moment later, with an unmistakable sound, the trapdoor dropped and so did the prisoner. In the thin, cold air, Luke distinctly heard the crack of Crawford's neck breaking.

He wasn't looking back, but Stallings must have been. The confidence man cursed and then said, "They didn't even put a hood over his head before they hung him! That's just indecent, Jensen."

"I'm not arguing with you."

"And you know good and well he was innocent. He was telling the truth about them framing him for that dove's murder."

"You don't have any way of knowing that," Luke pointed out. "We don't know anything about these people."

"Who's Ezra Hannigan?"

Luke took a deep breath. "Well, considering that the town's called Hannigan's Hill, I expect he's an important man around here. Probably owns some of the businesses. Maybe most of them. Maybe a big ranch outside of town. I think I've heard the name before, but I can't recall for sure."

"The fella who was hanging there when we rode up, the one they cut down, that marshal said he stole money

from one of the leading citizens. You want to bet it was
Ezra Hannigan he stole from?"

"I don't want to bet with you about anything, Stallings.
I just want to get you where you're going and collect my
money. Whatever's going on in this town, I don't want
any part of it."

Stallings was silent for a moment, then said, "I suppose there wouldn't be anything you could do, anyway.
Not against a marshal and that many deputies, and all
of them looking like they know how to handle a gun.
Funny that a town this size would need that many
deputies, though . . . unless their actual job isn't keeping
the peace but doing whatever Ezra Hannigan wants
done. Like hanging the owner of a spread Hannigan's
got his eye on."

"You've flapped that jaw enough," Luke told him. "I
don't want to hear any more out of you."

"Whether you hear it or not won't change the truth
of the matter."

Stallings couldn't see it, but Luke grimaced. He
knew that Stallings was likely right about what was
happening around here. Luke had seen it more than
once: some rich man ruling a town and the surrounding
area with an iron fist, bringing in hired guns, running
roughshod over anybody who dared to stand up to him.
It was a common story on the frontier.

But it wasn't his job to set things right in Hannigan's
Hill, even assuming that Stallings was right about Ezra
Hannigan. Smoke might not stand for such things, but
Smoke had a reckless streak in him sometimes. Luke's
hard life had made him more practical. He would have
wound up dead if he had tried to interfere with that
hanging. Bowen would have been more than happy to

seize the excuse to kill him and claim his prisoner and the reward.

Luke knew all that, knew it good and well, but as he and Stallings reached the edge of town, something made him turn his head and look back anyway. Some unwanted force drew his gaze like a magnet to the top of the nearby hill. Bowen and the deputies had started riding back toward the settlement, leaving the young man called Crawford dangling limp and lifeless from that hang rope. Leaving him there to rot . . .

"Well," a female voice broke sharply into Luke's thoughts, "I hope you're proud of yourself."

Visit our website at
KensingtonBooks.com
to sign up for our newsletters, read
more from your favorite authors, see
books by series, view reading group
guides, and more!

Become a Part of Our
Between the Chapters Book Club
Community and Join the Conversation

Betweenthechapters.net